W9-AHB-398

HIGH PRAISE FOR
MERCY ROAD

"Stunningly beautiful passages . . . Pagani clothes her story
in the shimmering language of magic realism."
—*Publishers Weekly*

"[*Mercy Road*] is the kind of novel too scarce on the shelves.
It is the kind of novel that makes us impatient for the next.
Dalia Pagani is an original, arresting voice, a realist who is
also magical."
—*The Philadelphia Inquirer*

"*Mercy Road* should take a place with the best fiction of this
and many years. . . . Poetic imagery and a musical sense of
rhythm drive a plot of family tragedy."
—*Valley Reporter* (Waitsfield, Vt.)

"Dalia Pagani has created a world of awesome and disturbing
beauty, with relentless grace and clarity, *Mercy Road* tracks a
family shackled by both poverty and place. I cried for their
tragedies and celebrated their unexpected miracles."
—Connie May Fowler, author of
Before Women Had Wings

Please turn the page for more extraordinary acclaim. . . .

"A marvelously moving chronicle of an incomparably individualistic family. *Mercy Road* is a beautifully written novel about real people struggling to survive in a hard land that, as Dalia Pagani eloquently puts it, still 'hums with secrets, lies, and legends.'"
—Howard Frank Mosher, author of *Northern Borders* and *A Stranger in the Kingdom*

"Wonderful, lyrical writing . . . filled with ghosts and mythological symbols, with overtones of contemporary Native American literature and a touch of William Faulkner."
—*Monadnock Ledger* (Peterborough, N.H.)

"This stark yet hauntingly lyrical first novel will call to mind the early work of Carolyn Chute and E. Annie Proulx, but Dalia Pagani's *Mercy Road*—with its moody, almost mythological resonances—reminded me more of Charles Frazier's *Cold Mountain*."
—Robert F. Jones, author of *Tie My Bones to Her Back*

"Compelling . . . eloquent . . . a wonderfully wrought first novel."
—*Library Journal*

"*Mercy Road* astonishes, moves and delights me by its utter accuracy: a book that belongs on a shelf with Annie Proulx's *Postcards*."
—Sydney Lea, author of *A Place in Mind*

Mercy Road

Dalia Pagani

Delta
Trade Paperbacks

A Delta Book
Published by
Dell Publishing
a division of
Random House, Inc.
1540 Broadway
New York, New York 10036

This novel is a work of fiction. Names, characters, places,
and incidents either are the product of the author's
imagination or are used fictitiously. Any resemblance to
actual persons, living or dead, events, or locales
is entirely coincidental.

Copyright © 1998 by Dalia Pagani

All rights reserved. No part of this book may be
reproduced or transmitted in any form or by any means,
electronic or mechanical, including photocopying,
recording, or by any information storage and retrieval
system, without the written permission of the Publisher,
except where permitted by law. For information address:
Delacorte Press, New York, New York.

The trademark Delta® is registered in the U.S. Patent and
Trademark Office and in other countries.

ISBN: 0-385-32356-5

Reprinted by arrangement with Delacorte Press

Manufactured in the United States of America
Published simultaneously in Canada

April 1999

10   9   8   7   6   5   4   3   2   1

BVG

This book is for Dorothy Tod.

Acknowledgments

I wish to thank those who helped me during the writing of this book with love, money, space, and kindness, in particular, my parents Federico and Antonia, my children Lucia and Luigi, Ken Liddiard, my friends Robert Solomon, Eugenie Doyle, Sally Stiles, Carol Lynn Marrazzo, and Philip Russell, and my first teachers in writing, Christopher Noël and François Camoin.

Mille grazie to Adrienne Aurichio. Thanks to Bob Jones for the grizzle and advice, and to Mark Breen and Steve Malesky, meteorologists, for their brilliant renditions of weather patterns in the Northeast. Special thanks are due to Charles W. Johnson, whose book *The Nature of Vermont* was a primary source of fact and inspiration in this novel. The work of Byron Dix and Jim Mavor on Vermont's stone mounds and sacred burial sites was indispensable. Thank you to Smiley Greenslit, trapper, who took me far into the ridge.

I am grateful to Yaddo, Vermont Council on the Arts, and the Vermont Studio Center for their support.

My deepest gratitude goes to Leslie Daniels for the dance that set this book in motion, and to the good hearts and keen minds of Joy Harris, Leslie Schnur, and Diane Bartoli.

To the hungry soul, every bitter thing is sweet.

PROVERBS 27:7

But the stillness and the brightness of the day were as strange as the chaos and tumult of night, with the trees standing there, and the flowers standing there. . . .

VIRGINIA WOOLF

Tell me the landscape in which you live, and I will tell you who you are.

JOSÉ ORTEGA Y GASSETT

The landscape. It boasts of an affinity with lonely rivers and the lonely people who come here hoping to find the challenge of something equal to or greater than their own bigness. It boasts of quickening days of summer when children skip stones across the flat clear streams. It boasts of women, dipping one leg at a time in the stream, reluctant, not knowing they'll be asked to go farther and deeper and all the way.

The ridge with its rock and sediment, fossil and fur, bough and sod, and its rotten stumps. At night, the big and the small, man, woman and child, gasp; so much is asked of them, so much is taken.

There are no seasons here except winter ending and winter beginning. Darkness and its contemplation. The late hour. The slumbering hour. There is never enough light, so what one sees is never fully clear. There is never enough warmth and what's remembered is the chill of exposure.

Here is the place where dreams are dreamt in overwhelming darkness and no one ever awakes fully.

DARLENE WOULD remember that year when Earl dug his first graves and made love to her every day. She had been out by the river in the village and watched the town folk gather by the cemetery. Earl was digging the grave that would hold the bodies of Azubah and Henry Mercie, a drowned woman and a hanged man. One grave for the two bodies. She walked closer, saw Earl leaning into the long-handled spade, saw children tumbling in piles of leaves, heard dogs barking at nothing. The pastor was under the shade of the yellowing maples with his heavy book in hand. Deadening lilies by the old granite pillars. Clouds on the ridge.

Earl had volunteered to dig the graves when no one else did. *Now, why in hell did I do that? I don't know the slightest thing about digging a grave,* and she told him there was nothing to it, just a hole in the ground. *There's more to it,* he'd said. Spade in hand, he had a pained look and she watched him close his eyes as if he were too tired to go on, though he'd hardly begun. *How deep do I have to dig?* And the men nodded at the marked spot and said, *Deep enough, till you hit rock.*

No one thought the Mercies should have been given a Christian burial because it was perfectly understood that it was the curse of the ridge that took their lives. But the pastor had insisted and had his way.

It was fall and the rush of cold was in the air. A scattering of town folk stood bundled in old gray coats, smelling, as usual, of homemade soap and tooth rot, and talking among themselves about the particularity of the Mercies. Those who couldn't walk outdoors opened their windows so later they could say, *I heard it, I wasn't there, but I heard it.* What they heard was Earl digging.

Deaths in the ridge were taken with the same lack of fervor as a birth or a marriage and all were foreseen, conjured up from a cup of water, a broken egg, a dark mirror. Only blizzards elicited formidable responses from them but the time for a blizzard was not upon them yet.

Darlene heard whispered talk about the Mercies. She'd heard it all before. Talk of the land and the things in there. How nothing was what it appeared to be.

You could've given me that land for nothing and I wouldn't take it.
Never saw them Mercies but one time, looked like glowworms.
That land of theirs is good for nothing but spirits.
They shoulda known.
They know now.
That they do.

Henry and Azubah Mercie had appeared in the valley one day looking like pilgrims in homespun coats. They paid no mind to the warnings that the land was cursed and they claimed it, seventeen acres in the hopeless ridge. Hopeless, rocky, unwanted land. Cursed land in the way old Indian burial grounds are. The place was studded with earth mounds, rock caves, rocks the color of old blood, rocks shaped like arrows, like giant cocks, and rising like a behemoth in the clearing was the old oak with its human configuration of twisted arms. Same tree where Henry Mercie hanged himself. Hunters stayed away from there, children were warned not to wander in. Nothing went in there, everything died there.

The only time Darlene saw the Mercies alive was a harvest years ago. They'd come down the ridge in a hand-hewn cart driven by Nubian goats. Their children sat on heaps of yellow corn.

Azubah, like a woman stunned out of an old Flemish painting, ochre and cracked, dreamy. Henry with the reins, a stiff man, wearing a white shirt, suspenders. A whip in his hands, a straw hat, red stubble on his face. And now they were dead.

The digging was taking longer than Darlene thought it ought to. She watched a woman in overalls offer Earl a cup of water and peer down to see just how deep the hole was and said, *Goodness.* Ruddy-faced men rolled their collars up and nodded sternly at the grave.

Takes a tragedy like this, don't it?

Ain't no tragedy in this. This here is a common thing.

Well it's done now, bound to happen, always knew it.

A crow flew across the grave and hovered there long enough for Earl to stop and raise his head. She saw the bird's shadow fall across his face. Wondered if he knew she was there, watching him dig, and if they'd make love later. Thought of his blistered hands and the sweat on him, smelling of death. No, she wouldn't have him like that.

She'd been with him the day they found the Mercies. They'd been in the hunting cabin, three miles up from the village. Not a soul around, not a sound except a woodpecker tapping on the rotted elm. The cabin was dark and small and smelled of old men, old fires, and whiskey. A hunter's cabin. Deer taken out of season were dressed there. *It smells,* she'd said and he told her it was supposed to. He had to duck to clear the front door. Inside, one small window faced north to the pines. From a post hung yellowing rope and iron hooks. Piles of bones, matted fur, spent shells, an old blue shirt, and the rusty handle of an old knife lay in a bed of ferns.

Inside, the cabin was bare except for a cot, a table, two chairs, and three pegs on the raw plank door with an iron bolt inside and out. The cot was built into the wall and was so short their feet dangled and was so narrow one of them had to be on top, they couldn't be side by side. A ratty brown quilt covered the stained foam mattress.

He'd talked about the baby foxes he'd seen creeping out of the woodchuck hole, how he'd stood for hours watching, taking it in, and she imagined the splash of sun warming the back of his neck. He talked with his arms around her, he talked all the time, talked to distract himself from saying what she was sure was on his mind. Didn't tell her he loved her, best he could do was say, *Damn it, Darlene, you're such a honey*.

They were in each other's arms, scent of moss and pine mingling with the scent of their own bodies, when they heard the screams. She sat up and looked at the pines and wondered if trees could scream. *Sound like children*, she said and then the screams came louder and then a pounding on the door.

Two small children with no shoes, shivering and pale. *Mama's dead*, they said at the same time. The Mercie kids. Darlene opened the door wide. The children stood so close their breath was one, four feet, two heads, one body. Little waifs with big dark eyes and small cold fists wiping tears away. They smelled of woodsmoke and clean sharp air. Come in, she'd said and led them to the cot. She put her coat around them and felt their tremors pass out of them and into her.

Earl went to the village to get help and later told her how they'd driven the truck as far as it could go on the rutted logging road to the Mercie property. How they carried guns and rifles and lengths of rope not knowing what to expect and then they saw him. Figure of Henry Mercie but not so much the figure of Henry but the shadow of a man hanging from the oak. *Hands flat and wide, he was swinging side to side, and his eyes were open, looking down at us, eyes real wide. I noticed the kind of rope he had around his neck, noticed he had on a belt with a shiny silver buckle, and his shirt was clean, like he was heading to church or something*. That's what Earl saw, that and the still composure of a hanging man.

He told her they'd hoisted Allen, the thinnest and tallest of them all, and he'd shimmied up the coarse bark and walked across the limb and cut the man down. *Never heard a sound like that in my life. Sound of a dead man's weight. Birds took off from the ground just as he hit, big fat birds. Grouse, partridge. Heard the scatter of hooves, the call of a crow, I swear, as if things were flying off the land.* Way he fell and arranged himself on the ground looked like he was in deep sleep. His eyes closed in the fall.

The men said something about going to the house to see Azubah, and they stood around looking at the dead man as if waiting for permission. They walked a few yards, close to the river thick with ferns and rotted logs and Queen Anne's lace browning in the stalk. A chill in the air, no wind, light on the river. *Then we saw her.*

Azubah in the water. Her long black skirt swayed around in the eddy. Hair around her like seaweed. Blouse swollen with water bubbles, and boots laced at the ankles. They pulled her out. *But we couldn't look at her face. Eyes were gone. Mouth open in a perfect* O.

And not a trace of blood on her anywhere. Not a bruise, not a ripped button, twenty buttons. Earl said, *I counted them. Twenty small wooden buttons turned on a wheel and carved by hand, burl-eye buttons.*

Was the devil himself that took them, the town folk said.

Was the Indian curse, said those who thought they knew.

Conjecture, said others, *whatever happened, happened.*

What you do with the drowned is let the river take them.

What you do with the hanged is you let them hang.

The bodies were put in the ground in a single pine coffin. The pastor said, Dust to dust, ashes to ashes. He buried his head in his hands and had visions of black-hearted birds, thousands of them, loosed upon the land. Nobody said amen.

The funeral party disbanded early. The day had been long enough. The children, Zeke and Sibyl, were washed, their hair parted and combed, their coats buttoned, their belongings stacked neatly in a trunk. Azubah's lacy shawl, the family Bible, a black satin ribbon, a carved bird, a whistling bamboo, a lock of Henry and Azubah's hair. The children were led by hand into a car, a bus, a train, and taken out of the valley by the oldest one among them, Jigger, the riverman. The light-haired, dark-eyed children said nothing during the funeral, said nothing and looked at no one as they were dressed and taken away.

They was like quicksilver, like little ghosts, something about them.

Don't talk like that. Likely to fall on us.

What's going to fall on us?

That, whatever did them in.

Don't be ridiculous.

It ain't ridiculous.

No one talked of the curse of the ridge or the Mercies if they could help it. It was understood the talk itself was dangerous. *Mind you,* a mother said to a child caught talking about it, *mind your tongue or it'll fall out.* That dawn, in a house turning cold, someone poked the fire and read the configuration of fate in the way the embers settled. Come sugaring season, they'd take a trickle of the boiling sap and let it drip in the snow and see the first letter of the next person to die in the ridge.

Looks like an S to me, don't it look like an S?

The Mercie house was quickly boarded up and the edge of the town road, where the two ten-ton boulders marked the entrance to the Mercie house, where the rise began in earnest, in darkness, was posted soon after. The name Mercy Road was carved on a weathered plank and nailed to a tree.

"That's the wrong spelling," Darlene said, noticing the sign.

"Makes sense, though, don't it?" Earl said and so it stayed.

Earl and Darlene made love again under the old elm.

"And you, Darlene," Earl said, sliding his sore hands under her, "how do you intend to go?"

"Fast," she said, "real fast."

"Why's that?"

And she let him have her the way he wanted, he looking into her eyes and she into his. "Because everything in life is so slow, so goddamn slow."

Part One

THE RIDGE is the crown of the land. A crusty scab of wilderness running 360 miles across the highest mountains in Vermont. It is really three ridges falling off or rising above each other like three crowns. It is a circular massive rock with chasms and a notch shaped like an ax where the river has gouged its way. The road follows the river. The valley floor is 1,500 feet above sea level.

An inland sea once covered the land and signs are everywhere: blue sand, coral, whalebones.

The ridge is altered, brooding rock.

Near the Canadian border the ridge is twenty-one miles wide, near Massachusetts it is thirty-six miles. It rises 4,300 feet and the icy winds gust a hundred miles an hour or more, pinning lost birds to thin air. The timberline has miles of black spruce with trunks growing sideways for twenty feet or more but never rising more than a few inches off the ground. The killing wind and snow and ice have made all arrangements here.

In 1853 the historian Zadock Thompson wrote, "Going over the mountain is a real obstacle." He meant the crossing, going east-west. The mountains block human travel and mark the limits of growth, the free mix of species. What belongs to the tundra cannot grow in the boreal.

Nobody travels the ridge from October to June.

Nobody calls snow snow or rain rain; everything that comes from the sky is called precipitation. The north-facing slopes have the shortest growing seasons, the coldest temperatures, heaviest precipitation. Severe weather is marked by snow-whitened death. In the bog lies a herd of frozen deer, huddled in hopelessness.

Weather builds, erupts. Snow crusts the tips of lichen. It is perfect ice. Crinkled and pyramidal.

The most precipitous fall is a drop of 2,500 feet. Snow-white pines below. Descent is a small gasp. A mere pause. Given the days one lives, the fall is profound.

There are monadnocks, or intrusions, where young rock has squeezed into preexisting rock.

The farther ridge is frost covered ten months of the year; the other two months it is heavy with birds, and the air smells sweet, of oats.

Sometimes a moose in rut will ram a tree. A small animal in a hole will come out and watch the operation of a big animal in the heat of summer, ramming a tree for want of a mate.

■   ■   ■

Earl summer and Darlene Hank grew up in the shadows of the ridge. First thing their infant eyes focused on was the granite walls of the valley; first sound was the roar of the Fulfillment River, sound of loss. In its flood whole houses had gone down, barns with newborn calves, cars and tractors, hundred-year-old trees, weak dogs, wheelbarrows, one moose, and seventeen children. The river had taken the wooden bridge so many times it was with a joke and trepidation that cars crossed it. A little bit of everything had gone down in that river but over the years the river grew tired, its rage was small, its pebbly bottom was visible, and sometimes, if the sun was right, the river turned a deep rose, like flesh with the quality of new skin, but most of the time it refused light, content with its dark polar beginnings.

The source of the river was high in the ridge, a slow mass of dark water seeping out of rock and into a wide basin. A mile into the village the river fell off into hundred-foot falls and pounded the boulders smooth as skin. Earl lived on one side of the river, Darlene on the other, their century-old houses shrouded in mist and spray, in strangeness.

Lost travelers looked at the vagrant river, heard the call of birds, the shifting houses, the breathing boulders. *Where's this road end up?* they'd ask. The answer was always the same: *Depends on where you want to go.*

The same road in was the road out and travelers were never quite sure what was meant by *You take the road in and head out.* Twelve houses lined this road, the only church was on the left, but the places of real commerce were on the right: Town Hall, post office, the store. The boarded-up one-room schoolhouse with its useless bell in the cupola was in the woods. The old cemetery stood in the center of it all, rising high, and from a distance all you saw was a town made of gravestones.

Earl and Darlene learned about each other from their parents' table-talk chatter, which always came at the end of the day, in the quiet of a house after the animals were fed and dinnerware was dried and put away. Then they talked. *Them Hanks. Them Summers.* Talk of misdeeds and misfortunes. No one was spared. The misery of one and the gout of another, the bad herd, the bad checks, the woman who put on airs, the man who talked too much. It was dished out without apologies and with little wonder. Blessings and omen came wing on wing. Superstition mingled with the ordinary.

If a sparrow sang at noon it was understood a life would be ruined by dusk. A ring-necked dove without a mate signified love was gone. A thunderstorm on the first of May meant poverty was at the door. The calm heat of a summer day, forked branches pointing north, a fluid field of corn, the green taste of a timothy stalk, caverns of gritty snow, high-headed mist, it all added up to something, it all mattered, it all had the potential to yield, to rob, to speak of the shifting, migrating moods of hearts.

The talk was the only thing Darlene could count on to be given freely, daily, and she took it in like a supplement. The Bible remained at the center of the table but the bowls of uneaten bread and plates with cold peas in a puddle of butter were moved aside as her mother's halting voice began:

Did I tell you about the yellow snake, yellower than this butter here, glowing as if it had some light in it, the snake that appeared night after night on the grave of the Summers' boy? Well, it was not a snake in itself, if you know what I mean, I mean some things take any shape they want, and this thing, this thing that was disturbing the Summer boy's grave had something to do with the snake but I can't tell you what that was. And what does the father do, tired as he was of seeing that yellow snake curled up on his son's grave? First he does what he thought he ought to do, sweep it away on a stick. Tosses it out in the woods. But it comes back, so then he takes a stick, beats the snake to death. Next day what does he see if not the likeness of the same snake, I say the likeness because it couldn't have been the one he had killed. Same color. Same disturbed presence on the stone. Thinks it's a message from his son and decides then and there to dig up his son's grave. Everybody seen him digging all night, truck's headlights shining. Thing is nobody saw him take the coffin out, everybody watching and nobody sees a thing. Stone's gone in the morning. Earth disturbed. Nobody asked and he didn't tell a soul what he did with his son's body. Nobody knows.

What about the snake? Darlene wanted to know.

Well that's the strangest thing. Lucky came home every day to find a yellow snake on the doorstep, coiled and lifting its head like they do. . . .

Darlene cried.

Child, I haven't said anything to break your heart. Just a snake story, that's all.

It was more than that. It was life itself. And she knew then that no matter how hard she tried to make the bad go away, it would be there in the morning, smiling at her.

. . .

Earl was a Summer, brown-skinned, golden-eyed people not to be trusted with tools, money, or women. Generations of men, no daughters born in two hundred years. *They ain't got no kindness in the heart. That's why.* Hunters, trappers; they bartered for everything. *They all got Indian blood in them, grandmother I think it was.* And by the way her mother said that, Darlene understood they were expected to act like savages. Earl's mother, *the missus,* had been too attractive, too out of place with the bare rock and grit of the land. *Took off on high heels down the road, left a trail of perfume, headed south.* Gone for years. One brother was pushed away, ignored, given to an aunt to raise. *Something about him, couldn't figure him out.* The other brother was dead, buried somewhere. Earl's father was known as Lucky on account of six fingers on his left hand. Lucky because he smoked Lucky Strikes, and Lucky though he was known to be unfortunate in everything. *And Earl, well, that's another story. Don't take to no one and no one takes to him. Got an attitude about him. Smell like skunk meat. Briny fellow.*

And when Darlene asked how she knew these things, her mother wiped crumbs off the table into her hands and, only after giving the crumbs a good thoughtful look, said, *Darlene, there's no such thing as asking how, it just is sometimes, just is.*

Stories washed down with a gulp of warm milk. Lights went out, fires glowed, dough was left to rise, spiders worked all night in the dark corners of the house, foxes moved in a circuitous manner, acorns fell, blackbirds folded their wings and slept. Some nights Darlene left the table and teetered up to her room feeling wholly changed. She pulled her braids to make sure she was really there. The talk was calamitous and left her shaking. Her heart was full of stories. Slice it open and there they'd be, the little terrors.

The moon rose bloodred one day and a child, so it was said, was born marked and the town looked upon him from that day on as a proper creature of the ridge, peculiar. Sometimes, if the wind was contrary, and the window was open, you could hear cries in the night.

Darlene was a Hank, meaning proud, sharp, quiet people with no real wealth, no history of fits, no passion of any kind. Old woman Hank was a hunchback who kept to the house and had the colorless and odorless ways of the lonely. Prayed loudly, cursed quietly. Eyes small and sunken, the color of a bog. Voice like a single cicada. Up close, her face showed no surprise, no pain, no joy. Only time her features changed was when she played piano, then the full impact of sound made her eyes open wide.

Old man Hank was soft in the head. A well cover fell on him one day and cracked his skull. Smiled a lot after that. Mouth full of teeth whiter than milk. A sweet man, harmless. Lived with the knowledge of one who had stepped in a beam of light and never stepped out of it. They had three sons and a daughter, Darlene.

Their houses were old and ugly and had buckled with time. They weren't built to be beautiful, that was never an intention, but they were measured in terms of the labor, the chosen arrangement of land to its inhabitants: a solid oak door carved by hand from which, if one stood at a certain place, say the parlor, one could see that flesh-colored light on the river. Or the beveled glass in the pantry doors from which, again, one could reckon, one could gaze, see more than was intended. Most of all, the houses were valued for their exposure to southern light. Few had it but those that did stopped their chores to watch the light pass over the crisp mantle on the piano, over the bushel of apples, and out through the mud room. *There it goes,* they'd say. They paid attention to it as one would a prodigy, with rapture and disbelieving awe. But it was common light, scant and thin, and it fell at random.

The Summers' house had one window facing south with a view of painted birches, the stone wall, tiger lilies. Birds crashed against that window all the time. It was a red house, red like the farms of the land. A house without a woman. Furniture was shoved where it was needed. A couch against a door. Chairs faced the fridge. Extension cords dragged everywhere, lights clamped on backs of chairs. Cane chairs worn thin at the seat. Painted chairs in red, blue, green. White enamel pantry table. Pantry with mud boots and guns and brooms and an occasional jar or two of gift jelly and preserve, pickles. But the mirrors were clean and spotless because Lucky was a vain man.

Going out, he'd say, looking over Earl's shoulder. Earl fixing the beak of a dead bird, trying to see down its tiny throat with a flashlight. *Don't leave that dead thing in the house,* Lucky said. He didn't understand death. He'd carried his own dead son far into the ridge and laid him in a dry cave on a bed of leaves where he hoped he wouldn't be disturbed by yellow snakes. His body sheathed in white canvas. Then one day he saw a flash of white up there and thought it was his son calling him back, asking him to take him away from that dark cave. Lucky put a curtain and tall dresser against that window. Mirrors everywhere else. He patted his stiff brown hair down and said, *How do I look?*

Earl didn't turn around, didn't answer. Knew just what his father looked like with his Wranglers and his studded belt and his studded shirt. Enough studs on him to line the road in. Lemon cologne. Earl pinched his nose and took his dead bird out the screened porch, stepped over the junk of tools, the clutter of traps, and out back where the shed was. The outside wall was lined with weathered racks of deer and elk. The space in the middle where the ten-foot brown bear had been—facedown, teeth bared, marble eyes, legs pinned out, tail too—that space was still empty. Somebody stole that bear.

Wet field full of carnivorous plants: sundews, bladderworts. Air full of damselflies. Bobcat, moose, pheasant, and grouse. Animals extinct, or about to be, common or not, congregated on the land baying and howling and honking.

Earl kicked the shed door open, snapped on the overhead light, laid the dead chickadee down, pinned its wings open, and put a twig in its half-inch jaw to hold the beak open. Then he stood back to think.

There was no noise but the roar of the river, which was the noise of silence after a while. But you could feel the houses shifting, feel one timber splitting open, one flat stone breaking, the ring of a tree pushing out, expanding.

The Hanks' house begged forgiveness for being so ugly. It was a sorry mess, sorry in the way houses are, turned inside out, with the hope of receiving a kind gesture, a thing of beauty from its dwellers. It had had it, that thing, but it had run out of it. Its walls were made of peeling paint and rotten beams and yeasty pine; it had horsehair for insulation on the north wall and it smelled of decay. Its rusty tin roof leaked, water ran down the chimney in summer, and mice and squirrels had made tunnels from attic to cellar and were heard scuttling up and down with the business of hoarding, mating, and killing each other off. No matter how many scented candles were lit or how many pomanders were stuck in corners of closets, the house smelled of incessant animal life.

The windows couldn't be opened because of too many coats of paint, but the side door flung open in the slightest breeze. Grass high except for a hand-cleared patch of crocuses, daffodils, lupines. Those flowers and the sound of the piano kept the illusion of abandon away. Three times a day you could hear the old woman sing, *Oh, rest thy weary soul.* . . . Bare floors, bare walls except for a framed calendar with the bleeding heart of Jesus and a tinted photograph of old man Hank in his youth, a soldier's cap shading his sore eyes.

A house is an open door to the soul of its inhabitants, and, in the country, where the wild land is a road that leads to a doorstep, a house holds no secrets—the way it's kept or not, way it holds up to storms and seasons, it all speaks of love or lack of it. Everyone looks in, looks out. Threads separate ridge dwellers' homes. Everyone watches the swollen shadows move across the windows.

And so, exposed, Earl and Darlene grew like a path with no apparent design. As children, both thought fireflies were fallen pieces of the moon. They'd seen foxfire over the bog and knew the ridge was occupied by something other than their own kind. They grew quick and fearful, dark in the heart. By their teens they were sharp mouthed, ill at ease. They longed to find luck and make it stick. To find love and make it matter. Beauty, they thought, could keep the powerful yellow snake away.

Earl looked for beauty in the velvet coat of a fox, in a single feather. He gnawed hard on his tongue and watched girls. The ones he liked most jumped out of his way. He swallowed too hard when he spoke. He had split-pea stains on his shirt. *Cut it out!* the girls said if he touched them. *Doing nothing, just getting a fly off your hair!* he'd say.

First time he came close to Darlene was at Town Meeting. He'd seen her from a distance out in the meadows with her dad, the two of them looking like children, swinging their arms, and he'd envied her then, wondered what kind of secret joy she had. She wasn't allowed out of the house much, rarely made it to school on account of some Christian belief her mother held that a child ought to be brought up with home learning and not book learning, and the school had consented. He'd been two grades ahead of her and had, by some accident, been given a high school diploma with a gold emblem which he cut into the shape of a star and upon which he pinned the first monarch of the season. He still had it, framed and encased in a glass box.

But that day at Town Meeting he saw her walk in the room and though she was a full ten feet away, his skin pricked when she gave him an almost imperceptible glance and he stopped talking in mid-sentence and watched her pick up a metal chair, slam it open, set it down hard, and sit. He looked around to see who else was admiring her. She didn't turn around to catch anyone's eye, she just sat there.

Liked her right away. Knew she'd stay long enough to cast her parents' vote for town marshal and town clerk, she'd skip the noisy lunch in the basement and then she'd leave the same way she came, with a sense of purpose he'd only seen in animals. Caught a glimpse of her eyes as she walked out. Mud season eyes. Brown and wet. Hair the color of a butternut.

After that he took to walking near her house, heart throbbing, watching the door swing open and shut and nobody coming or going. Pictured himself on his knees asking for love. Took to carrying the thought of her like a satchel, full and his. Saw her walking round the rooms with hands over her ears cutting out the sounds of the piano. Took to talking to her, heart to heart. *Darlene, it's me, Earl. Come out and talk to me.*

Darlene wasn't aware of him or of anything much. As a child she was never alone, not for long. Her mother made sure of that. *Come here and lend a hand,* she'd say, swinging a mop, a rag, a pail. *Work is what life is about and work is what you seem to be allergic to.* Rambling on and on, Darlene's mother, a gaunt figure in men's overalls, the smooth hunch on her back rising like dough from the neck to the spine so when she looked to the right or left she had to turn her whole body.

Darlene, then, wearing her father's shirt with sleeves rolled up, took the pail and the sponge and waited for her mother to say, *Cobwebs, you see them cobwebs, wipe them off the ceiling.* She'd get the tall pole, stick the wet sponge in it, and wipe the ceiling. Then the sideboards. *Grimy with grit, wipe them off.* Or the chickens. *You fed them yet? Get the eggs. They just sitting there waiting to be fed, who's going to feed them?*

Darlene did. Then she scurried to the sugarbush where it was cool and damp and she sank into the tall grass and stared at the sky.

Come dinnertime it would be *Darlene, hell, where you gone to? You're always where you ain't supposed to be.*

Darlene at the shed looking at tools, mauls, axes, saws swinging from pegs on the barn roof, hanging from rafters. One man's tools. Her daddy's. She'd seen him swing the sharp-bladed ax over many a chicken's head. *They don't feel nothing, they just chickens, they live to die. Peck and peck all the way to their death.* Then wham, the ax would go down.

If he saw her idling, braiding dandelions for crowns when the fields were yellow and the day moved forward with new spring light, quick faint green light, he'd call her. *How 'bout if you and me go trumping in the woods?* He'd lay the ax, the hammer down. *How about if we go see what's in the woods?*

Best of times. Skunk cabbage popping out of the soggy ground, river with chinks of ice, rocks split and laid facedown on the river's edge. Once they found a large crow, wings flattened, head and belly gone. *Fox did that,* he'd said. They took off down the path intent on finding signs. *Here,* he'd say, *look.* A tuft of rabbit fur at the base of a rotten tree. Woods still open, leafless trees, buds, birches creaking, whistling.

One day, hand out, squatting low to the ground, he told her to sit still, don't move. She was no more than five and did what she was told. And they watched the moose. *Big bull moose. Antlers on him this big.* They tried to recreate the moment for her mom and she said, *You going to eat or what, you going to let the gravy get cold, you know you don't like potatoes when the gravy gets cold.*

Nights in summer he'd take her to the high meadow and set brush on fire. Rotten apple, ash, maple. Little singe of smoke and then whoosh. The whole world on fire. *It's wild, ain't it, whole world is wild.* And she watched his long hair cresting in the night wind. Wild. She went to bed unwashed, smelling of smoke, and he told her stories. *And then this here big fat pig just went down the road, tired he was, just plain tired of all that building and fighting and messing with things. Just walked down the road. Nobody ever saw him again. The end.* You mean he died? *I reckon he did, eventually.*

He died in the rocking chair, cup of tea and whiskey, on a

Sunday when the church bells tolled at ten and the ladies of the town dressed up in fine colors went down the road, in a rush, to make their prayers heard. Last words he said were *There they go, the ladies of the town,* and then a hard pain knocked him off the chair and he fell at her feet.

She thought it was a stunt. Waited with a laugh ready to say, *Oh Daddy.* Her mother heard the loud fall and ran out, held the door open, one foot in and one out, looked at Darlene and without sending her off, said, *Dear Lord.* Darlene knew he was gone then.

Didn't cry till weeks after the funeral and when she did her mother said, *Keep your sorrow to yourself, stop running tears in front of me. You think I don't want to cry, you think it don't pain me none? Stop that crying or leave my sight.*

Her brothers left one by one, big-jawed men with big shoulders and big hands and big names following them out of town. Rupert Michael Hank. Trevis Woodrow Hank. Harwood Earl Hank.

She saw them leave with their brown coats and brown boots as they walked in the brown shadows of a day in fall. They didn't turn around once to look back to see what they were leaving behind. And she wondered if that was what was meant by good-bye, not looking back, not even when you hear your name being called, not even when there is somebody waving and jumping in the air, shouting, then whispering, *Good-bye . . . good-bye.*

They'd been eight, ten, and twelve years older than her, and her fondest memory was the summer they let her ride with them on the vintage John Deere in the Fourth of July parade. She was given a full bag of peppermint candies and told to set them flying into the crowds of children. But she'd been terrified some eager child would slip and fall under the heavy tires and so she aimed far above their heads and the candies fell into trees, on roofs, into dogs' yawning mouths.

And then they were gone. And their rooms were cleaned and stripped of unwanted possessions. Albums, socks, seed caps, and a heavy shoe box full of arrowheads. Rooms that would never be opened again. And her mother, with a gleam in her eyes, said what she always said after a satisfying day spent cleaning house, *Well, that's that.* Darlene asked if she thought they'd come back. Her mother closed the doors, jiggled the keys in the latches, and tried all the doors to make sure none of them would open and they didn't. She looked at Darlene and said it again, *Well, that's that.* And then she added, *If they have any sense and keep the Good Lord in their hearts they won't be back. Means trouble if they do. I didn't raise men to come back broken or begging or worse. . . .*

Gone to jobs, to roam, to other states. Gone and never wrote back except to say, *Well, here I am.* Postcards from Colorado, Missouri, pictures of big skies, mules, statehouses.

She wrote to them on pink paper, saying, *Hello, Mom and I miss you, love and beans, your sister, Darlene.* The beans were what they played bingo with, and monopoly and checkers. Beans because they'd lost the pieces over the years.

She held on to memories that came with the smell of lemon polish and soapy water and the sounds of an ugly old piano. Sundays, just the two of them, and the house quiet except when her mother said, *Praise the Lord.* Sunday dinner was ham, always ham, greasy sweaty ham. Baked apples and yams.

Come Monday she was the first up. *See that pail, now fill it.* She reminded her mother it was a school day. If she ran fast enough she could catch Mrs. Marshall going to town. The bus didn't go into the ridge and the school was thirty miles south.

Her mother was sick, often, and Darlene stayed home fetching. *A glass of water. A cup of tea. A cool cloth.* Once, she brought a book to read to her mother, who'd been feverish for days, but when she saw the book she sat up, said, *What's that in your hand?*

A book.

Where'd you get it?

School.

What's it about?

People, a family in the Midwest and—
Take it back.
Why?
Don't ask, just take it back.
But why?
I'm telling you. You want to read books, tell me what the Bible says, or tell me about how your father and I got to be here, tell me about the people of the ridge. Read what's real.
But—
Learn where you come from, that should keep you occupied for life. Read the Bible.

Years later she would bury her mother's Bible in the circle of flowers but first she would rip out pages. She would keep the Book of Kings because of Elijah who was fed by ravens, nothing of Chronicles, all of Job, and the Gospel According to St. John. When she dreamt she was burnt and resurrected she told her mother and her mother said, *Bah! don't bother me with such thoughts, ignorant thoughts, idle thoughts, thinking of death when you're alive is playing up to the devil's heart and resurrection is more than rising in the air, you know, and as for fire, well there's fire and then there's fire. Might as well die by the sword or the plague.* Darlene shook for a full hour after that and even when she was in bed she could feel the iron springs quivering under her. Death and fiery messengers and punishment by sword, it was too much, too brutal, too dreadful, and her life thickened with fear so she couldn't look at a common thing without thinking of death.

Yes she would bury her mother's Bible under the lupines which would crowd the garden and wouldn't be dug up for years, maybe never. She'd be grown by then, and gone.

■   ■   ■

SHE MET Earl face to face at the Grange dance a year and a half after they'd seen each other at Town Meeting. By then her oldest brother was in jail for having told some kind of lie, her older brother had fallen off a fishing boat and drowned, and the youngest had settled down in Utah and became a sober Mormon. She hadn't been in the company of happy people in months, years. Missed the monotone of men's voices. Missed music that had nothing to do with the Lord, missed laughing. Day of the dance she changed clothes a hundred times, slipping the same worn church dress on and off, cinching it at the waist, rolling it up, rehearsing smiles.

Everyone was there. Big tarp out back, big tent in front, bandstand, corn in mounds, pies, pickles, zucchini bread, zucchini cake, zucchini in barrels, everything free. Earl came at her like a ricocheting bullet meant for somewhere else but fell straight in her path. He looked like Tarzan dressed as a lumberjack. "Hey," he said, grinning. "Ain't you Darlene?"

"Of course I am." Voice too high, confident. "And you're Earl. I got a brother named Earl."

"Earl Hank?"

"Same one. He's a Mormon now." And she blurted out the fate of all the others. "Only one left at home now is me."

A hunter's moon rose over the ridge that night, and everyone danced to fiddling songs and stomped their feet and sang and they all had too much to drink. One by one, they drifted off to cool houses with slate roofs singed by the sun. They went home to make love and sleep and dream in their high beds, to have one long last drink of cool water, to let the dogs out or in, to make sure the stove was off and the kids in bed. It was night and the land was quiet and the lamps were turned off and darkness fell.

But Earl had his eye on her and she knew it as she sipped the tenth cup of birch beer from a paper cup. She wasn't surprised when he said, "You still here?"

"Can't you see I am?"

"Where's your ma?"

"Mother didn't come."

"I want to talk to her." He jumped off the bandstand, threw his weight against the lattice, rubbed his pant legs up and down.

"What about?"

"Something I want to ask her." He surveyed the hill, the sky, the lights on the windowpanes, then her. Dress the color of a quail in fall.

"Like what?"

She was thinking he'd want to hire himself out, help out fixing things. The roof, the cellar doors, the pipes. But they had no money to pay and she was about to tell him so when he spoke.

"Marriage."

"Who's getting married?"

"You and me."

She laughed and watched him toss a corncob high in the air. Watched him wipe his mouth on his sleeve, a gesture she'd see him do years later and loathe. But then, that day, she only laughed.

"You silly thing, come here," and he kissed her. Butter taste to his mouth.

She pulled away and said, "Silly is something I'm not."

He rubbed his nose. "Pretty, then, you're *purdy*. Is that better?"

She told him she didn't like people poking fun at her, and if he had something on his mind he should just say it and not bother flattering her. "And I don't like jokes, either, nor fools. I hate them." She crushed the cup and looked away, nervous.

"What else don't you like?" he said.

She meant to tell him it was none of his business what she liked or not, meant to say something clever but couldn't think of anything. When he said he'd walk her home she said okay. Their hands touched and their feet were dragging, slow. She could see she'd fit right under his arm and if he'd wanted to hold her then she wouldn't have minded at all.

They stopped at the covered bridge and looked down at the river. "I live right there," he said, pointing to the yellow light on the porch.

"I know that," she said.

"And you live right over there." He swung his arm slowly and brought his face inches away from her. "And we've been here all our lives and we just met."

"I know that too." She lowered her face.

"I been afraid to look at you." He lifted her face toward his.

"I ain't that ugly."

"No, you're not. That's not what I mean. It's the way you look."

"Sorry. I can't help the way I look."

"Not what I meant either."

"I have to get back to the house."

"No, you don't."

"Of course I do."

"I don't want you to."

She was about to cry. "I have to."

"Wait, I have to tell you a secret."

"That's another thing I hate. Secrets."

"That makes four things you hate. Tell me one you love."

She ran all the way home and he didn't follow and her mother said, "That you?" and Darlene said, "No, that was the door slamming shut," and her mother said, "Oh."

Months passed. Didn't see him again until the day a tractor trailer tipped and dumped a hundred logs on the road in. Someone said a dog was crushed in the mess but it wasn't true. The rescue squad showed up, so did the fire truck, ambulance, town vet, pastor, postmistress, all the women home with small children, and all the dogs in the neighborhood. Earl climbed over the pile, saw her, and waved. "Hey."

"Hey yourself."

"I've been waiting to tell you a secret." He took her hands and put them on his heart. "Here, here."

"What, what is it?" She thought maybe he had one of those electric gadgets in his heart. People were watching.

He felt like a lumpish fool. He'd always wanted to do just that, to take a woman's hands and place them over his heart, but he'd been too rough and held her hands too tight and now she was glaring at him. He let go of her hands and shoved his own deep in his pockets. Felt shame.

He'd expected more from her. And she from him. And from the pressure of their bodies came knowledge of pleasure. By the way he held her she knew he was capable of pain. Way she retreated she knew he'd have to hold her tight, tighter than anything, if he meant to keep her. What they felt had something to do with love but just what kind of love neither one knew.

Not long after he led her to the hunting cabin for the first time. "Don't seem right," she said. "It's right," he said. Down the soggy road full of tracks, scat. He couldn't help it, he veered off and went looking, told her to keep going, he'd catch up with her. She waited, irritable, by the cabin door. Hours earlier, she'd had her first violent thought, murderous really. It started when she told her mother she was going out. *Out?* She'd raised her hands as if asking for the meaning of out. When Darlene didn't explain, her mother started in about how it would give her some great satisfaction to see her daughter caring about the things of the world that needed caring for. Darlene had smiled angrily and said, *Would it give you great satisfaction to see me leave?* Her mother's jowls collapsed and her shoulders sunk and the hump on her back took on a great dimension and she flaunted it then by moving sideways and letting Darlene see just how hunched her back was, how heavy her burden was, how tiny, really, she was, and how big her pain. *I confess I've had my* . . . she started to say but Darlene cut her short and told her she wasn't asking for confessions of any kind, she just wanted a simple yes or no, and she asked again, *Do you want me to leave?* Her mother was silent, transfixed, which meant she was preparing to say words. Words meant to hurt, words Darlene would never forget, words she wished she hadn't heard, same words she'd come to repeat years down the road. *I don't know why you stayed here so long in the first place.* Darlene shook the echo of the words off and walked out and in her mind she saw herself turning in slow motion and tossing a hand grenade toward the house.

She was thinking about the consequences of that thought while she waited for Earl, didn't know why she was there except it was better than being where she was no longer wanted. Wondered what Earl wanted with her. Swallowed the thought as she saw him come down the path, mottled light falling on him so that he seemed familiar yet strange. He had burrs on his hair and that wild look in his eyes. "Bobcat," he said, "back there." His yellow eyes fixed on something beyond her vision and when he looked at her again he said, "Why you so angry?"

"I don't like this place. It's ugly, it's dirty, it stinks." She kicked the broom in the corner which fell on the metal garbage can which tipped and out poured soda bottles, beer bottles, empty cigarette packs. "I hate this place."

She was relishing the sound of the word *hate* in her mouth and looked around to see what else she hated, wanting nothing more than to tell him she didn't expect him to like her, or want her, and that it was fine with her, and she was about to tell him she wasn't wanted in her mother's house anymore and what did he think about that when he said, "Honey."

"I'm not feeling real sweet right now, and I don't have a single sweet thought in my head, and if I were you I wouldn't say another word."

He ignored her. He talked as he put himself between her and the door and slid the bolt. He talked about how the fisher's trail is a zigzag while he stripped her of coat and jacket and sweater. He said the fisher's trail always leads to the oldest trees in the forest. He pulled her thermals off her and then she was naked. Then he was overcome. *Jesus almighty, honey*. He choked trying to make his voice low. Grabbed a handful of her hair and held her close. *Damn it, honey*.

She listened for sounds outside. Expected her mother to rush in, yelling, *Look at you, just look at you!* Knew her mother could smell her undoing miles away; knew that later she'd be on the porch sniffing the air around her, saying, *You been out there again*.

Like this, Earl instructed and talked his way into her. *Open up, open up, honey*. Then he made a noise like a wounded man and his mouth clamped down, and she liked him quiet, saying nothing. And she took in the sight of his neck, his odd-shaped jaw, the big arms, the rough warm body. Felt protected, tended to. Better than that, she felt wanted. Later, away from him, she couldn't remember anything about him except his yellow eyes on her like lamplight.

She didn't talk much but when she did it was about her mother and how poor they were. "Electric's cut off again." Told him the only income they had was the widow's pension. "A hundred and ninety-six dollars. That's it. And she sits there praying, or crying, or flipping through catalogs. She wants to buy me a new coat."

He talked about hunting and when she asked about his family he pointed out the window. "That's my family."

"That's just the woods. I'd hardly call that a regular family. I was asking about your *real* family, Earl, your folks."

"You know all about them, right? Rumors. Talk. What else do you want to know?"

"Sorry, I wasn't asking that." She fought the urge to ask about the yellow snake, about his good-looking mother. Wanted to know if it was true what she'd heard, that at birth he'd been smothered in musk and laid in the carcass of a lynx, wrapped in hide and fur.

"It's true, everything you've heard," he said.

"I have to get going," she said, suddenly feeling out of place.

"There's just two kind of families," he said, "those that have beauty in them, those that have it outside of them."

"What about the ones who don't know beauty, who've never seen it?"

Earl looked beyond her to the light outside and she turned to look at it too. The light had shifted and what had been lit was now dark.

"I have to go," she said and remembered how she'd left her mother that morning.

"Listen, Darlene . . ."

He had that Tarzan look to him again, that first-man-to-ever-walk-on-the-face-of-the-earth kind of look. She pulled her clothes on fast and with the coat on her and her fingers shoved deep in the pockets she walked around him. Like a wife. Like she'd known him forever and was sizing him up, looking at his body, up and down. Green plaid shirt, khaki pants, boiled wool socks. She was making him nervous, felt him shake like quaking grass, his lips were wet, eyes on her, and she was enjoying it, the little moment of power.

"You caught any foxes yet?" She felt dizzy and sat.

He smiled, sat next to her.

"What do you use for bait? What's the price of a single fox, one nice-size fox, what's it worth, really? And who do you sell it to? Who buys the pelts?" She wanted to tell him he should get himself in another line of business like the quarry, or the logging operations in Maine. To be careful, that trapping would taint him, make him smell. *Briny fellow. Smells like skunk meat.* And who knows, down the line, he might get confused with what he did for a living. Might start thinking she could be trapped too.

"Honey, when *you* talk about trapping and *I* talk about trapping it's two different things." He raised his hands, noticed they were dirty, and lowered them, hoping she hadn't seen. He bit his lip and told her. "My grandmother killed a lynx. She hunted it, killed it herself. . . ."

"I know," she said. "I heard all about it."

"She fed me a heart, my first solid food. . . ."

"I heard that too."

"I still got the lynx pelt. Fifty-seven pound, male. This big." A little over a yard.

She believed every word of it. *The Summers. Got Indian blood in him, grandmother I think it was.*

He felt frustrated. He shouldn't have said a thing. Didn't like speaking about what was deep and private. Besides, it hadn't come out the way he wanted it, didn't sound right. There was more to it, more than blood and hearts and a hide. He'd been touched by creatures in a way few men had, but he'd never put it into words before, he couldn't. He was among those who believe that to speak of one's origins is to do injury to one's soul.

"I've never seen a bobcat," she said, "nor lynx. Dad said they are phantoms. Said every place has its phantom and that's ours. He said some creatures exist just to be feared, but very likely don't exist, not really, not beyond the fear we have of them." She glanced at him quickly to make sure he was listening. She had her own notion about the creatures of the ridge and they all meant something other than life. And he was a creature of the ridge, marked like her, but in different ways. Their path would differ, she knew that much. She knew even then.

He was picking at his bootlaces and listening. "I've seen them frozen in place for so long their coat turned solid ice. Seen them waiting by a rabbit run, slinking and sprinting. They go for the throat, you know. Four, five quick bites and that's it." He clamped his hands five times on her wrist. "Like this."

"Well, I don't know." She rubbed her hands till the warmth came back. The dark pines made her feel cold and wrong, something was very wrong about being there with Earl, and now that they were quiet, the room vibrated with everything they'd shared. "I'm very tired," she said. She felt like crying. She'd been looked at, talked to, made love to, held. The light in the woods was like spilled wine. The sun was setting. "It's a Beaver Moon tonight."

"Bad moon. Lock yourself in, shut the window, and don't look out," he said. "You know what they say. Beaver Moon, wild and mean." He rubbed his hair back. He was superstitious. Beaver Moon, that second full moon in fall, it took men, made gentle women go crazy. Animals went wild. "Nothing good about it," he said and wished he was home with a cup of whiskey in hand, a fire, warmth running through him.

She pulled on her coat. The zipper was stuck, the lining was ripped, the pockets had holes, it was flimsy. It would have to do another winter, a long one. "You know the price of a good winter coat?"

"What?"

"And the price of a good high bed?" She was talking about the price he'd have to pay for the things she wanted, needed. It was a way to avoid talking about other things.

"Honey"—he grabbed her by the shoulders—"you don't need to buy a coat. I mean the land here . . . I'll make you a coat like no other." His voice low, full of promise. His boots by the door were caked in mud. His brown coat hanging, the jacket sleeves held the shape of his arm, crooked, bent, with the shape of the rifle in hand, ready, aiming.

It was beyond dusk and all the talk had ruined their desire. They wouldn't make love again. The trees began to blend with the dark. Out the door she saw the foxfire, the will-o'-the-wisps out by the cedar swamp, little slips of light. "I think they're souls."

"Hell, honey, that's just gas bubbling up from the earth."

"You ever want to chase them, see where they go?"

"Who's 'them'?"

"Them, the souls." The wavering white flames rose and fell. She didn't want to think of it as gas, as something strictly physical and of this earth and wholly explainable. "You think they burn, Earl?"

"Hell, Darlene, don't talk like that. I just told you what they are." He checked the cabin to make sure everything was in place.

"Let's chase them!"

"What?"

"The lights!"

"I ain't chasing no ghosts."

"Ghosts? So you think they're ghosts?"

"I didn't say that. What I mean is that chasing lights is like chasing ghosts, same thing. Nothing to grab." He made a move toward her but she opened the door and the lights scurried up the hill and went right through the trees.

"Let's go, Darlene." He held her by the sleeves and led her out. "I'm going to talk with your ma. Tomorrow. That's that."

"You going to do what?" Smell of the land, pungent.

"You heard me. Talk with your ma. We'll get married."

She'd heard him say the same thing before and always she laughed, but this time she laughed halfheartedly. The thought of marrying Earl was like a leaky faucet; something she knew she'd have to fix or abandon altogether. Wanting him was like wanting rain in a storm. She wanted to be washed clean of the dust of her old life, wanted to be done with regrets and fear and the miserable expectations of a childhood. Wanted nothing more than to start again, to wake up in a different bed, a different room, hear new words, be given new instructions on how to live, and if love came along that would be fine, but it would be extra, not at all expected. Maybe it was like her mother said, that love and books were as unnecessary in life as warts. Or maybe not.

His coat opened up in the wind and he looked like a muddy swamp creature moved by forces that had nothing to do with her. She felt small, reduced.

"What if I don't want to marry you?"

"You will."

"Don't be so sure."

"I am."

"What about my feelings?"

"What about them?"

■

The riddle, the curse, the homespun tale. The ridge plates moved, ground under them, foxes danced in the saffron light, the swamp bubbled with life, and then the sky, wrung of all color, allowed the moon to move in. The beavers congregated on the shore of the pond and as if on cue they dove in and slapped their tails in unison. Those who'd heard it before said it was the Indians chanting a warning. Some said it was nothing, just beavers' ways. Most said it was hogwash, craziest thing they'd ever heard. Just the same a thousand beavers slapping their tails in the middle of the night on a full moon is enough to make the blood chill.

It wasn't the middle of the night yet, but they could see how it would be, later. The sun was done and the moon was up and the wind stopped, and they felt singularly alone as they walked through the woods and back to the low valley floor. Had they seen themselves from above, like the owl did, they would have seen two figures making their way through an opening in the fractured path. Rabbits and grouse watched in the stiff grass, as was their custom.

She turned to see a wisp of foxfire that burned vague then thick. She thought of dead beasts ruminating in the night.

He turned to see it, too, and smiled. The lights wound their way up solid rock and floated in the air ten feet away. Out of reach. Despite the coat and the extra socks and the lack of wind, he was freezing cold. She came straight at him, bumped into him. A clumsy night walker. "I can't see where I'm going," she said. Just then he knew one day his heart would break and there was nothing he could do about it. It would come at him like she had, stumbling, in a night of no particular weather.

The land smelled ripe and as they walked they put their hands out to the bark of trees to feel something solid within reach.

They walked on like this in silence with their boots sinking into the loam and the moss and the old growth of summer, and a thin veil of frost descended on them so when they emerged from the woods they both glistened and their faces had the spectral bewildered look of those who've walked out of something big.

By the bridge he kissed her and said, "Good-night."

The village was dark but the darkest of all corners was Darlene's house. The mist from the river had not touched it.

Darlene could hear her mother whacking the dust mop against the porch. "You missed dinner," she said.

"I know."

"This ain't no restaurant, you know."

"I know."

"And the power's shut off again."

"I see that."

"And there's just one candle, so don't go blowing it off till I get in the house. Lord help me. How's one supposed to live, I ask you Lord, how in the world. . . ." And she raised the mop to the heavens.

"Stop it, Mother."

"What, what did you say?"

"I said it's time to get in."

.   .   .

THAT NIGHT Darlene stood in her room, naked and shivering, spinning and turning in the moon's light, head up to its cold white spell.

Her childhood was over. She'd leave this room, this house, her mother. The coarse bare walls, the rough wool blanket, the borrowed life. *Be thankful for what you got. . . .* She wasn't thankful. *Don't be so resentful. . . .* She was. *You're going to pay for being the way you are. . . .* She would pay. *I can't figure you out. . . .* True. *Don't look at me that way, you got the devil's hate in your eyes, you got the curse of the ridge in your heart. . . .* She did. *Child, child . . .*

■   ■   ■

Rained every day in April. Land spongy and foot-deep in mud. Boulders were nudged out of their hold and rolled downstream in brown water. Darlene's wet braids mildewed overnight. Lichen grew thick and high. Moss spread quick on trees. Colonies of mushrooms everywhere. Birds grew wild, tiresome, and forgot to sing. The new aluminum siding on the Summers' old house reflected white light for miles, and in the Hanks' house the heat ruined the piano and several ivory caps fell off and were lost, so that every time old woman Hank sat down to play she frowned at the roughness of sound and touch. There was no money to fix another thing that broke. The sink dropped one day, suddenly, while she was washing her white underwear; it fell through the rotten floor ten feet down into the damp cellar. A rough board was placed over the hole. The hose snaked in from the back door and was used to fill a basin to do dishes. Because of the hose, the back door wouldn't close, and the house filled up with large green crickets which at first were never seen, just heard; they grew comfortable in the dark musty house, then they turned black and were everywhere. In closets, in shoes, in gardening gloves, in coffee cups left on the cutting board. Darlene grew accustomed to the sound of a hundred chirping crickets in the house, and to the sight of them leaping from room to room, down the hall, following the smell and sound of the leaky water tap in the bathroom where they congregated around the drain each night. And then came the newts, slimy and cold and orange. Bullfrogs moved in, too, and, confused, jumped into the dark walls thinking they were puddles, deep and cool ones.

During a rainstorm in July, the butternut tree cracked in half, its branches shattered two windows, quickly patched with duct tape. The tree missed the house by a foot or so but the impact of the heavy tree hitting the ground made the house sink several inches that night. The roof sagged even more. From a distance the house looked pinched in, top to bottom, like an inverted accordion. The parlor roof still leaked, the car hadn't started since June, and now it was September. Earl was still talking about marriage. Some nights he'd wake thinking Darlene was there by his side in his bed, in his house, his bride. Then he'd walk the floor, look at the moon if there was one, at stars if they were out, at the darkness which was constant, and with his hunting jacket on and slippers he'd sit on a chair waiting for a sign that the day was near. He cut his hair and shaved daily until his face was rough and marked with tiny scars. He took the habit of waking and pacing, imagining Darlene everywhere. What he could not see was entering her house, the Hanks' house, and standing face to face with her mother. He looked at his nose and found the flaw in the bone, looked at his eyes as he opened them as wide as he could then narrowed them to slits and tried to find the right kind of look with which to face the old woman. He knew she'd be looking at him for signs of shortcomings in his appearance. He cleaned the house and bought new pillowcases thinking the woman would demand to see the kind of bed and pillows he had in mind for her daughter. He had stilted conversations with himself in the middle of the night, in which he attempted ways of being courteous and smart. He found a pair of Wranglers, Lucky's, and put them on but they were too long and too tight. He made a list of the money he owed and money due and money expected by the end of the year. He took inventory of his life and tools and, feeling ready one day, trembling from head to foot, he came across Darlene out by the front of the house and told her, *Let me in there, I come to tell your ma about you and me.* But she had laughed and said that could wait and they went out to the tall grass and made love instead.

But now it was fall, the river had the quality of water found only in the imagination. It moved over everything, silent and fragrant.

.   .   .

IT HAD been a year since Lucky, Earl's father, left town in his baby-blue Honda. He'd said, "No need to worry. Hog's butchered. Plenty of meat out back. Smoked and fresh and whatnot." He lifted his hand to his son but just as Earl went to shake it, Lucky pulled his hand back, thumb out. "See you around, Earl." That was good-bye. "I'll be seeing you." Then as if remembering who he was talking to, he added, "Son."

"Left me with a pile of bills and a blank check and a pen," Earl told Darlene. The blank check was good for a hundred and fifty dollars. The house, once a home for twelve, then six, then two, now housed only Earl. He boarded up the rooms to keep the heat in. Slept, ate, and washed in the kitchen. Day he took Darlene there, first thing she said was *What smells?*

"There's a high bed upstairs. Didn't you always want a high bed?" He removed boards and took his flashlight and led her up the stiff staircase and opened the door and there it was, a hand-carved wooden bed with a crude carving of a rosebud in the headboard. Closet smell of mothballs. Spiderwebs big as the moon. She stood on the painted step stool and hopped on the bed, legs dangling like a child. "Oh, Earl."

.   .   .

DARLENE'S MOTHER wore the green dress with a row of pearl buttons down the front. Her face had a line for every unhappy thought she'd ever had. She was a countrywoman with one eye on heaven and the other in the kitchen. Her days were spent confirming her suspicions about the difficult business of living. She disdained the nature of life itself. She had, all her life, been preparing for death. She believed in resurrection. In her dreams she ascended through perfect clouds and orbited the world as a risen soul, wordless.

Day Earl came to the house she watched him, wondering how he'd greet her, if he'd shake her hand or what. Was glad he didn't. He followed Darlene in, left the door wide open. She'd never been close enough to a Summer to see their eyes. Yellow, like chunks of old marble seen through the iron-rich water of the lake. One look and she'd measured him for what he was and would never be.

That same day she began to resent her daughter for bringing him in. Looked at her with disbelief and horror. Couldn't see how she could lay her body down next to his. Imagined the dark hair on his back, down his loins, imagined him wrestling with her daughter, overpowering her. Could see him years down the road—angry and foul mouthed, slapping the child that was her daughter. Closed her eyes to be rid of the vision.

Was grateful Darlene didn't say anything foolish like *Mother, I'd like you to meet . . .* She'd never had a shot of liquor but wanted one just then so she could slam the glass on the table and maybe slam her hand down and maybe say no. She wanted to make him see into her eyes the same way she saw into his.

She didn't like this man. It wasn't love. Of that she was certain. Whatever was between her daughter and Earl had nothing to do with love. The air was leaden. She wanted to slam into it. Saw from the corner of her eye how Darlene crossed her arms, her father's habit, how she tilted her head sideways, also her father's habit. So, there it was, she thought, the girl's her father's daughter and like him she'll do what she pleases.

Took her seat at the table and served corn bread, lamb chops, and peas in the white unchipped china. Nobody made an attempt at conversation except to say the food was good. She couldn't remember having prepared it. It was tasteless and she chewed with the cautious contempt one feels toward what is truly unpalatable and unsavory. With each bite she tasted her own unsuccessful efforts at everything—the duty of her marriage, her mothering, her piano, her prayers—what had they taught her? She couldn't stand it and pushed her plate away. She tugged on her ears, folded her napkin, looked everywhere except toward this man who she felt was with-holding some deep and terrible secret. She had the urge to take away his food and say, *No, you may not have any more.* Who was he, after all, and did he expect, just because he was being fed, that she would accept the full measure of his worth? She looked at Darlene and wanted to beg her to think, and maybe tell her she hadn't meant it, about not wanting her in the house anymore. She wanted to say she was sorry but in fact she wasn't. She wasn't going to stand in the way. She was sure Darlene was acting out of spite. Marrying a Summer, of all people.

She looked at his garments. He had a rip in the cuff of his pants, his face was like hardened clay, baked-on features. His brow had three folds, deep ones, and he had boil scars on the back of his neck.

"Darlene, come over here. I want to talk to you, in private." She rose, dignified, without scraping her chair at all. Then by the side of the piano she leaned toward her daughter, who was no more than a foot or so taller, and she said, "Your father"—she paused long enough to let her fingers glide on the keys without sound—"your father always thought the Summers were kin to the devil." There was another short pause, long enough for Darlene to smooth her hair back and to lift her voice so Earl could hear. "Daddy was right. In fact he said he preferred the company of one simple devil to that of ten noble ghosts with airs about them."

The old woman watched her daughter walk back to the table and take her seat and rest her chin on her open hand. They stared at each other. *I made you that way,* the old woman thought, *I ruined you.*

Earl clinked the plate with his fork too many times, the food fell onto his lap, he pretended it hadn't. The folds of the curtains looked like prison bars. Elbows on the table he said, "I intend on marrying your daughter."

That was not what he meant to say. Not at all. He'd come to ask for permission but realized he already had what he wanted and there was no sense asking for it. There she was, at his side, sitting pretty, sulking, lips red, eyes done up in blue. He'd come prepared to say he knew how to make a living, and that, yes, he had hopes and dreams, and that the thing he loved most was sitting next to him and that he was weak with love, dawn to dusk, but saw no need to speak so openly. "Yes, ma'am. I intend to take care of your daughter."

She didn't say a word. Air stirred up the smell of ripe watermelon left in the sun too long, going sour fast. She glanced at Darlene's hands and said, "You up for this?"

Darlene felt hot and cold and wanted to throw up. She'd lain with Earl in the grass for hours that morning. Even her hair smelled of Earl. "I guess so," she said. The sky turned red.

Old woman Hank set out warm beer in a thick glass for Earl, said, "Well, then, drink up." Hands on her hips, waiting, looking up, imagining herself rising out of the house, right through the roof, up to the clouds and beyond. Couldn't wait. Earl took a long swallow, lips stuck to the rim, put the glass down, and tried to smile.

She took the glass and emptied it in the sink and rinsed it. Set it up in the drainboard, turned the lights off, said, "Well, then, goodnight."

"What the hell's going on with her?" he whispered. "She doesn't like me, does she? I mean, are we getting married or what?" He clutched Darlene's hand. His stomach grumbled, he was starving, the old woman hadn't offered seconds. Not even coffee.

"That's the way she is, always, with everyone, and no, she doesn't like you and don't expect her to, and yes, I think we can get married."

"How old are you, Darlene?"

"Old enough."

"The law says you gotta be sixteen, right?"

"Eighteen, I think."

"You old enough?"

It was awkward. He cracked his knuckles and looked away. She heard her mother upstairs closing the closet door, which meant she had changed into her nightgown and the next sound would be the creak of the bed. Felt the ghost of her father near her, right behind her left shoulder, saying, *Well well well, who have we here. . . .* He still felt alive to her. And it was because of him she finally said, "I think it'll be all right."

．　．　．

DARLENE'S MOTHER gave her a fifty-dollar bill, trimmed her hair, washed it, and made the wedding dress out of yellowed linen and old English lace. Talked about how she never had a proper wedding in a church or anything like that, but that it, her marriage, had done her good and she hoped hers would too. Saw her out the door dressed like a bride, said she wasn't feeling too well, that she'd have them over for supper or something when they settled down, not to worry, to have a good day, and she closed the door.

Darlene waited on the side of the road for Mrs. Marshall to drive her to the town clerk's office where half a dozen neighbors stood around. Women with too-pink lipstick, too many ruffles, smelling of Avon. They'd decided on no church, no pastor, no blessings.

Earl was there. Kissed her on the cheek, said she looked real pretty. *Real purdy* is what he said. Earl, gleaming, in his borrowed suit, borrowed shoes, borrowed tie. Judge stared long and hard at the book before he read the words: *Do you take this woman . . .* Didn't look up from the holy book once. When it was done, when the words were said and the ring put on, when the kiss was given, Darlene broke into a sweat.

The reception was outside between the parking lot and the old town cemetery. Two picnic tables pushed together, white paper tablecloth, four large rocks in each corner kept the paper from flying into the punch bowl. Nobody ate cake and the guests said they were busy and had things to do and left quickly. There was all that beer in a keg, plenty of tiny meatballs pierced by toothpicks, watermelon punch, and there was Darlene fanning the air around her as Earl undid his tie, tossed his coat off. A bird on a branch above the table pooped on the tiny figures on the cake. Mrs. Marshall saw it happen and she rushed to remove the figures, to wipe away the purple stain on the white frosting.

"I got you something." Earl, with a grin that could have been construed as too much joy. He kissed her thin gold wedding band, which she'd chosen and paid for herself from the money she got from selling her dad's tools. They left Mrs. Marshall to take care of everything. She was slicing the cake in big chunks and wrapping it in foil. The punch was poured into several empty milk gallons. The white balloons were released.

Earl drove her to the house and out back, in the shed, there they were. Fifty pelts. Gray fox, all lined up, neatly. She looked from them to Earl and tried to keep herself from asking, *What smells?*

"This here is what I told you about. Didn't I tell you? Didn't I say they were just begging to be caught?" His eyes to heaven. "God!" He walked toward the table and chose a pelt, hand hesitating among his bounty. "Now look at this will you, feel it, finer than silk. Pure gorgeous fox." He rubbed the fur against her cheek.

The pelts were grizzled, gray with reddish patches. Earl talked about pounds, nine pounds, fourteen pounds. And inches, forty-three inches counting the tail, he said. Up on a wall, she glanced at a disembodied fox head, bright eyed, mouth held open to show the pink tongue, incisors.

And it came back to her again: the table-talk chatter, stories about the Summers, their savage blood, the need to hunt and trap that spoke not of sport or real need but of something traitorous, criminal even, and the mother who'd gone off down the road, the buried brother, the one who was given up, the snakes, the man called Lucky. With the words *I do* she'd inherited a string of broken hearts. And now the pelts.

She could see where the heads and feet had been. Imagined them wondering in their animal way why they couldn't move anymore.

"They're all yours?" She turned away from the skins and closed her eyes until she was sure that when she opened them again there'd be a sight of the ridge, and there it was. Cold and familiar.

"What do you mean? Of course they're mine." The screen door swung in the wind and slammed hard as if a malignant force had come between them. She looked at the head on the wall again, so doglike. "What a shame," she said.

He looked at her as if he didn't know her. Felt powerless and light as if his body were hanging on a thin thread and his mind was twirling. He focused on the pelts and counted them by tens. Twenty. Thirty. He'd done nothing but work the traps for months, months! Heard a mallard call and wanted nothing more than to be out there, in the field, searching for that crazy bird, was sure it was mateless. He wanted him down. Wanted a bottle of whiskey, a six-pack, a smoke, wanted to fall down drunk under the stars.

Her wedding dress hung lopsided on her shoulder and she fixed it. Her arms were raised with goose-bump flesh. *My bride, my goddamn bride,* he thought. He wanted to make it better quick, to alter the course of the night before it got any worse. He wanted to kiss her, have her naked in his arms, he wanted night to come and dawn to be gorgeous.

The fields were full of dandelions, milkweeds, goldenrods, thistles, burdocks, and beggarticks. Seeds were carried in the wind, roots were taking hold. He began to hate her then and she him.

■   ■   ■

FOX 4 SALE. GENUINE NATIVE ONE HUNDRED PERCENT GRAY. Jigger saw the news clipping for the pelts. It was on the table next to Caroline's cup of cold nettle tea. She was outside, wrapping her cherry tree. He'd tried to tell her that a nursery-bought tree was meant for suburban lawns with regular light and regular air and not for the ridge, but she hadn't listened, never did.

The thirty-by-forty cabin was pine. Tar. Tin roof. Rock chimney. Thirty miles up on the high ridge, in the rarefied air, on a bony sheet of land far from humanity. Two thousand fifty-eight land miles and ninety sea miles from his place of birth, Resolution Bay, Canada. He'd come south to work the river when the river was a place to work, met Caroline at Fellow's Fall B & B, and liked the way she looked. A woman perpetually battened down, waiting for a storm. They settled down, she in her gray felt hat, he in his caulked boots. Out on the pines hung his old peavey hooks, suet balls, and a whalebone. A velvet-cushioned Queen Anne chair waited for a new leg out on the porch.

Clippers in hand, she walked around the tree, wrapping it in thin black mesh to discourage the birds from getting the cherries. They paid no mind to the clattering tin plates or the hairy masks she'd hung in the branches, and she could see it now, the mesh would be useless. The birds laughed in the trees.

"You seen this ad for furs?" Jigger approached slowly. Yesterday she'd thrown a basin of water at him for skulking toward her when she wasn't expecting him. Day before she pounced him with carrots and onions because he forgot to bring home the bacon, the real coarse thick red bacon she needed for soup.

"Course I seen it."

"You want me to call him up? It's the Summers' place, you know."

"Course I know. No sense calling. We'll just go." She tied the mesh together with fine wire and studied the results. A giant hair net on the lollipop tree. "Dumb birds. Greedy."

"You sure you want fox pelts?"

"Yes." She made one-of-a-kind coats, sold them to fur dealers. Vests from lambskin, deerhide, hats and mitts out of coons. Had her own labels: *High Ridge Furs*.

"If this don't work I'm going to shoot one of them birds, string him up by his tail, and let the rest know what happens to a robber bird."

"No, you won't."

"The hell I won't."

Next day they made the thirty-mile trip down. Precipitous. Black smoke shot out from the nonexistent exhaust, the hood was red, the cab top was green, the sides were dirty white, and the steering wheel belonged to a '57 Cadillac. Through the mud-splattered windows they couldn't see a thing, but the truck knew the way down. Gravity drove it.

Darlene heard the rumble of their truck as they drove across the bridge, the road, the lawn, and back to the shed. Earl was there with his pelts spread out on planks above two sawhorses. Wedding-day pelts.

"Glad to be rid of them," he said. He'd seen the tiny imperfections, the stream and stain of blood on one, the rip, the cut of flesh in others.

Caroline poked her fingers through the thin dry hide to see if it would give. "Twenty for this one." Pulled on tufts to see if they'd been dried too hastily, if they'd been in the sun too long. "Ten for that one." She stuffed them into a green lawn bag, pulled the string, threw the bundle over her shoulder, and walked out. A hundred and fifty dollars in tens and ones in Earl's hands.

The couple drove away. Red leaves floated in the wind, long spirals of clouds over the ridge, and the grass was high and singing. Earl stepped back in the shed. Wanted to cry.

He came in the house while Darlene was cooking. It was a Friday. She always made fish on Fridays and the house smelled of hot oil and flour and burnt flesh. Pepper in the air made him sneeze. She talked about how hot it was, how she couldn't remember it ever being so hot in October, and how she'd seen two gigantic birds. "Herons, I think. Never seen them around here before but I'm sure that's what they were."

Earl poked the fish to make sure there were no bones. Ate

gingerly, with one side of his mouth. Nodded every now and then but didn't look Darlene in the eye. Didn't give a hoot if an army of herons landed on his dinner plate. He was mourning his pelts. Mourning his beauties, that's what he called them. His beauties were gone. She hadn't wanted them, refused what was most alive in him. A circle of light formed around the ridge and dissolved, he looked at that, then he peeled back the skin of the fish but he had no taste for fish and left the table.

That night she was limp in his arms and he wanted to bite into her, make her scream and cry the way he couldn't. Wanted to tell her how he hurt and why and wondered if she cared. Wondered what it was about her that he thought he loved. In the morning she stretched and showed the whiteness of her belly and smiled at him in a way that made him cold. When she served trout for the tenth day in a row, he threw his arms up and screamed. "What the hell are you doing to me?"

He sharpened his tools, tuned the truck, bought new lengths of rope, and when he talked to her, it was low and hushed. She had to lean into him to hear. The nights were moonless and still. The dog-yellow birches were the last to lose color before the night settled in and she watched the trees losing definition. And they stood by the door, or at different windows or at the table where they put out their hands and steadied themselves, backs against the wobbly chairs.

"What's wrong with you?" he said if he saw her sulking, and she waited long minutes before saying, "Nothing." She, on the long green couch, studied seed catalogs and tried to imagine a garden in bloom.

He stayed up late finishing his new trap. A ten-inch bolt with wire and a spring. Tugged, heard the clamp click. Good, he thought. He'd set more lines soon. That's what he was talking about, that was the garbled talk, the mumbled words, the stuff he spoke of which she couldn't hear.

When the prices for fur got good in Canada he drove with the last good pelts hidden under the seat, smuggling for a living. "I'll be back soon," he said, a kiss on the top of her head, and drove away.

"You'll be what? You're going where? I didn't hear you, what did you say?" Cup of coffee in her hands all morning. Stood there all day.

Gone, she thought. *He's gone and left me.* Her mind put her to bed, kept her from sleep, told her to get up, to get dressed, to put on her shoes and get on with things. Sat on the high bed and wondered if Earl was being spiteful. Leaving her alone so much of the time. A tiredness set in and lay heavy in her heart. The ice days came and then the mud.

■ ■ ■

*T*HE ROAD *in also leads out. In winter it's white wet, in summer it's brown. It's a fissure, an opening in the land, and it oozes all the time.*

The road leads to a place some call home, and those who've been away return only for the memory of cool air, to see again the green knoll below the intense blue sky, or the old bloodred farm with the rusty sign that once announced that maple sugar was sold here, the gigantic maple-leaf emblem reduced to a brown stalk, skeletal after so many winters, and of course, they come to hear the hooves, the thud and patter and vibration of approaching horses, coming for the apple or carrot held over the edge of the fence. They are visitors, all, even the primitive sturgeon in the muddy shallows, the camping children waiting for shooting stars, lovers under the Northern Lights, everyone leans forward to see some-thing they will remember as the heron descends on the bare rock by the dark woods.

■ ■ ■

W HEN WORD came that Darlene's mother was dead she threw two coats over her, the long brown scarf dragging, and went to see her mother. She was in bed, in her green flannel with a pattern of ivy. Her buttons were buttoned. Her hands were at her sides. "Oh, Mother." Darlene turned to the doctor. "That's the way she *always* sleeps. She always looks like that." Of course she knew she was dead but she wasn't prepared to see her dead, not yet, and so she went about doing the things she'd been taught to do.

She'd spent many nights at her mother's side during her many sleeping fevers in the same room, humid with perspiration and the breath of illness. Now she rubbed her mother's cold hands. The doctor said, "Darlene, you have to understand . . ." Darlene ignored him; she would understand later. She took off her coats, both of them, and placed them over her mother's breast. She opened the Bible and tried to find the pages, the right ones, but they were gone. A gap between the Old and New Testament. Closed her eyes and tried to remember a prayer, but she'd forgotten the words. Worse than that, she'd completely forgotten how to say them.

Imagined her mother momentarily coming to, brushing damp hair away from her face, tongue sliding over cracked lips, asking for a cup of strong ginger tea. *With maybe a bit of honey if we can spare some.* Darlene stared, waited for instruction, and when she realized it would never come she laughed, and then she cried.

The old woman had risen according to plan, and was slowed down by the intense pull of the ridge below, but she kept her eyes up, and up she went, forgetting quickly how it was that one looked back.

■   ■   ■

THE BABIES came quick after that. With each one the certainty that she was pregnant came not with the doctor's confirmation, not with morning sickness, but with a nightmare. Always the same one: the walls tumbling around her, burying her alive. Awake in the quiet room, panic in her heart.

Spent the day cooking. New potatoes, ten loaves of bread, two different kinds of soups, custard pie, apple pie, cranberry relish.

When Earl sat to dinner, she said, "I'm expecting." He looked at her, then at the split pea, the corn chowder, the heaps of ginger beans, the mounds of boiled potatoes, the crusty bread, the ham. "Who's coming?" He picked up a fork. She said, "A child, Earl. I'm expecting a child."

He lost his appetite but she ate plenty. After the third slice of pie she yawned, slipped her hand under her hair, and smelled the day's cooking mingling with the fake fragrance of strawberry shampoo and she was sick.

"Don't count on a girl," he said. His heavy arms fell on her and she moved them off. Didn't want his thoughts interfering with hers and she fell asleep thinking of names, knowing children were feeble beings needing to be coaxed into life by a name. Of course she'd have a girl. She'd give her a name with no particular history. Gladys, Sylvia, Rose.

Her nightmares faded as her belly swelled. Slept all the time, slept standing, leaning against a wall, and while she was cooking. Woke to scorched pots, smell of smoke. Sometimes Earl was in bed, sometimes on the couch, and she watched him sleep, wondering what else would change.

Then the tears came. Cried all the time. Cried when she saw herself in the mirror, cried when she saw a bird alone in the air, cried listening to the weather. Couldn't bend over to tie her boots and so she went out in the muddy yard, laces dragging. Searched around for wild herbs. Tasted everything. Berries, bark, even the salt lick. Wore Earl's denim shirts, bought large bras. Set up her mother's Singer sewing machine in the kitchen and made baby quilts, stitched cotton lace around blankets. Once she made a maternity dress with a huge billowing waistline. The print was of tiny pink rosebuds. Held the dress up and was shocked to see her face above such a hopeful-looking thing. Tossed it into the woodstove, where it sizzled to a crisp. Spent the rest of the day stitching *S*'s. Susan. Sally. Shawnee. A girl, it would be a girl.

Breeze through the open door let in the sound of the peepers, smell of cow manure, sound of Earl's high-pitched tuneless whistling as he walked in and grabbed a pinch of dough left rising on the warm stove. Sundays he brought home roasted chickens, cold beers, and sticky buns, and except for a short walk to the river where they both skipped stones, she sewed all day and into the night.

He painted shelves, straightened up the shed, fixed the radiator, the hose, changed summer tires into snows, listened to the weather for comfort. *Fifty and in higher elevations thirty.* That was them. Higher elevations. Dreamt of holding the warm hoof of a beast in his cupped palm and digging out the sod and pebbles around the shoe. Dreamt of holding a wet hot fawn. Naked on the high bed he watched Darlene undress and dress again for bed wearing her mother's ivy gown.

"Don't go wearing that thing again, honey."

"It's my mother's. It's all I got left of her." Buttons up to her neck.

"That's just what I mean. You shouldn't be wearing that."

He was superstitious. Thought some bizarre event might take place, some kind of transmutation. Flesh being called back to life. Waited a few days, then he tossed the gown into the woodstove where he found a charred zipper, remnants of fabric with baby roses, pink.

While she slept he pulled the sheets back to see the lumpy form of the child forming in her belly. Tried to imagine the child as a replica of her. A baby woman. No, he thought, it wouldn't be a girl.

He fiddled around the house expecting to be called to do, to fetch, to help out, but Darlene had taken on the armor of pregnancy and didn't need him at all.

In her dreams Darlene saw her unborn child dressed in feathers, hands clutching something heavy. She came on hands and knees to see what was in its hands and found little rocks. In another dream she walked through a pumpkin field looking for the best one and when she found it and lifted it, she saw it was a baby's head. She didn't let these dreams disturb her, knew it was only the ridge making itself known to the new life in her. *It'll always be with you, right there with you. Can't escape it.*

Whole days went by and she didn't speak. Nobody visited, the phone never rang. Every now and then a car with out-of-town plates stopped by the drive, and she stood by the windows, holding her belly, waiting for the car to drive away. Tired of mending, she grabbed a trunkful of tattered clothes and burned them. Saved the buttons. Made curtains with lace and, finding them too transparent, made new ones out of thick white cotton, thick enough so she couldn't see out. And she sat on the long green couch and waited, hours and days and months, and then it was time.

"It's time, Earl," she said, "wake up, Earl, it's time to get going."

"Going where?" He looked at the clock. Midnight.

"The baby."

He talked about corn and the price of oil and the ditch that swallowed his truck. He talked to the nurses, to the doctor, he talked until someone finally told him to be quiet. Then he heard Darlene moaning, wailing, then crying. He'd never heard sounds like that. *Jesus Christ, somebody do something.* They finally asked him to leave.

The firstborn was a boy. Strong muscled and shaped like a little man, fists punching the air. He found her nipple and fed himself with both fists clenched on her breast and when he was done, he burped himself and turned as if saying, *I've had enough, now I want to sleep.* Butch, Earl called him, and it stuck.

My darling boy, she whispered, *my little man.* Earl didn't want him in bed. "Not enough room for the three of us here. I could crush him, or you could." He pulled the oak dresser close to their bed, emptied out the third drawer, laid thick flannels down, put the chair under the open drawer so it would hold steady, said, "There."

She stretched her arm out and held her baby's hand, a whole little hand in hers.

His first bath was with her, on the cavity of her flaccid flesh, the two of them warm, whole. A tremendous happiness filled her days and the spell of silence was gone. She couldn't wait for him to wake from naps and talk to him, look at his eyes. They were his own eyes. He was someone she'd never seen before.

First thing she taught him was the weather. Put his hands on the frost of the window, where he left his three-inch handprint. *Cold*, she said. She blew her breath on his cheek. *Hot*, she said. Hung prisms in the south window and waited for the three o'clock light, and said, *Sun*.

Earl's face contorted into grins as he tried to make Butch smile. Held him high. "Don't scare him," she'd say. "I'm not scaring you, am I? No, *nooooo*, you a big boy, you're not scared of anything are you?" he'd say but she stayed near, ready to catch, to hold, to take away. Couldn't stand watching Earl jangle the baby up so high. "Don't, Earl. Not so high. Be careful. Here, let me take him."

By the time he could say Ma-ma-ma, and he could walk, when she couldn't feel his soft spot anymore, when he was sleeping through the night and his fine white hair fell off and the new dark hair grew like a wig, she got pregnant again.

It was a Tuesday, and she was irritable, and it was raining. She had put the iron away, the baby was crying, the rain was a loud drumming on the tin roof. Butch sat on her hip while she stirred the corn mush. Turned the tap on, rinsed the cup, poured apple juice, took out a handful of eggs, cracked them gently in the frying pan, sprinkled pepper and salt, bent to search for the lid, put it on the eggs, poured milk in the mush, more butter, put a lid on that, too, turned the stove off, grabbed a box of crackers, and turned to see Earl looking mean.

"What's wrong?" she said.

He kicked her mud boots out of the way and went out the door.

"Bye-bye, Daddee." Butch waved in his two-year-old back-handed way. On the porch, with a shawl over them both, she held Butch's hands out. "Rain," she said, "lots of rain."

That night with Earl shivering, muttering, his hair parted in wet strips, his mouth open, he made a sound as if trying to say honey but all she heard was huh, huh. And she had the nightmare again. Buried alive. Woke in the dark and rushed to see Butch, who was in the corner of the room now, in his own cot. He opened his eyes immediately, and she sighed with relief.

The weight of the new child left her breathless and every step was painful with Butch on her back, Butch at her side, Butch wanting up, *Up, Mommy, up.* Dirty snow lined the road, nothing was green, but it was April, and the sun was trying. She rocked Butch to sleep on the porch and she dozed off too. Nothing woke them, not even the sound of Earl's truck as he drove up and found the two of them clutched in sleep.

She took to eating spicy foods and when Earl brought home a pheasant, she speared it with ginger and a hundred cloves of garlic and ate the whole thing. Her belly did not protrude, her breasts hardened like potatoes, she wanted love all the time, and on the seventh month Sid was born, dead and blue. His life fell out of hers. The nurses held him away from her and shook their heads and said, *Oh no no.* She threw herself at them and took Sid in her arms and screamed. Screamed him back to life is what she did. His eyes cracked opened and he took a painful gulp of air.

It happened then: what was to come, what would matter later. She forced him to live though he'd already chosen not to. It happened then.

She held him close to give him some of her own substance. His head lolled and his eyes didn't stay open for long and his mouth was reluctant about taking milk. His shoulders were thin and the slightest touch bruised him. She woke him from naps, shaking his little hands, pulling his toes to make sure he was alive. Rocked him constantly, thinking the motion would keep his blood moving.

Earl didn't touch him, ever. Didn't think anything born dead could ever be fully alive. Looked for signs of resemblance in the eyes, feet, hair, disposition. None of it was his. When she wasn't around he stood by the cot and called him *you little runt*. Measured himself in the failure that was his son, and it was a failed son, he felt it. "Something wrong with him. We got a sick child, don't we, going to take all we got to care for him, right? What did the doctor say? You didn't tell me. What did he say? That he'll never walk, never talk, won't be able to keep up with things, right?"

"Nothing wrong with him, Earl. He's just weak, that's all." But she was afraid for him. That startled look of birth never left him.

Earl whittled bears for Butch, climbing bears, sitting bears, mama bears and cubs. He sat on the floor and staged battle scenes with rubber soldiers while Butch watched. Sid struggled to pull himself up in his crib. Earl kept his back to him. When Sid cried Earl hollered for him to shut it and Darlene rushed him out of the room, away from Earl. *My baby*, she'd say.

He wore little caps all the time, slept with blankets even in summer, and she fed him by hand, spooning rice or noodles into her fingers and into his mouth, thinking the contact with her flesh would strengthen and nourish him more.

He was two and light as a feather. Butch held him like a puppy, scratched his ears, kissed his nose. On a rainy day she took them both across the bridge and walked into her mother's old house which had been for sale for four years but not one person had come by with an offer except a town selectman who wanted to buy it and torch it. Everything was as it had been, as it would be, for the house would go into the earth gradually, with everything in it. From the pantry she took the five-gallon jars of black beans. She opened the trunk and took the remnants of fabrics. Calicos. She found the old wheelbarrow and loaded the boys in it, surrounded by stacks of squares of perfectly cut cloth and the large jars of beans, and crossed the bridge home. Sid propped up in Butch's lap, Butch singing a sea song. *This is a song about the sea, about the sea, drunken sailors in the deep blue sea, deep blue sea, and the mighty captain in the mighty sea, ship to shore yelled he!* "Where'd you hear that?" she said.

"I made it up," and then after a smile, he said, "I heard it in my dream. Somebody comes in my dreams and sings these songs to me."

It rained all night and she sat up sewing little bears in yellow and blue, stuffed them with her mother's beans, and left them on the boys' beds, little offerings for their little lives.

Summer had come and gone. Monarchs and robins and blue jays marked the days with their predictable song and flight. And one day she was looking out the window and there were shards of ice on the roof and the ridge was blanketed in snow, and when the dream came she wasn't surprised. Pregnant again.

A girl. She came in her own good time, three weeks late, with a headful of hair, and long nails that tore at her breasts and refused mother's milk. A girl. Thirty-six hours of labor and Earl out in the lobby, mumbling, while Sid and Butch slept in a makeshift bed in the broom closet of the hospital.

First girl born to the Summers in two hundred years. Born wild, scowling, and angry, as if she'd been called away from a secret place. Earl came around, staggering at the door like the ghost of a ghost. "A girl?" he said. "You're kidding." And he circled the bed a hundred times before he said, "Can I hold her?" And when he did it was with great tenderness. He took in her eyes, one at a time, her head, the shape of it, the pointy ears flattened back, the stiff legs that kicked him back.

She kicked Darlene, too, bit down on her nipples until they bled, until Darlene screamed and said, *No!* and put the child down, both screaming at each other.

Kicked off her blankets though born on the coldest day of the year. Couldn't be picked up, wanted no cuddling, no rocking. When Darlene hummed a lullaby the child wailed. Her eyes were open from birth and fixed on Darlene at all times. The child stiffened when Darlene walked in the room. A bottle of milk was propped in her hands and arranged just so. Darlene walked out without a word, afraid the baby would hurl the bottle at her back. *The child hates me,* she thought.

Months passed with everyone calling her baby, until Aunt Mattie, Earl's aunt, said, "For Christsake call her Tina. I used to have a red hen just like her, got her spurs up and attacked me one day."

The child would remember her namelessness, her power, how everyone sidestepped around her and left her alone. She would remember their fear of her and how she drank her warm bottled milk, alone. *Alone* was the first word she said. Six months old and straight as a rod, hair like a storm on her head, eyes shiny and strange, deep. She was given a room of her own where she looked at the sky, the rare patches of blue in whiteness, and laughed when she saw all those blackbirds looking in at her from their perch on the maple. She became familiar with their astonished eyes and their shrieking call. She watched their beaks and mimicked them. She understood light was temporary and darkness was long and she knew stars and wind were kin to her, had to be, they came every day. And when summer burned like a coal she learned to pit her fire against it and learned to rage.

"She's just feisty, that's all," Earl declared one day. "That one there, that's the one you should worry about." Nodding at Sid. Butch hung to the side, looking from parent to parent, and when he offered a licorice to Sid, Earl snapped it away. "Don't give him none of that. Bound to choke on it." Butch put his hand on his brother, and Earl said, "I wouldn't go around touching him either."

Earl's contempt for Sid grew from his refusal to touch him at birth to outright bursts of cruelty. *Get that kid out of my way.*

Wouldn't sit at the dinner table if Sid was in his high chair, couldn't stand the sight of him. Mumbled to himself with the intention of being heard. *That one ain't in the world for long.* The boy was mute. His small pale face was empty of emotion except sadness. He never spoke, nor attempted to. Every now and then he moaned. That was it.

She ignored Earl until she couldn't. *Stop it, Earl. Stop being so mean, stop looking at him that way, stop saying those things, stop.* Picked up a chair and slammed it down, eyes on him. Glanced around at what else she could slam down. That night she told him, "Sid's just a child, be careful, don't do damage, don't."

"Face it, Darlene. He's the runt."

That night the raccoon got in the hen coop. She didn't hear the squawking but heard the gunshot. Thought Earl had done the worst thing and threw herself out of bed and rushed to the children's rooms, and, seeing them alive, sleeping, fell to her knees and stayed there through the night.

"Coon got that dumb hen of yours," Earl said in the morning. "About time too."

It was Sugar, her favorite hen, born half blind and lame, never laid eggs, but Darlene loved her sweet nature. She buried what was left of her in the morning. Butch gathered all the feathers and twined them in a wreath of sorts. "Does everybody die?" he said.

"Yes, but not this way. Nothing has to die this way." She wondered how to tell a six-year-old about the law of the land, how the strong and the weak balance each other, but then she heard Junior, the rooster. He was perched on a tree, crowing. Looked like a bundle of old rags. Looked like a fright. The other hens were hidden in the flower beds.

She raked the blood-soaked earth and fixed the wire fence and weighed the roof down with ten cinder blocks and dragged a thick log to the door. Enough to keep vermin and varmint out. Butch worked a crude cross made of twigs and shoved it in the ground. "Where did you learn that?" She pointed to the cross. There wasn't a cross in the house, nor had they been to the cemetery, her and the boys. "How'd you do that?" He shrugged. "Did somebody show you that in your dreams?" If he had said yes she would have believed him, for she knew dreams offered instruction even to children. He looked beyond her, to the house, and there, by the window, hands flat against the glass, was Earl. For a sick moment she thought he was going to break through it. When he stepped out he called Butch.

"Get in the truck," he said, "let's go for a ride." Butch didn't move. *Don't go*, Darlene said with her eyes. But then Earl was there and had Butch by the hand. Hour later they were back. Butch limping. "Cut his foot," Earl said. The cut was on the heel, jagged, rimmed with grass.

"Drainage pipe out in the field," Darlene said, "you were running in the field, weren't you?" She held the foot. Butch said nothing as she led him in and washed the cut. She showed him the blood. "This shouldn't have happened," she said. "From now on, you put your shoes on, you stay out of that field, you listen to me."

"Let him be. It's just a cut." Earl rubbed Butch's hair.

Sid crawled to the door and from another room Tina wailed.

"Some boys grow up to be men, others, like that one, don't amount to much. . . ."

"Stop!"

Later, when the boys were in bed, she told him, "I don't like the way things are, Earl. . . ." She held on to the wall, leaned hard against it. "The way you are with Sid is wrong."

"Don't go starting on that again."

"I wish you'd stop."

"Fine. I stopped. Won't say boo to the kid from now on. He's yours, all yours. Never liked him and that's the truth. And as for Butch"—he pointed a fat finger her way—"A cut's nothing. Worse things will happen. Worse things."

He was red and sweating and his voice boomed in the closed

room and she was sure the children had heard. She said, "Quiet, not so loud."

"Quiet? Quiet? I'm supposed to keep quiet? Can't talk, can't do a flying fuck around here!"

Morning and they were there, Butch and Earl, eating cereal. "Morning, Mom," Butch said, licking the spoon.

She nodded. "How's your foot? Let me see your foot." Butch said his foot was fine. "Let me see it." She got on her knees and lifted his leg, though he resisted.

"He's fine, didn't you hear him say so? He said he was fine." Earl stood and dropped the cereal bowl in the sink.

She pulled Butch's shoe off. The bandage was bloody. She held the foot up. "Look at this. You call this fine?"

"It's just a cut, Mom." He pulled his foot back. "It's all right." He looked like he was about to cry, trying hard not to.

"It's *not* all right. Can't you see?"

"It's fine, Mom, really. It doesn't hurt. Really, it's fine."

"It's fine," said Earl.

"It's bleeding. Your foot is bleeding. And you're trying to tell me it's fine?" She looked from Earl to Butch. "Nothing's fine."

Butch grabbed his shoe and went upstairs. He walked right past her. *Butch?* He did not look back, didn't answer though he heard her call. *Butch?* He closed the door gently. He knew the consequences of a slamming door. Even then he knew about the fragile order of the house. Knew when enough was enough. He'd had enough.

She looked around the house one day and felt a blackness settling in. Had nothing to do with light as the sun was bright and it shone out there, on the ridge: it was a blackness of another nature. Then Butch came into the kitchen and told her, "I shot ten birds." She was doing dishes. *"Really? You shot ten birds?"* She put the sponge down and he put a blackbird wing on the table. She dried her hands and looked at the wing with its serrated bones. The feathers were silky and iridescent. *"Ten birds?"* she said, *"Ten?"*

He shrugged and stroked a wing, turned it around and around.

"But you're just a boy. You don't even know right from wrong yet, I mean, this"—and she picked up a wing—"this is wrong. Who on earth do you think you are to go shooting birds?"

"They're just birds."

"Just birds?" She wiped the table clean of them and they fell at random around the floor, but she couldn't stand the sight of them like that so she bent to pick them up, stacking wing upon wing. "I don't want to hear about you shooting birds anymore, young man, I just don't." She put the wings in his hands and just before he walked out she said, "Tell me, killing these birds, did it make you feel good?"

"No." He looked like Earl, morose, indifferent. But Earl would have said yes, that it made him feel great.

Again she wanted to tell him things that a ten-year-old might not understand—how they would come back to haunt him, all those birds, how he'd pay. Imagined him just then, walking around the ridge, blind, eyeless.

He went on a spree after that. Trapped a whole family of weasels, kept the tails. Caught so many rabbits that he started selling rabbits' feet at the store. Dyed them blue, orange, pink. Sold for two fifty apiece. Smell of lye and wetness followed Butch in the house.

She knew he skipped school but didn't know how often until the teacher came to the house and told her Butch had been absent thirty-four days and was there a family situation the school should know about. She laughed. Thirty-four days. She shook her head and counted. "He was sick a week, then we had the snow days, then he was sick again. . . ." She couldn't go on, no matter what, the days didn't amount to thirty-four explanations.

"If there's a family situation maybe we can help. . . ."

She didn't look at him as she closed the door and after she heard his car start up and drive away she put on her mud boots and went out to the shed. Butch was in there picking on some coils of wires.

"You owe me an explanation, young man."

She didn't see Earl in the corner. "He's stopped. No more hunting. I told him so already." He had a spatula in one hand. "Besides, there ain't nothing around anymore. He got what there was to get. Might as well hit the books now." The two of them laughed as she walked out.

Allies, buddies, the two of them. It terrified her.

Some nights the smell of food woke her and she found Butch and Earl cooking steaks at midnight. Butch was almost as tall as her. "You have school in the morning, young man," and she removed his plate of food, and tapped his shoulder, and when he didn't move she pulled on the chair. *Now*, she said.

"He's hungry, for Christsake!" Earl, fork up.

"It's fine, Dad, it's fine. I wasn't that hungry anyway." And Butch walked away as if from snakes.

Butch threw the wings out the window one night. They'd been in a cardboard box in his closet for years. Never opened it until the night he had the dream: birds with his face on them, greasy black birds folding their partly severed wings over his face. Woke and got the box and tossed them out. In the morning he buried them.

The ridge was smoky blue every morning of that summer and then winter moved in quick and set itself between the sky and the rock and got into the serious matter of ice and snow. But first there was a strong Canadian wind that stripped every maple of every leaf and sucked the warmth right out of the land. A strong enough wind that blew the tops of trees off in the lower ridge and carried them airborne for miles down into the village where they fell on houses and barns.

It was during this strong wind that Butch couldn't sleep. He tried reading his textbooks with stories of Ethan Allen and his Green Mountain Boys, which always put him to sleep, but it wasn't working anymore. He studied his driver's manual, though he had all fifty-seven pages memorized in preparation for the day he would have his own license. He turned fourteen that year and spent hours having wide-awake dreams, dreams in which he dipped and swerved and no matter how he tried to escape he was always shot down.

Looking for comfort he went to his sister's room but she was snoring, deep in the center of the bed, curled like a mole in a nest of leaves. Sid had the darkest room and because he was so pale he looked like an angel, arms on his chest. "Sid, wake up." He called him a dozen times and shook him and still he didn't budge. Had an urge to walk into his parents' room just to see how they slept. Was it arm in arm, back to back, how, exactly, did they sleep together?

No one woke, no one heard him roam around the house alone as he wandered into all the rooms and sat on all the chairs and looked out of all the windows, and wondered what it was the others saw, what they felt. Didn't know if he was happy or not. Went to the ridge alone when he wasn't supposed to and if he found his father up there, he didn't disturb him. Nights they cleaned their guns on the kitchen table and when she came around and told them to get that stuff out of the house Earl ignored her. Sometimes he lifted the gun and sighted her through it. *Stop that,* she said. But her complaints got weaker and weaker.

And Butch heard the arguments, like black fringes around the night. He heard footsteps, doors slamming, curses. As a boy he knew he could do all the wrong in the world and it would never be as bad as the wrong his parents were doing to each other.

He was no more than a yard away the day Earl cut his finger off. Ax slipped. Butch watched the finger do a loop in the air and land flat on the ground, twitching with a life all its own. *Jesus, Dad.* Earl grabbed his finger, wrapped it in his shirt, and told Butch to drive. *I can't! I don't know how!* Earl looked at his bloody hand. *Start the goddamn truck!* and Butch did.

He turned fifteen the day a flare backfired and knocked Earl off his feet, blew bone and flesh off his shoulder. The blood formed petallike shapes on his father's chest. But he wasn't there the day the truck rolled back and crushed Earl's knees. That spring Butch carried the fear of death in his heart. Watched his mother in the kitchen and expected pots to catch on fire, for the knife to slip, for the water to burn her. When Sid tumbled down the stairs he picked him up and rushed out the door, ready to drive him somewhere, when his mother yelled, *Stop, put him down. He's all right. See?* True, there was nothing wrong with him just then but there would be something wrong later, he was sure of it.

At night he listened to the river grating the shore, carving land away. He knew when he awoke the river would look different, the house too. Heard a marble rolling across the floor, a stand-up doll tumbling off her chair, a stack of plates collapsing on the shelf. Things going, falling, crashing, and he rushed downstairs expecting to see everyone there, fixing, mending, patching. But no.

Kept his eyes open on the corner of things for it was there, he knew, that they changed first.

Crouched by Earl's side, the two of them silent, doing nothing at times but smoking. *Here, have one.* Learned to flick it in the air. Learned the names of weeds. Devilweed. Polar weed. Sacred weed. Learned to curse like Earl. *Fuck this shit.* Learned how to slip his body into the bare night and lie stiff and sweat through his fright. Grinned when he was supposed to laugh. Held his lips taut, stretched out, showed no teeth. Looked like a simpleton. Learned how to walk as if he had no care in the world, eased in and eased out of the house as if nothing mattered. Couldn't show what he felt. Couldn't tell a soul what he knew. Days didn't shimmer. Nights were long.

That summer their winter-whitened legs turned brown and their arms swelled with bug bites and their knees were scabby. They poked their pointy elbows at each other and ran to the river and dove in and emerged, shimmering, like seals, except for Tina.

Cut it out, guys, I don't want to get wet. She resisted water, frightened by its depth, stepped in a foot of water and went no farther but spent hours making pools for minnows and gathering the long beaded trail of frog eggs into the safety of the shallows.

From the house Darlene heard their sudden squeals and laughter and she dropped what she was doing and rushed out to see them backlit in the silver river. Her children, oblivious, intact, so animated.

In fall, some school nights they could be seen in their rooms, on the floor, a bucket of wet newspapers cut in strips and a bucket of paste. They shaped maps of countries they had never been to. They painted everything too bright green, too bright blue. Their clothes were stained with grape juice. Their baby teeth had fallen out long ago and she had been the tooth fairy who left quarters under pillows. She kept locks of their hair in her dresser drawers and their first scrawled writings, talismans. Kept the shiny rocks that were shiny only when wet. Closed the doors to their rooms, closed the shades and went to bed with the fine salty heat of a long summer day around them.

When she least expected it they'd ask her, *Tell us about the foxfire, the yellow snake, the red-eyed crows, the Mercie kids.* It was Tina then who wanted to know, and Sid, and they brought her twisted lengths of rope with feathers and asked what it meant. Strange cloud formations, a trembling in the earth, dark dreams. *What does it mean. Tell us.* What they really wanted to ask was: *Tell us why it feels like it does, why it's so enormous, this feeling, and why it doesn't go away.*

She sat by their side and looked at their eyes and Butch watched her, a little off to the side, no longer in the center of things, furtive, quick to leave, always ready to say, *I'm out of here,* and down he'd go, down or up the ridge. Sid's eyes were golden, like sap, spilling with light. Tina's eyes were small and dark like berries. Butch's eyes were often squinted but under his thick lashes you could see the gray in them, like Black Sea pearls. *Tell us.*

Loons and geese and ducks appeared on the banks of the river. Deer in their delicate poses. Everything a few feet away. Owls, hawks. *Tell us, tell us.*

At times the three of them appeared in the doorway, surprised to find themselves alone in the house. *Where's everybody?* Tina would say. *We're everybody,* Butch answered. *No, you know what I mean, where's everybody else? You mean Mom and Dad? Yeah, where are they?* And they held their breaths and strained to hear through the silence of the house.

The day ten monarchs and two blackbirds crashed against the window, Earl called her out. *Darlene! Come here, look at this.* She ran out and saw the birds, the butterflies. *What the hell do you think this means?* She looked at the sky, at the ridge, at the house. I have no idea, she said, but maybe a storm's coming up. *Must be a hell of a storm,* he said and went to the river and set his feet in it. They all watched him, the figure of a man with pant cuffs rolled up to his knees, head bent down, looking at his feet in the water, waiting for the storm to come from the bottom up.

She mended, cooked, cleaned, and listened to four conversations at the same time. She grabbed two chickens by the legs and rinsed their cavity, trying not to think about the bony frame inside. Walked outside on the porch, where Earl was fixing a broken ax handle. She asked him, "The chickens, Earl, you want them baked or fried?"

There, next to aprons and brooms, on the middle shelf was the old white box with her wedding dress. Mold and moths had eaten the corner of the box. She was afraid to read in its yellowing lace and old smell what the future was turning out to be.

Some nights she walked out to see the foxfire. Heard lots of things, small cries, her own children tumbling around in the old house, heard the river going like it had forever, heard the wind, but the little magic lights of the ridge were gone.

When the kids were small, she knelt by their beds and said their names like prayers, the only prayers that mattered, and fell asleep that way. A penitent by her children's beds, a guardian angel, a mother done with cooking and washing, a woman standing watch in the dark night. But now, she rounded up their years in a gaze: saw what each would be, what ills, calamities, glories, would come their way. She improvised their futures to please her heart. She dared herself to look at the unknown, to imagine it, every single cry of it. Grew scared and bitter at the world for all the harm it could do, would do. Looked away when she saw grass blades like daggers, yellow snakes in the garden. Didn't believe the call of an owl at midnight was an omen, refused to. The vanished foxfire, yes, it had been gas after all, a mere physical thing that had the right to cease. She yanked strangling vines from the lilacs, dug into the earth for the sheer sake of uncovering the soil, to see what lay hidden below. She shoved bulbs into the soil and told them to grow. She cleaned the house with a new fastidiousness, emptying cupboards, filling them up again, dusting cobwebs, scouring pots, scrubbing stains, and patching every hole in every coat and making sure all the buttons were on tight. If the ridge was what she had to live with, the least she could do was keep its ragged edges out of her home. And when spring came she burned winter brush. The children watched her at a distance.

■　■　■

THROUGH YEARS of feedings and fevers Earl had slept badly and now he wanted sleep, said so. *You'd think a man could get some sleep!* Closed the shades, took off his clothes, and with hands on his balls he slept. Like a man on a high wire. In his dreams he always fell.

He watched Darlene as she washed herself and looked in her dresser for that gown, that ivy gown, and not finding it she wrapped herself with the coverlet and slept as if in a cocoon. Reached for the hair and pulled it from her face. *I just want to look at you.* He grabbed his balls. Wondered if she felt the same loss, if she knew it was gone.

Sometimes she was willing to be aroused and thought back on the days in the cabin, the two of them alone and how even then it had seemed wrong.

There had been a connection between them, some unspoken understanding that had to do with reserve, stores, and safekeeping. The more he hunted and trapped and generally brought home, the less she felt she had to offer in return. She'd see the gutted fish lined up on the sink, dressed birds, the venison steaks jammed in the freezer. He expected her to say thank-you. He said so. He opened the fridge and stared in there and said, *We won't starve this year.* No, she nodded, we won't. Their hunger was of another sort.

They were failing each other. He was not the kind of father she wanted for her children. Good or bad, she'd been taught the sacredness of life—it had been in her mother's readings of Proverbs, Song of Solomon—it had been the reason her father had taken her out to see the wild things in the woods. But Earl's vision of wildness revolved around a slaughtering, a capturing, and she wondered if he'd set a trap for all of them, including himself. To go down, with pain. And she couldn't pretend she didn't know.

She didn't try to stay awake nor sleep at night, she went to bed because the day was done. And there he was with the steam of his tobacco breath, his eyes wanting to see nothing but her flesh, his mouth moving, whispering stories about the beauty and the horror of something, and the motions would begin. He expected her to cry out yes or no, and he kept his eyes closed even though she asked him, *Look at me now, Earl.*

God almighty, he said.

Some nights the children screamed in their sleep and she stood by their doors wondering what scared them. And when rain fell hard, late August rain, and their rooms were hot and airless and the windows were glazed over with the heat of shut-in bodies, nobody slept. The wind-wrecked trees crashed against the roof. Lightning struck the fields and split the rock of the ridge. Tina sat by the window, illumined like a specter, taking it all in. Sid shivered and turned his back to the storm. Butch waited for his mother to come in and say, *You all right in here?*

The aftermath of a storm, all storms, was as usual. *Mornin', Mom, Mornin', kids.* She sent them off to school and then went through their rooms wondering who they were, who she was.

None of them took to school except Tina, who couldn't keep her hands off books. Tina would be advanced another grade. She'd been advanced three times in three years, so by the time she was ten she was in the seventh grade. A teacher came by and told them. Darlene served Oreos and coffee, then sat back and watched a trail of black ants make their way from the window to the floor. She caught some words, *attitude and demeanor* and *reading ability,* and so forth. She pinched her nose and turned to look at the cold stove and the salt pork left on the counter. Earl studied the teacher's nose and her dress and her hands and nodded each time he heard the word *skill.* He finally asked, *Skilled at what?* Teacher didn't blink as she said, *Academically skilled. That so?* Earl said and turned to look at Tina, who had a moldy book in her hands and sat so close to the edge of her chair he thought she'd fall off if she took a breath. *Tina, where's the sun rise from?* he said. Tina shrugged and was about to stand. *Stay put,* Earl said. *Just proving a point here. Basic knowledge,* he said, tossing a scrap of something into the sink and missing. *Basic knowledge.* The teacher looked at Tina and Tina looked at Darlene and Darlene looked at the trail of black ants on the wall. Earl walked to the sink and splashed water on his face and dried his hands on his pants and walked out. The teacher looked around the dark room and Darlene followed her eyes and said, *Hard to know where the sun rises from in this house.*

By the time she was fifteen Tina was done with school. And as if it were enough to have one with brains in the house, the others slacked off, barely made it without flunking all grades. When

Darlene showed curiosity about Tina's love for books, she was shunned. Her daughter would close the book, leave the room, shut the door, shut her out.

Gradually, whatever little certainty Darlene had about her life with the other children also faded. Her methodical ways fell apart. One day she'd apologize for everything. *Sorry, I forgot to make your lunch. Sorry, I can't find your other shoe. Sorry, I didn't know you hated cheese. Sorry, I didn't mean to stare at you. Sorry, I wasn't listening.* The next day she'd snap at them. *Sit up! Hurry up!*

She demanded peace. *Stop fighting! Calm down!*

She demanded to be heard. *Listen to me!*

She struggled to make herself clear. She could say, *Here I am,* when they asked, *Mom, where are you?* but she didn't mean it, she didn't know where she was.

■   ■   ■

EARL SAW her sitting on the steps. Looking pretty. Blue bowl of peas in her lap. He mud splattered and aching all over. "You expecting company or what?" Wasn't what he meant to say. Wanted to tell her she looked good and that he'd noticed the garden was finally coming along. Meant to tell her the house could use some paint and what did she think, should they paint it white or what. But instead he stepped over her bare legs and went in and got a beer.

She pretended she wasn't really sitting there with a dress put on just for him. Didn't want to tell him she'd been waiting for him all day, that she'd lain on the grass in the morning and thought of him. She wanted to talk. Simple, easy talk. But he wouldn't be listening to her. She stayed out until the birds settled in the trees and the blackflies bit and drove her in. Long enough to know he wouldn't sit by her. She would have sat out all night and into the next and the next, and still he wouldn't have come out.

Later he mumbled about the heat, the dryness, the lack of rain. "July, ain't it, it's still July?"

She swept the kitchen though she'd already done that, but something about the sweeping set her at ease. Song of the peepers in the pond, call of barn owls. When Earl went to bed she sat on the porch and counted fireflies, wished on them like candles on a cake. Pieces of the moon. She wanted talk.

What do you want to talk about, for Christsakes? It's midnight. Can't you read a clock?

Watched him change year after year. Watched him to make sure he was really there. A figure in a hall. A man going out. Someone across the table. A man behind a wheel. Called him honey. "Honey?" That's what he'd called her. Honey. She still wanted the simple things of a simple life recognized. Like a plate on a table, something she could easily identify and say, *Yes, there it is, the plate is on the table. And there is my man. There are my children.* But the need was gone and she couldn't call any of it back.

Stood by the bed and watched him put on socks. Black with little red hearts. "Where'd you get those socks?"

"You got them for me."

"I've never given you socks."

"Well, maybe you should."

"What does that mean?"

"Nothing, it means nothing."

He looked at the socks, looked at Darlene. "You like them?"

"Yeah, I like them."

He looked at the mirror, caught her looking at him. He looked in the drawer for his shirt.

"Shirts are in the closet."

They had closets for everything. Linen, brooms, food, his stuff, her stuff. Empty closets.

"Honey?" she said.

"What? What do you *want?"* He tucked his shirt in.

She took a deep breath. Saw him walking around the world in black socks with red hearts. Thought someone had given them to him, someone who cared enough to buy him socks, and she felt betrayed.

"Where did you say you were going?" She opened the closet and grabbed his coat. She had taken the stains off the front and fixed the buttons. She dropped the coat, let it fall right out of her hands, and she stepped on it. She had done yard work and her feet were grimy with manure, mulch. She had set in a bed of petunias, something purple, to cheer her up. She stepped on the coat and wiped her feet on the coat. Her toenails, though painted red, were filthy.

He looked at the coat, then at her. The very air between them turned against him. He didn't tell her the socks came in the mail, addressed to another box number but he'd opened the box and seeing the socks, unlike anything he'd ever had, decided to keep them. *Stupid socks,* he muttered when she was gone. *Stupid woman.*

She walked down to the root cellar where the cool and damp stones wrested some of her heat away. Sat on the butcher log and stared at the crate of Red Delicious apples, rotting. She knew the smell of rot. Could have taken the bad one out but didn't. Went down every day just to smell that smell and then the whole thing went bad. Took the crate of apples out by the low sumacs and berry bushes, to the tree where Earl had carved their initials, *ES and DH*. A crude heart. A broken arrow. Sniffed the air and rushed back to the house knowing exactly what she had to do.

Got the rags, the matches, and ran back into the woods. Heard her mother whispering in the air, descending from her mounted clouds, saying, *Child, child.* . . . She hurried. The light wouldn't last forever. By the time she reached the cabin the sun was doubling back on itself. Two deer were feasting in the woods, their necks long, white tails twitching. They ignored her. Soon they'd be staggering drunk, bellies full of fermented berries.

The cabin was empty, had been for a long time. The cot no

longer had its brown cover. She twisted the rags and brought in kindling. It would catch. The matches spilled out and she got on her knees and from the dusty floor she saw what she'd never see again: the cot, the door, the table, the two chairs, the window so filthy the pines outside looked like apparitions. She saw herself lying over Earl's body. The sun was gone. The match flared. She stayed long enough to see it catch.

She burned the cabin down. People talked for days.

Did you hear about the fire?

No, what fire?

The cabin, the old cabin in the ridge.

No, what happened?

Kids, kids set the place on fire.

Shame.

Then it was forgotten. Other fires raged. Bully's old farm burned, took a whole day to put it out. Old forests crackled and the mountain was ablaze for three nights. Confused turkeys and grouse were seen on the road in. The wizened crows hustled in the corn stubble. Then lightning struck the church and blew out its tall windows. Then it rained. Then the moon rose like a dove, content, harmless, and without prophecy.

* * *

BY THE time Sid was four they knew for sure he couldn't speak. Spoiled rotten, Earl said. Give him time, Darlene said. Sid put his hands in her mouth and tried to figure out the right way to shape his own mouth to make sounds just like hers, but he couldn't.

He was eight the day Earl walked into the room and told him to shut it. *Shut it!* He picked him up by the shoulders and flung him across the room. No one was there to see him do it.

He despised himself for doing it and he despised Sid for letting him do it, for being the object of his anger. And, in the twisted way things have of going wrong, he thought the child was out to do him in. Thought the child had fabricated a world of his own, one in which he didn't figure at all, thinking him unworthy. *To hell with you.*

Sid was silent when Darlene came home. He was silent that night and the next day and she coaxed him and talked to him but he didn't try to answer, nor did he smile. He was altered, completely.

What do you think is wrong with him now?

Why isn't he talking?

Sid listened. He avoided his father. He looked at the ceiling as if he could bring it down.

His silence became a curiosity to others and everyone tried to shake him out of it. And as he grew he tried the cures, all of them. Aunt Mattie believed in nettle tea three times a day to loosen up the phlegm which she was sure was holding his sound box tight. A doctor slapped his back repeatedly. Another doctor put his finger down his throat. Speech therapists talked about the impediment, called it unconscious, automatic. They spoke as if narrating a difficult tale. They talked about trauma, deformity, and nervous disorder. They tried biofeedback and urged him to not give up, to go slow, to try again. They smiled in medicinal ways. Sid's only terror was that they might succeed and cure him. He did not want to be like them.

. . .

Y EARS PASSED in the way they do, with the waking and sleeping, yearning and loss following the thin chill, the thick heat. Nothing settled for long, nothing stayed. Late at night you could hear breathing and sighing and the little screams compressed into sounds no one recognized as hope escaped through parted mouths in sleep.

Cramped in the house, the children sat motionless like angry crows on a telephone line. Teenagers. The distance between them was wild. Whatever secrets they had in their hearts they kept in there. They didn't dare say, *I think this,* or *I think that,* because by then they knew what little knowledge they had might be used against them. They could be pried open, shaken up, tossed around. Better to say nothing.

Same with Darlene. Didn't trouble her at all to have no one to talk to. And the children had no one. No girlfriends, no boyfriends, no social events. The nearest movie house was sixty miles over the mountain gap but the bridge across had collapsed. Travel was impossible most of the time. Snow, flood, mud, or fires. The nearest restaurant was fifty miles in the other direction, across another mountain gap. Earl took her there one day, ordered the biggest steak, the tallest drink, the thickest dessert, and she didn't touch any of it. Cried silently into her napkin. *That's it*, Earl hollered, pounding the table and leaving his raspberry mousse unfinished. *Last time I bring you out! You don't deserve this, you don't know how to be nice.* Left a wad of dirty dollars on the table, walked out, opened the door, started the truck, and would have driven off without her if she hadn't run for it. Drove as if he meant to crash. *Nice*, she thought, *nice. I don't know how to be nice.*

In the dreary months before actual spring they brought out the nuts and cracked them open with a hammer. The butternuts had soured and were tossed out. Earl shot a wild turkey and spent the day dressing it and stuffed it with onions and potatoes and cooked it till the skin crackled. He tied the long turkey feathers in a bunch by the door. After dinner, Darlene brought out the Ouija board.

Sid had a cold and reeked of Vicks VapoRub. He had three sweaters on. She called the kids over and told them to think of something to ask the board.

"I hate this game," Tina said. "It's so stupid."

Butch put his arm around Sid, said, "You go first, you ask."

Earl walked by and said, "Don't mess with that stuff," and the kids all looked at him. "That's spooky stuff," he said before he left the room.

"Okay, now," Darlene said, rubbing her hands and smiling, "let's all think of a question, you don't have to say it out loud, just think it." She put her hands over the board and the kids watched her and soon her hands were moving in erratic circles and Butch picked up a pencil and wrote the letters where her hands seemed to stop.

Get on. Get off.

"I told you it's a stupid game, I told you," Tina said.

"What does that mean? 'Get on, get off,' " Butch said. "I don't get it."

"Neither do I," she said. "Let me try again." She formed a question in her mind and again her hands moved over the board and the board answered, *The door.* She asked again, and again the words formed, *The door.* "This door, that door, which one?" she asked. *This door.*

"I still don't get it," Butch said.

Late that night Sid walked into Butch's room and woke him. "The board . . ." Sid said.

"What about it?"

"The board . . ." he said with a great deal of effort.

"I hear you. The board. It's nothing. Just a game. Forget it."

An hour later Butch was still awake and so was Sid, each wondering about the meaning of a door.

■ ■ ■

In the morning Earl was always the first up, tossed a few logs in the stove, made his coffee, and was gone, out till supper at six. Left a cloud of diesel fumes in the air. Sometimes Tina was up, too, and she'd open the door and look at him. In her red pajamas, her bare feet, her wild hair around her face. She looked like Darlene and sometimes he wanted nothing more than to hold her. Sometimes he waved and called back, *It's early, go back to sleep,* but she stood there and looked at him, just looked at him. He drove a ways and stopped by the bridge and saw she was still on the porch, eyes on him. Just like a dog or a wolf, he thought, she had those senses about her. At night, when he came in late and everyone was asleep, he walked in their rooms just to look at their faces. The boys fast asleep but as soon as he opened her door she was up, eyes on him. *It's all right,* he'd say and close the door.

Every full moon he took Butch hunting. Sid came if Butch asked him. If there was a thin trail of snow the tracks were clear and they followed them for the sake of seeing where they ended up. Mostly hare and woodchuck. Sid crouched in the dark woods, poked his gloved hand in the snow, wrote his name. *Sid was here.* He didn't look for anything. One night they shot a rabbit and three coons. Earl ordered the boys to make a fire. "Get it hot and high enough so we can see what we're doing," though there was plenty of light from the moon. The boys dragged dry growth to the clearing, moving fast to stay warm, and the fire was big. Earl gutted the rabbit, cut head and feet off, and passed a strip of burnt rabbit across the flame, ate it mostly raw, and said, "Nice out, ain't it?"

They tacked the raccoons in a single file up a tree by the house. Heads up and tails out and paws to the side. Darlene didn't like it at all. "Can't look out the window without seeing something dead."

"They're just coons," Earl said. He was proud of them.

They stayed there all winter but by summer Darlene couldn't take it anymore. "Take those poor things down," she told Butch, and he pried them loose. She carried the carcasses by the tail and laid them in the narrow dug-out wedge and buried them. Two wild doves skirted from pine to pine and cooed and she thought they were thanking her. "Yes," she said, "that's much better."

"Dad's going to wonder why we took them down," Butch said.

"I'll tell him I couldn't stand the sight of them," she said.

He dropped his head and dug his bootheel into the ground. His jacket was too short. Over winter he'd grown tall and broad and he looked encased rather than dressed. "Dad says the ridge is cursed." He drew a hard line with his bootheel across the earth.

"A lot of people here think that."

"Do you?"

"Sometimes I do. Sometimes I don't." She grabbed the shovel and started back to the house but the way Butch looked kept her from moving. His eyes turned red and watery and she said, "Don't, Butch." She erased the mark he'd made with her own bootheel, still the soil was disturbed.

"The ridge is just rock with a little bit of earth over it. Hard to see what's underneath it all. And if it's cursed rock, then you have to believe your life is too. But a curse is nothing unless you let it in."

He didn't take his eyes off her. She glanced at the brown edges of the shady river and the blue smoke of sky.

And she understood how it was possible to die from lack of hope. She saw it in his eyes, how fragile and how bitter and how steady it moved in the human heart.

"My brothers left the ridge," she said. "I was very young. I watched them leave, and when I couldn't see them anymore I wanted to run after them and look at them just one more time. I remember that." She stabbed the earth a few times and hit rock. "What I can't remember are their faces. Not a whisker of them's left in my mind."

They watched each other.

"You might leave someday," she said. "You're bound to."

"You think you'll remember my face?" he said.

Turning away she said, "Of course I will."

A hundred yards ahead Earl was making his way across the gouged creekbed. Sensing them near he turned and waved once, then watched them from that distance until they walked away.

That summer Butch spent a lot of time on the river, tossing in pieces of wood, watching them float. He spent a lot of time alone, quiet, watching and listening. He was studying things. He took everyone's winter boots and rubbed mink oil on them, and set them back in the house so the first thing you saw walking in was five pairs of old boots in a row, nice and shiny.

"You intend on doing some walking?" Earl said.

"How about using your head and getting out of my way?" Tina said. Sid grabbed his boots and put them under his bed.

"They look like they're ready to walk away on their own," Darlene said.

He spent hours on the porch. If she sat next to him he said nothing when she nudged him and joked about his three-day growth and where was he last night and why did he come home so late and *what are you thinking?* He said nothing. When she walked away he followed her with his eyes and heard her in the kitchen slicing lemons, filling the pitcher with ice, turning the radio on and off.

He sharpened his knife and carved weapons. Bows and arrows, spears, knives, and daggers. He lined them up like a personal arsenal on the porch. But they were crude and thick and imperfect and useless. He made a two-foot dugout canoe from a birch log and launched it. Ran after it along the banks, watching it, waiting for it to sink or tip but it didn't. He'd build a bigger boat, big enough to get away.

■　■　■

THAT SUMMER Sid developed sloping shoulders, and seen out by the river he could have been mistaken for a boulder. He scratched his name everywhere. *Sid was here.* He tried to speak when no one was around. *Hello, I'm Sid.* He had large white circles around his eyes and the pinched look of someone much older. He read the Bible, read it under the covers until one night, when his father saw the flashlight under the sheet and yanked it off him. *Thought you were jerking off in here, thought you were doing yourself harm*. Looked at the Bible and at his son, grabbed the sheet, and tossed it off the bed leaving his son exposed.

Butch was given a hog to butcher. He was given keys and taught about idling engines and throttles. He'd been given his own gun on his tenth birthday, a rifle on his thirteenth. He was taught to stand real still and feel. Water down the river. Wind in your hair. Clouds overhead. Mist. Sleet. Snow. Rain. Sun. *Stand still, son, watch it happen.*

Darlene regarded all of them with a sidelong glance. Held her breath for long periods of time, held her head, her hands, kept herself from screaming, from tossing plates of food out the windows.

.   .   .

TINA, IN her room with its whitewashed walls, window facing the cold north side. She'd rid herself of the dolls and the paraphernalia of youth long ago, including the three child-size quilts in rainbow colors. The room held a highboy, bed, and lamp and three shelves stacked high with books, though her favorites were under the bed as she thought they helped ground her. Their pages yellow and musty smelling. Discarded used books. Bought-by-the-box books. Ten cents for ten years of *National Geographic*s. Fifty cents for *The Nature of the Physical World*, a dime for *Hiawatha* and Edgar Allan Poe. Butch knocked on the door and didn't wait to be asked in. He jiggled the latch and walked in.

"Two days and three nights," he said.

"What are you counting?"

"Since you had supper or anybody heard a peep out of you."

"Peep."

"You starving yourself for any particular reason?"

"Character."

"You don't need character to die."

"Who's dying?"

"Mom says to get down for supper."

"Not hungry."

"She says hungry or not you got to come down."

She pulled her hair over her face, long brown matted curly hair that had never been cut since she was born. It fell below her waist and covered her like a shroud. She opened her book and went on reading. *The Evolution of Ice*. He sat by the edge of the bed and looked at the posters on the wall. Glaciers, polar bears, northern lights.

Five minutes went by and he said, "Chopping wood builds character, too, you know. So does sitting at the supper table, picking up a fork, chewing. Bet you can get a good pound of character that way." Her legs poked out of her pants, sheer bone.

He smelled like he'd been in the kitchen while the fish was frying. "Brookies and peas for dinner," he said.

"I'm holding out. Declining. Interminably," she said.

"What does that mean?"

"Means leave me alone."

A few days later she came down with that ghostly shut-in look about her. Her brothers stared. Darlene sat with an elbow propped up on the kitchen table, looking at her. She was mending something in bright red and put the needle down. Everyone held their breath while Tina glided toward them, then she spoke. Maybe it was her tone of voice, so childish and thin, or maybe it was because it had been a long dry spell without a good joke, but when she addressed her brothers as *thee* and *thou* they both cracked up and roared with laughter, and couldn't stop, not even after they barged out the door. Her mother put her hand to her face and fought back the urge to laugh. She dropped the red cloth. "Tina," she said, "what on earth . . ."

"It's not funny," she said. "There's nothing funny. . . ." She held the book she was reading to her chest.

"Tina, really. You should see yourself. . . ."

She wasn't seen again for several days, though Darlene heard her making her way to the kitchen at night. Saltines and oranges left on the counter, a slice of bread and jelly. She left the milk out all night.

That girl, Darlene said, *holed up in that room*.

Those books, Earl said, *it's all those books*.

Leave her alone, Butch said, *the more you bug her the worse she gets*.

She went to the river hoping to see bullfrogs and stayed out longer than intended and when she came back to her room found her books gone. Stood there, couldn't walk in. Finally she rushed and looked under the bed. Nothing. The posters were gone too. Nothing but little pinholes in the walls. Through the open window she smelled smoke and looked out to see her mother and Butch by the old burning drum. Darlene tossing the books in. Big licking flames shooting up, pages flying out like winged messengers on fire. Saw Butch with hands in pockets, standing back, way back. Couldn't hear a word they were saying.

"This is the worst, the worst, Mom, I don't know how you could do this. I just can't—"

"Leave me alone, Butch. I know what I'm doing. You have no idea, no idea. She never talks to anybody, never bothers to say a word to me. Day in and day out, like a ghost. Well, I didn't bring up a daughter to be a ghost. To treat me like I don't exist." She stepped back from the fire. "You don't understand." She was crying.

"Mom, really . . ."

"Quiet, Butch, just be quiet." She wiped her face. "She'll have to listen to me now. She'll have to. She won't have a place to hide anymore will she?"

The *National Geographic*s went last. She dumped the whole box in. A gust of wind picked up and a huge gray cloud of smoke formed over the drum.

Tina stood still and watched the last of the flames from her window. She did not move for a long time, even though she heard a knock on the door, heard her name being called, her mother hollering, *Dinnner.*

Darlene slammed the burnt casserole on the table. The house smelled of bad food. She shouldn't have bothered to cook.

Butch and Sid came fast and so did Earl, who for once, sensing something terrible near the sink, didn't wash up there. He wiped his face and hands with the blue kerchief and made a big show about pulling the chair out and in again. "I'm hungry as a bear," he said, grinning. Darlene looked away. There was nothing she loathed more than optimism when it wasn't called for.

The boys looked at the crust of casserole and Earl peered at it too. "Looks like we got some baked rubber and some rusty iron here," he said. Then Tina came down. Quiet as a cat, one foot at a time. Hands on her heart. All eyes went to her. Darlene put her hands on her hips and raised her head, waiting for the words she was sure would come. If her daughter had walked up to her and slapped her she wouldn't have been surprised, she was waiting for it. *I despise you,* Tina said with her eyes, and when she was sure the feeling had registered she walked upstairs.

"Eat up, boys," Darlene said. "Eat while it's hot."

In the kitchen she turned the radio on, poured herself a glass of beer, and lit a cigarette. She wanted to see something on fire.

Earl was agreeable that night and held court at the table. He served himself and ate, nodding at the plate, at the boys. He leaned back on the chair and started talking.

"You boys got any plans?" He was asking for help fixing the car and the truck.

Sid couldn't say what was on his mind, that he hated the smell of gasoline and the sound of metal on metal and the sound of his father screaming get-me-this-and-get-me-that and how-come-you-can't-hold-a-fucking-tool-in-your-hand-huh-goddamn-it-how-come, but he couldn't say it though he tried and stuttered.

"Man, it's all right," Butch said.

Sid, hands shaking, got up and took plates to the kitchen, dropped them on the counter. His mother jumped, surprised to see him. That look about her, too much sleep, too little. Gone, she was absent even then and he hadn't seen it, none of them had.

"Surprised me there for a minute, son." She took his hand and turned it over as if she were about to read his palm. Sid pulled his hand away.

That night, like other nights, Butch and Sid waited until Earl was asleep on the couch. TV on. Their mother upstairs. Tina in her room. They got in the car, the old Lincoln, and pushed it, coasted, then drove until they reached the tar, drove over already-dead animals, skunks, chipmunks, birds. They blasted the radio, drove fast, flying. The car with its leather seats and ashtray full of peppermint gum. Butch drove, slapped his thigh. "Man, oh, man, we did it again."

Earl wouldn't let them take the car if they asked. *What for?* he'd say. *What the hell is out there? Can't you walk?*

∎ ∎ ∎

ONE COULD say more now, how what was sharp became dull, and how the peace of an evening star was something to be looked at and disposed of quickly in a blink. Smiles turned into grimaces. Frogs hurled themselves in the air, mad. The pungent fruits in the cellar rolled off the shelves and dropped.

What I'd like to know, said Earl one night, and he lifted his beer glass to all of them, the amber liquid splashed on his face and he grinned and wiped the beer off and said, *What I'm trying to say is . . . what I mean is that . . . Butch, come on, boy, help your old man out here.*

Nobody said a word. They watched him take his beer upstairs.

Nights were long. Darlene eased herself in the bedsheets, taking only what Earl hadn't clutched. She lay still for hours. A leg exposed and growing cold in the night air. An arm numb, unbrushed hair smelling of fried onions. She would not move and disturb him. She would not walk around the house and open doors.

One could also say that time slackened around them or they grew weak with time, careless in each other's presence, so that words no longer mattered. She avoided talking so he wouldn't curse. He avoided looking at her, afraid it would be the wrong kind of look. Dreams came howling and woke them. There was nothing to give themselves up to, not even the numbing promise of sleep. But they tried. Butch dreamt of boats and open water and Sid got down on his knees and prayed and Tina grew witless and scrawny and damaged. She hated, hated, hated.

Time locked them in. It slipped round their feet like cold work boots. Moonlight caressed the open fields far from the ridge. Moonlight stung the tops of trees and rushed down the earth, deep into the foundations, and up the floorboards where it rose like a wish, claiming their cold hearts. Moonlight seeped in and altered the children too. Through the thin walls they could hear it all.

Earl. I want to talk, his heavy body on hers.

Shut up. Don't go ruining everything. He came again and again.

Cold nights with stars guiding those who expected guidance, cold nights with a fire in the hearth and nobody there to see the flame. Cold nights and nothing. Time took it. Time moved in. Time made trouble in the heart. Made the soup go bad. Made the pots burn. Made the house swallow the moon. Took the stars, trashed them. Dampened the brows and made the bodies sweat in the coldest of nights. Time straightened the chairs and did the dishes. Time combed its hair in the yellow mirror. Time said, *Look at this mess.* Time said, *Forget it.* Time said, *Shut up.* Time was the spasm of cries and the hearts pounding. Time licked its lips, wiped its nose, and sometimes it said, *I'm sorry.* Time asked if it was going to rain or snow and time put on its coat and boots and time had a cup of tea. Time was forgetful.

Did any of you see where I left my hat?

What hat?

My hat, the only hat I have.

Never seen you wear a hat. What hat you talking about?

Time made them forget who they were and what they wore and what they looked like. Time stared out windows, at the river, at the ridge. Time rushed in and stayed in.

Out the back porch, across the river, she could see her parents' house. The FOR SALE sign was rusty and had been banged down innumerable times by the snowplow. No light shone through the windows but she imagined her mother in that dark misery. Only her talk had survived and it was in her now and in her children. They'd let it in. She was ready for them now to ask her about the curse of the ridge, she'd say, *Look, here it is,* and lay her open palms on them.

No one visited except Aunt Mattie. She was all that was left of kin. Darlene's mother was buried near her apple orchard, where no good apples were to be had. Her stone was under the path of the stars, slanted, alone. The carved words read: *My soul cleaveth unto the dust; quicken thou me according to thy word.* Lucky was still living out West, loving his good times. She hadn't heard a word from her brothers. That was it.

Earl became like a rooster in the perpetual act of crowing, his chest was too high, his voice changed. The days he feared had come. He moved his feet carefully over the land, afraid he'd sink in, disappear. *Son of a bitch,* he said, *you are one sad son of a bitch.*

He looked at Darlene like a mooring in the water, something he wasn't meant to reach, or latch on to.

To Darlene he appeared heavy and dull, altered into what she always knew he would become.

Earl saw her coming at him, curved like a gust of contrary wind.

At times Earl talked for the sake of talking though he knew she wasn't listening. "So I told old Gus I wasn't going to buy that wood from him and he said just as well because he wasn't going to sell it for nothing and I told him it wasn't worth what he was asking. . . ."

She pulled on the gold ring on her finger, tried to get it over the swollen knuckle.

"I don't see how my beers can disappear so quick. Had a six-pack here and not one left. You drinking my beer, Darlene?"

The ring would have to be broken off. She'd go to a jeweler, no, a doctor, and say, *Take this thing off me.*

"I know it just like I know the back of my hand this winter's going to be a bitch. Seen the geese today. Ain't nearly time for them to go and that means they moving for a reason. Going to be colder than a witch's tit."

She tried soaking her finger in cold water, tried rubbing oil, tried beeswax, still it wouldn't budge. Has to come off somehow, she thought.

And beauty, that thing they had carried in their hearts like wings long ago, vanished. When they saw each other the word that came to mind was *ugly*. He said it. *You are one ugly woman.* She said it. *You're so ugly.* And the house was ugly, even the children looked ugly.

The land was often black and dreary and when it rained too long or snowed too hard or the sun beat down too hot, it was all ugly. They lived on the opposite side of beauty. Nothing was gay, nothing surprised them. Everything was neglected, crowded, and failed.

When one of them laughed or sighed, contented, the others looked and wondered what caused that rare emotion.

■　■　■

IT HAPPENED over years, in a moment, for no reason at all; it happened because they took so much for granted, because they'd heard it all before, because they waited too long and they couldn't wait anymore, because it was always her, it was always him, it was always something; it happened because under their bed was a transparent web in which two silver moths were trapped; it happened because she sold her mother's piano, *and the piano will go to my beloved daughter Darlene,* she sold it because she was not beloved to anyone; it happened because Earl left her in bed in the mornings without saying a word, because he never said anything kind, because she stopped expecting him to, because, after all, the language they needed was unknown to them. And by then, of course, the foxfire had burned itself out. The cabin was burnt. And the children, she followed them at a distance, out on the porch, to the road, around the corners of the house and they stood there, away from her, always at a distance. She waited, dejected, staring till one of them snapped. *What do you want with me?* There was nothing to distract them from each other.

So it wasn't a surprise that day in late summer when the corn was high and the maddening crickets shrieked, when the sun was done burning and the moon rose dull and tired, when the geese were thinking of flying and the fish were easy to catch, when a lightning storm took the power lines down and the house was lit with kerosene lamps and candles, when the children were sulking and the dog out back was acting listless, dreamy, that's when things changed.

Darlene, how long you think you can keep this going?

He was talking about her silence, her indifference, her way of making do without him. He was also talking about the land, another winter creeping up and no money. He watched her hold on to the back of a chair, lift it, let it down hard.

What?

She had food to cook, clothes to wash, the children's rooms to clean up, wood to stack, her daughter needed talking to. It was suppertime and she hated suppertime. Meant she had to dig in once more, dig in to the empty fridge, the half-empty cupboards, she had to make something out of nothing, make it look nice, had to sit there and pretend, she had to try, all the time holding her head in her hands wondering where was it, that wild joy, where did it go. She was tired.

You know what I'm talking about.

He could get a rise out of her most of the time. He could say anything, call her a name, and she'd get furious. He could call her a bitch, that always worked. Or something worse. *Goddamn slut.* He'd rather have her hollering mad than like this, so unfeeling and quiet.

No, Earl, I don't know what you mean.

She was tired, that was all there was to it. Couldn't he see? Couldn't he tell? She hadn't washed her hair in days. Hadn't changed her clothes. The little flowers she'd dug up from the yard, thistle and goldenrod, were sitting in briny water. The dog bowl was empty. Couldn't he tell she was the approximation of herself and couldn't he just leave her alone, just tonight, just this once? Couldn't he just shut up?

There wasn't time to rethink the thought nor time to look at him or at the potatoes which were boiling on the stove or at the small portion of meat she'd have to cut and serve and hope it would do, there wasn't any time at all to think of the waking pain or the past or the bewildered look of the children, nor the darkened staircase that led up to their rooms, nor was there time to think about dreams and longing or nights as profound as a screech owl's call as it made its way through the tall mastlike trees, as it plucked from the ground the small, the frightened, the easy to catch. There was no time at all before she removed the boiling pot and set it down on the white

Formica counter, no time at all before she turned around and saw Earl as he lifted his hand and hit her.

You son of a bitch.

She meant to correct him, to tell him no, she was not a son to any bitch, never had been and never would be, and if he wanted to call her a name he should think first and maybe call her a plain old bitch, but there was no time and she was so tired she let herself fall, slumped on the floor, head against the stove. Her eyes caught the sight of a blue ball under the table. And a small tomato from some year had lodged itself in the heat vents along the floor. It was blackened and small. How was it she never noticed? She took a view of her world from the floor. The way his shoes curled up at the toes. The dirty linoleum. The ugliness of it all.

There was no time at all to consider the how and what and where and why. Candlelight shone through Darlene's cupped fingers covering half her face. A light from the table set with five plates, five glasses, five napkins. Eloquent in its startling evocation of what she had intended for the evening. She had planned the best meal under the circumstances: creamed potatoes, roasted pork in cubes, peas, hot bread pudding with caramel sauce for dessert. It was the best she could do.

He looked at her, felt his stinging hand, thought it only existed in his imagination. Thought for a moment a confused thought: he had *not* hit her, had *not*, rather he had found her in one of his open traps, and he'd only attempted to pull her out. The thought brought him to his knees. . . . *Honey, I'm sorry.*

The only one who could have felt what was about to happen was Sid, and he was the first one down the stairs and the only one to come to her and push the kneeling shape of his father away and say, *No.*

The other children stood in different poses at different angles on different steps of the long straight stairs. Tina held a book in her hand, it was folded in half; the spine would break, the pages would fall out, she would never read it to the end, it would no longer matter.

Butch stood behind her, looking at his parents as if surprised, as if someone unknown had unexpectedly walked in and now he was supposed to do something about them; he did not want them in his house, whoever they were. He turned around and went to his room. His door closed gently.

Tina stood still and looked at her mother on the floor, back against the stove. She took in the table, the settings, the smell of the food, the white salad bowl, empty. The dessert plates stacked one on top of another. She said only one thing before she went up. *The stove's on. Somebody better turn it off.*

. . .

THAT WAS the first night the ladies in the attic came to Darlene. They approached her like the ghosts they were. She'd felt them before, denting the side of her bed, whispering, gliding in a cold chill about the room, but she'd never seen them. They opened her dresser drawers and fingered the lace, the satin of her things, they moved her purse from one corner of the table to the other, they put her shoes under the bed.

Three old women. One with the midwife's bloody apron, one dressed with Sunday best, and one in a man's shirt, dungarees. They talked to themselves and asked, *Do you think it's raining yet? Where's the potash? Is sap running yet?*

Ghosts as old as the house itself. Women who'd been pushed out by death and roamed around like ancient and decorative and useless buffalo. The women of the attic, the benevolent, sad, lonely women who came back that night and made their presence felt in the centuries-old air, women who wanted to sit primly on a chair and talk about how the house needed a coat of paint and the flowers needed pruning and how the children were too solemn and the man too boisterous, but it was Darlene who concerned them and made them forget about themselves, dead as they were.

Darlene kept her eyes open and watched them fade as they took their brisk haunches to a place she could not go. Their papery air and dark breath swept over her and then they were gone. The faint light came through the curtains, then the screaming crows announced a new day had begun.

The mist was miles thick that day and took all morning to burn off and by noon the river looked like a massive slab of black quartz.

Part
Two

Stone and rock, what is the difference? One is loosened from its grasp, the other holds on to something bigger than itself.

Creek and stream. The difference is in where you stand when you come across it. A stream can be crossed in a single leap; a creek can't.

Love and hate. Difference is minute. Thin as thread and just as likely to break.

Up north, bogs are spreading their dark wetness and stunting growth. There is much speckled alder, red maple, gray birch. Lichen spreads like a map across the alpine tundra. What grows, grows. What dies, dies. It is in the threshold of what can be, in the confined areas, the raised or marginally claimed lands, that one can see what is central, what belongs and what does not.

The summer had been a long procession of dying animals—raccoons, skunks, solitary deer, all acting strange, rolling on the dirt, digging holes in her flower beds and scratching on the front porch. A rabies alert was posted, campsites closed, and children kept pellet guns loaded and were told not to go into the woods but they did anyway.

But now it was the end of summer and what had to die was dead. Eagles flew out of tall trees. The heron stood still. Geese started their flight. The garden was a heap of weeds and browning stalks and nothing but a red dahlia clung to its fiery color, defiant, like a harlot. The grass was matted under damp leaves. Skunks had dug around the porch and their stench was strong.

Darlene wasn't surprised when she saw the mangy-looking fox in the river, lapping water, disoriented. She towed it in with a long pole to the river's edge, where it arranged itself in a half-sitting position, too weak to shake itself, too weak to hold its small head up, eyes bugged out, ears raw and down. The long brush thin and limp between its legs. Mouth opened and closed. You stay right there, she said and got the gun from the shed. The fox was exactly where she'd left it, sitting like a puppy, licking its paw, looking at her when she shot it. Surprised to see blood bubbling out through the fur, thought it was empty inside. Surprised to find her daughter at her side.

"I can't believe you did that." Tina.

"I had to, it was sick," Darlene said. She looked at the fox and waited, in respect for its life, thinking all creatures need some time to rearrange their soul in the passage of one life to another. The blood flowed.

"I can't believe you did that. You *killed* it."

"What was I supposed to do? Let it drown? Take it to the vet? Rabies, Tina, this fox was very very sick."

"*You're* sick. You're *very very* sick." She ran to the house and slammed the door.

Darlene thought about the fox. If it had rabies, which it did, she was sure, she was supposed to cut the head off, place it in a cooler with ice, and take it to the vet where they would verify it had rabies. No need for that, she thought, and heaped the small fox onto the shovel, buried it under the crab apple tree, placed twenty flat stones over the circular mound, tossed a handful of wild asters, and said, There you go. Wondered who would show her a kindness like that when the time came. And it had been a kindness, a mercy killing, she was sure of it.

She put the gun back in the shed and the smell of dried blood stopped her. It was in Earl's things. In the cup with old coffee, the pint of whiskey, the ashtray, tools, resins, wax. The smell of Earl. It was outside too: his truck, his woodpile, the rusty chains. Wondered how a man could have a life with a woman and not show a trace of that life anywhere. No picture of her, no old trinket, no sentimental object that spoke to him of her, unless she was there, in the preparation of traps and the smell of blood.

Pulled her hair back, the way Earl did, until she felt her scalp rise. *I want to look at you, Darlene, I just want to see your face.*

It was a Tuesday in October. The day had the certain color of bad weather. Rain or snow. Hard to tell. It was the kind of day that forced its way into the senses and demanded you take notice. The only definite thing about it was the sweetness in the air, ridge air.

She wasn't thinking of going but looked at everything as if for the last time. Remembered her brothers, three tired brown shadows, going down the road. And saw her father in the rakes and hoes and garden gloves caked with mud. She saw her own life in the unpainted steps. The maples, the dirt road. Chokecherry, goldenrod, thistle. The little bed of purple petunias which she'd let die once again; they'd looked so hopeful she couldn't stand them. The crimson bee balm, the ancient lilac, the bridal veil, the irises, everything choked in weeds. And there at her feet, the road, nothing but gravel and stone. Beyond, all around and forever, was the ridge.

The sagging porch was where she'd sat waiting for someone to talk to, waiting for foxfire, waiting for her children to be born, for them to go to sleep, for dinner to be made, for the night to end, for summer to come, for winter. The signs of neglect were everywhere. Not a thing of beauty anywhere. *How was it that it changed?*

No use asking how, Darlene, things are sometimes, they just are. Voice of her mother in the air.

Imagined walking down the road with the house and the land trailing behind her, following her out. She'd wear it, the ridge, like a cloak miles long and miles wide.

Across the road, the familiar sound of Emma Darling's red

Honda. She was the librarian. When the children were in school she'd brought boxes of discarded books, encyclopedias missing volumes B–C, P–Q, dictionaries with water stains. *Huckleberry Finn, Treasure Island, Hiawatha* with full-page color drawings. Tina's books. Gone now. Books and the occasional basket of surplus zucchini were the only gestures of friendship they'd received all those years.

Maybe because the house was set in darkness, shielded and obscured, they were expected to be like the land itself, hard and resilient, and to do without. Maybe it was the talk, and there was plenty. Bad blood. *That child of theirs can't talk, that other one, the girl, never see her go out of the house. That Earl, I don't know how she puts up with him. That woman, she terrifies me.* Whatever it was, it was there. And the house itself with its domestic ghosts and the band of horned swallows and the acres let go. Sawdust and rue and the shed, the shed with the hide and heads of animals.

And their kind of poverty. Though not dirt poor, the slightest change of circumstance—too much snow, too little rain, illness—could have reduced them to nothing. Money still came from whatever Earl did. Clearing land, hauling logs, firewood. He set traps, hunted in and out of season, did what had to be done. Once a week Darlene still put out her hands and got flat dollar bills counted twice. *What you gonna do with that money?* Her answer was always the same: *Buy food.* She saved what she could. Six hundred and two dollars after many years.

Was about to go in and see about dinner when Moose drove up and hollered as if she were deaf. "Earl here?"

She hollered back. "No. He's out doing wood with the boys. Won't be back till supper."

Moose was a local, never married, never had a woman take to him, and so the question hung: What was wrong with him? His parents had land, lost it all, and became bitter, dumb, and skewed in their ways. Their house had a view of Route 100 going north and south, it cut across what used to be their good meadow. Moose did odd jobs, bought junk cars, fixed them, sold them for three times their worth.

"He got this running?" He was eyeing the Deadhorse, Earl's truck, a '79 Ford diseased with rust. "I'll make him an offer."

"Not for sale." Wanted to tell him he could take it if he wanted. Had to be toyed with to get it going and once it got running it couldn't be shut down. *Ought to just shoot that thing*, Earl always said but he kept it running as if it were a symbol of his manhood. An ugly broken-down thing. He cussed it, she cussed it. If it wasn't the starter, it was the battery or the clutch or the brakes. Hours hunched over it, under it, and then swearing and worn out he'd come in the house aiming to fix whatever. Nobody got in his way. *I ought to shoot that thing*, he'd say.

Moose stroked the hump of dented chrome as if it were a prize bull, something to brag about. She knew the kind of man Moose was. Knew by the way his clumsy hands fingered a hole of rust that he'd never make a woman feel good. His mouth clamped tight on his dangling cigarette and smoke curled out his nose. He was admiring another man's junk. He avoided looking at her.

Way you look at men is all wrong, Earl often said but what he meant was *How come you don't look at me that way?* She didn't look at him at all if she could help it.

"Wood green?" Moose said. Eyes everywhere except on her.

"Don't know." She crossed her arms and watched the ridge. She'd never been on the other side of the ridge.

Earl, what's it like on the other side?

Likely to be another ridge, just like this one.

Likely. Could be. Maybe was. Sameness. Conjecture. Neither knew more than what there was to see in plain sight. The dead-end road, the village, the bridge, the river, each other. Her long nervous hands. His clumsy desire. Her sidelong glance. His blunt approach.

Heard voices coming through a loudspeaker. The village was preparing to unveil a memorial commemorating its history. A marble slab told of General Warren and his soldiers who died in the great famine in the ridge. The men had cut into their horses for food, horses that were brought down by wolves, wolves which were heard nightly until the last of the soldiers froze. The year before, the village had put in a plaque commemorating the Abenaki. A stone sculpture of a brave on his knees, hand on the soil. Of her own history there was nothing left.

What remained of her parents' home was a stone wall, a cellar hole darkened by moss, and the muffled wind as it swept over the tall hedges. The house collapsed one winter into a heap of broken beams, rotted timbers. She'd scavenged the overgrown fields and found milking pails, wooden plows, carts, a silver teaspoon. Swarm of flies and wasps lanced the air. A damselfly led her to a tarp, rotted and brown, through which sprung tufts of timothy, wild and green. It was there she saw her father, in a thin blade of something wild. Bullfrogs called out from a dark pool of water ringed by stones; deep dark tremulous notes like those of the old piano. It was all dead; crocus, daffodil, lupines, and the wild iris. Childhood, she understood, was what you walked away from. Childhood was a bare room straining against its own emptiness, the parallel rows of cotton lace on a nightgown, the seashell-pink glow of a lamp, the unforgiving stories, the cooling rim of a bathtub, the scalding soup taste to a day, any day. It was gone, all gone.

Moose poked around the yard, picked up a quartered log, and whistled. "Looks like Earl chopped down a piece of history." He showed her the log. He twisted his mouth so his two front teeth hung over his lip.

She grabbed the log from his hand and saw it. *DH and ES*. Darlene Hank and Earl Summer. Twenty years ago Earl had carved the crude heart on an elm. History. That's where he begged her to say it: *Say it, Darlene, say you love me. . . .* But she hadn't. Neither had he. *Damn it, Darlene. Come here.* Here, here. The tree was winter wood now, ashes in somebody's fireplace. She tossed the log into the pile and nodded to it as if it were a nasty acquaintance.

"Yup," he said, to his feet, to the pile, to the day. "Yup."

Dirty-bottomed clouds hung low and the ridge turned black. She pulled on her brown sweater. A tired little cough escaped her.

"Cold's going round. Siberian flu. Everybody's got it," he said.

"I don't have a cold."

"School closed down, all the kids got the flu. Russian flu or something like that. Was in the papers. You seen the paper?"

Shook her head no. She kept the local paper stacked up for fire starter. Never read it. The *Reporter* was full of bickering between locals and out-of-towners. People complaining about fences, money rolling out of town, money not sticking to the locals' pockets, money and its bad impression. It was a skimpy paper subsisting on gossip and petty formality, and no, she never read it.

A sudden light fell on the ridge. The sky opened. The darkness passed. A cloud vanished. Light laced the river. The rain gutter sparkled, the tin roof shone like polished silver, everything looked good, clean, and then it changed again. The day became dark and soured her mood.

"Moose? How's your family?" She felt like crying.

"Fine." Moose scratched his crotch, but he caught himself, or else the need subsided and he stopped. He was awkward as hell and didn't know what to do with himself. His big head looked like a prize cabbage and his clothes were so faded it was hard to tell their original color.

And, as if planned, as if the day had begun just so the next moment could happen, she heard the geese and saw the dots in the white sky, their arrowed indentation. They seemed desperate to go. When the last bird disappeared over the ridge she felt abandoned.

Quiet, real quiet. Then gunfire in the valley.

"You hear that?" Moose turned east. "Earl huntin' yet?"

"Bow-hunting." She imagined Earl and her sons walking with the intense determination of primitives in a light-speckled field. Browns, reds, and yellows. Shadow and light playing tricks on them. Oblivious to splendor, governed to hunt. They didn't feel what she did. The fight of the geese didn't make them cry. Turned to see the door open slowly, then close just as slow. Her daughter, like a stranger in a dream. My daughter, thought Darlene, my daughter.

The lack of real light, the geese, the shots. It was more than she could stand. Crows gathered on the tallest branch and complained. Oh, shut up, she said, just shut up. The huge black birds drew close together and Moose wandered into the woods. He wouldn't go far. Mercy Road began and ended right there at his feet.

She rushed into the house which smelled of a little death. A mouse caught behind the fridge, festering. Smell followed her up the stairs. Worn treads. Narrow steps, low ceiling. Wood painted white, the grain showed. Ran to her sons' rooms, opened the doors, confirmed their absence. Knocked on her daughter's door. "Honey, Tina, you in there?" Nothing. Opened the linen closet and listened through the thin membrane of plywood that always let out the sounds in her room. Nothing. Both of them holding their breath.

Looked around long enough to feel how time had seeped in with gusts, in rain; it had stained the walls, cracked the ceiling. Cobwebs hung high on a corner like an abandoned show. Blackflies, spider eggs. Saw herself caught in there, going mad, fast.

The bed in her room was too soft for the hard kind of bargaining that went on in there. The night before she'd pulled all the covers over her, pillow on her head, lying still as Earl stood over her, asking, *You awake?*

She'd heard them again, the ghosts, the ladies in the attic, the kind and weary women. Had felt them quiver like cold birds, their presence like an open beak, like fledgling dreams. Asking politely: *Where's the potash? When's it going to rain? Sap running yet?*

Earl had fallen into bed like a sour curse. *You mopin' again?* That was his way of asking *Don't you love me anymore?* Then he called her deranged. *You deranged or what?* Called her silly. *Silly woman.* Said she was sick. *You must be getting that disease they talk about in the news.* Then he'd shouted down the hall so the children could hear. *Watch out for your mother here, next thing you'll know she'll be out walking nekked in the woods.*

The children had heard, she knew because in the morning they looked at her as if she were really standing there naked.

Now she saw the coat in the closet. He'd given it to her years ago. A fox coat. He'd said: *Now look at this, try it on, look at this will you, hey kids, come see your mom, look at this will you?* and he'd made a show of putting the fox coat over her, making the shoulders fall nice and heavy, pulling on the collar, showing her where the pockets were, then standing back saying, *Now look at you,* and he'd made her see herself in the watery mirror and she'd seen a thing made of fur but she didn't see herself at all. She didn't know where to put her hands. "You forgot to make buttons. It won't close." And she had stood there with the coat sides open to show him how impractical it was. Why hadn't he thought of buttons, or at least a sash, a belt, something to close it? "The wind will get right in, see?"

The ugly black suitcase was under the bed. She packed. Sweaters, skirts, shoes. Shoved the fox coat way back in the closet. Didn't look in the mirror, afraid she'd see something that might stop her.

She thought of the fox, the one she had killed that morning, and wrote a hasty note with a leaky pen. The room with its quilt, pillows stuffed with ancient feathers, a highboy, a chest, walls with two photographs. If she'd had a handful of ashes she would have scattered them over the bed.

The suitcase banged against the walls as she made her way downstairs, and she expected her daughter to come out and say *Stop that noise.* Moose was leaning against a tree watching birds darting from tree to tree. "You been in there lately?" He pointed to the woods, the overgrown path, the old road. The sign for Mercy Road had rotted long ago.

"No, I never go in there."

She could have told him the obvious, that a road stops being a road when it's not traveled, that nothing went in there except darkness which fell like a mourning skirt, pleated and thick and dignified. She could have told him that birds lost their song in there, and that creatures halted in the path, paws up, noses in the air, then turned and ran the other way. Crows perched on treetops like guardians. Owls thrived in there. She could have told him about the summer berries fermenting on the vines turning the soil blackish blue, and the foxfire, how it used to burn its silent little path into the woods.

Moose looked at her and she felt a pull, a loosening rush between them, but it wasn't much. His face had the pessimistic pendulous weight of one who's been alone too long. His shoulders seemed to exist for no other reason than to hold his big head up, and it was a big head. His mother said it was carbonation. *Drank way too much of that seltzer water. Got all that air in me, bubbly went straight to his head. Doctor said he'd never seen a head like his. Carbonation.*

"You going into town?" Darlene lifted her suitcase. Silver buckle straps shining.

"Town? What town?"

"Town."

"You mean Smallford?"

"Exactly."

"I reckon I could go if I had a reason to."

"You got a reason now." She shoved the suitcase up on the seat. On the dash was a brown hat pinned with flies, silvery feathered things.

"Sure you don't want to ride in front?" Moose hollered as he drove away. She waved her hand no. She was in the back of the truck between two old tires, greasy ropes, a can of gas, and a wet bale of hay. Wind on her face. She was wearing a brown skirt, a black sweater, her blue coat. She had opaque stockings and boots with rubber soles. She had six hundred dollars in her purse, a brush, gum, matches, a crossword puzzle. It was a strong wind, Canadian cold front. She wouldn't be home when it hit. Wouldn't hear the rifle shots or listen to the men talk about the kill. She left no dinner cooked.

"Stop! Stop!" She pounded on the hood.

"What's wrong?"

"Go back! I forgot something. . . ."

Moose swung the truck around and sped all the way back. Darlene jumped off, ran to the back of the house, and there she was. Missy, the dog, chained and with an empty bowl of water. Darlene slipped the collar off, filled her bowls with food, fresh water. Held the dog's face and reckoned with her. "Go on now, Missy, eat and get the hell out of here. You hear me? Eat and then run. Run, girl."

Missy wagged her tail, happy for the attention. She cocked her head one way, then the other, struggling to understand what was expected of her.

"What was all that about?" Moose said.

"Nothing, just something I forgot. Let's go."

"You know what you're doing?"

"Yes." She jumped in back. Thought she saw someone in the upstairs bedroom. More like a fragment of light moving between the curtains. Wind howled and she thought of Earl. *Told you, didn't I tell you all? Didn't I say it? Gone down the road nekked or something.*

Well, she wasn't naked. She wasn't, however, dressed for the day that would drop to twenty by nightfall. She realized that as soon as Moose let her out where the bus stopped. Nobody called it a depot or a station. It was just the parking lot in town. A bus to New York came at four-thirty daily. It was the only bus that came into the ridge and she'd often stared at the letters, New York, and wondered what kind of person lived there.

"You can change there for whatever destination you wish," the driver said.

"Yes, I will."

"What?"

"Change my destiny."

"Lady, I said destination."

"I know what you said." She held his look until he looked away.

He shut the door and the bus started and she closed her eyes because she didn't want to see what it looked like, the passing, the leaving. Didn't want to see the ridge and what was left of its miserly light. Knew it by heart.

You never been happy with what you got.

What have I got, Earl?

Aw, shut up. Get lost then, go on, get out.

. . .

W HAT SHE left behind was a sugar spoon rimmed with coffee, a grocery receipt, dried mascara, an old lipstick, soiled sheets. Two pairs of high heels, soles shiny from wear. She left her old pink terry robe hanging on a peg in the bathroom; in the pockets was a wad of tissues. She left eggshells in a plate and a salt shaker turned upside down on the kitchen table. She left her toothbrush and her thin gold wedding band on the sink. She left the stove clean. She left her closets bare except for the coat; the pockets were empty. She left on a day when the river shimmered, naked and taupe, like a long silky leg.

She left a note on the table: *If I take you back shoot me.*

It wasn't Earl or Butch and Sid who found the note, but her fifteen-year-old daughter. She read it by the light of the window and at first didn't get it. The handwriting was the usual, a sloppy cursive slanted to the left. *If I take you back shoot me. Shoot me.* Birds called from the trees, darted out, swung over the river. A truck went by on low gear. *Shoot me.* Why would anyone want to shoot *her?*

She took the note to the bathroom but didn't read it. Thought of flushing it, making it go away, instead she folded it in small pieces. Ran up the stairs, tripped on a loose tread, and slowed down. What was the rush? Looked around the room, hoping she wouldn't see something she'd regret.

Opened the closet. Smell of pine freshener, a plastic bag from A&P, two old shoes, and the fox coat. She put it on. The soft fur bristled at her touch and she felt a connection there, something wild and recognizable.

She remembered the day Earl carried the coat into the house like a child and put it on Darlene. They'd taken a photo. *Take the picture already, will you?* And so it was recorded, the gift acknowledged. A photo proved it. But the coat had meant nothing to her and when she left she took the blue nylon coat with snap buttons and pockets deep as shovels.

The room seemed emptier than empty, as if nothing and no one had ever been there. Light through the windows, smoke from the chimney. The maples looked ghostly.

And there on the walls was the photograph of the five of them. Aunt Mattie had come along one Christmas with her new Polaroid and told them to line up. *Line up and stay real still.* Clumped like logs in a river jam. Each one jutting out at a different angle, refusing to come together. It was awkward, all that closeness. Everybody had their eyes set in different directions except for Darlene, who seemed to dare Aunt Mattie to go on and take the shot. There they were. Five broken grins. Best they could do. Next to that was a framed clipping of the man in the moon in the white grainy light of space.

When her dad came home, clothes smelling of diesel, wood chips on his cap, face red and sober, he said, "Where's your mom?"

"Gone."

"What do you mean gone?"

"She left this." She flicked the note toward him.

He read it, put it down, and nodded, a stiff up-and-down nod. "Had supper yet?"

That was October, first week. River out front was still running, wouldn't freeze till the cold of January hit. She'd remember the day for the sound of the men in the house. The way they came in and kicked their boots off, hung their coats, and washed their hands in the sink. They looked at her like she was out of her mind as she pulled out *her* chair, and sat on it, unbothered, contented.

Butch leaned way back on his chair and put his feet on the table. "Get your feet off the table," she said. She didn't sound like herself. He knew it, she knew it.

"Where's Mom?" he asked.

"Gone." She pushed the note toward him. He read it several times. Earl cleared his throat. Butch slammed his hands on the table.

"Cut that out," Earl said.

She'd remember the day for the smell of food. Fish.

She set the table with four forks, four knifes, four cups. Ripped two paper towels in half and folded each one on top of the plates. Yellow plates. Roses worn out in the bottom. Green roses. Who ever heard of green roses?

From the fridge she took four thawed brookies, heads and tails still attached, dusted them with flour, salt, and pepper, fried them fast until the eyes turned white and the tails curled up.

Poured milk over boiled potatoes and whipped them up. Opened a can of pineapples. Rings. Placed two on each plate, a dollop of mashed potatoes, a brookie for each one.

"Anybody want anything to drink, you get it yourself." She poured water for herself and drank it fast.

The men looked at the blackened skin of fish, then at her. Earl sliced through the head of his fish and sucked the eye out. Always did.

Only one who didn't ask to read the note was Sid, but he caught her eye and she held his stare, painful as it was, and raised her head as if to say, *That's right, she's gone.* His eyes, big and watery, honey colored, were too much to look at.

That first day they expected something to happen, something more than the sound of their forks, their gulps and swallows. They ate without conversation, looked up whenever a car passed by, all of them expecting *her* to walk in and say, *Well, here I am,* and to roll her sleeves up and sniff the air looking for signs of foul play, foul odors, for anything to be out of place. They expected *her* to come in with a blast of cold air following her into the house and to all of them she'd say, *What smells?* And they'd look ashamed, the whole lot of them, arching their necks out and away from the sight of *her* disgust.

She'd remember the day by how suddenly night came. Earl shoved wood in the stove. Sid went out back to see about the dog. He'd found her collar attached to the leash, her bowl full of food, but she was gone. Wasn't like her to run off. Butch stretched out on the couch in front of the TV. She went out back and saw the dog had returned. Sid was pulling burrs off her tail.

"Told you she'd come back," she said, though she hadn't really said that. Sid ignored her.

"It's freezing out," she said and rubbed her hands. Sid started in then. Trying to talk. He coughed out sounds, shook his hands as if a little shaking would make the words come out.

"Come on, Sid, take it easy, relax."

"Heah—heah—he-he-he . . ." He slapped his hands on his forehead, wiped tears away. Face full of hollows.

"Take it easy, Sid. . . ." She reached for his hand but he pulled away. "I know how you feel but listen, she left all of us, not just you, and it's not like she was happy here or anything."

Sid shook his head no, and turned away.

The cold wind came off the river and slapped the trees down. The house darker than the night. Thick stream of smoke shot up the chimney. Light illuminating chairs, dressers, lopsided pictures on the walls. A bare bulb in the back. The ground hardened under their feet. Sid scratched the dog's head. A half-moon shone between the cracked arms of the trees.

The house was warm and silent except for the TV and nobody said good-night. They all closed their doors. They all prayed in their own way.

Earl kicked the wall and pounded fists on the pillows. His curses were the same as his prayers. *Goddamn it, damn it all.*

Butch was watching the news—wars, bombings, fires, calamities of all sorts. The spectacular was holy to him. In others' sorrow he felt kinship. His prayer was quite simple. *God.*

Sid prayed, choked in his usual silence.

Tina pulled the big fox round her shoulders and fell asleep hearing someone in the john, flushing and flushing.

She'd remember the day by the dream that came minutes or hours later: her mother rushing in the room, telling her to get up, get out, hurry! *But why?* Woke with the question, fur in her mouth, a puddle of drool on the coat, a burning smell to it. Wondered if the men had the same dream, if together their dreams amounted to a clue. But gone was gone, and no dream ever leads the dreamer to its origin.

∎ ∎ ∎

OF COURSE she left more than her children and husband and a house behind. She left the black woods. The hard rock. She left her sore feet and her sidelong look, there, she left it in the corridor, by the pantry, near the long-gone beans. She left the luminous light that flickered too briefly to matter. She left what hadn't mattered, what stopped being absolute, what was behind her, always, or rushing in front of her, always. She left what was crouched and slumped and drunk and boring and despondent. She left without saying I'm sorry. She left with two feet and two hands and two eyes intact. She left the little terrors in her heart and the sounds of her dreams and the old ladies in the attic. She left what was disembodied and not hers anymore. She left aimless, alone, sad as ever. She left.

∎

She left me, she left me, she left me.

Tina took the name of Fox that night on account of the coat. Fox, sweet little fox, she said as she stroked the fur and put the coat on and turned to look at herself in the mirror. She pulled the collar up until her face was hidden. She pushed her arms in and crouched low and tucked her legs in and sat with the coat forming a cave around her. It smelled of mothballs.

She imagined her mother rushing in and yanking the coat off her, saying, *Give it back, this ain't yours.* Saying, *I'm back, I had a change of heart.* But Fox knew it wouldn't be a change of heart and she wouldn't be back.

She spent the night with the coat on, falling in and out of the same dream in which her mother dragged her out of the house and tried to make her fall into the same hole where the dead fox lay.

In the morning she found Sid hugging the dog. It was unusually bright out, arctic light. Everything was exquisitely acute. Even the shadows fell with precise distinction. The maple was maple, the birch was birch. There was no mingling, no confusing anything in that light. Imagined herself spending the day crouched under the trees near a crushed bed of ferns like a fox, watching, waiting.

The coat resisted the wind but she pushed her hands in the pockets and opened the coat like wings.

"You like the coat?"

Sid scrunched his shoulders.

"She never liked it. I found it in her room. She took that blue one."

The coat hung inches above her ankles but she figured if she wore the boots with heels it wouldn't look like it was dragging. She rolled the cuffs up. The shoulders were padded and gave her the feeling that somebody's big hands were on her, kind hands.

Sid looked at his sister as she knelt beside him and whispered, "I changed my name. It's Fox now. Just plain Fox. Don't ever call me Tina." He grinned in a sad way and he put his arm out and jostled her by the shoulder. He opened his mouth but she knew he wasn't trying to say anything, it was just the way he showed everything was okay.

"You think she'll be back?" She pulled the coat open and Sid moved into it. Even the dog nudged his face under it and sighed.

"I saw her leave. I was standing by the window and saw her drive off with Moose. I saw them go." She turned to the mound where the fox was buried and told Sid, "See that? There's something buried in there." Her brother's expression said, Hurry up and say what you have to say. The dog picked up on her tone of voice, its ears and nose twitched in the direction of the tree.

"I don't think she'll be back."

Sid sighed and looked from her to the tree to the dog and long minutes passed without either one talking. He wanted her to speak for him and tell him that she, too, was terrified, that something big and sad had happened to their mother and that nothing could be made better.

"Sid," she said. She could hear him breathing. "Sid."

He stroked the dog between the ears and ran his hand down the dog's long nose and listened to his sister. Her eyes looked like blackberries and her voice was like a sound he once knew but it was disturbing, all of it, the coat, what she was saying. He moved away from her.

"You think I should get a job or something, maybe work at the store?"

Sid stood and looked down at her and shrugged. She wasn't talking about anything that interested him anymore and he walked away.

The store, the only store in town. No, she couldn't work at the store. Luke worked at the store and if she ever saw him again she'd pull his tongue out and make him eat it.

Luke with his blue-bead eyes like marbles. Scrawny Luke with his broken tooth. She remembered him and the day, it had been green, yielding, end of June, hungry swallows in the buggy air. Luke with brown sagging pants poised like a skink on a rotten log, eyeing life's sweetness. She saw him step in the same sunshine as hers. Was close enough to see him suck in air and bite his bottom lip. Saw his too-blue eyes. He came right up to her. *Where you going? What you doing? Want some pie?* Mouth open, scooping air. Said he had lots of pies back at the house. *Apple, rhubarb, blueberry.* I don't like sweets, she'd said, and walked around him, feigning indifference, wondering, if she had to run, would she make it clear across the meadow, could she? *Hey, I asked you nicely.* Her legs took off before she knew she was running. The long meadow blurred into a sea of green and she was above it. Felt the cold sweat down her forehead, then her head was jerked back. He grabbed her by the hair. *You bitch, I told you to wait up.* Head to the side, hair in his hand, his leering face inches away, his hot breath on her ear. Blue jay screamed. She fell or he knocked her down. Her face twisted in his hands. Eyes on her mouth then his big fat tongue all over her face. Forced his tongue inside her. She bit down hard and felt the blood soak her mouth. His blood. He fell off her or she kicked him off. He slapped her. She slapped him back. She ran, he ran after her. Then she stopped and opened her mouth and what came out were loud curses made up on the spot, not really words but sounds born of the ugly day with its bloody bloody taste. He wiped his hands, pulled on his pants, and left. She watched him go. She was thirteen.

She's convinced a particle of the boy's tongue is still in her, a sliver of his flesh lodged between her teeth.

No, the job at the store was out. Sid disappeared in the back and the dog sniffed around the tree. She walked across the bridge and down to the other side of the river where sumac grew tall. Smell of dog urine in the ground. The land, protruding here and there. Wind coming down, pulling warmth out. And at a distance, the house. Wondered who'd be the next to go.

■

They all felt marooned, like missionaries dragged across a harsh land for many years only to find they'd arrived at a harsher place, an incomprehensible one. Abandoned to what and why? To whom were they now accountable? They didn't recognize the house anymore, nor each other. And when they washed their faces they lingered over the bathroom sink and studied their faces in the mirror. Who were they now? How had they changed?

They moved through the house like needles, aware that anything they touched might burst. They tried not to touch each other in passing.

The boys looked at Tina more and more. They watched everything she did. The way she moved through the room and stopped for no reason at all while she was holding a load of laundry was enough to startle them and make them suddenly think of their mother. They listened for the female sounds of her voice and it occurred to them that they were looking for memories. *Her* absence had displaced them and they were no longer sure that what they were looking at was what it was. Tina spent days rearranging furniture and moving mirrors and removing light bulbs from lamps so that at night, when they were thinking of settling down by the fire, there was only this immense darkness. That darkness confused them and forced them to bed, where they dreamt wild and tortured dreams.

They thought of what they might have meant to their mother. Tina thought of how she'd been told she'd been born spooked. *Even as a baby you pulled away from me.* And she imagined herself as an eight-pound infant testing her strength against her mother's. *You just never warmed to life, never wanted anybody's love.*

And Sid wanted to talk. He thought if only he had talked to her she wouldn't have left. It was his silence, he was sure, that had forced her away. *Let me go and I'll find her.* But he didn't have a clue where to begin or how to look for her, and he gave the thought up before the day was through. And of course the words never came.

And Butch, with his feet on the bed and his head on the pillow, looked at the ceiling and imagined his mother's face and was satisfied he could still see her, but he wondered how many years it would take before he forgot what she looked like.

Earl went through her things in the closet. Did she have a scarf, a hat, which shoes did she have on, and how much money did she have and where did she get it? He turned the dresser drawers inside out, he threw the furniture against the walls, he pounded walls and he got drunk and drove as far as the ridge allowed him and then he came back to the dark house, stepping softly upstairs, breathless, stopping to scoop up a necklace from the floor. *So you're gone.*

They ate supper in silence. Sometimes Tina turned on the radio but if a love song came on she snapped the radio off. The very word, or hint of the word, *love,* was not tolerated.

And they remembered how she'd been. Doing dishes and saying, *Somebody ought to help with these damn dishes.* But it wasn't just the dishes. *Doesn't anybody hear me?* they'd heard. They just didn't know what to do. *What on earth does it take?* They had no idea.

They understood why Earl woke them some nights, drunk and out of his mind, saying, *Your mother, you wanna know what your mother is?* And he'd say it. The ugly words. And it would be Butch who'd stop him and say, *Dad, stop it, she's not here anymore, all right? She's gone, leave it alone.*

It was a little thing, a handmade thing like a coat made of fifty skins, and a birthday cake left on the fridge for a week because nobody could make themselves sing "Happy Birthday," it was bedtime and nobody saying good-night. It was the way summer got out of the way fast so winter could move in, it was the reason she was gone.

Butch saw Tina walking toward the house with her head down. She looked stricken.

When one sees someone through glass, one is no longer seeing that person as is but as the person has been, will be. In the frame of the window what Butch saw was his mother standing in the cold. He saw her confinement, a young woman on the porch, saw her tattered beauty, engrossed in her protective silence as she had been, was, would always be to him. More than anything, he felt her as the mood that clung to the day like a cloud. She was in the house, there, in the pantry, there, by the stairs. Everywhere. Imagined her as she must have been flanked by them as babies, toddlers. Her hair was the same color as the fringes of the curtains. Her face was in all the corners of the room. She was in the unhappy light, white bony pale light.

Tina stared at him. "What's wrong with you?"

He opened the door to let her in. "Get in here, it's cold out, what are you doing out there? and what's with the coat, anyway?" She looked like a weasel in that coat and she was shivering. "You're trembling, what's wrong with you?" The coat was so thick he could have put his whole hand in and it would have disappeared in there.

"Nothing's wrong with me." She left a wet trail on the floor. "I was talking with Sid. He doesn't get it. Mom leaving and all."

"I don't get it either." He closed his eyes.

"I know why she left." She tugged hard on the coat.

"Quit that," he said, "you'll ruin the coat."

"She hates me and she won't be back. I know that for sure."

"What else do you know for sure, Tina, tell me."

"You don't believe me."

"Doesn't matter if I believe you or not." He put his hand out to her but she shoved him away.

"Don't touch me!"

"Her leaving has nothing to do with us."

Out the window Sid was playing sticks with the dog. She wished the dog had taken to her but it never had.

"So," she said, "are we orphans or what?"

"Orphans don't have parents, they have nobody."

She turned away, furious, but he followed her up the stairs and went on talking through her closed door. "Orphans have nobody!" He stopped himself from saying, *We have each other.*

.   .   .

T HE BUS let her off at Port Authority. She had never seen so many people in motion in one place. She kept her eyes down and followed the crowds, like a minnow in a school of big fish. A woman ahead of her pulled a young boy by the arm, yelling at him to hurry up. She followed, propelled by the same command and ran behind them until she reached the street.

The gray city came at her like a solid wall of noise. She leaned back and watched people. She felt all wrong. Her coat smelled of hay and sour milk. Her skirt was too short for where she was coming from and too long for where she was. It ended at her knees and gave her a matronly look, calves too wide, ankles too thin. And her shoes were not shoes but mud boots which she had slipped into as if she were merely going to fetch the mail. Her hat was a wool cap that had been her daughter's, then her son's, and had been in the basket by the door, an available hat for anyone going out.

She stood close to the edge of the sidewalk, and when a yellow cab stopped, she leaned into the window, expecting the driver to ask her something. When she didn't move, he said, "You getting in, or what?"

She pulled back, and a couple rushed up and yanked the door open and got in. By the time a third cabbie stopped, she knew just what to do, except she got in the front. *"Lady, passengers go in the back. It's the law."* She apologized and got in the backseat. She caught his eye in the rearview mirror, tired blue eyes, then he said, "Lady, where to?"

"I'm not sure."

He turned and faced her. "In that case I think you better step out until you know."

"A hotel, I want to go to a hotel."

"Which one?"

"I don't know. Any hotel."

"Any hotel?"

"Yes, a nice one."

He stared until he was sure he'd made her feel uncomfortable and he drove.

"Here you go," he said. "I think you'll like it here."

The hotel had a blue canopy, wide glass doors, a floral print on a worn carpet and a domelike ceiling with a forty-watt chandelier. She walked toward the long, paneled desk, past the oblivious old ladies who sat smoking like starlets in the lobby. She walked with the sad dignity of those who can't afford to show how wrong things really are.

"One hundred dollars a week, plus a three-week deposit," the clerk said. "No male visitors in rooms."

He didn't look at her. "Male visitors in the lobby only, and they must leave by midnight." He took her money, she signed, he gave her the key. "Room 206. And no pets. No little dogs, no birds, no vermin." When he did look at her he took her all in, as if at some point, when asked if he recognized the face in a photo, he'd say, *Yes, she was here*. She smiled. He yanked off his wire glasses and stared hard back at her. "No animals of any sort."

She thanked him curtly and followed other women who walked into what seemed like an elevator. Luggage in hand, purse in the other, back against the wall. An elderly woman with many rings on her fingers slid a metal grid sideways with a considerable amount of effort, she used both hands, and slammed the door shut. She pushed a button. "What floor?" Everyone called out a floor except Darlene. "What floor?" the woman said again. The woman pushed all the buttons. Darlene rode up to the twelfth, and all the way down to the lobby. She did this several times before she stepped off on the second floor.

Her room had the antiseptic smell of rooms that have housed many bodies with bad habits, ill-health, and nasty tempers. Alcoholics, drug addicts, perverts, liars, cheaters, arsonists, terrorists, defrocked nuns, the badly beaten, the runaway, the temporarily out of place, the moderately insane, and the common everyday loser had slept in that bed. She would too.

In the unnatural heat of the room she pulled out her suitcase, the ugly black thing with cardboard tags. *Northern Trails,* tangible proof that, yes, she had left home. Home, the idea of it, came at her like a theme park—pastoral, dotted with cows, a place where even trees said good-morning and rivers moved with common sense. It was a lie. She had only to close her eyes to see the home she had left awash in cold sameness, a muted, blurred, iced-over vision, a mess of a place.

Faces of Hog and Sarah Hawkins, Moose, Cant, Karl, and Birdie. Town folk. Square shouldered, paunched in the belly, short-legged people with bright corn-fed eyes and mouths fenced up with thought. Saw Misty and Fat in the garden pulling weeds; saw Guy tinkering; Sue plucking a head of lettuce out of the ground, saying, *Don't get better than this.* Saw summer, spring, and fall; *saw* winter; *saw* the steeple of the church in town and its sour-faced pastor sweating as he climbed to the bell tower on Sundays, at a quarter to ten, tugging on the rope to wake the sinful, the slothful, and *saw* him panting, taking his gluttonous weight down the creaky stairs and, in a rushed moment of uninspired meditation, *saw* him sit in a pew and stare blankly at the single gold crucifix and ask the Lord, *What is this all about?*

And she *saw* home. A place of collapsed bridges, broken fences, woodpiles, woodpeckers, shutters drawn tight, lamps left on all night. Bitterness in her heart, snow in the air. *Damn you.* Damn life for being less than a dream.

■

Room 206 measured sixteen feet the long way, nine the short. One window. View of a dirty brick wall with a fire escape and a window across the way with splintered glass patched over with tape and cardboard. A street below illuminated by yellow traffic light.

Cinder-block green walls, a sink with rust stains, bed bolted to the wall. Cheap wooden dresser. A linoleum floor, spongy, with green and red squares. Green like dead grass, red like old blood. Green like a chewed-up stalk of timothy. Red like winter-old sumac.

Above the sink was a small, metal-framed, water-stained mirror. Saw herself there. Ugly, she thought. Ugly.

She didn't leave the room for two weeks except to get food and to use the bathroom down the hall. A young woman brushing her teeth, mouth foaming white, said, *Hi, I'm Myra*. Darlene didn't answer but walked quickly back to her room, fumbling with the fat key, and stood for a long time listening from the door, praying no one would knock.

To get dressed and walk out, down the elevator, across the wide lobby and out the door, took all her strength. She ran across the street to the deli on the other side, where she ordered a coffee and bagel to go. "You want that buttered, toasted, cream cheese, plain?" Yes, she'd said. "Yes what?" She hadn't understood she was being asked to choose. After four days the cashier said, "I know, plain to go."

She learned to be a pedestrian, to look at traffic lights, to watch for a break in the rush of cars. She understood the loud rumbling sound in the ground was the subway. Nights she prayed the city wouldn't collapse with her in that room. Never took the subway. Walked. Wore her boots out, developed calluses on her toes, blisters on her heels. Saw herself a hundred times a day in window reflections, and always was surprised to see herself. Got lost one day and found a river. Leaned over the railing and inhaled deeply but it didn't smell like river air. Looked for a way down the banks but there was no way down, no banks. She made notes to herself to tell the children later, at some point, how *there was this huge gray river, wider than the Fulfillment, and it flowed deep on both sides, no rocky banks, no trees alongside it, couldn't see the bottom and there I was standing fifty, maybe a hundred feet above it.*

And then what? What would she say then? That she thought of flinging herself over air, just to land on water? That she thought she could do it and emerge whole? That it was the only thing she thought of, immersing herself in water, and stroking, furtively, across it, in the hope it would lead home? No. That wouldn't do. Couldn't see the kids anymore, nor the house. Closed her eyes and saw wild animals prowling around her abandoned garden and the ridge swollen like a black eye and nobody around.

It was black, the dream she had that night. There they were, her children when young. They lifted their heads, lifted their arms, which, for no apparent reason, were bleeding. *Do something, stop it!* they cried. She ripped her dress and tied tourniquets around their tiny arms. *There there,* she said, soothing them, over and over, trying to convince herself and them that the blood had stopped, would stop, had to. *Do something, Mommy, do something!* The more they screamed, the calmer she had to be, she knew that, she couldn't let on how she felt. She tied, she cleaned, she stroked their faces, she kissed them and said, *It's all better,* she held them to her. She did her best and still they bled, they screamed. She didn't see any cuts, couldn't find the source of the blood. They were leaking from their pores. *It's fixed now, it's all better.* She lifted their heads to keep them from seeing the blood which rose around them. It almost killed them, swept them away, then she woke up.

Babies. She'd had them, now they had her. She was gone but they were present. She'd stepped out of their lives for lack of reasons to stay.

I don't know what you expect me to do, she said to the suitcase.

. . .

Tina WALKED into her mother's room looking for the scissors. They were by the table with clippings of recipes for tuna mousse, tuna croquettes. There were piles of clothes on the floor, mostly Earl's, but some were *her* things. A dress with a price tag, a strapless bra, summer shirts, boxed soaps, ribbons, trinkets.

She didn't look in the mirror while she cut her hair. Stopped when she felt an inch of hair on her head, like spikes. Then she bleached it white, whiter than frost.

Look like a scarecrow, Earl said in the morning.

Whatcha do that for? Butch said.

Sid looked at her as if he were saying good-bye to someone he once knew.

She tossed the hair out in the woods for the birds to make a nest. The hair was exactly like her mother's. Earl always said it, *Best thing about you is your hair, just like your mother's.* Long enough to strangle me with, she thought. Now that it was gone there'd be no confusion about who was who.

Friday Earl pounded on her door, said, *We gotta get some shopping done,* which is what they did every Friday. Earl waited in the truck while she bought chicken nuggets, whole chickens, drumsticks, four loaves of white bread, two jars of marmalade, lard, peanut butter, coffee, two gallons of milk, five pounds of sugar, onions, yams, six tomatoes, and ten packs of Jell-O. She ate a banana while she shopped. Didn't pay for it. Bought the carton of cigarettes for Earl. Six pack of twin blades for Sid and Butch. Deodorant, tampons, shampoo. On the way back, Earl stopped at the post office.

Handful of white envelopes. In the truck he said, "These here are all for you." He opened and read them. *Dear Tina Summer . . . We are proud to inform you . . .*

She grabbed them and read them, couldn't believe it. "It's just school stuff," she finally said. Earl started the truck and she folded the letters and stuffed them in the grocery bags between her legs.

"You graduated, didn't you? What school you talking about?"

"College. Scholarships for college," she said, and moved her legs, careful not to bruise the tomatoes.

"To do what?"

She couldn't explain, didn't want to. Stared out the window and counted chimneys, counted clouds. She moved as far as she could from Earl and his stick-shift arm. He smelled of diesel and boiled wax.

"Anybody giving you money?" he said. "If they are, then we have something to talk about."

"Leave me alone. It's not money. It's nothing," she said.

"You got a nasty mouth on you," he said. "I'd watch your mouth if I were you. You and your . . ." Then he stopped. She'd sounded just like her mother.

Later, in her room, wrapped in the coat, she wondered how different the day would have been if her mother had seen the letters. *Guess some people think you're smart. Smart enough to pay you to go out and think. Is that it, is that what this is all about?* She'd fan the air with the letters, maybe slap them on her palm. She wouldn't have understood either. She had burned her books. They had been books of poetry, of physics, novels. *Books aren't making you smart. You think you're smarter than all of us, different. Only thing different about you is that you don't know right from wrong. Sure I burned them, of course I did, and now you know why. Books are an extra thing in life, unnecessary as a wart.*

Without the books she would have to use memory, and reconstruction. It would take hours, lots of them, quiet ones. It was better this way, she decided.

■

Winter moved in. The men were sullen and avoided each other. They left Fox alone. The dark fell. The nights grew cold. The river slowed.

The coat lost the smell of mothballs and took on her own smell, that of a tired animal after a chase.

Dream: Crouched by the tall wet grass near the well. Night. She heard the riders emerge before she saw them. Riders like pictures of riders, equestrians on sleek dark horses. The riders wore wool and leather. A rich smell, the smell of wealth and the trained hunt. The black wool riding coats, the felt stripes on the collars, red, yellow, the long fitted coats, the thin and supple boots, the riding crops and the gleam of the beasts' dark eyes as they leapt over her. They knew, of course they knew she was there. It was torture. Waiting to be found out. Above her she felt the huge stretch of muscle, the silent velvety hooves forming a wide and high arc before they came down. Then one of them whispered, *Let's go*, and they went back into the woods. Riders and beasts. Gone the same way they came.

Sleepless, she stood by the river, which she believed was ruinous and curative. Whitetails came down from the woods and stood on the opposite banks of the river and studied her and flicked their tails. They feared the water as much as she did, and after a careful drink they moved away in single file and zigzagged through the old-growth forests and bedded down in the shadow of standing trees.

■　■　■

*T*HE RIDGE. *Like all things, it has its source. It began underwater. A jumble of rock, pebble, sand, and clay heaped up and heaved out, melted down, and dumped in piles, mounds, and sheets. Bedrock and moraine.*

Shaped by glacier flow and its debris, the ridge has been scoured, rounded, smoothed over; gaps widened to notches. Ten thousand years ago the ice receded and carried boulders, huge erratics, and rolled them high and far, in open fields and tops of mountains, to form the crown of the valley, the collar of the sky.

The sun rises over the carcasses of enormous beasts, pulverized now, but once they were ruminating, swimming beasts. There are remains. Whalebone, woolly mammoth fur. There is evidence.

This is what there is to see: violence in a shallow lake, a river loosened of itself, microscopic time in a bog. No one can belong to this, yet it invites all, it asks for immersion. It offers the deranged more of the same; and to the blessed, more blessings. All night long the snowy owl calls out from its boreal woods. It cannot imagine its own absence.

■ ■ ■

WINTER, CRAMPED like bears, wobbling from couch to bed to fire to food, and nobody said a word. If it hadn't been for the TV, some nights there would have been no human sound.

Earl dressed each morning with a sense of foreboding, feeling old and mortal. He layered on thermals and shirts and jackets, three pairs of socks. Hands in his pockets fingering bolts and nuts, short strings, matches, pencil stubs, and the thick card of the private investigator. *Who's missing?* the man had asked, and when Earl said, *My wife,* the man said, *What do you want with her?* and Earl didn't know what to say and walked out.

Butch heard his father pacing between bedrooms, outside, turning lights on, off, opening doors, slamming them shut. One day he saw him in the truck, head bent over the wheel, and for a moment thought he was dead, but then he raised his head and wiped his face with the back of his hand. He was only crying. Good, he thought, good.

The snow and moon and river and trees and the dog out back sometimes howled as if pleading, and the deer herd refused to freeze so early in winter. The cold wind formed sheets of new ice under the kitchen door. The mountains at dawn were like frozen beasts. It all spoke of the wild profusion of things. Under it all the bones of old Indians shifted and rattled and their curse spread as their bones became sand, which settled in deep wells and became part of the water everyone drank.

She became part of them in the same way. Enormous with the pull of her absence, and *she* thrived in the confusion she left behind so that even the beams and floorboards and rock foundation shifted under the weight of her abandonment.

She was the reason the sun faded and left a pink glow in the sky long into the night. The reason pots were burned and dinner was tasteless. The reason Earl walked around drunk one night saying to his children, *It hurts like a sonofabitch*. He held his hand to his jaw and when the children looked at him he asked, *What's your problem?*

■　■　■

"Butch?" Tina said.

"Yeah, what?"

"Want to play the Ouija board?"

"No."

"Come on, let's. I'll let you do all the asking."

"I thought you didn't like this game. You said it was stupid."

"I can't sleep."

"All right, bring it up here, I'm not going downstairs."

She stepped carefully like a thief, knowing what she was after, afraid of being caught. She saw the game in a corner by the kitchen window and when she heard Earl cough she froze, she leaned against the wall, terrified. Of what? Why? By the time she walked back to Butch's room he was asleep and wouldn't wake.

"Sid? Sid, you awake?"

"Huh?"

"It's all right, it's just me. I can't sleep. You want to play the Ouija game?"

Sid, feet dangling from the bed, blanket around his shoulder.

They whispered as the wind blew snow and piled it high on their roof. They asked, *Is she alive? Is she coming back? Does she love me?*

The old apple tree broke under the weight of snow. Not far, on the road to the ridge, a car swerved to avoid hitting a fawn but it was too late. The fawn stood in front of the car, her foreleg raised. The driver stepped out and walked timidly toward the animal saying, Oh, my God. Bright red blood poured out of the fawn's nose and mouth. Eyes unblinking, steady on her feet, she did not know what happened. Not far, high in the forest, a pack of coydogs raised their heads, crazed by the scent of blood.

■   ■   ■

THE MEN hunted all of November. Fox packed their lunches. Cold ham, rolls, pickles, hot Thermos of coffee, matches. They left early. She heard the alarms go off in their rooms, hard feet stomping down the stairs, doors slamming, truck driving off.

Night after night, they came home looking enormous and cold.

Something happened to them out there, changed them from the outside in. Felt it in the cold air that followed them in the house. Something about them standing in the cold, waiting, rifles up, shooting, not shooting, it altered them.

She waited for the boots to go off, the hand washing, the coat hanging. "You guys want something to eat?"

Nothing, they said not a thing, but sat at the table expecting to be fed. Heads bowed, arms over chest, they rubbed their faces, pressed hands down on their ears. Red eyed and squinting, they focused on her.

"Ham with pineapple sauce." She passed plates. It was a Sunday and they always had ham on Sundays. Poured cup after cup of coffee, looked up when one of them burped or cleared his throat as if something else was about to be said. Didn't want to miss a thing.

Wondered if this was what *she* had seen in them all those years. A hapless bunch of men, uninterested, unattractive; and her, the daughter, amateur at everything. They amounted to nothing, less than the man in the moon.

"There's more of everything," she said. "Help yourselves. Ham, potatoes, salad."

"You got that car running?" Earl said, fork up.

"Yeah, water pump blew, but I got Kirby to take a look at it," Butch said.

"Got no heat in the truck. Windows frosted in and out. Can't see a flying fuck." Earl blew his nose on the napkin. Damp spots on his orange quilted vest. "Need the car running in the morning." He pushed aside clumps of pineapple, moved them as far off on the plate as he could without tossing them out. "I ought to shoot that thing."

They all looked up.

"Fuckin' Deadhorse is gonna die one of these days."

Three pairs of eyes looked out the window toward the logging operation, that half-assed attempt Earl called his living.

He pushed his chair back and tossed the napkin across the room. Hit the tea canister with a silent puff.

"You guys seen anything, tracks, anything?" she said, using the fork and knife to move her food around. She chewed softly. Three pairs of eyes fell on her.

"Warden took a sixteen-pointer."

"I ain't seen anything bigger than my own shadow."

"Too damn cold is what it is."

"Gonna get colder, though."

"That it will."

"Shit, that damn truck don't start tomorrow I swear I'm gonna shoot it to kingdom come."

"Wanna pull out the Lincoln?"

"No way in hell I'm gonna put that on the road. And it ain't registered. Last thing I need is the constable slapping me with a fine."

Eyes out the window, anywhere except on each other.

"You check the traplines like I told you?" Earl said.

"Nothing there. Hare tracks is all," Butch said.

"How far'd you look?"

Butch pierced a potato with his fork and talked to it. "Far as you can get." Dropped the fork with a clang.

"How far's that?" Earl leaned over the table, voice low, mean, arms crossed and hands tucked in the folds of his wool jacket.

"Right to the brook. Ain't that as far as they go? To the brook?"

Earl coughed, spat, and talked at the same time but this time he looked at Sid. "Quit that moaning! Sound just like your mother."

Sid, red-rimmed eyes, mouth open to show red gums, his pasty tongue flicking this way and that. Veins like serpents on his forehead.

It was true, he looked like *her*. Bone white, transparent skin, same pouty lips, like hers, tongue, like hers, licking the taste of things away. Moaning was his way of clearing his throat thinking nobody could hear him.

She reached for plates. "Well, as long as you're all done . . ."

Butch tilted his chair way back, lit a cigarette, tossed the match on the Jell-O salad.

She cleared the table. Looked at their hands. Kin. Bunch of ornery men. Pigs. Earl picked his nose and burped. Butch wiped his mouth on a sleeve, then picked at his back teeth. His fingernails were dirty. Earl spat stuff out the side of his mouth. Ugly men. It was the business of hunting, that's what it was. They wouldn't be happy until they brought something down.

Sid hadn't touched his food. Held the plate in both hands as if at any minute he might hurl it across the room. Like *her*.

She nudged him. "What's bugging you?"

"Cat got his tongue," Earl said.

"Leave him alone," Butch said.

She piled dishes in the sink, ran hot water over them. "I'm going to bed," and to Sid she said, "Don't leave your food out."

Sid was still hunched over his plate.

"You going to eat this?" she said. "No? Yes? Come on, Sid."

In one sudden jolt, Sid got up, grabbed his coat, and walked out.

"Jesus," Butch said.

"Cat got his tongue. I told you," Earl said.

"Stop making fun of him." She wiped the table.

"I ain't making fun. He don't care. Ever see him act like he cares?"

"You miserable bastard," she hissed, but he heard.

"Watch your mouth, young lady." Earl, eyes on her.

You miserable bastard. Those were Darlene's words. Exactly *her* words.

"Don't use all the hot water!" Earl yelled as she left the kitchen.

Sid in the yard. The dog licked his face. He undid the leash and the dog ran in circles and jumped into his arms. The leash was tied to the run between the house and a maple. Thirty-foot run. She was a big dog, white with a black chest. Blue eyed. Sid had found her near the traps as a pup with a mangled tail and hind leg broken.

The hot water wasn't hot enough in the shower.

"Hurry up in there!" Earl pounded on the door. "Hurry up!"

She'd do without a shower. Ran up the stairs, to bed, lights off, and waited for the dream but when it came it was not of riders and hooves but of her mother strangling her in her sleep.

■　■　■

Mornings came like a jolt, bright, fast. She waited for the men to take their rifles and go. For their smell of coffee and smoke to go out the door. When she was sure they were gone she turned the TV on to the weather. Loved the prophetic voice of the weatherman. How he elaborated and paused, lowering his voice, holding his pointer in both hands, looking at the satellite map and taking his time to say the milder weather would soon give way to bitter, *bitter* cold. He looked into the screen with apologetic eyes as if to say, I'm sorry for the hardships of weather.

Shook the floor mats outside. Crows screamed. Slammed the door and a sheet of snow slushed down the roof. Plugged in the vacuum and blue sparks shot out. Vacuum snagged on the rug, spit out pieces of metal. Pennies, screws, bent nails, junk. She expected to find something of *hers* in the rug. A pin, a link of gold chain, something broken and forgotten, a sign, something she could hold in the palm of her hand and say, *This is it, this is why you left.*

Emptied ashtrays, did a ton of dishes, found dirty cups under beds, beer bottles on the sofa, on the porch. Bagged trash, rolled newspapers into tight logs, put boots in the pantry, hung up shirts, coats, and hats on the peg wall next to the gold clock which was the only thing bright and shiny in the house.

Sid had won it at the Grange raffle years ago; wrapped it and gave it to her for her birthday, two days late. Bought a card to go with it, a funny card with a mouse chasing a cat. Inside, it read: *Time to get even.* She hadn't seen the sense in it but thanked him anyway.

Clothes in the dryer, frying pot off, drumsticks sitting in their own grease. The men liked them that way. She had peanut butter on a spoon, Jell-O pudding. Saltines.

Caught a glimpse of herself in the mirror and thought she saw *her* again, thought she heard her say: *Be somebody. Somebody.* But who the hell was *she? She* was gone like daylight, gone like a dream. Colorless and smelling of nothing. A starling chased by a band of crows. And here she was cleaning up in a house of men.

The weatherman talked fast as if he had no time to lose, as if the storms in the global air were upon him as well. Hurricanes, palm trees bent to the ground, boats heaved up on land, a young couple huddled under a thick gray blanket, a house, or what remained of it, splintered on a beach. Disasters.

The worst that happened on the ridge was the cold. Ordinary cold and snow, tons of it. That was to be expected. Every now and

then there was a botched killing, a minor robbery, collisions between man and moose. The week *she* left, the front page of the local
paper had a photo of a two-hundred-foot spruce toppled over a
farmhouse, roof collapsed, split in two. The tree's roots up in the
air like a scream. The back page of the paper had a photograph of a
skier also up in the air, tree line far below. Grainy, black and white,
unreal.

Winter was full of bright bloodstained roads; in the woods
small animals howled as they tried to drag themselves out of traps.
In the ridge irrevocable things occurred all the time.

The blue streak of a jay against the white sky. Air frozen. Day
grizzly. White upon white upon white for days. A flicker of light off
the ridge like spun metal. The men were up there, walking in
silence, waiting, ready to shoot. They wouldn't be home till dark.

Coat on, she walked down the unplowed road, snow above her
ankles. It would get deeper, more trees would topple, the ridge
would appear like a scar in the land, the scream of gunshot would
echo for miles, the river would freeze, calamities would occur,
houses would burn, and church bells would toll. Winter would
come and go and come again.

Walked far enough from the house to see it for what it was. A
ramshackle place. A makeshift arrangement.

If it hadn't been for the tepee at the far end of the town there would
have been nothing unusual to see. It rose out of the ground like a
flesh cone, canvas and willow poles. A stream of smoke up the top.
The mailbox was painted iridescent pink: SANDRA LOOS-LAND. HIDDEN
LIGHT, GRAVITY FIELDS, INC.

Earl hated the tepee and the woman in it. Called her a goddamn
witch, *Indian witch*. She had no indoor plumbing but had a spring
that never froze. Had no electric, a blind crow for a pet, had her
blacktop drive dug up. Built the tepee after the house burned down
in a chimney fire. *Witch*. Earl spat out the window every time he

drove by. When he plowed the road in winter he turned the blade around, encasing the woman's car in snow boulders. He tried to have the town slap her with a fine, something having to do with building codes and such, but there was no law that said you couldn't put up a tepee and live in it.

Fox walked by the tepee and Sandra saw her and waved. "What a snow! Isn't this *beautiful*? I just *love* snow, don't you just *love* snow?" She spoke in halting tones, as if in a spell. Eyes like river water. Smell of lavender. Face flushed with life.

"Yeah, it's nice." Fox had never said anything like that before. Snow was snow. Cold was cold. A day was a day. In fifteen years she hadn't given snow a thought, except to say, It's snowing again.

Sandra leaned toward Fox. Fox pulled back.

"We're having a little celebration tonight and we'd love it if you could come. Food and music . . . and a chance to talk." She breathed the word *talk*.

"What do you mean?" Fox said.

"Tonight's the solstice and it's very special, there's going to be a lunar eclipse."

She wasn't about to ask what was so special about that.

"Why don't you come? *Share* with us. It'll be just us, just women."

She could not believe she was being asked to a party, even if it was just to look at the moon. She'd never been to a party. At school she'd been the youngest, shortest, ugliest, and unfriendliest girl in her class. "Okay," Fox said, "I'll come." The words rushed out, and embarrassed for sounding almost happy, she turned and walked away.

Sandra's friends were transplants, they'd come to the ridge from somewhere else and built houses in the sunny hills outside of the ridge, houses so new they made the old farms look like pictures in old postcards. They had windmills, solar panels, ponds shaped like hearts, Victorian gazebos purchased from catalogs. They had llamas for pets and pretty horses. They jogged, they knew about Skin So

Soft, and the count of *E. coli* bacteria in the Fulfillment River's swimming holes, they swam naked. *Nekked, seen them women nekked in the millpond!* Earl would announce. *Oughta be against the law to be ugly and nekked.* Women who posted the land against hunting, trapping, trespassing.

Back in the house she did her eyes and lips. Dampened her hair until it pricked.

You look like a headful of needles. Like somethin' struck by lightning.

Set the table, fed the dog. Sprayed the house with perfume so the men knew she'd cleaned up.

The weatherman said: *Accumulation of five to six inches by nightfall in higher elevations.* . . . Out the window the clouds looked distorted and enormous. Sunlight filtered through clouds like lamp-tinted light.

Didn't want to go out but didn't want to stay in either. *Her* words rang clear: *Do something, anything—join a club, go to church, get a boyfriend, a job, something. What's wrong with you . . . scared of daylight, scared of people? . . . go on . . . do something, will you? Go on . . . get out of the house . . . what's wrong with you?* . . . And to Earl she'd complained: *That girl, holed up in that room. Nose up in the air.*

In the air. Holed up. In that room. And here she was, out the door, going somewhere. It wasn't fear of the outside but fear of what held her in. Afraid it was stronger than her, afraid if she stepped out she'd never be let in again.

Gunshot bounced off the river. The men were out there with hands stiff and eyes burning trying to make things out in the dark, things which weren't there. Later they'd cramp the kitchen with their gloom.

She took clothes out of the dryer and changed in the kitchen. A white cotton T-shirt with long sleeves, a black wool sweater, white underwear, jeans, wool socks, a pair of black impractical boots up to her calves, a red mouth. She rolled the coat sleeves up and felt that tremendous weight on her shoulders. Grabbed a lighter from the table, a pack of cigarettes, and walked out.

■　■　■

THE RIDGE is a land of waste and damage. It offers no relief. It serves no purpose for mankind except it is one place that cannot be had. In that sense it serves a purpose against vanity and ego and wishful thinking. It cannot be had. It will shelter no one. It has disruptive patterns, darkness and cold. It is, in the end, what holds everything at bay, at a distance.

Earl cursed the cold. *Fucking cold.* He cursed his luck. *Goddamn fucking luck.* He held the rifle up. Stopped to read the signs posted in the open land. NO HUNTING. NO FISHING. NO TRAPPING. NO TRESPASSING.

No fucking shit. He blamed women, vegetarians, hippies, tepees, Saab drivers, flatlanders, game preserves, wardens, trophy hunters, and Darlene in one sudden curse. *Fuck you.* But one look up at the hard ridge and he felt at ease. He wouldn't find their kind up here.

Toes numb. Fingers stiff. Stepped over the barbed wire. Spat on a posted sign, a hard yellow phlegm. Unfolded the earflaps of his cap. It cut the wind but also cut the sound he most wanted to hear. A rustle, a step in his direction, the sweet sour breath of animal life nearby. Wind cut through the trees, snapped branches. He walked across cornfields, stalks like spears, and over heaps of stones, into the woods, climbed an old tree, sat on a limb.

It was nasty, semifrozen sleet and rain. That morning he'd pounded on the bedroom door to wake the boys. *Get up!* But they were already up and waiting in the kitchen. Drank his coffee and was out the door with neither of the boys saying a word. *You boys enthusiastic this morning or what?* They'd looked away. *Well, the hell with you, go on and be happy if you want.*

Low clouds and rain. They'd driven up to a higher elevation where it was darker and snow quickened. Stopped when they saw deer tracks across the road leading to a clearing of cut pine. Yearlings traveling with does. Timber jutted out in interesting shapes like huge freak racks. Rough and gnarled lumber. He'd told the boys to make their own way, and seeing Sid lagging behind he told him he'd better take a shot at something. *This is the wilderness,* he said, *go out there and shoot something.*

The wind slowed him down and he wished for snow, tons of it. He wished for that mammoth buck, the once-in-a-lifetime buck, the buck with his name on it. But the wind, the high-driving rain, and the heavy snow that was promising to come were against him and his almighty buck. Nothing was moving in that weather except him. He knew this kind of weather would give deer lock-legs and they'd stand still, their sense of smell, sight, and hearing would be diminished, gone. Frozen in place, they'd lie up and wait for a break in weather. He stalked, moved like molasses in winter. Looked at the outlines of gray, expecting to see the gleam of an eye, the flash of a white tail. Saw track trails in a straight line, sign of an undisturbed deer. Farther on saw the trail meander into small circles, deer searching for bedding site.

Disguised, clothes the color of bark, parka over fleece, aloft, temporarily, aboveground, like a bird, he listened for the murmur of change. Felt foolish. A grown man with a rifle sitting on a tree. As a boy he dreamt of flying, thought he could grow talons and become feather streaked if he put his mind to it. Called himself Raptor, his best friend was Kestrel, and they greeted each other with a screech, *keeeer-keeer,* flapped their arms like wings, and with pocket knives they skinned whatever they brought down.

Loved birds, their noisy scattering, the squawk, the call, their heavy flight, the deliberate way they came across the sky, wings full of intention, the sudden surprise of seeing one fall. Loved to shoot the sons of bitches just to watch them fall. Loved to pluck their feathers. Loved the smell and feel of raw flesh. Most of all he loved to put his hands inside the warm cavity of their bodies and yank out the tough hearts. Loved to eat them.

First thing he ever shot was a bird. He was six, no more. *Now what in hell made you do that?* Tom said. He was the man who taught him to hunt, man who was more of a father than his own father had been. He picked up what was left of the robin's blood-splattered wing, and told him, *If you think hunting is shooting, then you shouldn't hunt.* He made Earl bury the wing and gave him a shovel. Made him work in the yard and fix roof leaks. When he turned twelve he got the rifle. *This here is no killing toy.* Tom told him things Earl hadn't forgotten. *In everything you see there's a killing, in everything you kill there's a living.* He also told him there was nothing wrong with hunting . . . *nothing wrong at all. Just put your heart in it, your whole heart.*

Well, he wouldn't get his buck, that much he knew, because his heart was out of place. *She* was crowding it. Darlene.

Shot rang out from the ridge and his eyes fell on the spot where the sound came from. Granite and sunlight resisting each other. Light and dark. Soft and hard. Near and far. Another shot, then another. *Goddamn. Hope you boys know what you're doing.*

Butt sore, he climbed down, away from the clearing, across a frozen ditch where a fox left her tracks, big brush dragging. Dim sun. Light without warmth. Lifted the rifle and sighted lichen-covered bark. *Something in there,* he hissed, *I know it. Come on, move into the light, you sonofabitch, step out.*

Too damn cold. Velvet moss under a pine glistened with frost. A leaf heavy with mold fell on the surface of an almost frozen pond. Like an animal through a well-worn path he made his way to the truck. Didn't see the boys and didn't want to know if they got something or not. Headed home on foot. Thought he heard an owl, he cursed it. Cursed his life, his old age, his cold need, the ruin of a cold day with wrong thoughts in his head. *Goddamn fucking bitch.* Kicked snow, kicked trees.

Home was down there. A steep hike down and across the posted field, over old stone walls, past the cedar swamps with its jagged stumps, down there, by the river. A darkening place.

House had lights on in all the rooms and he saw her. Same way of leaning into things, of looking up, a curious way of walking, same smart mouth as her mother. Same way of holding her arms out, ready to fend off a blow. Used to have the same hair but not anymore.

Hid and watched her walk down the road with the big coat on. *Where the hell you think you're going?* he thought. Hiked up his pants and stepped over the frozen stone wall and watched her go down the road. *Hell*, he said in a long cold drawn-out voice, *hell*.

◾ ◾ ◾

THE WIND was sharp and cold on her head. The river was shutting down with ice. The tepee glowed like a living thing. The women's voices carried over the water like the buzz of mad flies. The women laughed and hugged, hands all over the place. The thought of all those hands on her terrified her. Knew hands had the power to do you in, keep you back, hold you down. Curled fists, flat open palms, even the fidgeting, trembling, itchy hands. They all had the power. Earl tricked her once. *Hey, got a surprise for you but you have to close your eyes and put your hand in.* She'd closed her eyes, put her hand way down in the bag, pulled out a bloody chicken's foot. *Gotcha, didn't I?* He'd laughed, mimicked her for days, jabbing his hand into an imaginary bag and jolting back with make-believe horror, exploding with laughter. He'd butchered the hens that day. Had fricassee for dinner that night.

The house seen through the broken birches was like something scratched with light. The men would be home soon. They'd see she'd cleaned and made dinner. They'd make a fire, get the house real hot. Earl liked it eighty year round. They'd drink a beer and wait around.

She walked between the parked cars, which ticked with the sound of cooling metal. Women approached her, said hi, hands out to her. She tried not to look at their eyes but when she did she saw they were naked and pale as if the intention of eyes, of sight, had been neglected, erased from their otherwise featureless faces. Or maybe it was the way eyes looked at night, she wasn't sure. *Witches, goddamn witches!* The boom of Earl's voice in her. Wind buffeted a limb and snow crashed down and she felt cold as a seed deposited on turf that would yield no life.

■   ■   ■

T HE BOYS. Hardly boys. Sid and Butch. One reed-tall, the other short and tough. The thick and thin. The strong and the weak. Red-faced and hardened boys who had been talked to by their mother about right and wrong, about girls and bed-wetting, about clothes and manners, and the proper way to hold a spoon when eating soup; they'd been given a hint of manners. Taught what to say and do in the best and worst of times and now they couldn't tell what was good and what was bad. They were young men who had been boys who had not stepped in and held back the hand of the man who was their father when they watched him swing his hand up and hit *her;* men who had not sat with *her* in the sun, who had not asked, *Can I get you something, can I get you a cup of coffee, a drink, a cool cloth;* men who had been conned into thinking, the way men are, that women can take anything, men who thought a woman's superiority lies in her tolerance to pain. There they were, boys in the woods, cold to the bone, looking for something to shoot in a snow-covered world.

Their minds were not so much on the deer they were supposed to track and shoot and bring home, no, their minds were on how empty they felt. They wouldn't call it that; they'd say weird, strange, *I feel kind of weird and strange,* but they weren't talking.

On this particular overcast day, a Tuesday, Sid and Butch had their minds on that singular feeling they couldn't name. Was it the weather, what they ate last night, or did it have something to do with *her?* Whatever it was unsettled them both and they walked away from each other.

Sid walked with head down, rifle couched in the crook of his elbow, the Indian carry. Scarcely any light to the day so he cast no shadow. Gray oversized coat with a rip near the elbow patched over with duct tape, blue jeans, brown leather boots needing new soles. Orange cap. Heavy gloves, fingers numb. He'd emptied the rifle of shells this morning. Had the dream he always had before he went hunting: he was a buck on a trail, walking with the long stride of a buck, relaxed, unaware of anything except of his sex. He was a buck who stopped and listened to the deadly steps of the hunter. Turned his vision inward, waited, heard a shot but thought it was ice breaking, rock falling, and he bolted, unaware of the wound, aware only of the beautiful snowcapped ridge ahead. That was the dream.

Didn't care for hunting, never had, but he'd been out on the first day of rifle hunting, one of 103,000 hunters tracking 150,000 deer. Vermont's unofficial holiday when barbers, mechanics, builders, and country store owners put up signs: CLOSED FOR THE FIRST WEEKEND OF DEER SEASON. He'd been out in bow hunting season too. Forty-five hundred deer killed. Rifle season was bigger, the kill would top 20,000. The numbers made the front page in the *Reporter.*

He and Butch and Earl packed a three-day-supply of beer, one box of ammo, .30-06, twenty rounds, and food. Steak, salad, potatoes, oleo, sausage, eggs, coffee, bread, onions, garlic, cookies, and chocolate for the cold weather in the woods. Sleeping bags, underwear, socks aplenty, boot oil, moccasins, ax and saw for firewood, toilet paper, and a shovel to bury the shit.

They drove shoulder to shoulder in the unheated truck to Bog Cabin. Up at dawn they walked miles through well-used deer trails, said not a word. Out in the snow. Sid had removed the shells from the rifle. His teeth chattered with cold. His eyes burned. Tried to stand tall but felt no bigger than a feeble switch of willow.

Lift your feet up. Pick up those goddamn boots. Stop coughing. Jeez, do you have to piss on the trail? Take that cigarette out of your mouth. That's no way to carry a rifle. Don't you got any sense? Can't you see what we're trying to do? For God's sake.

They'd heard crashing sounds, soft stepping, they'd seen a large-bodied deer through binoculars. They'd had dinner. Steaks and onions and potatoes. They cleaned up. Bagged and buried their trash. No need for vermin in camp. Then they played poker, nobody won. Earl cursed and they went to bed.

In their dreams they readied their rifles. In their dreams they shot straight to the heart. In their dreams they put their fingers to the frothy light-colored blood. All for nothing.

Came home after three days without a kill, and Earl, feeling heavy handed, went out back and shot the plastic buck set up between two bales of hay, firing round after round. He'd thrown the bottle of scent into the woods, the love potion with the randy scent of a young buck and the urine scent of a doe in heat. It had failed Earl, and so had his enthusiasm and so had his good eye and the wind and the weather. It had all been against him. So he said. And Sid had watched his father eyeing the other hunters in the field, dressing their bucks, dragging them to the trucks. *Bunch of bullshit artists,* Earl said when he heard them bragging at the local check stations about the bucks weighing two hundred pounds, ten-pointers, the near impossible shot, the sure shot, the perfect thirty-yard shot, and the goddamn good luck they'd had and he hadn't. *Bullshit.* Earl blamed them, Sid in particular.

That boy . . . something's wrong with him.

Nothing wrong with him. Let him be.

Let him be, let him be. That's all you ever have to say.

People need to be, Earl. Stop complaining.

That's how it was. He listened, took it in. Eighteen, barely made it through school. His writing was illegible except when he carved his name. The initials *S.S.* like twin eels. He liked geography, was the only subject he understood. He could feel it, touch it. The raised relief of peaks, canyons, trenches. Silent places. There he left his message: *Sid was here*.

Always thought his family had supernatural powers. They could talk, scream, laugh, at will. They had tempers, used words like firecrackers, big, magnificent words, wild and prolific curses. They could call the rain *rain*. All those years, his mother had said, *It's all right, you don't have to say a thing, I understand you*, but she was wrong.

He gauged the time of day by the angle of light and stared long and hard until his mind's eye took over and he was no longer looking at the trees but at the shape of his mother as she materialized and when he had her clearly in focus, when he saw the stitching of her coat and the wrinkles on her face and the thick curl that hung down her cheek, when he saw her face fall sideways and smile at him, she spoke. *I had to go, Sid*. She lifted her arms, turned, and vanished. She did this often. Showed up. Out of the blue.

To him she was already dead and had the ability of the dead to materialize; she also had the reluctance to go which he associated with unhappy souls. Sometimes he had to coax her to move out of his vision. Sometimes she refused and he had to turn his back and do something foul, something she wouldn't approve of seeing, like pissing on a tree. He'd read the Bible, gone to church, and once he stared at the water stain on the ceiling so long he thought he saw the face of Jesus. Scared him. Same with her, he wanted to see her but once he did he wanted her gone.

Heard the groan of the trees. Bird shot out of a low bush and struggled to rise. Heavy fat bird. Heard steps behind him and he lifted the rifle and aimed.

"Hey, it's me, put that thing down." It was Butch.

Sid sighted the enlarged vein on his brother's neck, the stubble of a week-old beard, the dry fat lips, his thick nose, his animal eyes.

"You crazy or what? Put that thing down." Butch did not move, though he felt like running. Felt a cold slice through the back of his head. Felt the numbness of his ears and realized his brother might shoot him. He lifted a hand and unzipped his coat and jacket, his sweatshirt read HARVARD. He had others like that. They read YALE. TUF STUF. And very slowly he said, "Aim right here, Sid, go for the heart, right here."

Sid felt the cold weight of the rifle pulsing through him.

"Shoot or put the rifle down, Sid. Put it down."

"N-n-no . . ." He was trying to say it wasn't loaded, that he wasn't going to shoot, but he couldn't move the rifle away.

In one quick motion Butch yanked the rifle out of his brother's hands and raised his hand to hit him. "You crazy?" He lifted the rifle high and fired into the air. He quickly worked the bolt and fired again. Shot cracked the air and bounced off the hills, everything expanded, vibrated around them, then it was all still.

That morning Sid had removed the shells but Earl saw him and loaded it again.

"I can't believe you aimed that fucking thing at me, you god-damn son of a bitch, you lunatic, I can't believe that." Butch gripped both rifles. "You son of a bitch, you crazy goddamn son of a bitch."

Sid covered his ears but Butch yanked his hands away. "What's wrong with you?"

Sid shoved his numb fists in his mouth, bit down hard, felt nothing. Pressed his cold hands hard on his throat looking for the place where words could form, inside pockets of air and bones, nothing.

"You crazy loon, come on, let's just go. It's fuckin freezing out and your brains are probably frostbit. That it? Too cold for you?" Butch punched his brother on the shoulder in a lighthearted at-tempt. He was shaking. "I can't believe it." He held a branch back so Sid could go first but the branch snapped and hit Butch on the cheek. "Goddamn!"

Butch led the way. Icy brambles and wet snow. After a few yards he turned and gave his brother a spiteful look. "I can't believe you aimed that fucking thing at me. I'm not against you, you know. I'm not the enemy." Sid put a hand on his brother's cheek and showed him. "Blood," he said. "Forget it," Butch said.

The ridge in self-contained misery. The unpleasant, unwanted common feel of pain. Two brothers unsure of what has happened. Sid followed Butch, stepped in his tracks, until they reached the truck.

"Dad's been here." Butch pointed at the tracks. "Glad to hell he's not here. Not in the mood for his stinking company anyway."

Sid climbed into the truck, hands between his legs, shivering. "So you okay now or what? You see something out there?"

Sid shook his head. No.

"I didn't either. Fucking cold is what it is. We'll come out later this week, what do you think, want to come out later, try again?" Butch started the truck.

Sid shook his head no, then yes, then no again. He was freezing.

"Good. We'll try again."

No doubt about it. They'd come again and again, year after year, soon as the stalks of corn were dried, soon as the chill got in the trees and turned the leaves gold, soon as the jack-o'-lanterns' devilish eyes were lit and glowed from every window and every porch of every house, they'd come again. When the crows burst out of trees and made dark wide arcs in the sky and all the green was gone from the land they'd be back. Drawn to the fierce cold, gripped by need and familiar ways, hopelessly tangled with misery and thinking of love, they'd be back. The eleventh of November would come again and again and so would hunter's moon.

. . .

THE RUTTED road was iced over and the wheels spun and Butch shoved his foot down hard on the gas, cursed, slammed his hand on the wheel, and the Deadhorse bolted out of one patch of ice and fell in another. They were glad when they reached the paved road. Glad to see a familiar car, Skunk's old Chevy with the rack mounted on the grille. They exchanged honks and half-raised hands.

"Sid,"—Butch spit on his hand, rubbed them together—"she hasn't called yet, has she? Mom?"

"Me-me-me . . ."

"Means what?"

"G-go-gone. . . ."

"Yeah, well, I know that. She's gone. I know that. I think we all know that but what the hell do we do? Shouldn't we do something?"

"She's g-g-gone. . . ."

"I know Sid, I know. We all know."

Truck hit a boulder and the side door, which never closed properly, swung open. Butch grabbed Sid by the pants. "Hold on to that door. You don't want to fall off."

Several hundred feet below was the river running like a black serpent.

"You want to go out later? Have a drink?" Butch said.

"N-n-no. . . ."

"See Suzanne's old house? What do you think? Maybe she's back. Want to drive by? Just for the hell of it?" He blew on his hands.

"C-c-can't. . . ."

"Hell, why not?"

■   ■   ■

IT WAS unfair of Butch to ask, to even mention her name. Sid wrapped his hands around the door handle, holding himself in. Saw himself flying out into the trees, lost without a sound.

Suzanne had been their girl. She'd done it with both of them. Night when the cornstalks hissed in the little night wind. A year ago. October. He and Butch had the old car, the '72 Lincoln, rolled it down the drive, into the road, coasted for a half a mile before they started it.

Suzanne was out there. Her house was right on the road in, and behind it were rolling grasslands and the steep sharp slab of rock where kids spray-painted their names, class of '86, class of '92, and a swastika, a marijuana leaf. Her old man had poured acid on the swastika but it still glowed eerie green in certain light. Suzanne with her curly mess of hair and her vanilla scent and her girlish voice and her crazy ways. Suzanne living alone with her old man, Gus, who was bound to lose his wife, his farm, and his mind all in one month. He told her they could have everything, everything they wanted, except the horses, and he was out there one night telling Suzanne to lead them out of the barn one by one and then he shot them. Suzanne, left alone to figure out her life, ran to the boys, to the dark leather seats, and fidgeted with the radio dials until she found a song she knew by heart and she sang real pretty as the cold night rushed past them and she laughed at nothing. She held the boys' hands in hers, she called them crazy boys, she squeezed their hands tight in hers. Wearing her father's army jacket and a T-shirt and nothing else.

"You guys are crazy. *Crazy.*" Her laughter hard, fast, immediate. She sucked in her breath. "You guys got a smoke?"

No.

"*Noooo?* Well, let's get one." Rocking in the seat, twisting her hands around the boys' knuckles, turning in her seat to see who was following.

"Relax, nobody is after us." Butch, head barely above the wheel.

"Could be, way you're driving."

"It's the speed limit."

"Sixty?"

"Yeah, this time of night, sure it's sixty. Right, Sid?"

Sid nodded.

Suzanne laid her hand on his thigh, squeezed it.

"Man, you guys are *craaaazy*." She rubbed her hands up and down Sid's leg, then she screamed and pounded the dash. "Oh, you *passed* it. Slow *down*! Man, you *passed it*!"

"Passed what?"

"Just go back, go back!"

"Why?"

"Go back, reverse!"

He did.

"There, park there."

It was a little gravel spot off the road. It was a dented spot in the land. A little clearing. It was in the cornfields. It was Butch first. She grabbed his hands and ran out the car. Then she came back, alone, jacket over her nakedness. Kissed Sid, said, "Hey, you."

She called him *you crazy crazy boy*. She kissed him in the mouth and rubbed him till he was hard; her plain lips tasting of cold air, her body heat coming out of her hair, her legs wide open. She kissed him and made him kiss her the same way. She undid his shirt, his pants. *Hurry, hurry up, come on, come on*. He could hear her words and then she was crying or laughing. She told him she loved him, said he was *crazycrazycrazy*.

He didn't see much of her after that. Hard to track down. Not home, not well, too busy or something. Whenever they could, they drove to her house, parked, and turned the lights off. Sometimes they saw her walking through the house. She didn't come to them, though.

Last time Sid saw her was the day his mom caught Butch and

her in his room. His mom called her a little bitch. She called Butch you little prick. She told Sid to get lost, to stop staring, to get out of the way.

Thought of Suzanne now came to Sid like thunder. Disturbing, like everything else.

Whatever thoughts Butch had of Suzanne he wasn't sharing. He drove. "What do you think we should tell the old man? That we saw something and we missed, fired and missed? Or we didn't see a thing?"

He was talking about the cold again, the night, the hunting.

"No-no-nothing."

"Yeah, okay, we saw nothing. Was nothing out there to see. Nothing at all. Nothing worth shooting. Didn't see a thing."

The night smelled of frozen river water, hardened soil, everything beaten back, cowering under cold. It also smelled of brakes burning. And their hands, when they put their hands across their faces to shield their eyes from the light on the porch which went on like a flare as soon as they drove up, their hands smelled of green summer trees.

. . .

THE RIDGE has no human dimension, it is not of human design, it is made of terms that have nothing to do with human determination or courage or need or want. It is vast and nourishes only its vastness. Water and fire, air and earth. It all feeds on itself.

. . .

THEY DIDN'T want to go in. Earl stood by the window, staring out. Damage in the night. The very heavens warned them not to go in.

Butch opened the door.

"Cold's getting in, shut the fuckin door," Earl said.

Sid turned like an uninvited guest and went out back. Butch stepped in, closed the door. The click of the doorjamb was loud.

Something about the way his father was standing—arms crossed, unlit cigarette in his mouth—was wrong, whatever he was thinking wasn't right.

The house smelled of perfume and fried chicken. Butch stood by the door waiting for instructions but there was no one to tell him to get washed up, to take his boots off, to have a seat, no one asking, *You hungry, you want coffee, beer?* no one saying, *You look a mess, is something wrong?*

There was plenty wrong.

"You see any fuckin thing out there?" Earl said without turning to face him. There were two Earls. The one in the flesh, who spoke, and the one reflected on the frosted window with patches of ice on his face.

"Too cold," Butch said.

"Not asking you the fuckin weather. Asking if you saw anything out there."

"Nope, nothing."

"Nothing?"

"Nothing. Didn't see a thing moving."

"Who fired them fuckin shots, then? Sid?"

"No. Me. I tripped."

"You what?"

"I tripped, I had the—"

"You didn't fuckin trip."

It was no use. Butch gripped the edge of a chair and stared at his father.

"What's that blood on your face?"

"Told you. I tripped."

"Go wash your face. You look like a fuckin Indian."

Butch looked around, expecting to see his mom. The perfume

in the room was hers. Trapped in the heat. Butch expected her to come down the stairs, hands on hips, and give Earl one of her looks to put him in his place and say, *Dinner's ready, sit down. Peas, want more peas? Have some of this bread, it's fresh. Butter. Coffee, you want more coffee?* He wanted her sharp presence between him and Earl.

"Dad? What are we going to do?"

He was asking for trouble, asking for miracles, asking for a fish to fly. He wanted lightness, somebody laughing for no reason at all. He wanted the old kind of pain, not this new one.

"What do you mean? Do about what? Your sister's out, I suppose. She left the house with all the lights on. Dumb kid." Earl turned to the stove, pointed at the black cast-iron skillet as if that explained something. "She's around here somewhere, she made dinner."

"No, Dad," and only after a while he said, "I mean Mom."

Earl put his unlit cigarette carefully in his shirt pocket and looked at his son. Air escaped through the cracks of his front teeth. Back straight, pants hung low, dirty shirt, dirty face.

"I don't have eyes in the back of my head, son, and I don't give a hoot about what I can't see, and I can't see your mother anymore."

So. He couldn't fly.

Earl stepped behind Butch and for a minute he thought his father might touch him. He was waiting for it. To be hit or hugged. An embrace like a freak wave, embarrassing them later. But no, Earl reached for the pot on the stove, lifted the lid, slammed it down on the counter, and grabbed a drumstick and tore at the greasy skin.

Butch rinsed two beer bottles and put them under the sink. He wiped the counter. He rearranged the canisters, four of them, in their right order, small to big. Flour, sugar, tea, coffee. Black canisters with white-capped mountains and pink cherry blossoms. *Her* things.

"Better eat," Earl said, "and tell your brother to get in here. We're going out again." Mouth full, he sucked his greasy fingers.

"Going where?"

"Out."

"I don't want to go out."

"I don't give a damn what you feel like. We're going and that's that. Get your brother in here." Bones fell with a thud in the sink.

The dog growled when she saw Butch. Sid was on the snow.

"Hey. Get your butt off the snow. Aren't you cold?"

"No."

"The hell you're not. Bet your butt's blue. Bet your balls are frostbit. Bet you. Shit, it's cold."

It was twenty and dropping. The weatherman had said: *A cold weather front is forming out by the Great Lakes, bringing a lot of mixed precipitation. It should come into our area by Tuesday, early Wednesday, mixing snow, freezing rain, and fog. Higher elevations expected to get a total accumulation of ten to twelve inches by morning. . . .*

"Dad says we're going. He wants us to come."

"Where?" It took him seconds to form the word.

"Out."

"Out," Sid repeated and the dog wagged her tail. He patted the dog's back, kissed her black nose, said, *You good dog, you good good dog,* without stuttering. Clipped the leash on the dog's collar and they all sighed, high and long, boys and dog. For shelter, the dog had the woodshed with her pile of old blankets. Sid snapped his finger and the dog jumped on the blankets.

A light went on in the bathroom and through the white curtains they saw their father pissing.

"He's going to get her," Butch said. He said it twice.

．　．　．

THE MOOSE, the nomad of the wilderness, wades out of Joe's Pond and uproots weeds, disturbs ice that wants to form; confused and brain sick, it moves out of its wild range and crosses the interstate to join a herd of placid cows in a pasture.

■   ■   ■

IT WAS strange and delirious being in the tepee. Candles, incense, women's voices like chants, a woman waved a smoking brush of sage across the room.

The women sat around the potbellied stove and passed bowls of bread, cheese, fruit. Their hands cast long shadows. They sat on rugs and pillows embroidered with tiny mirrors. The walls had masks with feathers and beads. The floor was hard and gave off the smell of trapped earth and wetness. Fat candles flickered from earthen pots. Fox caught herself smiling, sighing, she sat on a crimson cushion and listened to the conversation. *Sooo beautiful . . . sooo peaceful. . . .* the women echoed each other, voices like clouds. A basket of cards was passed around. *Angel cards,* Sandra said.

The women read their cards aloud in a solemn way. Fox read hers and shoved it in a pocket. *Travel a clear pond like a dragonfly.*

"It's time," Sandra said and the women put on their boots and coats, except Fox, who hadn't taken hers off. A tall woman with a beak nose and bangs down her eyes touched Fox's coat, rubbed her fur, and asked, "Is this real?"

"What?"

"The coat, is this real or faux?"

"It's fox."

"Oh." With two pointy fingers she parted her inky black hair and in a squeaky voice said, "Are you a Summer?"

She'd never been addressed by her last name. *A Summer.* She thought of Earl's truck trimmed with coon tails; the rusty clutter of chains and traps, pelts piled high, the box with bait, broom and shovel for road kills. He carried an ax, a twelve-inch knife, his rifles were always loaded. The coat was testimony. Yes, she was the trapper's daughter.

"Yeah." Fox nodded. "I guess I am."

The woman's nylon coat swished as she walked away.

The women talked of a lunar eclipse and the solstice and Fox understood they took nature as a sign of something besides weather. Watched the moon disappear and wondered what it meant. Couldn't remember looking at the sky for any real length of time, ever.

They followed Sandra to the wide circular maze in the snow, the path lined with sweet-smelling hay, and at the center was the fire. Nothing else seemed to have life except the fire. Even the ridge fell away completely. The fire drew them in like fires do. Snow kept it from spreading. The cold wind fed it.

One by one the women walked the labyrinth to the fire and made tossing motions with their arms, saying, *I release you.* One woman released her lover, her desire, her need, *All gone,* she said, *all gone. I now release you. Go.* The fire, as if beckoned, moved toward the woman.

Fox felt foolish. She didn't have anything to release. Didn't understand what it was all about. She didn't want to be there anymore and moved into the tangle of old lilacs. The women howled. *Ooooouuuuu . . . oouu, ooouu, ooouuuuuu . . . uuuuuu . . .*

Out of their minds. Had to be. Howling like wolves. Heads thrown back and necks strained with the effort of getting the sounds right. Short howls and long ones, on and on and on. A desperate human sound in need of violent reassurance. High above the howls Sandra's voice instructed: *Call back the light! Call it back! Bring the light back! Hooouuuuu . . . hooouuu.*

They didn't sound anything like the wolf she'd heard a day long ago when Butch called her out and said, *Come see what we got in the traps.* It was a she-wolf and she was whimpering, her back leg in the clamp. Seeing her and Butch standing so near she had pulled harder and cried but it was a weak cry like that of an infant. The wolf's yellow eyes fell on her and stayed on her and she understood the meaning of the word *mercy.* Butch slammed the butt of his rifle against its upraised head. It was looking at her, pleading, trying to make a pact, when it died. *You killed it for nothing, Butch,* she said. He'd poked the animal in the ribs to make sure it was dead. *It was going to die anyway,* he said.

"*Call the light back . . . bring us light.*"

The women didn't have the pain of the wolf in them and their howling was comical and out of place with the darkness and the fire. The moon was gone and the stars dragged their mystery across the sky and were too far away to matter.

■ ■ ■

T<small>HE RIFLES</small> were in the rack. The moon was no longer full. Ice on the shallow banks, on the upraised roots of ash, on the broken maple, on the splintered spruce, ice on the land. The vanishing moon cast shadows that would never be seen again, not like this.

Butch sat between Earl and Sid.

Sid held on to the door of the Deadhorse, eyes closed.

"Fuckin cold, ain't it?" Earl said. The boys said nothing.

The moon was full of darkness and dead ahead.

Earl quit the engine and coasted downhill. Same hill where he'd pushed them down on sleds as children while their mother screamed as they went flying out of the sled. She'd picked them up, wiped their faces, only to have Earl hurl them down again, yelling, *Way to go!* The same wild and uncontrollable fear was in the boys now. Panic in their guts.

Earl tapped the brakes. The Deadhorse skidded to a stop. He opened the door, passed out the rifles, and without a word Sid and Butch fanned out to the sides like coydogs stalking.

The tepee glowed like flesh. Thin smoke curled up from the top. Six cars by the road. A huge bonfire in the meadow. The women were out there, howling. Butch and Sid looked at each other.

Earl walked quietly, lifting his legs high. Rifle in arms.

The river here was deeper and open and rushed loud but not as loud as the sound of a dozen women howling. The fire blazed ten feet high. The women's heads were thrown back to the changing sky. Howling and laughing.

Jesus. That's what Earl said. *Jesus fucking Christ.* He said it over and over until the blast of his shotgun shut his words down.

■ ■ ■

THE HOWLING was so loud she couldn't hear the river, the fire, the truck, nor the men but she heard the shot and then the women screamed. Another shot hit the tepee and made the same sound the wolf had made the day Butch crushed its skull. Air escaped. Life went out. Fox moved away from the clearing and into the thick bushes until she felt taken in.

The women saw the barrel of the shotgun and the man's arm. A gash of light on his face. Two men around him like dogs.

"Thought you were a pack of goddamn wolves. Could hear you screaming for miles. What the hell is this?" It was Earl.

"Put that rifle away!" Sandra with her white cape and the fire behind her.

"You goddamn witch! Disturbing the peace round here. Acting like a pack of goddamned animals. I ought to shoot the whole lot of you."

"Get off my property—now—or I will call the police."

"Hell, go ahead. Law says nobody got the right to go acting like crazy and you all acting crazy. Howling like fucking bitches."

"Go away." She spoke as if to a child, slow, clear words. She moved away from the fire, away from the center of a world she knew and could control by breath, out of the maze. She wanted to look at his eyes.

With the same careful deliberation, with his eyes clearly focused on her, with the weight of years lived in training for unexpected moments, his hands on the familiar shape and feel of steel and wood, tired and irritable, he shot above the woman's head.

Sandra jumped back, fell in the broken circle of straw, too close to the fire. Her white glove caught on fire. She stood, stared at her hand on fire, and waved her hand at him, or so it appeared, waved her burning hand as if she were going now, as if she were waving bye-bye. One of the women pulled Sandra down and rolled her in the snow like a carpet.

"Damn witches!" He stepped away, bothered by the frenzy. "Tina! Where the hell are you?" He walked to the dark tangle of small trees beyond the meadow where she stood.

Knew she was there, could sense her. "Come on out! I can stand here all night or I can shoot the whole goddamn place to pieces. You hear me? Come on out!"

The straw caught fast and Sid kicked snow into the fire. Butch held his rifle as if at any moment he'd have to shoot something.

"Tina!" Earl called, then, remembering she had wanted them to call her Fox, he almost called her that way, but he never had and never would. "Tina!" He poked the branches with the barrel of his rifle. Old sumacs, old lilacs.

The women, a huddle of scared flesh and muted sounds in the immense cold night. The moon was gone. The fire raged. The river broke.

"Tina!"

He was holding a rifle that could have blown a hole right through her heart, a hole big enough to kill her and her mother, too, had she been there. In his fury he wanted to force the two of them out of wherever they were and face him and tell him what it was, why they were gone. "You're just like your mother!"

That would do it, he thought, she wouldn't like that, she'd have to come out now, she'd hurl herself out just to talk him down. "Come on out."

The fear in him was dangerous and he was trembling. "God-damn it, you hear me, come out of there." *You're my only daughter, only one born to my kind, I want you home.* "Come out!"

She heard him, knew his words, his voice, but she wasn't going to move. Couldn't. She saw his hands and legs and face scratched in the bramble. She knew him but he didn't make any sense. He could grab her and pull her out, she was within reach, if he wanted her out he could come and get her and stop yelling at her. She waited for him to grab her. But that was a dangerous thing to think. *He can't, he can't, he can't find me. You're nothing, nothing.* Her eyes were fixed on him and she saw him change into many things—bear, beaver, a huge black crow, he was her mother, her brothers, the house, the moon, he was all these things at once and he grew twice his size then became smaller and shrunk before her eyes until he was nothing, nothing at all. Something was between them now, whatever it was kept her in, and him out. She was keeping vigil, watching herself watching him. She was in that part of the world that had been his until then, a world she had never known, a world of scents and feelings and disappearing life. She knew nothing of it, had cringed away from it all her life. *Whoever you are, you cannot harm me.* Peace. She felt it settle in her like a wing. And in that instant she became completely invisible to him. Hidden by more than branch and darkness. He would never see her again.

Nothing was there and then something was. A deer, next to her, a hand away. A hot animal presence. The black jelly eyes, the long bone, the beautiful face. Her fear passed into the deer and she felt it pass, she shuddered and so did the deer. Its eyes opened and closed in resolve, and for a second, none of it made sense. *Tina! Come out! Come out of there! I'm giving you one more minute! One minute, that's it!*

It was a small moment. Much had already happened. The deer looked at her as she was, as she would always be from then on, and she looked at the face of the deer, and in that way the pact was made, eye to eye, one would survive, the other would die. The moment passed, the fear passed, the voice stopped. She lowered her head.

She felt the hooves of the long-legged creature rise from the ground as it leapt over her head. The rush of heated animal air. The branches exploded. Then she heard the shot and dropped to her knees.

Earl stepped directly in front of her, not seeing her, then he turned and knelt by the deer. "Dead."

Her brothers also looked through the branches. They couldn't see her either.

"Dad . . ." It was Butch. His voice broken.

"Shut up." Earl took the knife and plunged it into the deer's throat. He cleaned his hands on the snow. Rubbed a handful of snow on his face. The deer bled. It was over.

The men dragged the deer to the truck and drove away.

The women were silent and found their way back to the tepee.

The moon began to fill itself with light again.

They had all looked at her but not seen her.

I release you, she whispered. The river screamed. *I release you.*

Nobody saw her crawl out of the brush to the cold bloodied spot in the snow where she put her face. Nobody heard her say, *I love you.*

The river clamped shut after that. It closed down from the bottom up. It made the sound of a slap, hard and quick. It was done.

■ ■ ■

THE RIDGE doesn't give out secrets. Doesn't let on how much death is in the flickering light, how much cold the stones can hold, nor how long any itty-bitty thing can make it, wing on wing, across the land. But it knows desire, and desire makes the patterns of the sky.

Not far, the flash of black-and-white wings, snow geese, flying high. The others left, too, dropping down to rest in the evenings and rising again in the morning. The blacks, mallards, blue-winged teal, widgeons, pintails, shovelers, wood ducks, gadwalls, and the green-winged teal. That one day, hundreds of snow geese stretched across a cornfield and descended on Dune Creek like they have every year since 1954. They came upon the marsh like a blizzard of feathers.

■ ■ ■

"DAMN IT, Dad, stop the fucking truck, will you? Stop the truck."

"What the hell for?"

Too late. Sid, gagging on his own puke, hurled himself out. Butch jumped out, too, he rolled, and grabbed at a stump off the road. Sid buckled over. Butch put his arms over him and waited. The wretched night. The goddamned night.

Earl saw Sid on his knees and Butch rolling down—his jacket shone like a ball of fire in the mirror—and he cursed them. *Damn 'em.* He gripped the wheel and drove, brakes screaming, clutch popping, and the smell of puke all around him. Headlights shone high on the land that seemed stranger than ever. Boulders like carcasses, tangle of dead wood, mist like a corpse, all of it came swirling at him in the desolate darkness of the ruined night. Spat into the cold and the ridge opened up, let him in.

Almost shot her. My own flesh and blood. Almost killed her. Those were his thoughts. She was in there. He knew it. He'd shot at her. *At her.* Meant to hit, not miss, didn't miss, didn't miss at all. Buck took the shot for her, that's what it was. Those things happened. Shook the cold off him, sat up straight, and held the wheel as the Deadhorse screeched downhill.

Sight of the house cornered by cords of wood, blond and naked, needing to be delivered. A thousand dollars sitting there. Money for bills, gas, electric, food. Had a hundred pelts but nobody was buying. Thought maybe he'd get Caroline up on the ridge to make fur-lined mittens, fur-trimmed hats, and sell them come

Christmas. Thought of fishing come spring, thought of shoveling food in his mouth—rind of salt pork, sweet ham, yams drenched in maple syrup—thought of these things to forget what he'd done.

Walked to his shed and turned the light on. Tableful of tools: surgeon's scalpel, broad-bladed butcher's knife, sheath knives, penknives, shiny carbon-steel tools, all those sharp cutting edges, no blood groove on any of them. His Arkansas stone of pure silica, the scrapers, needles, nippers, forceps, and his mixing bowls, his plastic buckets. The slicker used to finish off the leather, the fleshing beam clamped to a bench, Borax in gallon jars, Plastilina, beeswax, wires, cotton cord and salt, all in a row, ready and waiting.

The last fox he'd pulled out of the trap he'd had to step on, crushed his chest near the back leg. Plugged all the openings but forgot the mouth; blood and bile gushed out and that was that, ruined. The mess was impossible to wash off the fur. Ruined. He'd never forgotten to plug up the holes before. Nose, ears, asshole, whatever, certainly the mouth, and one day he forgot the mouth, of all things. What was he thinking? Took the beast out, wrapped in burlap, and threw it in the river. Nobody saw him do it. Since then he hadn't caught a thing. Wouldn't either. That much he knew.

Thought of himself in the past as if others were talking about him: *That Earl, he was always good at it, trapping, skinning, tanning.* Fur, he liked it, didn't matter what it was. Weasel, mink, marten, fisher, fox, skunk. Knew how to case better than anybody. Could do it blindfolded: hind legs ripped heel to heel, skin around the vent to the back legs, tail skinned down, stripped, hung the animal by the hind legs, peeled the skin from the body. If it was still warm he used an old coffee spoon. Slit up the belly, careful not to rip the hide. Stretched out on the hoop to its natural shape. His skins sold as superior pelts; never hung anything by the nose, never gave it a shape it didn't have, never put it in the hot sun to scorch, always soaked and worked it till it made him moan with pleasure. It had to be that soft.

That was who he was. That was his work. To make another sort of life from life, to capture quick, make it good, keep the beauty.

You like it? Hey, you like this or what? Ain't it a beauty? He'd draped the fox coat over her shoulders years ago. His prize furs for her. And now his daughter was out there covered in fur. His fur. Hiding like an animal.

Thought hit him, but it was more like a vision: daughter and wife and fox turned into one—one beast larger than him, more powerful, more dangerous. She wouldn't survive out there. She'd come home. Nobody stayed out. Too many things out there to struggle with. She didn't have the skills. Didn't know north from south. Would see her own shadow and die of fright. *Hell, you don't know what you're up against.* He meant his daughter, he meant his wife.

The thick night settled down again. It had been wild for a moment. Nearly did him in.

■   ■   ■

DARLENE STOPPED to give a dollar to a woman with a scowling bloody face. The woman inspected the dollar on both sides and walked away mumbling. What would it take, she thought, to end up like that?

No one ever told her what to expect from marriage, how to cradle it, hold it. She fumbled in her pockets. What was it, exactly, she had left behind?

She stepped into a glass lobby just to see how the world looked from there. Fractured, smooth. Cream-colored walls and cream-colored floors, an oversize black bust of a man in a glass case. Snatches of conversation. *You know what it is, Al . . . And the damn bitch . . . I should have canned him. . . . You going uptown? . . . Did I tell you . . . Tried to call but . . .* Faces intent on going or coming. Delicate ringing elevator bells. Two women dressed in the same coat. A couple holding hands, the man going much faster than the woman who looked at her feet as if begging them to go faster. The effort to move, to talk, to get up and go. How did they do it? Life as an errand. Quickly, with hands out, she entered the spin of the doors, but the spin was greater than her and she went around like a child on a merry-go-round. Dizzy, she fell into the rush of the street to see a waif of a woman wearing robes and holding a large glitter star above her head. Somebody's guardian angel, Darlene thought, lost in the crowd. *Get a look at that.* . . . Men laughed.

The shop was dwarfed between much taller buildings, shabby with an Old World look. The sign was written in crude markers: SEAMSTRESS NEEDED.

A cluster of bells on the door. A shelf lined with sun-bleached blue taffeta. Hand-painted boxes filled with sweaty chocolates.

Smell of cotton, dust, old dust. Walls lined with remnants, calico prints. An old yellow couch with pleated upholstery, a tufted chair in orange and brown, a musty-smelling Oriental carpet, a sleeping yellow dog who lifted his head from his paws to look at her and let himself down again as if he couldn't be bothered.

"Hello?" Darlene said.

"A minute." A tired voice, foreign, female.

The lunchtime crowd outside was dizzying, so Darlene looked at the dark chocolates; two were missing. A pincushion shaped like a heart. Another sign: ALTERATIONS, CUSTOM-MADE CLOTHES, FREE ESTIMATES.

"Yes?"

Darlene turned to see a woman three times her size, large from top to bottom, with a huge head of hair wrapped in a turban, a head the size of a heifer and a body enveloped in a red caftan. She wore running shoes.

"You're looking for a seamstress?"

"I need seamstress."

"I can sew."

"Yes?"

Darlene nodded.

"Sit here." The woman pointed to the tufted chair; the dog opened an eye.

"Do you like chocolates?"

"Yes, I do."

"Try one. Go ahead, take the box."

The woman smelled of mayonnaise. The chocolates were rounds and nut-sprinkled squares. Darlene ate a square one, smiled, and said, "It's very good."

"Yes? Take this one."

Darlene took a round one and bit into it. It was soft and bitter.

"Bourbon balls. My own recipe."

"It's very good."

"Yes?"

"Yes."

"Come here." The woman led her through a curtained doorway into a small cramped room with a large black sewing machine in the center. "I need hems here, zippers here, this needs ironing." *This* was a lemon-yellow tulle evening dress which filled the room as if with sunlight.

"I'll pay you minimum. You start now. Yes?"

The woman cleared the table, turned a light on overhead, removed a stack of cut fabrics from a wooden folding chair. The curtains swung for a long time after she left the room. There was a fan on. Darlene sat, put her foot on the treadle, and watched the needle go up and down, sewing nothing but air.

When she was ten she learned to cut a straight line. She mended, darned, made dresses, aprons, pants, curtains, bedspreads. *You need to do things with your hands,* her mother had said, flattening the muslin out. *You need to do it like this,* and she taught her how to lick the thread before she inserted it through the eye of the needle. *You need to make your seams wide.* She learned the measure of an inch. *You need to make it give.* She learned the trick of the bias. For

Christmas one year, her mother gave her pinking scissors, her own tomato-red pincushion, and a bundle of squares for her wedding-bed quilt. No whites. *Whites stain in the awfullest way, they yellow too.* Her mother gave her crimson and indigo, copper-penny red, and mustard colors. *Anybody can do this,* she said, talking with pins between her teeth, cutting, marking, stitching. *No whites, whites stain.*

Darlene had ruined her wedding-day quilt because she was thinking of Earl. She made the straight lines curve. She made uneven edges. She broke needles, ruined the pins by sewing over them. She ruined her marriage by making her bed, on her wedding night, with a coverlet bought at Sears. *How do you expect to make anything that lasts with that?* Her mother had humphed her way out the door.

Now she pulled on the thread and it broke. A blend. To make it last, the stitch, it had to be one-hundred-percent cotton. She threaded the needle over and over as if she were paying for a lesson she should have learned long ago. *It's all in the give and take,* she could hear her mother say.

Her seams were hard earned but straight. She had to undo a lot of thread. Her ironing was wrinkled. Her skills were sloppy. She almost burned the tulle. After an eight-hour day at the machine, with the fan on her head, she sneezed into the satin-lined bodice. It stained in the shape of a teardrop.

"What is this?" the heifer said.

"What?"

"Ruined?" The woman pointed at the stain.

"What?"

"You ruined perfect dress?"

The woman who said her name was simply Madame picked up the dress and took Darlene outside and in the sidewalk, where everyone heard, she yelled, "You see stain? Yes? You *ruined* me."

She did see. A splotch. On another woman's dress. A dream dress. Ruined. She could see that with her own eyes.

"I'm sorry," Darlene said, casting her shadow on the handheld dress.

"Sorry?"

"Yes."

She spent the rest of the week at Madame's cutting coarse cotton for aprons for a restaurant. She embroidered the name Gus twenty-six times. She was given seams to undo, polyester pants to shorten. Seams to take in. She was called in to measure sweaty women, skinny women, and she was told to come, to go, come back, sew this now, and then after two weeks she was told, after being offered a single chocolate, *Go away, you ruined me*.

Nights after she dreamt of needles and straight lines; she dreamt of edges, of fabric gliding easily under the foot, of zippers ripping open with a sigh and seams coming undone in a sneeze, of needles splintering on metal teeth, of plastic that wouldn't give, and of inches, quarter inches, eighths and tenths of inches, and in her dreams she walked with a white chalk and marked everything. She smelled like cotton for days.

At Madame's she'd made enough money to pay for a week's rent. She did without lunch and dinner. For breakfast she went to a new deli. A dollar sixty for coffee and a bagel served with sweet butter shaped like a seashell, which she sliced thinly. She walked to Third Avenue to smell food cooked in real kitchens. Cloves and curries, onions and peppercorns. She watched the preparations in open kitchens—a hand on a ladle, the long-handled blackened pot, the swift hand lifting a top to let steam out, the flambé, the heaps of rice, the rack of lamb, the ever-so-green garnish. Her room smelled of unwashed linen and every night she opened the suitcase hoping to find something she'd overlooked. Nothing there.

WAITRESS WANTED. And so came another job. She chopped garlic, washed broccoli, served turbaned Muslims endless glasses of water and tea, and left with a two-dollar tip after ten hours. Giuseppe, the owner, told her at the end of the day to *go on, take anything in the fridge*. She took a slice of cheesecake, the most expensive item on the menu at $3.50 a slice, and in her room, with feet up on the black suitcase, she ate the sweet thing.

She could tell by the give of her bra that she was losing weight. It was all going fast. She laughed with the other waitress, an Italian with a thick head of black henna hair who said, *Who needs this?* Darlene took to saying the same thing in her room late at night as she fingered the cheesecake. *Who needs this?* She took to showing up half an hour late, she chopped garlic in a panic. *Who needs this?* She flirted with customers, hoping for bigger tips. She grabbed leftover rolls, stuffed them in her pocket. She carried a hundred pounds or more of dirty dishes in and out the swinging doors, and her skin, even after showers, reeked of garlic. She cleared the mist from the bathroom mirror, and dried herself. *Who needs this?*

She yelled her orders to Giuseppe. *Table six, ten orders of sole and broccoli.*

Giuseppe, thin, dark, ragged, needing love, said, *What? What?*

I said table six is ready to eat. She slammed the tray down.

Please, he said, *you say please.*

It was too much. The man who never thanked her for coming in early, for staying late, for walking home with a ten, a five in change, the man who made her hate humanity's hunger, was asking her to please say please.

I quit, I've had it. She tossed her paisley apron on the stove. The strings caught on fire.

No! Giuseppe said, *You don't quit! I fire you!* He tossed the flaming apron at her feet.

You can't fire me, I already quit, didn't you hear me? I quit! The apron burned.

I fire you!

I quit!

He pushed her aside. *Get out, you talk too much. You fired.*

It was so easy to do, really. The tray was loaded with glasses, plates, and serving dishes ready for table six. She saw the other waitress flash a smile, her Italian hips sashaying from table to table, but she could tell the smile was made up, the hips were tired. The place was packed. She moved the tray an inch or so off its place and it crashed.

I fire you! Get out! Get out!

The customers clapped as she left.

The idea of food came with the memory of all that was cruel in the world. She would never eat cheesecake again. She walked the twelve flights of stairs to the roof, pulled out the plastic lawn chair, and with head back, stared at buildings, at airplane lights. It was freezing.

When the door opened and slammed shut, she turned, expecting to be told to get up and leave. But it was a couple, they didn't see her. It was the business of love they were after. They got into it. The slapping motions of flesh on flesh took over the sounds of traffic in the night and she thought how little time the grand moments of life take to happen and how quick, how suddenly, they end. The couple left, slammed the door. They hadn't said a word to each other.

■   ■   ■

T HE BOYS were swept in the cold and guided by it as they walked. Butch held his brother by the shoulder and felt his bones rattling and his flesh pounding. "Get ahold of yourself, Sid, we're almost home," but the thought of home made the two of them sick and Sid dropped again. "What I mean is that we'll make it, don't worry. And Tina's fine, I know she is." He didn't know but he spoke as if he did. *Stay out there,* he thought, *wherever you are, stay out there.* The eclipsed moon shone meekly on him and on the bent body of his brother choked in tears.

Out of the bush stepped a large buck no more than a few yards away. They felt him before they saw him. It lifted its heavy head, eyes without fear, and recognized by their heaving that they meant no harm. When he'd had enough of looking at them he made an exaggerated noise and bounded across the road.

Earl saw them walk in. Butch by the open fridge, head tilted back, a can of beer to his face. Sid moved like a line cut out of softening wax. Thought of calling them out to help with the deer but it was late. They'd be clumsy. He'd have no patience. Funny how things are, he thought. Had hiked miles, endured blistering cold for weeks and no luck, and then tonight of all nights, beast jumped right at him. Take me, it had said, here I am.

Drove out again. Cracked seat stiff with cold. The road was black ice. Headlights like fallen moons. The sanding crew would be out later. Nobody in the village needed their drive plowed tonight, and if they did, to hell with them.

Didn't look back at the house or at the tepee or the river. Watched the shadows on the road expecting to see the half-crazed shape of his daughter running. She'd be back. Rolled the windows down and yelled. *You'll be back. I ain't looking for you. You're out there now.* Rolled the window up and drove with the ridge high around him. Leaned on the wheel, chin grazing the coiled leather. *You're out there now. Gone's gone. You ain't mine.*

Drove straight to the Pig's Eye. A rewarding place in the right frame of mind, a forlorn place that night. Most nights he found the locals talking about haying, upgrading the herd, do-it-yourself-and-get-rich schemes, and mourning love. Most nights he could sit for a spell, drink, and get out without a scratch. But this was hunting season and he expected talk of monster whitetails and step-by-step recounts of the hunt, the weather conditions, rattling calls, and scents used. The knowhow and superabundance of confidence is what he expected. Two cars in the drive, though. One was Carm's, the owner, the other was Jigger's.

Jigger, the old riverman, talking in the smoky air to himself.

A poster of Madonna with a metal bra hung over the cash register next to three rows of bottles with spouts. A blue light on the wall-to-wall mirror, a clock with Miller time. The register was old, silver and gold, engraved on the side. A ten-point buck's head was mounted over Madonna. Everybody called the buck Dick. Called her Jane.

Quiet nights at the Pig's Eye meant the TV was on without volume so everyone could hear the sound of the cars outside as they slowed down, parked, and checked out who was in there. Whose wife, whose husband, whose lover. There'd been shootings, crashes, brawls, men dragging women out by the hair, women dragging men out by the feet. The constable stayed away. That was good.

Loud nights were Fridays and the band played broken-hearted songs. Patsy Cline, always Patsy Cline. Sometimes the fiddlers came, a wiry trio with pointy boots keeping time on the dusty four-by-four stage. Saturdays a woman named Magic sang, brought the mike to her open mouth, held a note as long as she could and barely moved as she sang with eyes closed and the room swelled with desire. Even the walls buckled with longing, and when she was done, men hooted and called for more while their women looked away, sipped warm margaritas, and went outside to look at stars. Those nights Earl paid the extra dollar to watch the woman sing and he drank too much. And if anybody looked gloomier than he, he'd buy them a round.

But it was a quiet night. News on TV. The jukebox was lit up but shut down. Place had the rank smell of dirty rinse water. The mop in its bucket by the corner. Garbage bagged. Half hour to closing.

Earl swung his legs over the black plastic-covered stool, near the john, which reeked of Pine-Sol even with doors closed.

"The whole thing's gone to hell. Can't win long enough to call yourself a winner, can't lose enough to stay out of the game." Jigger, the old river driver, like a gloomy hunk at the far end of the darkened bar. A plate of beet-stained eggs in front of him. A bottle of beer, a chaser of schnapps. The usual. Hair over his forehead, raw and red hands like boiled lobsters clamped around the bottle.

"Two shots of bourbon." Earl pulled the heavy coat over him. He was bone cold but kept from shivering, knowing if he gave in to it, it would never end. It being the longing, the need, the god-damned need.

Carm poured the honey-colored stuff in two shot glasses. Earl drank quick.

"You wanna try these eggs?" said Jigger. Eyelids fluttering like moths.

"I don't like eggs," said Earl.

"These here are no ordinary eggs," said Jigger, pointing to the purple-shaped things with the tops bitten off. He licked his fingers. "These here are Caroline's eggs. Made them fresh this morning." He laughed, coughed, and the bullet shape of his head fell in his hands. When he got his breath again, he said, "Ain't that so, Carm?"

"That's right."

"Been sitting in beet brine long enough to make a man turn blue." Jigger laughed, spit out some beer and egg white. "Best pickled-egg maker this side of the Mason-Dixon line."

"What's on the other side?" said Earl, weak, halfhearted.

"Beulah," said Jigger, "Beulah and her wet snatch."

Carm picked up his rag. Earl downed another drink.

Jigger's hands trembled in midair. His hands broken by logs and scarred by cant hooks. Had the agile brutality of a man who's worked the rage of the river and seemed as if at any minute he'd hurl himself clear across the room, disturbing nothing. Had worked the river from the time he was a boy till the mills closed down; he'd seen the horses, then steam, then trains go. Wore his red wool cap all year long and his yellowish white hair stuck out from under his ear, over the collar. High rubber boots, thick woolen pants. Claimed he could spit farther than any man, could indeed spit clear across the parking lot. Looked a hundred and ten but was probably a randy eighty. Lived in a camp up the ridge, no electric, no running water. Nobody went up there. He was the ridge's own noble savage. Twenty yards from his door was a fifty-foot pole with a flag. Got patriotic pride when the local state representative heard about him fighting a war and coming home empty handed. They gave him a commendation, a plaque, a flag in a glass case, and a meal of baked beans and chicken pie in Town Hall. Since then he keeps the flag flying. Middle of nowhere. Up a pole. High on the ridge. Winter through winter. Gets a new flag when the stars fade and the stripes rip.

"Caroline waiting up for you?" Carm said, switching the TV off.

"Nope, never waits up. She knows I show up, sooner or later." Sweat on his forehead, Jigger turned to Earl, said, "You got any pelts you want sewn up?"

"I ain't trapping." Didn't want to bother talking.

"Heard it's a good year for chipmunk." Jigger laughed, spit splattered. "Need about a thousand of those little critters to make a hat." More laughter, more spit.

Earl pushed his empties to Carm.

"Near closing," Carm said. He noticed Earl's eyes on the buck on the wall. "You have any luck in the woods?"

"Luck? Luck is for those who don't know nothing."

"I mean the hunting. The boys, they got anything?"

"Yeah, they got one. In the back of the truck now."

Earl downed another shot. Shook his head and turned in the seat.

Carm stared at the TV though it was off. "How's the family?"

Earl looked at Carm's small twisted shoulders and his dark hair. Italian hair. Sculpted and painted-on hair. An expression of mild impatience, voice hoarse, slightly vicious. Carm smoked and sipped watered-down cold coffee all night long.

"What did you say?" Earl said.

"How's the family? Boys? Tina?"

Way he didn't ask about Darlene meant he knew. Meant everyone knew. Was expecting some stupid drunk to make a joke about women gone out of town. Gone. Running naked down the road. It was no joke. Gave Carm the eye, let it sit on him long enough to bite.

There were stories, lots of them, about how somebody's wife just up and left. Juke Jenkin's wife of thirty years went to have her hair done, left a stew in the oven, took off in her son's Firebird, never came back, called from Toledo to tell Juke to go to hell. Carl's wife, Terry, everyone saw her by the fire station on a Thursday night, six P.M., just as the volunteer fire squad was taking the trucks out for a run to empty their hoses in the river like they did every Thursday night. *Should've seen her!* Talk was of her too-tight jeans and her strutting with a strange man whose car had Jersey plates. They said they'd seen her with her pants down. Up on the memorial. With the Jersey man and her pants down.

For the poor sucker left behind to twiddle his thumbs and burn in shame there was sympathy: *Poor Carl, poor Juke, nice man, such a nice man, didn't deserve her is what it is.* About the gone women, well, names were called. Spit was spat. *She had that look in her, was written all over her face, always knew it.* It was Earl's turn now. His woman gone and running. And now his daughter, a howling witch.

Maybe it was the bourbon, the way he smelled, rangy, fire fed, but the memory of Darlene, naked, scrambled into that of the bloodied buck in the back of his truck and he couldn't tell, not really, who was who and what was what. Where did the animal end and the woman begin? In the hooves, in the hide, in those deep jelly eyes, or was it in the blood at the base of the long neck? He could still see it lying in the frozen bed of ferns at the base of the old lilac. Had it been lilac or sumac?

Last time he'd made to love to Darlene he'd seen a stain of semen and blood on her side of the bed. It shocked him, put his hand into it and smelled it, felt it. Blood, all right. Wondered if he'd hurt her. Hated the sight of blood in his own bed.

"You okay?" Carm wiped the counter where Earl had spilled his drink. Fumes from the drink stung Earl's eyes and he lit a cigarette and the smoke made him cough. The lit match burned for a long minute like a tiny blue dancer in the tin tray.

"You tell me this," said Jigger, voice too loud, face small, monstrous up close. He moved next to Earl. "You remember the best night you ever had? Best night. Not talking about next to best, or worst, we know them all too good. I mean, the best." His beady eyes scanned Earl's dirty face and dirty coat and the rough turkey skin of his neck.

Earl smelled the boiled egg in Jigger's breath, smelled urine down the hall, smelled himself—dried blood, gunpowder, wood-smoke, air. "Yeah," Earl said, "I had a good night once."

Of course he did.

Jigger put out a shaky hand, gnarled and trembling. "You a lucky man, then. Ain't he a lucky man?" he said, tossing his head too fast to the side, losing focus. "Man's lucky. Remembers things."

Earl put his hand out to Carm, who was pouring another shot. His head was tight and knotted. "Enough."

"Next one's on me," Jigger said, finger up in the air. Just then the door opened and what hit them first was cold air. Smell of fresh snow. Sweet.

Schoolkids, Earl thought. Schoolkids in trouble. Two boys and a girl, sixteen at the most. They stood by the heavy wooden door not sure if what they needed would be found in such a place. The boys wore wool navy coats, suits, white shirts, and heavy-duty boots with rubber soles an inch thick. The girl had glasses which quickly fogged up in the heat and she took them off. She wore a dress of some sort, shiny and red, stockinged legs in workman's boots. She squinted, mouth turned down, about to cry. They looked as if they had come from some occasion, a wedding, a graduation, and maybe taken a wrong turn somewhere, ended up on the ridge. By their ghostly faces and their skittish way, the men knew what the kids were about to say.

"There's been an accident," said the girl. "We hit something. It was *right* in front of us." She put her hand out to measure a foot's distance. She looked over Earl's head. "I think it was a deer."

"You hit a deer?" said Earl and watched her eyes, trying to focus on the face that belonged to the voice.

"No! It hit us!" A high shrill voice just like his daughter's.

"What she means is that we hit the deer but we didn't mean to," the taller of the two boys said. His voice broke and he cleared his throat, and straightened his shoulders like an actor rehearsing for an important part. "Whatever it was it came right at us and it was too late when we stopped. . . ."

"The car's totaled! We can't move it! We walked here." She was maybe six inches from Earl's face and he could see into her myopic eyes and smell the cigarette smoke in her breath, perfume, booze. A bad girl, he thought.

She drew back. A boy took her hand and she said, "We need help, we need to call, is there a phone, we need help. . . ."

"Where is it?" said Earl. "The car."

"My mom will kill me, she'll *kill* me . . . ," the girl said.

"Nobody's going to kill you. But it seems to me like you killed something. Where's the car?"

"It's up the road, the car, I mean, we can't even move the car."

"Where's the deer?" said Earl.

The other boy's hair was so white it looked like a silver helmet. He said, "It's *under* the car." He had an accent of some sort, or maybe it was plain and simple education that made him speak that way.

"You mean you hit it and drove over it?"

"No! It came right at us and it slipped under the car. We walked here! We can't move the car. The deer, or whatever it is, is under the car," the girl said.

"Deer's under your car?"

"Yes, sir," the two boys said.

"You sure it's a deer?" Earl felt the bourbon buzzing through his brain, thought of wild honey hair down a long white neck, thought of long legs, broken, thinking, not thinking.

"The deer came out of nowhere, *I swear!*" The girl turned her head to the nearest shoulder and cried.

"I understand," Earl said. Those things happened. Deer, women, spirits, big cats, fish this big, stuff like that. It could happen. "Happens all the time," he said. "Deer just bolt out of nowhere and hit your car. Happens."

The kids moved aside as Earl walked out. He made it up the hill in second gear. He saw new snow on the road with the kids' deep footprints and the black ice beneath. The Subaru had its front heaved up, the deer, a doe, was under the front left tire. Still alive and trying to get its hind legs working. Still alive. *Jesus.* Earl tried not to look at its huge scared eyes and the thick white plumes of its breath. The tire was sitting on its belly. Earl walked back to the truck, pulled out his rifle, and shot the doe in the head.

He didn't know they were there, the kids, didn't hear them coming, didn't hear a thing, didn't even know what that sound was, that crying, until he turned and saw the girl with her face in her hands and the boys holding her shoulders while she screamed.

"Who's driving?" he said.

Nobody answered.

"Who the hell is driving this thing?"

"It's my car," said the girl. "I'm driving."

"Then get in and start the car."

"What?" She looked at the boys as if they could tell her what to do.

"Somebody's got to drive it." Earl adjusted the rifle and it must have scared them because they ran in the car, slammed the doors, all except the girl who took her time, buttoned her coat to the waist, wiped her face with her coat sleeves, and got in real ladylike. She gunned the car, it bucked, the back wheel rose over the doe's body and fell back. The car stalled, started again, and made it over. Earl kept his eyes on the doe.

"You can go on now. Car's fine," said Earl. "Garage down the road won't be open till morning. But you can drive as long as you go slow."

The tires were badly out of alignment, hood crinkled up, muffler dragged but the car was going. Soon as he lost sight of their taillights, Earl stooped and held the doe's face up from the gritty ground, wiped gravel off its forehead, and closed its eyes. Wiped fresh blood off its nose. He brought his truck up alongside and heaved the doe up, with an effort, and laid it side by side with the buck, and drove home.

. . .

Butch ran up to his room. Sid to the bathroom. Both doors slammed at the same time. Butch sat on the bed, hands to his ears. Couldn't get the sound of shots out of his head. Shots fired through the tepee, at the women, the woman's hand on fire, the buck, the way it leapt out of the bush, how it fell, struck dead. The sound of flesh cut open. In the silence, in the bush, he'd heard his sister, felt her fear, knew she was in there watching it all. *In there.* Heard the river, its rush under the land, nothing gentle about it. Heard the sound of the deer drag. The sound of the truck. Sid puking. The stomping of their boots on the floor mat, as if they should care tonight of all nights not to drag snow in the house, as if anybody cared. And the sound of their steps in the house. The house screaming, although nobody was making a sound. Heard his father take off down the road and was sure he was going after her again.

Hell was a cold place, he was sure of it. And he was in it. Somehow he'd slipped out of his life and into a savage one where a father hunted his own. Could have killed them all. Would have taken less than a thought, a mere shot, a simple trigger action, nothing more.

Bile and tears and the need to scream, to rip into the walls of his life. The corners of the room tightened around him. He felt small, scared. Watched a small spider cast its web in thin air and he brought it down with a swift stroke of his hand. Spider curled into a ball at his feet, he watched it unfurl its legs and make a go for it. He let it.

. . . *That gun you holding like a spoon ain't for puddin'* . . . *that gun's better than your arm, it's attached to your heart* . . . *let it think for you* . . . *it knows more than you.* . . . Earl had taught him about the extra eye, the extra ear, the sense that would make him *know*. And Butch had tried, never letting on he was repelled by the deadness of things.

First he kicked the wall, then he put his fist through the light fixture, and ripped everything off the walls. Threw the rack on the floor, his first eight-pointer. Waited to hear his mother crash into his room, hand on hips, eyes like bulldozers, saying, *What's going on in here, young man?* Young man, that's what she called him. He stared at the door, waiting.

Ran to his sister's room. Nothing but nothing in there. Down the hall, the bathroom light on.

■   ■   ■

IF BUTCH could have seen through the walls into the night he would have seen Earl dazed on the road, drunk and tearless, staring up at the newly full amber moon among the stars. He would have seen his sister looking up at the same sky, afraid, thinking that if she blinked she'd die. He would have seen his mother in a city, not knowing what it meant to go downtown, uptown; he would have recognized her no matter what, she'd be the one looking out of a grimy diner window with a too-heavy cup of coffee in her hands, she'd be the one trembling. And he would have seen Sid open the medicine cabinet, push aside bottles of aspirins, cough syrup, a tin of bandages, and up on the third shelf, up there, he would have seen him find what he was looking for. The new pack of double-edge razors. He would have seen him slip one in his hand, feel the blade, and with eyes on his own gaze in the mirror, he would have seen him calmly slice his flesh, first his arms, then his neck. Quickly, very quickly. And he would not have heard him cry. Never. He would have seen him slice his throat without a sound.

.   .   .

TRUE, SID did not make a sound but he heard plenty, especially his father's voice, which would now, right around now, if he had been there, let out a gargantuan cough. Same kind of cough he made as he approached a trap. He'd cough to let the animal know he was coming, then he'd signal to them, his boys, and say, *Come and take a look.*

Sid had looked too many times. He'd seen. The rotten luck. He'd seen.

Look at that, will you? And Earl would let out a whistle. Another cough.

Tuft of hair, jaws, little feet, eyes wide open, heads fallen, little bodies curled up in the sleep of unbearable pain.

Damn it, look at that, that little bugger is still alive. Give me that club, will you?

Once they came across the bloodied trail of a fox. It had chewed its leg off to rid itself of the trap.

Jesus, if you're going to be such a sissy about it, get lost then, go on, get out.

Earl, gingerly removing the animals off the traps. Sometimes if they were still alive he crushed their breastbone with his boot.

Go on, get out of here.

Afterward, in the sink, there'd be a plastic bag full of innards, purplish black and smelling. Bait. *That there's just what we want.* And Earl would take a kitchen knife and chop. The heart, the liver, the guts. *Good stuff.* He'd set baited traps all his life. Knew what smell attracted what. *Sweet stuff, wolf goes for sweet blood, lots of it.*

For a fox, Earl chopped the innards. And chicken guts, also chopped mouse. He kept his rubber gloves on. Smoked the traps outside and kept them outside. Never touched them with his bare hands. Foxes don't go near the scent of man. He kept his clothes and gloves outside, kept the skinning knives outside too.

Held a litter of coon pups in the palm of his hands once, fleshy hairless things, embryonic in every way. Popped the sack that held them together. Sliced them up.

Could imagine his father now, saying, *God what a mess!*

And try as he did, Sid couldn't get his father out of his body, which was the same thing as his mind. It was Earl's blood, his body, his life ebbing out of him. Thought he heard the word *son,* but it could have been *soon, soon.*

■ ■ ■

Butch stood out in the hall waiting for a sound that meant his brother was done. A flushing, the belt buckle clanging in place. Something. Heard the water in the sink, water falling without interruption.

The house was old and the same pipes that carried water into the house carried it out. Pipes rattled on every wall, vibrated under the floors, filled the house with the rush of soapy water, scummy laundry water, clean drinking water. In and out the same way. But there was nothing now, no real sound except a strange thud.

Butch called out. *Sid, you done in there, hey, hurry up.* He pounded on the door and the door swung open.

Jesus fucking Christ . . .

The curse went up to heaven. The Lord was called upon in a crude way, He was asked to goddamn do something. Something is always expected when the Lord is called upon, a miracle is often needed. *Goddamn it, God, help me.*

Butch thought it was the deer. The deer's head in the bathroom. Then he thought it was his sister. Slowly, the shape of his brother materialized under the blood. His eyes, dead eyes, rolled open.

Sid . . . A whispered cry, then a scream. *God!*

He didn't know how he got to the phone but there he was, talking to someone, saying, *My brother's dead. My only brother's dying. My fucking brother . . .*

The voice at the other end asked, *Where are you calling from? Where do you live?*

He knew it, he sure as hell knew where he lived but he couldn't begin to say the name of the town, or where the house was, or how to get to it.

The voice asked again. "South of the ridge or north?"

Mention of the ridge put it all in place. *In the ridge, in the valley, on the way up, Mercy Road.* Like a bird flying from mountain to mountain, elevated, he could see himself down there, in the hollow, where the old elm used to be, where the corn used to grow for miles, where the river ran fast, where the bridge was, where the house stood.

He ran to his brother, expecting him to have vanished like a bad dream, but there he was and he knew his brother was alive because his lips moved. Blood spurted from his mouth and onto Butch's face.

"Sid, not now, please, goddamn it, don't say a word. . . ."

He rocked his brother, head cradled in his arms, he moved the wet hair aside, kept his eyes clear, wiped the blood off his mouth. He'd never held his brother like this, like a child. It was so easy. He was so light, his body fell into the contours of his arms, his head fit in his hand. Sid's honey eyes swam in and out of place. Weather-filled eyes, his mother used to say, changed with the weather.

Help me, please, somebody. . . .

The ambulance lights flooded the house and the medics rushed in. Someone put a finger in Sid's mouth. Someone shoved a needle in his arm. Sid's eyes opened and closed. He was taken away.

Butch's hands were taken off his brother, somebody said, *It's all right, let him go, we got him now, let him go.* He was holding on to his hand, bloody fingers intertwined. *Let go.* He followed them to the ambulance and turned around to see the house, the door open, all that heat going out of the house.

In the hospital, arms without a face held him back, saying, *You can't go in there. You have to stay here, you have to understand.*

Butch didn't understand, not even when a nurse asked him to *please calm down, please just calm down, you can't help him, but we can . . . let us help him.*

All right. Fine.

Good, she said, sliding some papers across the table.

She asked him his name. She asked him if he was next of kin.

Fucking brother!

She asked him what he had seen.

What? He wanted to tell her of the deer, of the strong smell of its blood, of the sound of the shotgun, of the women howling, and more than that, he wanted to tell them about Sid, but not one clean thought came to him. Heard the ticking of a clock and it hurt him, the sound time made as it passed. Looked at the nurse's eyes and couldn't tell her how they, three men, had hunted a girl, one of their own, a sister. How they had stood and watched, waiting for it to happen. A kill in the family. Wanted to tell her about his mother, how she left one day, how her last words were *If I take you back shoot me.* Couldn't make his mouth open and say a thing. Knew only that what he felt then he'd always feel. It would never leave him. He would be this forever. This pain, this silence. He would be known to himself from now on by the misery he felt. And everything everywhere would remind him of it, always. He'd never speak of it. "You want to know what happened?"

"Yes." She passed him a box of tissues. Was he crying?

On a table, not far from him, he saw a copy of *Flyfishing* magazine. Next to it was a standing ashtray, the heavy kind one could pick up and take anywhere. The magazine had a photo of a man holding a bass. Knew the kind of bug needed to catch them, weed runners to fish the bottom, mid-depth, and surface, where bass feed on grass. Come summer he'd try catching bass. He'd take Sid. He'd take a small boat. He'd pack a lunch just for the two of them. Sweet pickles. Ham. Rolls. There'd be overcast skies. The two of them on a dark green lake. He'd talk to Sid. They wouldn't keep anything they caught, they'd toss it back. Later they'd make a fire, a good one. They wouldn't say a thing if they didn't feel like it. That's what he'd do, he'd go fishing with his brother.

"Are you all right?" the nurse asked.

He hated her for bothering with his thoughts and looked down at his old leather boots, the laces soaked in blood.

The doctor walked in. Butch knew it was a doctor by the way he put out his hand as if in apology. Butch shook his hand. He wanted to know about this man and if he was capable, was he the right kind of man to see about his brother. He wanted to tell him, *Go easy on him, he's not like all of us.*

"He might make it . . . ," the doctor said.

Butch heard other words that moved in his brain like a labyrinth with no way in and no way out. ". . . Lost a lot of blood . . . cuts are deep . . . stable . . . maybe . . .   Go home . . . rest. . . . Will call you in the morning. . . ."

"Is he going to live?"

"That I don't know. It's up to him."

"What the hell does that mean?"

"He'll make it back if he wants to."

"What do you mean *back*? Where is he?"

"He's in a lot of pain."

"Pain? *Pain?*"

Meaningless words, he wanted the man to speak his language, he wanted him to explain the meaning of life. He wanted the impossible. He wanted God to step between them and explain everything. In plain English.

"Do you know what made him do this?"

Again, Butch saw the deer, heard the explosion of skin, the woman's hand on fire, his sister as a mound of darkness, out there. "She's going to freeze out there."

"Who is?"

Smelled blood in the air, tasted it. Wiped his face in his sleeve and looked down to see the doctor's shoes, black and shiny, and his own boots, brown with blood, and he knew then he could not tell him a thing. He looked from the doctor's shoes to the doctor's eyes trying to convey the impossibility of his request.

Phones rang. Doors slid open. Air moved around them.

"Why would he want to kill himself?"

What Butch knew of killing was one thing, what Sid had done was another. In his mind Butch saw roads become arteries, the river a vein, the mountains were the flesh, severed, parted. In his mind, strange words formed stranger images: *Take and partake of my body.* Sid's body, the land. *Take and partake of my blood.* Sid's blood, the river.

"He's going to need your help. Counseling, therapy. We have a support staff to help families deal with crisis."

Crisis. Countries had *crises*, not people.

"Go home, rest." The doctor put a gentle hand on Butch's trembling shoulder.

"Thanks. . . ." Couldn't remember the last time he'd used the word.

* * *

BUTCH DID not go home. He sat in the lobby. His trembling was fierce and he held his hands between his knees and wondered when someone would notice his wretched shape and take him in. He wanted a blanket, a bed, he wanted love. He watched the nurses change shifts, heard phones ring, watched people walk in and out. A nurse did her nails, filing them with great care, then she read a magazine, put her feet up on the desk. Butch could have stayed there forever watching her yawn. He was afraid to leave her sight. She had blond wavy hair and glasses on a chain which dangled down her breasts. She had round shoulders which she rubbed as if sore. She had wide hips, thick white shoes. She was serious on the phone. She put her glasses on to write.

When he finally got up, he walked as if the act of walking couldn't be trusted anymore. The nurse said good-night.

The air outside was like an army of needles. He watched his breath. He watched a car drive up and a woman with a man's overcoat ran out clutching her belly, crying, *Oh God oh God.* . . .

So he wasn't alone. There were others like him making desperate prayers, pleas. He wanted to run after her, hold her hands, smooth her hair back, and lead her in, saying, *You'll be all right.* But he didn't believe it. Nobody was ever going to be all right.

And the night was old and broken and the moon was like an old pearl. He walked toward a blinking light thinking he'd know what to do if he made it that far.

Part
Three

SHE'D HEARD about those rivers that one day dried up and stopped being bodies of water and became the memory of water. Those wide and brown African rivers that dried up because the sun burned too close, or too long, or the gods forgot to keep their promises, or the people forgot to offer enough, the plenty required to keep things such as rivers flowing. It is known all over the world that a river requires more than water.

This river wasn't dry but she imagined how it could dry itself out eventually, tired of its own devastation and beauty. It could.

This was the river that flowed past her house. She walked along the banks as if she'd done this all her life. She didn't swim. Couldn't. This was the river where she'd seen deer stretching their necks and drinking. Where geese skimmed their wings and open beaks and settled in at dusk in a raucous manner and left quietly at dawn. Same river where Butch dove in and turned blue. Same river that made Sid shiver and made their mother see things. *This river took seventeen children. It will take what it wants, how it wants, and when it wants, so don't go staring at it, it might take a liking to you. Might remember your face, might call you in.* And Fox imagined herself among the seventeen children in raincoats and yellow rubber boots sitting at the bottom of the river, on swampy hairy logs bristling with green weed grass. They would have lunch down there and look up at the whitening light of days rolling high above them.

Same river that rose so high one spring it rolled the tank-size boulders from one side of the bank to the other. It swept over the yard and onto the porch and took the white rocker and the ten-year-old geranium bedded in a cast-iron pot. It took the fence. Uprooted a hundred-year-old maple. The cemetery slid down the bluff, and the town's sidewalks, those heavy slabs of marble, were swept away like cards.

Heard a crackling sound behind her and thought it was them, the men, lined up and aiming at her. Waiting to shoot.

The widest part of the river was straight ahead and looked like a frozen swamp with huge dead logs jutting out from the middle. Logs with sharp ends. Beasts of the swamps, Earl called them. She moved toward the ice banks and listened to the sound of ice forming and she looked back again. The men would follow her to the river and see her tracks. She had to cross it.

One foot, then the other. Anything can happen now, she thought, as she let her weight settle on the ice before taking the next step. Held her coat up to her waist. Walked toward the logs and the ice groaned and moved below her. It was unnerving, the whole thing, her, walking across the river. She expected to fall in at any moment. Imagined how it would be, with the coat billowing up around her like a cloud of fur, a furry jellyfish, bulbous, and she would go down and the coat would settle around her eventually, like a blanket of moss. She felt the pull of the water. She had no business walking on water. Arms out, she glided to the logs and held on. Aware that graceful movements, rather than fear, might do the trick. Aware for once that the water meant her no real harm; if she could only believe that, she'd get to the other side. The ice had cracked where two logs touched and she looked at its dark lightning-bolt shape and thought *here* is where the children are, wrapped in weeds, calling her in.

She let go of the logs and glided to the other side. Her feet landed on solid ice. Miraculous, she thought. She put her hand over her heart and turned to see what she had just crossed. Couldn't believe it. They'd never find her now, never. No one would believe she had done this. They'd come to her tracks, see the logs, the crack in the water, and they'd go back. *Swallowed up whole*, they'd say, *the river took her*.

Ahead was the rise and the rock and the thick dark trees like a shrine. She stepped in, hand on her heart. *Here I am*.

The trees moaned with the cold and the ice. The ash leaves rattled in the little wind. Tall birches leaned into each other and creaked. She was cold and shivering, but it was not a cold that belonged to her but to everything else and she let it rush in and out of her. After a while she pulled the coat over her head and tucked her arms in the sleeves and curled up under a very wide pine on a bed of pine needles barely touched by snow and fell into a wave of sleep like a turtle, protected. She had crossed the water.

Woke to a loud blast and thought it was Earl with a gun to her heart. What she saw was the fall of an ancient spruce crashing through the trees in slow motion and hitting the ground with a force that shook the land for miles so that somewhere in some-body's house a picture fell off the wall, a cup rocked in its saucer, and somebody looked up and said, *What was that?* The cone-laden crown was a few feet away from her.

A widow maker. The burden of snow had cracked it. She'd heard about a man in the ridge who went out on an ordinary day not thinking it would be the last walk he'd ever take, not knowing the sound above him was the sound of his particular death ap-proaching. The forest was deep in snow and not even the dogs had found a trace of the man. They found him in spring. The widow did. Recognized the open hand, the cuff of his wool shirt. Nothing else. The blow of the fifty-foot tree had imploded his flesh.

It was near dawn, the light around her was a light she'd never seen. The woods vibrated with the stillness of the fallen tree, and she stood still, waiting for the next crash. Though she couldn't see them, she was sure there were small animals perched on trees, looking down at her, as if she had, in some way, caused the fall.

The light brightened and what had been thick shadow was now

thin mist. Everywhere she looked she saw a piece of Earl. A head, an arm, his long wide back. It was a difficult thing to see.

The tree, like a broken arrow, pointed the way. North, south, she had no idea. She'd find a path, there'd be signs, she was sure. She looked back often, thinking she had missed a turn, but after what seemed hours she was back where she started from. There were her tracks around the fallen tree. This won't do, she said, and chose to go into the thicker woods where she had to duck and her coat snagged and she was pummeled by snow falling from branches. Every now and then she studied the shape of trees, gave them names. Monkey tree, elephant tree, long-sun-starved snake tree, witch tree, black tree.

The thick forest gave way to a strange clearing, flat and wide, and the sun streamed through. She wasn't cold. She ate snow and rested on a fallen log with her arms around her, knees close to her chest, rocking herself. Then she was cold and she walked on, climbing when she had to, sliding when she fell. The second night came and she pulled the greatcoat around her again and slept on a thick and curved low branch of a tree. Dreamt she was an embryo made of pure crystal and her mother's womb was the dark rock that held her in.

The moon swam in and out of trees and the forest was black.

The weatherman was right. *Snow with an accumulation of twelve inches by nightfall, more in higher elevations.* She was in the high ridge. Snow fell.

■　■　■

"Room's due this week," the clerk said.

"I know." Darlene had fourteen dollars and change. She needed two hundred for the room plus twelve for bagels and coffee for the week. She needed money for the bus. She wanted to buy things, she wanted something pretty.

Remembered a time with Earl, after Tina was born, cold of

winter and no money, no work, the truck broken down, gas cut off, electric, too, cupboards bare. She'd dug in the snow in her garden until she found a clump of chives and Brussels sprouts that had never matured, dug into the ice-rock soil until she came up with three red potatoes the size of Ping-Pong balls, dug some more and found the wild ginger root. Hungry, all of them hungry, she did what she had to do. Down off the main road, in a slanted hill and hidden by a stately blue spruce, was the white house with green shutters and the eagle wind vane, the Hutchinses' house, empty in the winter while they summered in Florida. Darlene aimed the rock and the back window shattered. Let herself in like a thief, stepping lightly, watching, listening. The cupboards and pantry were full. Canned foods, boxes of specialty crackers, cases of sodas, juice, wines. Coffee in tins by the dozen. Pasta in every shape and color. She read the labels and prices like a shopper. Filled a box with preserves, mustards, beans and rice, canned corn, tinned hams, yams, green olives. Threw in a bottle of wine, pickled herring. *Where'd all this come from?* Earl asked. *I made a loan, that's all.* Good enough for him, never asked another word. The herring sat on the shelf for years. Eventually it turned black and exploded on the shelf, causing alarm among them as they sat at the dinner table years later, wondering what that ungodly sound was. Then there was the stench of it. However, that winter, they got by, but barely.

It was being hungry, broke, and alone, all at the same time. It was knowing there wasn't anything in the suitcase, nor in her pockets, nor in her purse. There was nothing hidden. Nothing left to find. Face it, she said to herself.

That night she called Mattie, Earl's aunt. The phone rang and rang with the static of dread. Nobody home. Then the voice like a truck.

Yeah? What is it?

Mattie?

Yeah? Who is it?

Mattie, is that you?

I know who I am, who are you and what—
Mattie?
I said I know my name. . . .
Don't be angry, Mattie, it's me. Darlene. . . .
What is it?
Mattie, oh, Mattie . . .
Damn it, Darlene. Get Earl to take you home. You drinking or
what?
No, no, Mattie, it's just that—
Hell. You know what time it is? You got any idea?
I'm not home, Mattie. I'm in New York.
Don't they have clocks there? You have any idea what time it is?
It had been a silly idea. She couldn't beg.

. . .

*U*P ON *the gap the night is brutal. A herd of whitetail deer moves*
out of the hardwood forests and into the softwoods in search of food and
shelter. They have grown a new coat of hollow. Under their hooves, as
they pass single file, they hear the workings of the shrew deep in their
maze of tunnels under the snow. The great horned owl lets out its first
call of courtship. January, it is snowing, it is splendid, terrifying and
splendid.

. . .

DARLENE'S MOTHER once made her a dress she hated. She'd
wanted a scoop neckline, something rich looking, silky, nice to
touch. Instead she got dotted swiss. Looked like a candy cane. *Keep*
still, don't be moving so much. She itched in it, sight of it made her
sick. She scratched herself up and down her legs. Mother with pins
on her clenched lips for an entire afternoon. *Keep still, don't move.*
A year later she'd made herself a satin soft dress and she was

out the door with it on to see Earl. She was almost out when her mother stopped her. *Turn around, what you wearing under that coat?*

She didn't turn around but felt the force of her mother's hands on her as she tore the coat open and ripped the dress off.

You look like a slut. Look at yourself.

Hard hands tearing the silky thing. Hands that were used to doing the wash quickly in the soapy basin, hands that never lingered long enough to know what they were touching. Hands that said, *This is life, and life ain't pretty, get used to it.*

Darlene had never heard the word. *What's a slut, anyway?*

Her mother didn't tell her a slut is the name a mother calls her daughter when she shows signs of things to come. In a posture, in a gesture, a mother can see hell, fires out of control.

A slut is not what a mother wants her daughter to be, so she makes her room up pink and white. She buys her white undies. Places the white teddy bear on the pillow. Makes her dresses that look like cotton candy. Says, *There,* and arranges the white straw hat, *now stand still* while she takes the photo.

A slut is not photogenic.

The smile is always wrong or not there. The hands are clutching something, anything. The eyes squint, averted, or stare dead ahead.

A slut is someone with a trick up her sleeves, a tick, a habit, something which runs down her arms, into her pants, down there, and seeps in, makes itself at home in the heart of things. Later it becomes a mind. A thing with a mind. Unapproachable. A slut has a mind of her own.

Her mother had been the first to call her a slut, the first who threatened to do her in, to make her pay, to make her sit still. *Sit, sit still.* She didn't think anything of it when Earl did the same. *Look at me, why don't you look at me?* She with her purple lips. She didn't have a chance.

∎ ∎ ∎

SEVERAL MILES up from where Fox slept the wind spiraled the snow up and deposited it on the pitched roof of the small cabin where Caroline and Jigger lived. The door was blocked by snow-drifts three feet high. Jigger took the shovel and, with door open, began to dig himself out of the stuffy heat of the place.

But Caroline pulled him back. *There's no way you're going out in that weather. Why don't you make yourself useful around here?* She pointed to a heap of potatoes and turned to see him staring at her rump. *Go for a walk but don't go far. If you can't see the light of the window, you've gone too far.*

He dug his way out of the cabin and put on snowshoes. He couldn't see the light in the window and didn't need anyone telling him how far to go. Walked with the wind hissing round his head, eyes blurred, mouth open, legs working independent of his old man's body.

Went straight to the tree. Wolf tree, council tree, brother tree, old Indian tree. He raised his arms to the wild tree that made his heart stop every time he saw it. Approached it like a sacred being. Knew the tree had a nation of souls embedded in its trunk. In the wind he heard their song. Anybody else would have said it was the just the wind but he knew better. The tree was more than a tree. So wide it would take ten men linked arm in arm to round it. Walked to the other side where the massive bulge of roots spread high over the stone chamber below. At the entrance of the cave he removed his snowshoes and propped them up and got on his knees and crawled inside.

It was ten feet long, five feet high, and ten men could sit in a circle and not touch. The slab roof was lodged into the walls. Nothing had buckled, shifted, or fallen out of place. The earth floor was dry. His pile of kindling was still there. The opening was narrow enough for a man to crawl in. Through it he saw the cold white formless world outside. The wind did not come in. He stretched his legs and put his head down and closed his eyes. He'd slept here many times, untroubled deep sleep. Never told a soul about this place, not Caroline, and not the scientists who excavated the mounds in the lower ridge.

■ ■ ■

BEWILDERED, BUTCH walked around the rooms of the old house, old with the air of abandon. *How is it?* he said to the photo of his mother, but it wasn't for her to answer why she'd left. Everything in the room suggested he look elsewhere.

It's the ridge and its curse, isn't it?

It doesn't exist unless you let it in.

Out in Earl's shed he tried to understand the quiet in there and stepped out and again felt a quiver. Saw the house as nothing but a shelter for the deepest, most complete sadness. Lined up on the window, like little coffins, were the small boats he had carved.

The snow was ice and cut into his face as he walked up the ridge to the old Mercie place. *The critters here are skittish. Nothing worth trapping here.* He followed the river until he came to the boulders and the house. The chimney like a totem. A hawthorn, an apple tree, a maple, all twisted and broken.

Tell me, he said to the land, to the house, *Tell me.* But of course, houses don't talk. *Where are you?*

The windows were white with frost. The air was so cold it hurt his ears. He stepped back and heard the song of a bird, a summer bird. *Impossible.* He didn't move. The massive door was bolted and boarded down, so were the windows. A heap of branches lay like an offering on the doorstep. *Where are you?*

He had brought nothing. No food, no blanket. If he found her, what would he coax her back with, what could he offer?

■ ■ ■

IN THE denser forest the land was new with snow. Fox had slept on a tree, balanced on a fat branch that was wide enough for her to sit with legs crossed. Saw the mist rise out of the ground and out of her own body and lift itself over the tops of trees, where it hung suspended waiting for the warmth that would burn it off. Just watching it rise had taken an hour or more.

The snow was a foot deep, pure powder. Her back was sore and her hands were numb and when she opened her mouth her lips cracked and bled. She'd slept with the coat over her head and shook the snow off her shoulders and it fell off in a solid sheet. She'd dreamt of her mother coming to her barefoot through the snow, with hands full of berries and roots.

The sun was polar sun, far away and white, and it had come over the eastern ridge and hung in the sky that was fissured and corrugated with gray clouds. What little heat it gave off was spent on drawing out the scent of bark from trees and her coat, too, gave off a strong wild scent which was new to her. The snow smelled pure.

Her tracks from the previous night were gone. Hiked up the coat over her knees, but that was too much effort so she let it drag on the snow and clutched the sides together. The tracks she left behind were of her boots deep in snow, and the sides of the coat dragged like wings. Climbed the rise, told herself to climb. *Go on!* Birds screamed and lanced the air around her, admonishing her. They looked fierce, tremendously alive, propelled by their dark plumage. They swooped down close enough for her to hear the furious wingbeats. Hares darted around her. *Move! Move!* everything instructed her on.

On the third day she was hungry and tired and her feet wouldn't move when she told them to. She'd been awake for hours but had no idea if it was early morning or late afternoon. The sky was crude gray and dense and the weight of snow was in it. She stopped often just to look at the sky, at the trees, to listen.

She made a shelter in a clearing, piled snow to the sides, packed it in, shoved twigs into a rough weave for a conical roof which she placed over low branches. A crude cathedral. She broke off branches and bark and piled it high. Butch's cigarettes and lighter were in the inside pocket of her coat, along with the angel card. She read it one more time. *Travel a clear pond like a dragonfly*. Then she set it on fire and worked it under the wood, where it formed a little glow. She took her boots off and laid them side by side near the fire. She impaled her frozen socks on sticks near the fire. Her feet were colorless like larvae. Ice between her toes. Pulled the coat over her head and held her feet in her hands and watched the huge plumes of her breath.

When she slept the dream was of her mother again, pushing her out of the old house, saying, *Come on, move, move*! leading her out the back door, under the clothesline where Earl's dung-colored pants hung stiff, under barbed wire fencing, beyond the brush piled high for burning, past the heap of tires, into the woods. *Come on, girl, you need something to do*. Into the soggy darkness where the spongy ground soaked her shoes. Bugs in the air, wasps. Branches infested with caterpillar nests. The skull of a raven. Smell of earth. Rot giving way to life. In the dream she was forced to see, smell, and feel everything she was afraid of. The dark force of life with its incessant pull and gradual decay.

In the dream her mother clutched a handful of chickweed. *Eat, eat, it's good for you*. In the dream Fox nearly ate it until she saw the ugly shape of an earwig. In the dream she screamed. *Go on, eat, eat!* In the dream Darlene ate the weeds, earwig and all, with great pleasure.

When she woke the fire was nothing but dead and her boots were dry and stiff and her feet were swollen, but she forced the socks on and then the boots and looked for bark and branches and fed the fire. There was snow and snow and snow. But the night smelled of copper and wild onion. Closed her eyes and dreamt some more. Her mother again—with her upraised skirt full of mushrooms, twigs, leaves, roots. *It's wild, it's good.* Her mother, knee deep in a dismal bog, vanishing like fog.

The snow hardened. Does rose, startled, and quickly nudged their young into the thicket. They had slept near her. Fox watched them paw the snow and she did the same. Pawing the ground with her bootheel to uncover moss, frozen earth. The deer looked at her.

She fell into pockets of snow. At peace. Alive in the snow. *This is what I will tell them when they find me, surely they will find me, not him, not Earl, but somebody will and it will be spring by then and there'll be green everywhere, and when they ask me what it was like I will tell them about the feel of snow and how I was in it.* She talked to the trees.

Filled her pockets with pine needles, bark, scratched out hardened moss, and sour darkened berries.

If you ever fall off a boat in the ocean what you do is you take a button and suck on it. Suck on a button . . . keep you from dying of thirst. She didn't have any buttons. The bark was hard as rock.

Honey, you got to learn to fend for yourself. We're not always going to be around fetching for you. Her mother was in the taste of bark.

Resources, a person needs resources.

She slapped her hands together but didn't make a sound.

Swallowed up whole, her father would say.

I told her, I told her. . . . Her mother's pale face out a window.

She can't be gone. Butch would deny her disappearance.

Sid would know she was in the center of the world, intact, in a chunk of ice.

The trees gasped, then it was dark and silent.

Serves you right. Her mother.

Come on out! Her father.
Hey. Butch.
Stay in there. Sid.

. . .

Butch walked around the tepee and waited, and stepped under the old lilac. Wanted nothing more than to see what it was that had kept her safe, out of sight. Wanted to be transported like she had been. *Gone, you're gone.*

Beyond by a mile or so was Earl, crouched in the woods, thinking of his daughter, wondering what to do if he found her. Afraid to find her swinging from a tree, afraid to see her head-down in the ghostly river. *God, no!*

He had a rifle. He had his gloves, and a pair of blue mittens, Tina's. He had two beef jerkies in his pocket and a Thermos with hot coffee and whiskey. He stared at the river and the stumps. Looked for a break in the water. *No way in hell you crossed this water here, no way in hell.*

He'd been out other nights, wandering, lost, looking for her with his blanket roll and rope and knife. Thought she had fallen, broken a leg or something. Looked to the sky, had a shot of whiskey thinking it would make him strong but it made him weak and he cried, and he drank, and he cried some more and he finished the whiskey. Drunk, he spat out curses, and made his way home.

Woke before dawn knowing there was something urgent he had to do, fought his mind until the thought came back. Dropped his head in his hands. *Where are you, where are you?*

. . .

Fox made big fires that died out fast. She wanted the boys to find her so she could laugh and say, Here I am, and rise out of the snow, big as the universe.

Make a fire! she told herself and she did and sat with legs tucked in the greatcoat and sometimes she let out a wild howl. Sometimes she lay back, face up to the sky. Small and big animals passed through. She wasn't afraid of the sleepwalking deer.

In the fire she smelled the boys, it was so strong she thought they had to be near. Sid's wet-dog smell. Butch's tremendous sweat. Earl's bone-marrow smell. Her mother's perfumed skin. Her own body smelled like a sealed coffin, lavender and hyacinth. She wondered how long she could go without a bath, without changing her clothes, without sleeping in a real bed.

The snow fell sideways and the wind was strong and on the ninth night, when she was dreaming of falling into the lap of her house with its warm smells, her shelter collapsed. The fire died. The wind was a howl full of voices. Butch telling her to *move, get up!* Sandra was angry and said, *You must stop this.*

Not far, a snowshoe hare rose on its hind legs and smelled her and her dead fire and her cold flesh and the fox on her. Its ears vibrated with inbred sensation. Its whiskers twitched and its tail thumped involuntarily.

Fox saw it, accustomed as her eyes were to the night and to anything that strained forward, and she followed it on her hands and knees up and down and up again to where the land flattened out like the moon, it was so white and empty except for a large dark tree with branches like arms. The hare sought her out, drew her closer, and then it disappeared under the tree and she followed it to a narrow entrance of a cave. The hare rushed out. She didn't move, waiting for the hare to return. She slept.

She was in a stone mound, she was out of the wind, out of the snow. She dreamt of the hare. She'd kill it with her own hands. It would give itself to her. She would wait for it. She slept with her hands out.

When she awoke she saw it was still dark and she saw the linear juxtaposition of morning stars, whole constellations going down, but they meant nothing to her.

. . .

Yᴇᴀʀꜱ ᴀɢᴏ, scientists and archeologists descended on the ridge with Land Rovers and helicopters; they excavated more than thirty stone mounds. They drew lines in the northern sky from Polaris through Capella in Auriga. Betelgeuse, Rigel. It made sense. They agreed the sites were ancient ritual places. There was proof in the stones shaped like testicles, like vessels. They read the markings on the stones like a language. They disturbed everything.

On a fine day in June, before the babies were born, Darlene was by the river, when she saw a ball of fire in the sky. The sound came much later. The helicopter was carrying scientists and six sacred stones out of the ridge when it exploded. Earl swore the debris ruined his hunting grounds. Scared all the animals to kingdom come.

Darlene told the story often. The boys made fun of the story, as that is what they took it to be, a story made up to amuse or distract them. She had elaborated. Spaceships, she said, eyes wide as she leaned over the table, spaceships landed up on the ridge. *Oh, Mom, cut it out. Really.*

. . .

Gᴏᴏᴅ ᴘᴀʏ, flexible hours. A young boy with an emaciated little face, wearing leather pants and leather jacket and red high-tops, pressed the flyer into her hands. She felt his body rub against hers and turned to give him a disapproving look but he did not look back at her as he made his way through the crowds like a black cat rubbing up against everybody. The flyer had bold letters announcing *Good pay, flexible hours,* and an equally bold silhouette of dancing girls.

In her room with shades drawn she lifted her skirt and looked at her legs from the side and back. She hiked her underwear up thinking it would help, but it didn't. It had never occurred to her that she was aging in a mortal way and that one day her face would sag and her legs would ripple with softened flesh. She remembered being very drunk once and dancing with a man who assessed her body with a firm hand. You should be on a stage, he'd said, and the thought of it gave her a rush then; now it made her dial the number.

"I'm calling about this ad. . . ."

"Which one?" Grouchy voice.

"The one in the flyer. . . ."

"We got lots of ads in flyers. Dishwasher, bookkeeper . . ."

"Dancing girls . . . ," she said.

Silence on the other end, a deep inhale. "You dance?"

"Yes."

"What I mean, doll, is do you have any experience?"

"Of course I do. I've danced all my life." She'd danced with babies in her arms, at the Grange, every Fourth of July, danced drunk at the Pig's Eye, danced alone winking at her herself as she passed a mirror and nobody watching.

He gave her the address and told her to come right away for an audition. She changed her underwear, brushed her hair one way, then the other.

The Biloxi had two white pillars and life-size posters of two women with hair like Barbie dolls standing in a sea of feathers. Gold shoes. Perfect teeth, huge eyes. *Good pay, flexible hours.*

Inside, the darkness of a cave, the smell of old booze, old smoke, old dying air. An empty bar, a hallway, chairs stacked in a corner, upholstered love seats, tables for two.

"Over here, doll," a voice near the door marked EXIT. The man was dwarfish and his coat was cut a size too large.

"Mert." Distinct New York City voice. "You called about the dancing job?" He looked her over, then started walking, his hand signaling her to follow him.

"Attitude," Mert said, setting her in a leather chair, the swiveling kind. Between them, on the desk, a crystal paperweight shaped like an owl; its ears were translucent. "Attitude, doll, you need it in excess for this kind of business." He removed wire-rimmed lenses from his coat pocket and put them on and inspected her with bifocal vision, up and down. He took them off and wiped them on his lemon-yellow tie. His eyes were blue, dry, and damaged. Red streaks, yellow cataracts. Eyebrows like fur, a colorless small mouth. His body had the stuffed look of one made of bad air, as if he could be pierced and cease to exist. Darlene judged him, as he, undoubtedly, judged her.

What he saw was a thin colorless woman slanted forward, too eager, too ready. Scared, he thought. Running, he was sure. Her hands were worrying hands, too hard. But her eyes were sharp. "You ever been in trouble with the law?"

"No, never."

"Way you look is like you have."

"What do you mean?"

"It's in your eyes. You got a record?"

"No, of course not."

"You like purple?" He pointed at her wool purple sweater.

She shrugged. She'd bought it from a catalog, the color was all wrong but it was a wool blend, washable, didn't itch. She was about to cry, to tell him the story of her life, to tell him she needed money, lots of it, and fast. *Good pay, flexible hours*. In her mind she saw herself as a grown-up Shirley Temple doing a quick soft-shoe routine, then switching to a Carmen Miranda number, lots of swaying hips, then a tango, yes, she'd show him she knew the tango.

"Relax, doll. Tell me. You need money? You have a place to stay?"

He stood behind her, his hands on the back of her chair.

"I can dance. I need a job." Her words made no sense but it was all the sense she had in the world. Didn't dare swallow because it would have made too much noise. She wanted to take a deep breath but couldn't.

She turned to see him put his hand over his heart. "Talk to me, you can talk to me."

She almost did. "I can dance. I need a job."

The office was neat and dark. A dark wooden desk, a small carved elephant, the owl, pens, telephone, nothing else. The room hummed with the sound of electrical equipment but there was nothing except a tiny red light on the ceiling. Through the blinds she saw the skin of light, light that comes and goes, kind of light that makes things appear to be what they're not, dreamy, thin-skinned light.

"You into kinky stuff?" His voice was low, conspiratorial.

She looked at his shoes, wingtips. Her father once told her you could tell lots about men by the kind of shoes they wore. Laces meant control. Shiny shoes, scuff resistant, were for the narcissistic. Pointy shoes were bad news. Square-toed boots too. High heels were sure signs of a dubious nature. Soft shoes were for the soft at heart. Wingtips, he'd said and he'd made a face as if he smelled skunk. Wingtips. They told of unspeakable things.

"Had a woman working for me. . . ." Mert sat and crossed his legs, studied his own shoes. "She had funny ideas. Worked here for, oh, maybe two, three months, had the customers happy. Next thing I know cop comes in and says do I got so-and-so working for me, I say yeah, he says, well, she's under arrest. What for? I say. This is a clean business! we run a clean joint! I say. Cop says, here, and he shows me the photos. Saw it with my own eyes. The woman was nuts. She crucified a man. I mean that literally. Nailed him to the wall. Five-inch nails. You never saw that in the paper because the man was in government, family paid to keep the news out of the press. Woman took off. Pooof. Gone."

Darlene swallowed.

"You got anything against men?"

"Me?" Her hand flew to her neck, she laughed. "No, of course not." A little girl's voice. She felt like a fly pinned to a wall.

"Got any man looking for you? You running away?"

"No." She was leaning too far on her seat. She was smiling.

"No?" He, too, smiled. Light caught on his ring, a pinkie with a diamond the size of a pea.

And suddenly she saw him as a symbol of everything truly repulsive in man. Sinister, charming. He looked like a composite of all the bad men in the few movies she'd seen. A gangster, murderer, rapist. He smelled of recently committed crimes. He was the man waiting in the dark alley, the one at the top of the stairs. She leaned hard against the chair and let out the breath she'd been holding in. Not this, she thought.

She arranged herself to get up and leave, to say it was all a misunderstanding, to say she didn't need a job anyway. She stifled a yawn, hunger. She fingered the tarnished snap on her purse, saw the seams worn, ripped in parts, prayed it didn't show, none of it. The undoing, the unevenness, the hunger, the pain, the loss. How desperate was she? The thought scared her to her feet.

"Relax, sit down. All I'm saying, doll, is evil's evil. Attitude is one thing. Evil is another."

"Yes." Evil, she wanted to hear what he had to say about that, so she sat again and held his gaze. He was right, evil was evil. She wanted to tell him she knew a few things about evil, how it came in the middle of the night, how it held her down, made her take it, how it spoke, how it called her names, *bitch, whore, slut,* how it was always sorry, *so sorry,* how it longed to be forgiven, *please.* She could have told him she knew the taste of evil, that she gagged on it every night. She knew the kind of clothes evil wore, the way it walked, the way it talked, she knew evil's name. Knew where it lived. Evil wore ordinary boots.

"Relax baby doll, *relax.* I'm not going to eat you." He stood behind her and laid his fat hands on her shoulders. She jumped and faced him. His hands went up in surrender. "Okay, sorry, sorry, I won't touch you but tell me, baby doll, you got a life? Husband, kids?"

Nothing, nothing at all. Couldn't say a word. Couldn't draw a picture of her family, none of them, nothing but her daughter's high-pitched and hysterical voice saying *Reeeally, Mom, really.*

"Hey, doll, cheer up. Life gets good from now on." He bent to look at her face. "You want to dance?"

She wanted to slap him. She wanted to lose her composure and offend him, scar him for life. She wanted to say, *You've made a big mistake, I'm not that kind of woman,* but what she said in a too kind voice was "I can't dance. It's all a mistake."

"Did I scare you? Did I? I didn't mean to scare you, baby. . . ."

"No, you don't scare me. I have to go."

He opened a door and yelled "Toby" and a huge man, black as a crow, appeared. He wore thick red beads around his neck and dozens of studs in his ears. He wore penny loafers. Toby opened the door wide and Mert said, kindly, "Show the lady out."

The corridor was dark but she saw in the filtering light the racks of clothes and she put her hand out to feel the metallike thickness of body suits encrusted with millions of rhinestones and sequins, the supple floating nothingness of boas, the feathered illusion. It had almost been hers, there for the taking, and she saw herself gilded in light on a stage, hips and tits and the aged expression of a dream-ruined woman. She could not have danced for men like Mert. She would have spit into his eyes and given him something else to say about women. *Had a woman in here who spat in my face. Imagine that. The bitch.*

Outside was the day. Noon, lunchtime, and the city streets were full of hungry people. She moved quickly away from the door of the Biloxi, away from the porno shop and the sex-toy stores and the adult books and away from the hands of the same young boy in leather who swooned into her and offered her a flyer. *Good pay, flexible hours.*

■ ■ ■

THE SNOW began again and didn't quit. The entrance to the mound was a wall of snow which she clawed at, making a fist-sized hole with her hands. Then she noticed the kindling and dug herself out. The tree was there above her, rising out of the snow, like a giant preacher. She walked around it. Felt a tremor under her feet and heard a sound that was like no other sound. Her coat bristled like a hand had passed over it, a hundred hands. A witch tree, she thought. A howling witch tree. The kind of tree her mother had told her about, where the little lights lived, where foxfire died. Certainly, this was their source, their home.

Her face felt raw and burnt and she wondered what she looked like, if she had changed at all, if she was still recognizable. She ate snow. Fished two sourberries from her pocket and ate them. The hare darted into view and propped itself up on its hind legs and its face twitched like it had before and she did the same to it. Moving her jaw sideways and blinking. It darted into the cave and out again, in and out, as if inviting her to a chase.

There was a blurring form near her, something larger than her, alive, big and moving. Felt its size by the way the ground vibrated. Saw it then, an old man dressed in brown with a bright red cap. A ghost, she thought. She moved back into the thin stand of trees and watched.

The old man walked around the tree, turned three times, clockwise, and saw the tracks, hers. He bent and put his hands in them. Small human tracks. Deep indentations and something dragging sideways. He took off his snowshoes and crawled inside the cave. The ground in the cave had been disturbed. Came out quickly as if he'd been called and he stood there facing her direction. Again he looked at the tracks and up to where she was.

She shut herself down as she had once before. Invisible; he could not see her.

The old man rubbed his face. Nothing, he thought, whatever it is it's nothing. He put his snowshoes on and walked back in the direction he had come. Wasn't about to pursue whoever it was and he scurried away, knowing they'd meet, whoever it was, they'd meet.

That same day and at that very hour, Earl sat alone in the kitchen. A cast iron pot was boiling on the woodstove. His wet socks hung from a peg near the fire and his coat on another. He sat and listened to the sounds of the house and none of them were right. He knew silence. He knew what sustained silence and he knew that what he was hearing now had nothing to do with silence. When he looked down at the boiling water he saw his daughter's face looking up at him.

The socks were still wet and so was his coat and it hung heavy and made him colder than he'd been in a long time. The truck started after many tries and he headed down the road in, out to the logging road that wound around the river and led to the bog and to the rise of the farther ridge where it leveled out like a short mesa. The sky was nonexistent. Whiteness had obliterated every recognizable landmark. Snow fell with the softness of feathers. He talked aloud as if Butch were with him.

You'd think if she was up here she'd be easy to find.

Been out here long enough. Weeks. Hell of a long time for someone like her to be out in a place like this.

Ever heard of anybody doing this? Taking off out here and surviving?

What exactly are you asking?

Nothing.

Don't talk to me about surviving. Surviving has nothing to do with what she's doing.

She won't want to come back.

I won't be asking her to come back.

Then what are we doing out here looking for her?
Looking. That's all. Looking.
There's the river. Think she crossed it?
She'd have to sooner or later. Have to. Can't travel a line forever.

The Deadhorse climbed until the road died and the maples leaned into each other like tired ghosts. Here the strain of rock had forced the gorge to split open and rocks had tumbled. Earl looked at the seat next to him, empty, but for a while he thought Butch was really there. He nodded at the empty space just the same. He strapped on the snowshoes and looked behind, again, as if someone needed to be waited for. This feeling of being accompanied stayed with him as he walked the last wide space there was to cross. Above it was the thirty-six-mile rock stretch known as Purgatory Crest. Jagged. A wall of granite jaws open perpetually to anything foolish enough to go near it.

Every rock had a face and if you looked close enough you'd find your own. The rock opened up to caves and some of them led to the heart of the mountain itself. He'd been up here twice in his life. Never liked the feel or look of the place. Didn't think she'd be here and now wondered what it was that had led him here. He pushed through the snow and lost his footing once or twice and heard a rumble and turned to see the ground next to him give and fall away. A snowslide. *Jesus.* And when the cloud of snow settled far below he walked back to the truck and sat there trembling. That's what it was. He'd been led out here to see what had happened to her. Buried alive. *Jesus.*

He wanted someone to talk to but had nobody and sat up that night by the fire, kept it hot, and talked to the twisted flames. By morning knew she wasn't buried alive. He'd look again. He'd wait for the snow to stop, wait for Butch to show up. Tried not to think of Sid and when he did it was a thought that didn't stick long enough to matter. Thought of Darlene, of what he'd tell her if she came in the door. *Days,* he'd say, *Tina's been out for days. And Sid is nearly dead. And Butch is gone.* Wondered if she felt any of it, a tug on her heart. The condition of the home.

.   .   .

Fox waited a long time after the old man left. Jigger, the old riverman of the high ridge. Looked like a moving piece of bark.

The hare appeared once again and looked directly at her and went into the cave. She followed it in and this time it did not run. It was limp in her hands and didn't fight as she cupped the head and watched it close its eyes. She broke its neck with a sudden move that surprised her.

The dry wood took easily. She used a sharp rock to cut into the hare. She emptied its life into hers. Drank the warm salty blood. Removed the entrails and covered them with snow, and later, when they were frozen, she would cut them into strips and chew them like gum. She turned the cavity of its belly inside out and passed it over the flames. She peeled the blackened flesh and ate it.

She slept with hands smelling of burnt flesh and blood and in her dream she saw Butch looking down at her. *I did it,* she said, and he said, *You did what? I killed something,* she said. In the dream he turned away.

.   .   .

Down the twisted road, at the entrance to his wild property, Jigger had painted a sign and hammered it across the fence: ABANDON HOPE, ALL YE WHO ENTER HERE. Had liked the ring of those words, was mighty pleased to have thought them up. Plenty had seen the sign and word was out that Jigger had loaded guns, ready and set to go off if anyone wandered past the fence.

His land was in the ends of the earth, beyond the woods, the river, and the stillwater bogs. It was on the other side of Purgatory Crest, thirty miles from the village and the nearest neighbor. In the heart of the Hopeless Ridge. His mailbox, ten miles down, was a tin bucket with a lid, hanging from a tree. He'd painted a sign on that too: GOD-FORSAKEN RURAL ROUTE NUMBER 1. He prided himself in living as far away as he could and still get mail.

From here he'd seen stars close up, felt the wave of time, the barbarous explosions that set them free. He, too, had done his share of exploding, he'd raged, felt loss tug on him like a mad dog. Lost one wife, then another and another and another, four in all. To ills, bad hearts, birthing problems, men. Knew what futility was, and when he felt its tremendous weight, he drank.

He'd been to the Pig's Eye and drunk more than he'd meant to. Couldn't remember who he'd talked to. Drove home on empty roads slick with ice. Saw two of everything. Two lights on the cabin, two fires, two women greeting him saying, "You sober?"

Caroline watched him spin in, and said, "If you ain't sober stay out until you are." She meant it.

He went out, peed on a tree, sneezed, took a long gulp of cold air, and watched her light a lamp by the bed. He walked in.

"You've been drinking," she said.

"Yes, ma'am. I've been drinking with the intention of drinking."

She said dinner was no longer warm but there were cookies on a plate. Gingersnaps. He had two and fell into bed. She lifted his legs, pulled his boots off, dropped his legs hard on the bed. She pulled the covers over him. She turned the oil lamp off and let herself into bed.

Hours later she heard something that was not wind or snow. She woke Jigger and said, "There's something out there, I heard something."

"What?"

"I don't know, but something's out there," she said. She was kneeling on the bed looking out the window.

He pushed himself up, looked out the window long enough to convince her he had looked. Saw a hundred things meshed together by darkness. Lay back and grabbed the blankets, and said, "Go to sleep."

Caroline stayed by the window. She had one good eye, the other had clouds in it already. She'd stay up all night, and Jigger knew it, unless he paid attention.

"It's one in the morning," he said. "What you hear out there is time creeping up on you." He tried to stroke her backside but her hand shot out fast and stopped him.

"Look!" Caroline struggled to keep her balance. She was a hefty woman with an unbroken line from shoulders to hips. She lifted one knee at a time to untangle herself from the sheets and her long nightgown.

Jigger felt the booze in his head and said, "I shouldn't drink. I should never drink. I think I'll never take a drop a liquor again."

"Quiet and listen. Look."

He turned on his belly, propped himself on his elbows, and looked out the window to see the trunks of trees. Closed his eyes and looked again.

"Look! *There!* Jigger . . . something's out there."

He saw it. "Something is, probably moose."

"No moose moves like that. We don't have moose here." Caroline grabbed a straight-backed chair and went for the door.

"What the hell you doing?"

"Whatever it is, it's not coming in." She put herself and the chair against the door.

"Hell, it's probably raccoon." He laughed, but the way she looked at him, whole body rigid with fear, indicated he should not attempt to joke. He got off the bed, pulled up his pants, slung the suspenders over his shoulders, eyes out the window.

"See!" Caroline shouted, finger pointing.

"Hush, woman!" Jigger crawled to the other side of the room. The rifle was next to the glass case where he kept his medals. He pulled the rifle down and crawled back to bed, propped the rifle on pillows set up like sandbags.

"Careful what you shoot," said Caroline. "Might be nothing at all."

"If that ain't nothing at all, then it sure moves like something."

"What I'm saying is don't go shooting a real live human. . . ."

"If it's a real live human, then it has no business being around this place at this time of night." Then he remembered the tracks by the tree. What he'd seen was nothing that frightened him. Whatever it was meant no harm. Still, he was an old man. Shook the thought of his weakness off and reasoned things. He wouldn't leave the cabin, would stay put and wait for whatever it was to make another move.

"Want your glasses?"

"Don't need no glasses to see."

"You need them. You know you need them. Here." She tossed them on the bed. "Right there, behind you."

Jigger let go of the rifle long enough to pull the glasses over his ears. "Jesus, can't see a thing with them on."

"What do you see?"

"What do you expect me to see? It's black out there."

"Want me to take a look?"

"And shoot my truck?"

Just then he saw it move again. A small, slow, falling move.

"Nothing but a dog," Jigger said, turning to see Caroline lean harder against the door as if she could hold it back, whatever it was. Occurred to him then that he loved her just for that, for trying. Told her to get away from the door. She didn't move.

"There's nothing out there," he said and took one last look, saw the barrel that held rainwater but was ice now, saw the gleaming stack of tin for the roof he meant to finish off in the fall and that was now covered in snow, with its sides showing like ridged scars. Saw the truck, the green license plate that read MAD, and beyond the dark spruce forest crowded around the bit of moonlight left in the sky like a party ribbon, he saw nothing. Stroked his mustache and beard, looked at Caroline, who was still by the door, said, "Come on, whatever's out there is staying out."

She walked back to bed but left the chair jammed in the doorknob. "Really, Jigger, I saw something out there."

"I know," he said, "me too. There's lots of things out there this time of year." He felt his two front teeth jagged and sharp on his tongue, taste of gingersnap and whiskey. Closed his eyes and waited for the splintering window, the pounding on the door. Dreamt he was sitting on a chair in the field and watching deer make love.

. . .

THE SMELL of new smoke woke her. It was not her fire, hers had gone out long ago. The smell came from outside and had the familiar smell of home fires. Crawled out and saw the sky was clear and a crescent moon dangled upside down. The tree was in silhouette and she could see how much it resembled a giant preacher with tattered robes. She walked until her shadow fell inside that of the tree with no distinction between them. The smell of smoke was too strong to ignore.

She studied the stars for a sign on what to do. There was sufficient light for her to walk, and though her feet hurt and she wished for nothing more than to sleep again, she walked in the direction of the smoke. The snow was deep and she struggled to lift her feet up and over. The coat dragged. She felt the burden of her body and the burden of being alive and the thought of these things which she could not change occupied her as she walked between trees and up a rise which led to a darkness that appeared to be solid as a door. *Up,* she commanded her feet, *move up.* As she approached the dark trees she saw they were not solid and a light shone through them and the smell of smoke was strong. Beyond the last stand of trees was the thing she had feared and wanted to see the most. Light in a window. Two windows. A cabin. The smoke curled thick and gray up the chimney. Then someone opened the door and she heard a sneeze, loud and perfunctory. Snow sloshed down the roof. The door closed. The light in the cabin flickered like leaf light.

The snow was up to her knees. Her feet made her fall. She told them to stand and walk. *Just stand up!* She made them move between trees and she watched the light in the cabin go off. She fell and slid down and branches snapped underfoot and she tumbled and stood again and again. Jigger's place. Knew it because of the flagpole. She stepped back in the woods and circled the cabin and when she saw the shed she thought of apples and walked toward it, lifting the wooden latch and letting herself in.

■   ■   ■

THE SKY was lightening when Jigger awoke.

"Feel like hell," he said. Caroline pulled the pillow over her head. "My head's about to burst," he said. His mouth was balled up with the sour taste of old whiskey. Pain shot across his groin and he made it out the cabin with boots on and the first coat he grabbed, hers. The silky lining colder than his flesh. Clambered down the rough steps he'd set in, deep in snow now, swung the door to the outhouse open, and with eyes half closed he prepared to release himself when he saw a thing wrapped in furs sitting on the can. A thing, either dead or asleep.

He shuffled backward, tripped, and yelled, *"Caroline!"* but his voice was thinner than air. He meant to yell loud, real loud, but it had only been a gasp.

The fur thing moved. A hand shot out and covered her face. It was a girl. Her fingers white like splinters and so was the hair on her head. He strained to get her in focus as she jumped, pushed him down, and ran away. Jigger thought this was not a way to die, in the first light of a day, belly full of piss, wearing a woman's coat, flat on the ground, his parts showing. Closed his eyes and waited to die.

"I'm telling you! Now be quiet and listen. It was a she and it was a devil, all spurs and hide and fur, claws, and fangs. It was a she-devil I saw and I'm telling you I saw it clear as daylight."

"Shut up, Jigger, and listen to me. Sit there and don't take that blanket off you and don't go getting up to look out the window again, 'cause I'm telling you, there ain't a thing out there except the night and the night itself. And for one thing, there ain't no she-devils. Only devils in this world are he-devils, and you can't tell me you saw the devil himself sitting in the john at four or five or whatever time of night it happens to be. Don't you know devils don't have need of the john? They don't have needs like ours. No devil's going to use the john out here, for heaven's sake. And like I said, you couldn't have seen anything clear as daylight because you're blind as a bat and you haven't seen daylight straight as it is since you were born. It ain't daylight quite yet. This is fool's light, makes you see things that ain't there, you ought to know that. And another thing, there ain't no trace of nothing in that john, no trace, no trace, you hear me? I looked, I went there and saw nothing. Now, we can go over the whole place in the morning, call the sheriff in, get those dogs trained to sniff and find people, and still I tell you, they'll find nothing 'cause nothing is out there, nothing was. You saw nothing and neither did I because there was nothing to begin with."

Caroline caught her breath. She had her finger pointed at Jigger while she talked, a finger, no more than that, to keep him down long enough so she could talk sense into him. She tugged the blanket around her shoulders. Pushed the chair back to its place. Touched the doorknob, moved away from it, and looked at Jigger sitting on the edge of the bed, shivering from cold and fright.

"I'm telling you, Jigger, you take ahold of yourself now."

Jigger stared at a spot out the door.

Day came with frozen purple light. Caroline kept her eyes on Jigger and watched the small changes in the shifting light. She'd seen the tracks, human.

■   ■   ■

SOMETIMES, ALONE *in the woods, in the snow, walking, one has the sensation of traveling over water; only hope sustains, carries one over. Also, there is the distinct feeling that what one sees—shadows, snow, ice tears, one's tracks, those of others—will never be seen again, and that by nightfall, in the sudden and complete fall of night, in that intangible moment when day passes completely out of sight, for the briefest second, it will all be erased, memory of place and memory of self. Gone. It won't help to look back.*

■   ■   ■

LONG TIME ago, Butch tried to talk his sister into going up the ridge. *I can't go in there, Butch, let's go back.*

Scaredy-cat. Go on, what are you scared of?

That out there.

What? The dark?

Yeah, the dark.

It ain't nothing but trees.

It's more than trees.

Nothing but trees and a teeny little vole, a little mouse, a furry rabbit. You can't be scared of that.

No, not that. It's everything else I'm scared of.

There's nothing else but trees.

There is more than trees here. You can't see what I see, you don't know what I know. You asked me what I was scared of and I told you. If you didn't want to know, you shouldn't have asked.

Sorry, didn't know you were scared of trees. Trees are just trees.

More than that, I think.

Trees are trees.

I said there's more than that. I said so already. We should get back.

They got back. To the house. To Darlene. Supper served.

Wash up, you two. Where you been?

Out walking.

Walking where?

Just walking, Mom, just walking.

Hand on her hips, she tried to extract a measure of truth, a sign of trouble brewing. *You up in the ridge?*

No, we were by the river.

Humph. Get washed. Go on, supper's cold already.

Already. Dinner. The five of them.

Pass the peas. The butter. The bread. Please.

Sometimes, if their mother was in the mood, if Earl wasn't around, if there was nothing else to talk about, Darlene would tell them stories of people on the ridge. Fox pretended not to care. Sid smiled. Butch leaned back on the chair and asked again about the yellow snake, the thousand birds that settled in the bog one day, the hundred beavers in the lake, the little glowing lights up the cedar swamp. They chewed slowly and didn't interrupt the telling. They understood what was said had to do with what was and wasn't, the miraculous, the unbelievable. They took her words in with a blink of an eye and a sip of water. They sat until the fires went out and somebody said, *House got cold.* Or, *What time's it, anyway?* And if Earl hadn't come home and was not expected back for another hour, they would stoke the fire and coax her to tell one more. It was always Butch who asked, *How'd you guys meet, anyway?* And her storytelling voice would change and become plain and harsh. *Oh, I told you all, I told you a hundred million times.* And she'd turn her head, and push her chair away and stand, hands on the back of the old chair, rubbing the soft oak, which was no longer yellow but dark, nearly black.

Those thoughts came to Fox in a too clear way. They existed because nothing else had taken their place. Felt her mother closer than ever. Remembered all the words. *Listen and don't ever forget this.* In the onslaught of winter, under the incandescent light of rooms in winter, she'd held on to a fear and it held her now.

. . .

S<small>HE HAD</small> not walked into a shed full of apples but an outhouse, and she'd slept with head against the wall, feet off the ground. Slept and woke and saw old posters of bazaars, fairs, dances which occurred decades ago. Posters of old times in the ridge. A bottle of bleach, a broom, a wooden shelf with rolls of tissue, a mirror hanging lopsided, a wooden floor, a bucket, a door. Daylight came with a man's face.

She knocked into the man, he felt like nothing, less than wind. She ran and fell against trees and could not feel her feet moving but they were. The snow was confused with clouds and she felt guided and she pushed through the air with extreme effort. She did not feel pain but a strong and peculiar peace. She fell into the snow and the snow said, *Rise.* Her mouth opened and she understood what the women had wanted to say when they howled, understood the gentle eyes of the deer and why it died for her, and understood that anger and sorrow were made of ice. When she came across the tree she was surprised to have found it again. The tree looked down at her with judgment.

Gone. Swallowed up whole. Ridge took you.

She crawled in and under.

The night was illumined by miles and miles of snow. It was the light by which things are rarely seen and in which she slept thinking she had found the center of her world.

She dreamt the tree had taken on flesh and a face and it raised its arms up as if offering her up in frozen hallelujahs. But the sky didn't want her, and the tree, recognizing her worth, dropped its arms. She fell to her knees and began . . . *Our Father* . . . Then she remembered. She'd already been accounted for. Prayers, she was sure, had been offered for her. The town people would not speak about her except to say, *Gone . . . swallowed up whole. . . . Not even the dogs found a scent.*

Bullshit, she's got to be here somewhere. She imagined Earl carrying on the search alone and maybe he'd come across her trail and decided to disregard it saying he'd thought it was her, but no, it wasn't. Maybe he was walking the ridge, all three hundred miles of it.

A morning star shone. A faraway fire. Felt a burning in her belly. Imagined her stomach served piping hot on a white plate. Her kidneys in mushroom sauce. Pictured her pelvis stuffed with bread crumbs and something green.

You've never let anyone love you.

She made a deal with the preacher: *In your hands, in your hands.* The tree leaned into the wind.

She crawled back underground and slept. Awake, asleep. Awake. Asleep. A middle-of-the-day sun. A middle-of-the-night darkness. No moon. The world white. She slept and woke and slept again.

I'm gone, swallowed up whole.

Let her be.

Pass the peas, please.

Animals stood still, hooves in the air; unblinking eyes, breath suspended, they watched her.

She hummed softly, *Hi-ho, away we go.*

The animals went away.

She felt the heat of death approaching.

Cover your head. Heat escapes out the head. Don't you know?

Truth is nothing escaped her.

Hi-ho, away we go.

■ ■ ■

Bᴀᴄᴋ ɪɴ the shed, Earl looked at his traps, the number one jump for marten, the larger double-spring for fox. He looked for the small skulls he'd kept over the years; his favorite was the small head of a marten which he weighed like a ball. Pure bone. The animal had yielded its life; still, something remained ungiven. Thought of his daughter. If he found her, he wouldn't force her back, he wouldn't even try.

He hung his traps. Boiled them in a stew of birch bark and spruce twigs. He was done with trapping. Too much brooding in his heart. Too many years perfecting the intricacies of death for nothing. Walked up the spruce ridge, to the boggy creeks, and up where the wind was strong, where the Fulfillment River drained; there he crouched by the scorched remains of the cabin. Something big and wild was living around there now. He'd leave it alone.

Out by the river he saw where a beaver had built a new dam. He'd trapped a beaver once, not far from there. Watched it for months, working hard at bringing down poplars, swimming them out, weaving them into his lodge. He'd worked just as hard as the beaver, cutting through several feet of ice until the dark water bubbled up and then he'd set the trap. Next morning there it was, thick and brown and drowned.

Wasn't worth it, he thought. Went through the pages of his little black book where he kept a record of every pelt sold. The money was scant—twenty martens, two lynx, one fox: $300. He had recorded it.

He stood in the wind till it was dark and listened to the groaning of rocks freezing in place.

■ ■ ■

THE RIDGE is the rebellion of time itself.

One cannot get too close to it, nor far from it, without feeling its pull. It can be a home for a monk or a madman, but most people are not mad or holy enough.

The air is peppered with ice, always. It accumulates. White on white. Here one understands the sacrificial order of life. Not everything can survive, nor does it have to.

A mere ten thousand years have passed since the ridge rose out of the inland sea. Admit it, it says, I am old.

Part Four

THE YEAR started unremarkably. Snow fell thick and blinding like it did every year, except this was Earl's forty-seven winter and it was severe. He was not a man who looked at himself in the mirror but here he was in the hundred-watt visibility of the cold bathroom staring himself down. Golden eyes with the gold gone. Mouth twisted to the side where so many curses had been spat out. Hadn't shaved, couldn't stand the thought of putting a piece of cold metal to his face. Studied his hands. A missing finger, a chopped-off thumb.

The house was cold. The fire was burning but the house was cold. He was cold. Walked around with boots on. Glad for once Darlene wasn't around to say, *What you dragging ice in here for? Can't you see the floors are clean?*

The floors were filthy and it was cold and she was in the cold. She was in the timbers. She was in him and would be forever. She was his circumstance, his sorrow, a great thing.

What in the world did you expect?

Turned the radio loud to hear the weatherman's voice, earnest and full of advice: *Well, folks, last day of the year and it looks like a bear of a day. Thirty below for three weeks in a row and no change expected, not in the near future.*

Not in the near future? Was that tomorrow, the day after, or did he mean longer periods of time? Years, many of them, the rest of his life?

More precipitation expected through the night and into the morning. A major storm . . . forming off the coast . . . could be here by tomorrow, early morning. . . . Gusts of up to forty, fifty knots. . . . If you look out your window tomorrow you will see those tall strong spruces bent almost down to the ground. . . . By early afternoon the wind will taper off, but the snow will come down heavy, a total accumulation of eight to twelve inches, folks. Brrr, not a good time to be on the road, so if you can, stay in, and if you must go out, drive carefully. . . .

He walked out. Night like a solid muscle above the ridge bones.

When he reached the bridge, thought a cheap cowardly thought. *Jump. Nobody's gonna stop you. Jump, you son of a bitch.* But he wasn't in the mood to die.

The tepee, like a wounded animal. The hole he'd put in it had been patched up. Big white square of cloth. No fires in it. Nobody in there.

The village was down to its real cold self. Iced-over geography. Arctic. The wind blew out of the ground and in circles, with him as the target of its force. The glow of house lights through curtains. The shut doors, snowdrifts of ten feet or more, ten-foot-long icicles in gutters, and cars completely buried under the snow except for a thin antenna showing. The wind was a long moan in the storm.

He was limping for no reason at all. Couldn't remember hurting himself, but there it was, a cold pain in the hip. Boots laced up to midcalf. Wool pants, two thermals, two wool socks. Shirt, sweater, thermals, jacket, coat. Still the cold got in. *Catch your death in this cold.* Who spoke?

The church was lit up with floodlights and looked like a huge ticket for a place where he would never gain admission, nor did he care to.

The store was a two-story contraption built on stilts to allow for swelling waters. The Fulfillment River had flooded many times and gouged in the land so every house had a piece of the river in its backyard. The store used to sell only provisions for the mountain travelers and the sign hung still. Provisions. Feed and grains. The watering trough was next to the outdoor phone. Now the store sold jewelry from Timbuktu, but no feed, no grains. The potbellied stove glowed October through April and coffee was pricey, a dollar a cup. Diluted coffee with a stainless steel taste but better than making his own.

A bulletin board held notices of dances, concerts, missing cats and dogs. For a minute he imagined posting a notice: *Wife and kids missing. Reward. No questions asked.*

Inside, the silliness of Christmas was in the red and green lights, and a string of plastic black-and-white cows hung from beam to beam. Hadn't thought of Christmas at all. Worked his way to the coffee and filled his cup.

"Hey, Earl, cold enough for you?" Someone slapped his shoulder. A day for locals. Flatlanders were either thawing in their condos or stuck in ditches off mountain roads.

"Damn pipes froze last week. . . ."

"Car died. Can't get it going. . . ."

"Don't need a car in this weather, what you need is snowshoes. . . ."

"Hell, you'd sink in that stuff. . . ."

"Hear they closed the mountains. Sixty knots of wind up there. . . ."

"Hell, no, hundred and fifty knots. . . ."

"You guys got it all wrong. It's fifty below with windchill. . . ."

"Closed the mountain? Because of a little snow?"

"A little snow? You ever seen this much snow?"

"Colorado."

"Colorado? What the hell is that?"

"You ski?"

"Hell, no. Me? Ski? Do I look like a flatlander to you?"

"What you look like to me don't matter."

"Hell, no, I don't ski. I live here. What the hell would I see on a mountain that I haven't seen before? I don't pay for my views."

"Hey, Earl . . ."

Earl blew on his coffee, looked at the big white-faced clock, watched a woman walking a dog, black tail above the snowdrift.

"Earl . . ."

Listened to talk of weather, the years, the degrees. Winter of '92, thaw of '94, drought of '95; the year the river dried up, then flooded and turned black and smelly from seeping sewage, the year nobody caught a single trout in Vermont, the year four barns caught fire and killed a hundred and ten calves was the same year rabies struck and deer and fox wandered, dazed and furious, onto highways. Disasters and weather gave way to talk about other local phenomena: a herd of moose in pastures, wolves as pets, the catamount's return, the death of the last loon on Bitterberry Lake. Just like that, years were remembered by the severity of winter. The land's worth was measured by the absence or presence of beasts.

"Earl, you ignoring me or what?"

"I ain't ignoring you." Earl didn't turn. He knew who was talking.

"First I want to wish you a Happy New Year." Man put out his hand. Earl looked at it and turned away.

"Second thing is this, Earl. Got a report about you and some shooting, some damage done to Sandra's property some time back. I thought I'd give the two of you time to sort it. So what about it?"

Earl turned his face, enough to catch a look at the man, the constable. He was taller by a foot or so, boylike, hair the color of sunflowers, cut military short, neat around the ears.

"What about what?" Earl said, swishing the coffee in his cup.

"Is it true or not? You shot at the tepee? Maybe you and the boys were hunting, forgot about the posted signs? You know you can't do that in the village, Earl. Don't you know that?"

"Know what?"

"You can't shoot around here. Houses, people, pets. Earl. You know what I'm talking about."

"The point as I figure it is not whether I know what you're talking about or not but whether or not it matters. That's the question. And I'll answer that. It don't matter."

Everything matters, everything matters. Darlene's voice pushing his thoughts.

"The hell with it," he'd said to her, and to the constable now, and he finished his coffee and threw the paper cup in a backhand way and it landed right smack where he aimed. Unbuttoned the top three buttons of his coat and walked out. The cold was a good thing for him to feel just then. He'd hear from the constable later.

His tracks were gone. Windblown. Cemetery was a field of white-capped gravestones. *Earl, when you die I'm going to have those words carved on your stone: Here lies a man who thought nothing mattered.*

The waterfall was frozen in the act of water falling, huge wind-formed curls of blue ice. Gargoyle ice. Come spring it would explode like gunshot. Thaw always came like that, loud and wild.

Didn't bother to take his boots off or his coat as he walked in the house, up the stairs. Opened the doors to his children's rooms.

Happy New Year, he said to Butch's room, which was a mess. Glass, frames, posters on the floor. He laid the rack on the bed, exactly where Butch's head ought to be, on the single pillow.

You, too, he said to his daughter's room, to the air in there, fetid, swampy.

Kicked Sid's door open. Bed neatly made, blue-and-white-plaid blanket, slippers under the bed, books lined up on the single shelf, unpainted wood held together by metal brackets. The tattered black spine of the Bible stood out.

Happy New Year, to himself in the dark mirror as he walked out again. Plowed his way out the drive, followed a sand truck all the way to the Pig's Eye. Glittering lights accentuated the loneliness of the place. It was crowded, everyone had the high color of those who've been in the cold too long. Booze and smoke and the scent of perfume. Bodies jerked side to side, up and down, arms like wrestlers . . . *twisting the night away* . . . Wished for a moment he could toss his head back and grind into the dance with a girl who didn't know him, wished for one moment of blind fucking happiness.

Somebody kissed him. Sloppy gin kiss. The counter was crowded but Carm passed a bourbon over the tops of several heads. *Happy New Year.* Same gin lips kissed him again. Hated gin.

Drinking didn't make him feel better so he left, pissed on the snow, and the truck started with a jolt. At home, yanked his boots off, pulled his pants down, and lay on the couch. No sooner had he closed his eyes than he felt somebody near him. A creepy sensation. *Whoever you are, leave me the fuck alone.*

The house ghosts, he thought, Darlene's ghosts, the old ladies he'd never seen. *Look, just look,* she'd say, and point to the foot of the bed. *Goddamn it, Darlene.* He never saw a thing then, but here they were. Too afraid to open his eyes and see them.

The woman with the smell of apples, the midwife with her bloodied apron and her desperate look because she'd delivered a dead one.

An assortment of weary souls, unhappy with wherever their final resting place was, sure there was some mistake, positive they had forgotten something or left a thing or two undone, and now they milled around the house, aching to do chores. They made it hard for Earl to breathe.

Go away, just go away.

He swatted them as if they were cluster flies. Then he spoke. Figured he had to.

Where is she?
What?
Where is she?
Who?
The girl.

What girl?

The long-haired girl. He meant his wife.

Oh, she's gone.

Nothing else was asked. He felt them gliding up the stairs to sit on her side of the bed, where they'd mumble all night long asking, *What do you suppose happened to her?*

Enough. He slept, afraid of all that life might or might not do to him.

The wind settled down eventually. The snow didn't quit.

■   ■   ■

T HE SIGN on the door said OPEN and the red lotus sign blinked on and off in rhythm. A couple ate with heads bowed, hands around the bowls of soup. They didn't look up as she walked in.

"Coffee?" a waitress asked as soon as Darlene sat.

"No, tea, and some food."

"Menu's right there on the table," the waitress said.

Cup of coffee arrived anyway. "You ready to order?"

Menu open in her hands. "Ham and some boiled potatoes."

"We don't have ham."

"No ham?"

"No ham." The lady propped her arm on her hip. Her tag read ROCHELLE.

"What do you have?"

Waitress snapped her pad shut, walked away. Seconds later, a white apron stood in front of her table, an apron with a man's face and a voice. "You'll have to order now or leave."

"I did order. Ham and a boiled potato."

"We don't have ham."

"What do you have?"

"Turkey platter. Special tonight."

"Does it come with cranberries?"

"Yes."

"Then I'll have that."

Food was piled high on rimless white china; the potatoes were lumpy and salty, the turkey was thin and smothered in gravy, the cranberries were jellied. She took a bite and another, tried hard to concentrate on getting the food to her open mouth without crying. Ham, she would have liked ham, always had ham on New Year's Day, and it was New Year's, an hour and fifteen minutes into it.

The coffee was bitter. The bill arrived facedown. *Here to serve you!* and Rochelle's name under the total. $6.99. *And a Happy New Year!* the apron called as Darlene stepped out.

■ ■ ■

*A*NIMALS ON *the ridge are scarce. In the higher elevations, which mimic arctic conditions, in the sparse tundra, nothing but voles and mice. No mammals live in the tundra.*

In the lower ridge are the native scavengers, crows with their shiny black coats. Their sound is a metallic grawk-grawk. Unmistakable. Its nests are tucked in ledges or in the crowns of trees in the trackless forest.

The dark-eyed junco and white-throated sparrow, small seed-eaters, and finches are everywhere. Hawks, too, you can see them flying parallel to the ridge and spiraling up thermal currents.

But it's the crow that speaks. Go-go, grawk-grawk. Come here or go there.

■ ■ ■

EARLY MORNING in the city Darlene stepped behind a man walking a small dog. If the man had turned and smiled, she would have followed him anywhere, she was that much in need of companionship, of idle talk. Followed him for several blocks until she saw a woman run across the street to meet a man. Stunned, she stopped and watched them kiss.

She'd done that once, run to meet a man. A man who'd come

slinking around the shadows of the house, out near the shed, on a day when she thought she was alone, with the boys gone.

It had been a laundry day and she'd done three loads and hung them out on the line and was bringing them in, folding them carefully, patting each shirt down like a baby in the wicker basket. She had clothespins in her mouth when she heard the man call out her name. It was J.J., a man who'd been out hunting with Earl once or twice, a man she'd never seen up close until that day. He'd smiled and stepped under the old elm. The way the light fell on him and on everything around him was dazzling. Bushes and trees and the very grass seemed illumined, everything rose to the light of the day, three o'clock light.

First thing he said when she was close enough was *I've come to take you away,* and the words, the silliness of the words, the stupid promise, so desirable, made her laugh in a way she never had. She said something equally silly and he took her by the hand to the birches, where she leaned against him and closed her eyes and her mind too. When he started to walk away she called him back and watched him, perplexed, in the leaf shadows, and she ran to him, kissing him like the girl she'd never be again.

On her way back to the house she filled her skirt with radishes. She scrubbed them and served them for supper. Nobody ate them. Later she washed and looked at the limp blue dress on the floor, stained with moss and wet bark and smelling of another man's sweat. She tossed it in the woodstove and set it on fire, which made the house smell, and the boys complained all night of the unwanted heat in the already stifling house. She watched her dress burn. She was done with little scraps of hope.

■　　■　　■

Room 206. Washcloth around her neck, armpits, down her legs. Didn't open her eyes until she was safely away from the mirror, which she was sure was haunted by all the faces of previous inhabitants. If she stared long enough she'd become them, ragged, mad, powerless.

Friday and Saturday she did without food. Sundays she stayed in bed until she heard church bells, then she rushed out and walked many blocks and stood outside the cathedral. Imagined throwing the doors open and entering, back stiff, mumbling words of supplication. Mondays she sat in the lobby and read *Ladies' Home Journal* and *People* and whatever section of the *Times* was lying around. She folded the paper into fourths and read. Wednesdays and Thursdays she walked with the intention of getting lost and window-shopped, studying the mannequins' poses, their pretty boredom.

She ate Chinese food on Mondays, took her time ordering the bowl of rice, kept her head down and listened to conversations, drank all the dark tea that was offered, smoothed out the paper napkin, put the fork down on the side of the plate, cleaned up after herself so the waitress wouldn't have to do it, so she wouldn't feel so bad when she realized there was no tip.

On Wednesdays she had a large slice of plain pizza. Ham on Sundays. Three meals a week. Tested herself to see how long she could go without food, and when the pangs of hunger came, she took to bed.

Washed her clothes in the sink. Draped them over a chair to dry overnight. Blue skirt, brown pants, black sweater. Couldn't make herself wear the purple again. In cloudy weather she wore sunglasses with thick black rims and wide sides. She pulled her hair up under the wool cap. She was weatherless, undefined. She punched three new holes in her belt. Used a safety pin to keep her skirt from falling.

Wanted badly to call home, tempted every time she saw someone leaning over a phone, smiling, but what was there to say? *Hello? How are you?*

The children. Their faces came with a background of heavy weather, a thick buildup of clouds, gusting winds, blizzards, faces like comets and a trail of exploding stars. The world reduced to white on white held her babies, framed in ice and falling snow. In that light she'd seen them, slanting toward them.

I quit, she said in her dreams and she tossed dishrags, slammed doors, dropped trays, threw her shoes at men. *I quit.* She repeated the words in her sorry mirror but she was not convincing. *I quit, quit, quit!* She meant no more seams, no more cheesecake, no more broccoli, no more longing, no more. She dreamt she was lying naked in moonlight and had no desires.

She awoke with simple needs. A walk down Third Avenue to smell boiled cabbage. Down to the river to dream. Down the streets with pain in her heart.

■   ■   ■

IT WAS the night of the big snows in the Northeast. Cold enough to kill orchards. Winds big enough to blow barn doors off. Three days in a row. A triple storm. Drifting snows. Gales. Zero to minus five. Zero to minus ten. Thirty below. Zero again and holding. Zero, lots of below zero days. Overnight, bridges collapsed. Homes without power. More snow than seen in a century. So much snow. Wild windstorm then the freak thaw, early ice breakup and heavy rain. January thaw, to be expected. Three men washed away in their ice-fishing camps. Sudden drop and bitter again. Minus thirty-four. Minus twenty-three. Wind blowing at eighty miles an hour. Nothing like it since 1869. Sunrise promised snow again. Twenty inches by nightfall. Northern railroads closed for three days. Twenty-five-degree drop in four hours.

Holy Moses. God, it's cold.

Ain't it, though.

Yup. It's cold, all right.

Cold enough for you?

That it is.

In the ridge extensive damage was done. Three children died in a car while waiting for their parents to return from shopping. Their little hands froze together, noses pinched tight in the cold air, lips black, the whites of their eyes glazed under frozen lids.

Deer froze. Birds fell from the sky. Total storm fatalities: 143. Great storm. Sleet.

"Reckoned as cold a day as has happened here in the memory of the oldest man among us. . . ." So said the *Reporter* in Smallford.

.   .   .

I<small>N THE</small> dream Darlene saw Earl move toward her as if she were a shadow, a thing in fog, shapeless, hardly there the same way air is always there, and light is, and dark is. She tried to become solid. Tried to move out of the way before his big hands found her and pulled her in. He tried to touch her in a way she couldn't be touched anymore. He was drinking.

Damn it, he said. *Come here.*

You know I can't.

Come here.

I said I can't.

He rushed toward her knowing if he could just get a grip on her skinny arm he'd have her. That's all it would take.

I said come here!

You can't do that anymore, she said in the dream.

.   .   .

T<small>HREW HERSELF</small> out of bed. Knit cap pulled down, coat wrapped tight, hand over heart, she watched a crew of men on scaffolds hundreds of feet above the ground; they were laughing and looking down. She wanted to warn them. Laugh now, cry later. The sky was full of rumbles and ordinary light.

But the ordinary turned on you, she'd seen it happen. One day when her father was still alive, when they still had a herd, when the air of every morning smelled of hay and manure, she had watched cows bend their heavy heads over the watering trough, their fleshy tongues, their milky bellies, those huge open mouths, and then lightning struck. Burned them. But first their heavy bodies were thrown against the barn walls. Two were spared and had to be blindfolded when the men came to hoist the dead cows away. The barn smelled of sulfur for days. Then the silo caught on fire. Exploded one clear night. *Freak things happen*, her father had said, and he'd walked with his rubber boots into the fields, solemn, like a man looking for lost things.

Darlene was surprised to see herself in a window. Looked like Mrs. Marshall, the old schoolteacher, the kind of woman whose most treasured possession might be an old green couch, a cat nearby, a pot of tea.

She was a composite of everyone she'd known. A walking album. Her mother's desperation in her eyes, her father's vagueness, and when the wind slammed against her, she winced like a dog. Even her voice was no longer just hers.

She stared at the open display of love and longing in the streets, men and women kissing. She wanted to interrupt and tell them, *It's not that easy.*

On the corner of Forty-second and Fifth she saw a man wearing a purple shirt the color of eggplant. He looked at her, made a small gesture with his head. She turned back quickly and stopped at a newsstand, picked up the first magazine she saw. *Flyfishing*. A picture of a large rainbow trout on the cover. She was thinking of the boys and beds of fern and the smell of frying fish. The man behind the stand said, "Lady, you buying or reading?"

"I'm reading."

"You want to read go to the library, you want to buy you pay and leave."

"I'll do what I want." No sooner had the words come out than he was standing next to her. Slapped the magazine down, she bent to pick it up and saw his tennis shoes, filthy white. Did not see his knee as it came up and hit her across the face. The shock forced her down.

I'm telling you, Darlene, the way you look at men is enough to drive one mad. Earl, of course Earl.

I spared you the rod at home and what happens? Man on the street kicks you in the face. Her mother, naturally.

What's wrong with her? She all right? She drunk or what? She could see shoes walking away from her, pointy shiny shoes, lots of heels, lots of black pumps.

"Take my hand, please, let me help you." A voice above her, a hand, a purple shirt.

"Here, take this." His white kerchief.

"My nose . . ."

"You'll be all right." He led her a few paces down the sidewalk, away from the crowds. "Let's go in here." He held her by the elbow.

"Who are you?"

He wasn't Earl, he wasn't anybody she knew. He had a purple shirt, a black coat. No tie. No hat. She said thank-you, she said good-bye. She ran across the street, face in her hands. The man in the deli where she bought a bag of ice looked at her with disgust. She had a bloody face. She now knew what it takes to look like that.

When she walked into the sour, proudless lobby of the Allen House, two elderly ladies in pastel suits sat smoking long cigarettes with great pleasure until they saw her. Like a sepia photograph of aging dolls, smoke tinged and salvaged from an attic chest and propped up to look their best, their legs crossed at the ankles, ladylike, both women looked at Darlene as if saying, *What has this place come to?*

She had blood on her coat, a throbbing in her cheek, bag of ice in her arms. She walked past them mustering some dignity.

In the elevator two other ladies stood very still, like apparitions with airs about them. Huge rhinestone brooches on their coat lapels, old gold rings with rubies and other dark stones. Thin watches with crystal cases, rose tinged, the numbers too small to see even with good eyes. The kind of watches they had to wind every day. Darlene paid attention to all of this, to their heavy eyes, their silence, their immobility, because she didn't want to think about herself.

The hotel was full of women who had moved there years ago because it was a good address, far enough uptown for some, far enough downtown, depending on where they started. No husbands, no children to speak of, no real income. They never left the city, traveled only as far as the Cloisters with enough money for bus fare. They went just so far and no farther.

In the middle of the night, some nights, Darlene heard male voices, running steps, the whir of wheels on the worn carpet. The only time she heard male voices in the hotel was when the medics came for a dead or a dying resident. Then, Darlene, like others, opened the door to see who it was, what room. She saw a woman on a stretcher once, eyes metallic and bright, frightened. She was done for. They both knew it.

Darlene punched the button for her floor and waited for the doors to close.

"It doesn't seem to want to go," said one of the ladies, voice like a cracker.

"What?" said Darlene.

The lady blinked and swayed at the question.

"*What* did you say?" Darlene said, not nicely.

"It doesn't seem to want to work today. The elevator." The lady had a talc powdered face, white and dusty. She gave off the scent of paper flowers left in the rain, a slight hint of rancid perfume.

"What do you mean? Is it broken or what? What are you going to do? Stand here all night? Wait for a miracle?" Darlene slammed all the buttons. She was asking questions not meant to be answered. Questions that had nothing to do with the broken elevator. She took the stairs up, cursing until she reached the bathroom. Slammed the door open. Same woman she always saw, white bathrobe, white froth of toothpaste in the mouth, towel round her hair. "Hi, I'm Myra."

"I know." Darlene looked at herself in the mirror. The damage was visible. A swollen lip, a sore nose caked with blood, a tender spot around the eyes. She'd heal. The bag of ice dropped from her hands. She took a deep breath and asked the woman in the mirror, "How long have you been here?"

"Me? Long time. Home sweet home. This place shuts down I'm homeless with a capital *H*."

"How'd you get here? I mean, why here?"

"Circumstances."

"Yes. Circumstances." Darlene pushed the bag of ice aside and looked at herself again. What was next? Felt a series of bad changes had set in. Wanted her old high bed.

"And you?" Myra asked

And she told her she was passing through. Said she was traveling, and yawned to prove her exhaustion. Said she had no family. "House blew up one day." Told her she wasn't looking for anything special. "Nothing at all." And as she spoke she felt traitorous, fraudulent, and saw the house actually blowing up with Earl rushing into her arms, a ball of fire behind him.

"Cures you."

"What does?"

"Traveling."

She was tired, very tired. She did not want to say that travel reminded her of everything left behind—the dirty laundry, the unmade beds, the bills, and everything else, and that she was crowded with memories and that it didn't matter where she went, she was weighed down, unfree.

The bathroom was lit with large fluorescent tubes, the high windows were sealed and had a metallic grid over them. Two other women walked in, both with ice-blue hair, shuffling slippers and smelling of medicine. Myra rinsed her mouth, tapped the toothbrush against the sink. "At least they keep the johns clean."

"Yes." Darlene focused on the watery glass above.

"Some people live here until they die."

Darlene nodded. A large moth was caught in the window.

"I mean they never get to see home again. I guess most don't care. Once they get here, I mean, hey, what's the use, right?"

"Right." The moth was flattened against the glass. It flapped its wings, sliding up an inch and sliding down again.

"What's yours?"

"Mine?"

"Your room."

"206."

"Thought so. I'm 210. I had yours for a week. Couldn't take the smell of piss. Still smells in there?"

"No, no, I don't think so." The moth folded its wings and formed a large V on the glass. It thought, very likely, that the glass, with the reflection of light on it, was the closest thing it would have to a fire. It thought if it stayed still long enough it would warm itself.

"Six months ago I thought I was here for a week. That was six months ago today." She pulled a letter from her bathrobe, leaned against the sink, and opened the letter. The old women came around from the back where the shower stalls were. The women looked flushed, clean and pink.

Darlene watched Myra read the letter, her eyes skimming the page, and when she was done she folded the letter, carefully, put it in the envelope, and back into her pocket. "How long you here for?"

"Not long."

"That's just what I thought. See this?" She pulled the letter out again. "I have a man waiting for me. He's across the river, right in Jersey. But he's kind of, I don't know."

Someone walked down the hall, knocked on a door, called a name. "Mary? Mary?" She knocked some more, softer and softer. "Good-night, Mary." Then she walked away.

"Place gives me the creeps." Myra shivered. "At least it's safe, though, I mean nobody can get you in here, right? And the john is well lit. I like that."

The moth fluttered once again, lifted itself off the glass, and banged furiously against it to penetrate the light.

"Someday I guess he'll make up his mind. You know, the guy I told you about."

Darlene nodded.

"Sometimes I think this is it, that this is who I am. Myra of room 210. Could be worse. Sometimes it makes a lot of sense, I mean, what else is there to know about anybody, right? Name and room number. At least I got that much, right? Name and room number."

Darlene looked from the moth to the woman in the mirror and to the little bar of soap on a pink dish. The mirrors were clean. The sinks were clean. The moth was in the kingdom of light but it could not enter it or leave it.

"It's very bright here," Darlene said.

"I see you go across the street every morning. Get a cup of coffee and bagel, right?"

"Sometimes."

"I see you. Ten to seven most of the time. I'm always up. I don't sleep much. I used to but not anymore. Bed's too lumpy."

Darlene could see herself years later remembering this day and telling the story of Myra's life. She would clear the table of crumbs like her mother, clear her throat like Sid, toss down a shot of whiskey like Earl, shrug like Butch, and tell the story of this weak blue-lipped girl in the bathroom of a hotel for women. She'd make everything up. Say Myra had a fatherless child, say her knuckles were worn smooth; she'd give her a tattoo on her arm, big black letters with the name of her lover, Buddy. She'd give her scarred hands with moonstone rings. Her plain eyes would be transformed into haunted foggy eyes. She'd sit her by a big picture window, ground level, where she'd look out over a clear stream, a river maybe; there'd be ducks in the water, a blue sky, a nice day. Yes, she'd give her niceness and weather. She'd give her a chance. She'd invent an ending far from the hotel. She'd say she died in her arms on a day full of light.

After a long silence Myra sighed and lifted her head and shoulders as if her thoughts had taken her far away and she was surprised to be in the bathroom. She took the towel off her head and shook her hair, which was the same color as cooked pumpkin. She laughed like people do when nothing is funny.

"I see you got some blood there. Walked into a wall or something?"

"Yeah, I did."

"I've done that too."

The heat in the room kicked in, and they stared at the radiator.

Myra walked out first, said, "Well, good-night and nice talking to you."

Darlene said good-night. She stayed in the bathroom watching the moth. Then she washed her hands and face and rubbed ice on the side of her nose. She filled the sink up with water and dunked her hair in and her face touched the sides of the sink and when she opened her eyes she was suddenly afraid.

Her dreams were many and came quick that night.

Dream: she was in a park, it was snowing, her three babies huddled in her arms, blue faced but miraculously alive.

Dream: she turned a corner and saw her babies fully grown and solemn, passing her by without a word.

Dream: she talked into a tin-can walkie-talkie, the string was long and white and it wound around the house and out the door and into the woods. Her children took turns on one end, their high voices full of laughter then angry and shouting at her. *Mom! Can you hear me? Can you hear me? Yes,* she shouted, *yes, yes!*

．　．　．

THE WINTER storms of January came. The windows rattled and the hiss of steam was continuous and so were the sounds of the weary women in the hallway. Shuffling slippers, flip-flop. Everyone huddled in their beds, in their rooms, to bed early, and some nights the power went out and the hotel was darkened except for hundreds of pairs of bright fearful eyes staring out through dark windows.

She asked the clerk if there was mail for her. "No, there is no mail for you," he said, sneezing, blinking, bothered.

She had a job at a restaurant called Way of the Future. The walls had black-and-white photos of Einstein, Darwin, and others she didn't recognize. It was a small place near the river and she enjoyed watching the water. She was given a uniform. Black pants, white long-sleeved blouse. The pockets were wide and embroidered with the name of the café. She ate soup every day. Cream of spinach, minestrone, chicken noodle, lentils, black beans served with a dollop of sour cream. Her hunger vanished. Her dreams left her. She was content serving, walking from table to table; she did not ask, *May I help you* or *How are you this morning,* not even *What can I get for you?* She stood, flipped her pad. Sometimes she couldn't help it and smiled, and with a nod she took the order. She didn't say thank-you or have a good day or bye now. She worked, she got paid. She changed clothes at the café. She memorized the litany of specials. She didn't know what to recommend, couldn't. When someone looked at her too closely she said excuse me and she asked another waitress to please see about that table. Stayed in the bathroom until the fear was over.

She avoided Myra and the elevator. She stopped watching people on the phone, stopped rushing. She cleaned her room, made her bed every day, bought old postcards of the city in its horse-and-buggy days. She wrote simple words. Addressed them. Dear Tina. Dear Sid. Dear Butch. Dear Earl. On each she wrote something she did not want them to forget. Simple things. The yellow snake. The horned toad. The silver moth under the bed. The floating lights of the cedar swamp. She said she was all right. That she remembered them.

She wrote cards every day for weeks. She kept them stacked on the table. It was the first thing she saw when she walked into the room. She was spent when she wrote her last card:

Dear Sid,

Remember the day we walked up the east ridge? It was summer and we chewed timothy stalks and I told you I liked walking the east ridge best because it went somewhere (though we both know the ridge has no path anyone can follow) and you asked where does it go and I said to the west ridge and you laughed and I went on and on, trying to convince you that all roads lead somewhere. Well, I was wrong. There are paths that lead nowhere.

Love, Mom.

■   ■   ■

AFTER WORK she went to the park, to the river, stopped wherever the thought hit her, the thought of home. Felt for stones in her pocket, wondered how it was she forgot to take some river rocks with her. Watched people, looked around, read every sign she came across, all the stop, parking, no parking, no U-turn, so on. Expected to see one with her name on it and an arrow pointing the way out. Her feet hurt all the time. Walked the mile back to the hotel and looked at it from the outside. Never imagined she'd be living in a place where the illusion of grandeur—in the canopy, the chandelier—rang so wrong. The elevator grinded up to her floor and she looked at the room number for the last time. Opened the door and let herself in. In the morning she'd let herself out for good.

By five o'clock that morning she was packed. She left the room clean. The month was February. Left a kiss on the mirror. Went to the bathroom and swiped at the hanging moth, which had been there for weeks, caught in a spider web. She left a postcard for Myra of a gigantic tomato under blue skies with the words: *Some things are too big to ignore.*

Sat in the lobby waiting for the shop across the street to open so she could get her coffee and bagel. There were a few women already in the lobby. She sat next to the one wearing a bottle-green dress. She was motionless except for the thin hand that waved a cigarette. She'd be like that, too, Darlene thought, years from now if she stayed, an old lady waiting to die. The traffic noise started up and the streets were slushy and it was hard to tell what season it was. "February," she said to the lady in green. The lady had rat-colored eyes and said, "How are you, dear?" and for a moment Darlene thought it was her mother talking. "I'm fine, thank you. I'm leaving today. Going back home," she said. The lady stared, and said, "Did you have a pleasant stay?" "Yes," Darlene said. "I did." She didn't look like her mother but something about her was exactly like her mother, the sour eyes, her muttering. She waited for a sign to confirm that it was indeed her mother. Waited for the chandelier to drop, for a painting to fall off the wall, for the old woman to throw her head back and laugh and say, *Of course it's me, can't you tell, don't you know your own mother?* Darlene jumped from the seat and grabbed her suitcase and walked out. *Just keep walking,* she told herself, *you don't need to hear anything from no one right now, just walk. Go home,* she said, and turned corner after corner until she was on the avenue that would lead her to the bus station.

The city light was soft and wet and her shoes were soggy and her toes were cold. Bought the paper as a souvenir, something she would look at later and say, *It was twenty-five degrees that day.* She was heading for colder than that and pulled on her yellow wool gloves bought from a street vendor on Canal.

At Port Authority she rushed to the board and saw the names of cities she'd never been to. Cleveland. Milwaukee. Chicago. Denver. Albany. Pittsburgh. She looked at the times, the hours and minutes. Gates for departure and arrival. Travel words. Coming and going. Delays were broadcast over loudspeakers. It was thirteen below in Duluth. Sixty and calm in Miami.

She couldn't decide what to do. Tried to draw out sufficient reason to go back. Tried to imagine Earl's face when she said, I'm back. Cracked her knuckles and chewed on her nails and fidgeted with the suitcase. She felt no elation, no excitement, no real fear. Then she heard it, her father's voice: *Nothing's going to happen to you, just go back, go back.*

She moved ahead with the line. Her legs were weak and trembling. Her heart felt like it would burst. The line moved forward and her palms were sweaty and she couldn't breathe.

Nothing's going to happen, just go back. . . .

Plenty was going to happen if she went back. For one, she saw herself pounding on the door to be let in and it would be Earl at the door, saying, *Who asked you back?* Her daughter would certainly slap her. Sid would never trust her. And Butch would be gone.

Someone nudged and told her to get a move on.

The man behind the counter asked, *Can I help you?* "A ticket to Smallford," she said, in a tiny voice that surprised even her. The man asked her to speak up. Again she said, "A ticket to Smallford," and the man shook his head and asked her to write it down. Her hands were shaking and the letters came out wobbly. "Smallford?" the man said. "Yes," she nodded. "Well," the man said as if he were talking to a child or imbecile, "we have a Smallford in Virginia, a Smallford, Tennessee, a Smallford, Arkansas, Smallford, Vermont." She put her hands up and said, "Yes, Vermont." "One way or round trip? he said. She lifted a finger, one. "You sure?" He put the pen behind his ear and held his face in his hands. He had several layers of fat under his chin, he looked like a turkey. "One way," she said. The man took his time stapling, punching, and staring into the computer. He counted the exact change bill by bill, penny by penny. He held the ticket and waved it at her as if he were giving her an undeserved prize, then he passed it through the little slot in the window, and said, *You have a nice trip now.*

So, she'd chosen. She'd known she'd have to do it sooner or later.

. . .

M ORE SNOW fell on the ridge, as if enough hadn't fallen already. *It's enough already, all right, enough's enough.* The people of the ridge had had it with the snow and they talked to it from their windows. *Damn thing's still falling.* They cursed as it hit them from all sides. They cursed the snow shovel and the plow trucks and the dwindling or nonexistent woodpile. Backs were broken, legs too. Moose Hawkins hired himself out to shovel rooftops. Children sledded off the roof and into ten-foot snowdrifts. Everybody got dressed by the heat of the woodstove. Thermals were left by the side of the bed or were never taken off, except for showers, and showers were avoided because of that one minute of nakedness. Ice and wind cracked windows. Mothers with children went mad when school was canceled for the twentieth day in a row due to bad weather. Road travel was impossible or nearly. Planes couldn't land or take off. The phone lines were busy when they weren't down. Kitchens smelled of brownies and split pea soups and homemade breads and the food tasted good but was never filling. Preparing food itself was a task that took hours and everyone gave a hand. It was the only distraction from the real task of living.

Old lilacs and bridal veil were indistinguishable in the mounds of snow. Chickadees, no bigger than a thumb, fought the wind and made it from feeder to nest, their song was high and carried far.

Days were dark as night. Water pipes froze and burst. Cellars flooded, chimney fires raged, roofs collapsed.

It was endless. Made some think the end of the world would come by ice, but they were praying for the fires of hell. *Hell, I'll take hell any day.*

It was epic, it shared a moment in history with the *Titanic*. It took on metaphoric powers. It was no longer just snow falling, but a maelstrom. It swept over, obliterated and shut down the entire Northeast. Those who lived on the borders of memory told tales long into the night. It was a season for the hard at heart and the prepared. Those who'd made a stew that lasted a week ate well regardless of the power being out, and those who had plenty of venison, those who had wood, who could fix things, who could whistle regardless of entrapment and the wind howling, those who could make love and not hear the kitchen windows rattling, for those the storm was merely a storm though the substance of life had come to a frigid halt.

One weatherman exalted the weather's power and spoke of the storm's vehemence, its will, its fury, its trail of devastation. *Jeesus,* Gus said, *shut the damn thing off already, will you?* He was talking to his wife, who had the Sony portable in bed.

Updated satellite maps showing the storm for what it was, a solid mass of cold air, made the front page of the *Reporter* for four weeks straight. Everyone cut out the map and taped it on the fridge. They tried hard to make sense of it. *Hell, we don't exist anymore,* said Gus, who couldn't see clear across the front of the house to the ridge. *We're gone, can't see nothing there.* The long lake, the wide rivers, the high ridge, and the deep valleys. The accent of land. Gone.

Cows froze standing up. Horses were blanketed. Steamy slop was served to the hogs. Hens slept in huddles of six or more. Crows alighted singly or in twos on the telephone wires and faced the wind and called out, *More! More!* The trout slept in their deep mud holes and knew only what a trout knows. Deer froze in the ice forests, buck and doe and fawn. And the big catamount leapt across the logging road one day and was seen by Jigger, who followed its tracks until the snow forced him back. It was the forty-second consecutive day of snowfall on the high ridge.

■   ■   ■

Fox swam in and out of her visions; they were not dreams but visions. Her eyes were open and burning. The mammoth crow called her out, made her do the things of the living. Make a fire, kill that hare, eat it, melt the snow, drink it. Sleep, eat, rest.

She was in a stone chamber built four thousand feet high in the ridge, a hole framed in the notch of rock built five hundred years before Jesus said, I am the way. Built after empires fell and rose again, built after the Chinese introduced phrenological calendars, when real farmers, aware of indicators, knew that when buds burst into leaf or flower it meant something. It meant warmth. But this was not a warm spell and the wind whistled through the trees and broke them and she heard the crashing and nothing was growing except the storm itself.

She was in a circular beehive in the ground, with tons of snow above her, miles of it around her. She was twenty-five miles from the old Mercie property line, a mile from Jigger and Caroline's cabin, three from the sweet spring that never froze, thirty miles from her house where there were fires roaring up the chimney, and blankets, and food. She thought of the dog, Missy, and of Sid and his silence, and she had no idea that behind the horizon, down the irregular summit, at an angle of one degree and many miles away, her mother was making her way home.

Again and again memory took over and she wondered if they had looked, if they had bothered. Then she remembered: she was invisible. Even if they had looked they wouldn't have seen her.

Her feet, the pain in them gave her some comfort. If she was dying or already dead she'd feel nothing, but the pain meant she was alive. The nasty wind drew the warm air out of the chamber and put her fire out.

■   ■   ■

Butch followed the nurse down the halls of the hospital. She smelled of plastic sickness. White stockings wrinkled above her ankles and from her front pockets bulged pencils, sanitary pads, a hairbrush, and long-handled scissors. Her black hair was snarled and shiny like a new scouring pad. She pushed doors open and smiled, said just one more door, but there were many more doors. Her smile coaxed him on, down long white hallways lit up too bright for his pained eyes. He clutched his pocket and watched for her smile.

If it hadn't been for her smile, he would not have followed her. It was an eager, motherly smile, except his mother never smiled like that. Her smile and her white shoes led him to a particular door and then she said, *He's here.* When he didn't move she lowered her voice and stopped smiling. *Go on.*

She drew a curtain open and Butch saw the body under white sheets.

"That's your brother, that's him right there"—and she smiled.

What Butch saw was a face that belonged to an emaciated ten- or twelve-year-old. A little boy pulled out of the icy bottoms of a lake. Thought the nurse had a made a big mistake. The body in the bed looked like Bomber, the kid who'd dived from the big rock in the river and gone under while his mother and all the other mothers were having a picnic on the other side. They'd seen Bomber dive, a high sloppy jackknife, and the splash he made was big and they turned to smooth the towels around their legs and everyone forgot to watch for Bomber and it was minutes before someone said, *Hey, where's Bomber?* He didn't come up. Everybody watched as they fished him out. Looked like he'd been under for years. The river had robbed him clean of all he was. Didn't look like himself at all. Sid had the same look now, a liquid transparency. Had tubes in his nose and mouth and neck and arms. His bandages were very white. Butch wasn't alarmed by that as much as by the feeling that there was something else in his brother, something that begged to be recognized. The sound of his breathing was the sound of misery.

"He can hear you. Go on." The nurse pulled a chair for him.

"Hey, old buddy, it's me, Butch. Didn't think we forgot all about you, did you? It's snowing out and the roads are a mess, and Dad, the Deadhorse, well, you know how it goes. Took all morning to get it started."

Wasn't true, he'd taken the car, the old Lincoln. Had knocked on his dad's door, said, "I'm taking the car to see Sid. Wanna come?" He'd let the engine idle a long time, thinking his dad would come.

"Hey, buddy, the medics say we got you here in the nick of time. What a ride, though I guess you don't remember any of it." Butch watched his brother's face for a sign. An inflamed nostril, the left one, twitched with an unnatural rhythm.

"Does anything hurt?" Stupid, he thought, stupid thing to say. Wondered what it looked like, the gouged neck.

Shivered as his mind flashed on the memory of the day and the sink, the bathroom mirror, the blood-soaked towels, the tooth-brushes, the combs, even the light bulb. Earl had found him scrubbing tiles with a toothbrush. *What happened here?* Butch told him, said, Sid tried to kill himself. *You oughta have let him die.* Earl looked at the blood on the walls, the light bulb. *What a goddamn mess!* He stepped over the bucket, the mop, pulled open the shower curtain, looked inside. *Should have let him die.* He staggered up the stairs, dropped his boots, fell in bed. Floors groaned. Butch gathered the razors, the scissors, and all the kitchen knives except the butter knives, and buried them under a tarp out back.

Sid. Helpless. "Can you open your eyes, Sid? See what I got." Sid's eyes zigzagged under his eyelids as if straining to reckon with the voice. "Come on, Sid, just open your eyes for a sec." Butch willed them open, prayed they'd open, asked God to do it, *Make him open his eyes*. He needed to see his brother's eyes.

"Doc says you got to do your share. They're done patching you up. Now you got to do the rest." Sid's little finger moved, involuntarily, but Butch took it as a sign, meaning *Leave me alone*.

"Okay, okay. You take it easy, then, just rest, old buddy." He touched his brother's hand. Thought of the day, long time ago, first time Sid went fishing with them. They'd been on a rented boat fishing for lake trout or pike. They had a Five of Diamonds lure, the yellow and red, which showed well in the tannin-stained waters. They'd cast, then trolled. Only one who caught a pike was Earl and he'd tossed it at Sid, saying, *Now gut that sucker*. Threw the knife at him too. Sid mumbled, shook his head. *Gut it*, Earl in a calm voice, *gut it, for Christsake*. The fish was hurting, out of water, tail flapping, mouth searching for what it didn't have. Sid was looking at it, couldn't hold it in his hands any longer and tossed it out, back in the water. Earl grabbed Sid by the hair and tossed him off the boat. He grabbed an oar and slammed it in the water to keep Sid from swimming to the boat. Butch jumped, pulled Sid away from the oar, away from the boat, and, with an arm under his brother's shoulder, swam back to shore. Sid was nine then, maybe ten. Never took to waters after that.

"By the way, Missy's doing fine." Butch watched the monitor for a change. Nothing. Wondered if Sid's thoughts also came in a stutter, if his heart did, too, if it all went on and off.

"I got to go now, Sid, but I brought you something. If you'd open your eyes you'd see what it is." Butch pulled the stuffed bunny out of his pocket. It was the only one they had in the gift store, it was pink.

"I'm going to leave it here on the table for you." He set it on the table next to a glass of water with a long straw.

When Sid was a kid, a toddler, he had a favorite bunny, carried it everywhere, slept with it. Earl threw it away one day, called Sid a sissy, said he was spoiled rotten and wouldn't have a boy of his sleeping with a goddamned bunny. Sid was three, maybe more, cried all night long. Nobody slept. Butch found his bunny in the garbage, snuck it into Sid's room. But Earl found it, burned it in the woodstove. *That goddamn piece of shit is gone now, you hear me?* They'd sat up all night listening to Sid's wailing. Earl slept in the shed. Darlene went crazy. The house filled up with screams.

"It's a bunny," Butch said, choking on the words, "it's your bunny, I found it." He put it next to Sid's hand.

■   ■   ■

OUTSIDE, IN the car, Butch cried and begged his brother to live though he couldn't imagine Sid alive, not really. The hospital, all lit up, the windows darkened, he expected to see his brother taking flight out the window, white sheets around him, dissolving like a cloud.

He knew the delicate framework of Sid was no match for that of life itself; he'd known it all along. He'd seen him on a spring day, when the river broke and was full of rushing waters and debris, he'd seen Sid holding on to the tree rope by the river, watched him hold on with both hands, saw him walk backward to get a good running jump over the waters, knew what he was thinking, knew he couldn't hold on to the rope and make it over the high waters and onto the boulder which jutted out in midstream, mostly covered by ice, and knew that if Sid managed to swing and drop on the boulder he'd be stranded, he'd let go of the rope and have no way of getting back, knew also that Sid would not cry for help, that he couldn't, and knew also like he knew the natural laws of his family's ways that his brother could die that day and so he had yelled, *No!* Sid had let go of the rope and turned to Butch. There was nothing to say after that. He remembered the roar of the water was loud and the wind moved the hair over Sid's head, and they both knew his time would come again but that was not it, not then. And he wondered now, if

he screamed would Sid hear him, would he turn back from wherever it was he was going.

Butch started the car and drove farther north toward the last county
in Vermont bordering Canada. Along the highway was a stretch of
twelve miles where the road wound around square miles of rock
and you could see the river far below gnashing into it. Beyond that,
northeast of Painted Creek and farther north to Wild Gorge,
the ridge died, the land dropped and was no longer spectacular. The
mountains flattened out to bumps and the river lay flat on the
horizon where the lake appeared, glossy as a photo.

He drove to a city with paved streets. The place had the closed-
for-the-night look to it. Corner delis, shops, gas stations, all closed.
Houses, dark. Streets, abandoned. He ran all the red lights. Nobody
out. Drove straight to the house, hardly surprised that he'd found it
again. Suzanne's place.

He'd driven by her house once thinking she could feel him
near. Had parked and flashed his lights and waited all night but she
hadn't felt him and so he'd left.

Now he called her name as he drove up the streets. Suzanne. He
wanted her heat-soaked nearness. He wanted safety.

Houses so close together, no lawns, no big trees, cars on the
road. Houses with gingerbread trim, wraparound porches, windows
sashed, lace light. He knew why she'd come here, so far from the
ridge, away from the auctioned-off homestead, the empty pastures,
the rusted tractors, the miles and furrows and smells of newly
birthed calves, and the ash of a burning cigarette, and the drinking,
the screaming maneuvers that were her father's, now that he was
alone. She wouldn't have any of it.

Butch imagined her quiet now, sitting on the floor, cross-
legged, playing with her hair in a beam of light. Imagined her
sleeping naked. Sanctified, saved. She had resurrected herself by
moving a hundred miles north to a city where the roads all arched

up and the lake shone silver and gave the inhabitants a place to dream.

He parked near a phone booth. Sitting in the Lincoln with its peppermint-scented interior, he flicked the lights off and on and called her with his heart. *Suzanne.*

Her apartment was on the left, corner window. On the porch, a child's bicycle with streamers, a basket with a doll. Not hers, she had a boy. She had left town to give birth. Peaty, the father, stayed behind to work at the Blow Torch Garage on the outskirts of the ridge. Peaty, racetrack driver, Thunder Road fame, chiseled face restructured, refashioned, metal pins in legs, hips, and palms without lines due to burns. Peaty, driving rivets into metal, pumping gas, checking oil, he'd been the one to tell Butch about the kid. "Damn thing is he don't look a thing like me."

Tucked his arms around the phone, face on the mouthpiece, waited for her voice.

"Suzanne."

"Who is this?"

"Me. You told me not to get too serious about you. You told me I'd regret it."

"Butch? That you? What are you talking about? Is that really you?"

"You told me to leave you alone. You couldn't be bothered. Said you didn't want to end up with a broken life. Said I had the curse of the ridge on me, said I had a smart mouth."

"Butch? It's you isn't it?" An hysterical pitch to her voice. "I can't believe you're calling me. . . . I just can't—"

"The thing is I wanted you then, still do." Thought of her that first time with Sid in the car, the sandy spot off the road, cornstalks hissing, and all that beautiful moonlight.

"Where are you?"

"I'm right here."

"Where?"

"Here."

"Butch?"

"I have to see you, Suzanne."

"I don't believe this."

"Let me in."

"What?"

"In. Let me in." Sobbing, slow tears. Couldn't help it.

"Are you drunk?"

"No." Snow. Sky gone. Snow and darkness.

"Are you calling from the street? Is that you out there?"

"You know that's me."

"You're drunk. I know you're drunk. And you're in trouble. That's it. Is that it?"

"Suzanne, say you and I are out walking in the woods or something and we get separated, lost, and it gets dark and foggy and you can't see me and I call you, I call your name, you think you could find me just by the sound of my voice?"

"You crying, Butch?"

"Suzanne, just listen to me. . . ."

"What are you trying to tell me?"

"Do you think you can find me just by following my voice?" The silence was long and unexpected.

Then he was at the door.

"How'd you find me?" she said, holding the door open.

"I never lost you."

■   ■   ■

Nowhere near dawn, he awoke and pulled his pants on, looked out the window, saw a car's headlights in the snow-drizzled streets. Red digital clock by the bed. One, two minutes after four. Felt like a wanted man slipping out on a sleeping woman. Wanted for coming in, for staying, for surrendering, for taking what was offered. She didn't belong to anyone. He could have her if he wanted, and he did. He'd said a lot in a matter of hours. It had come easy. *I love you*. Out of loneliness, desperate, head nuzzled in her hair. *I love you*. Easy to fall, as if nothing. *I love you*.

Hands, face, all of him smelled like her, a perfumed metal smell. He could fasten himself to her, to the idea of her, out of need. He could ride around the air she lived on. Could worship her. Mother wife bride woman. His love for her would make him something he'd never been. Suzanne mumbled.

"What?" He moved toward her.

"Shush," she said.

Shivering. Shadows on the walls all lined up and aimed at him. Suzanne's mirrored skirt on the chair, a book of nursery rhymes with a little pig wearing an apron, the night-light in the shape of an owl.

For a moment he imagined himself as a fairy-tale papa wearing a tie, suspenders. He'd be a lightweight pig, a talking pig, one who believed in good endings, and hugs and kisses. He'd stand at the door on the petunia-lined porch and have no worries.

"You going now?" Suzanne's voice.

Cold metal belt buckle on fingers, he felt for the third notch.

"Butch?" Her words with that dry-lipped sound of sleep. She propped her head on the pillow.

Wind slashed snow, wind on empty streets, and the windows rattled. Where would he go?

"Butch?"

He couldn't find his shoes. *Man's got three things he has to keep track of: his money, his woman, his shoes*. That's what Earl always said.

His shoes were by the door but her hands were on his belt, undoing what he had just done. "Quit that!" His hands were too hard, he pushed her aside. "Sorry, I didn't mean that. Sorry." Sounded like Earl.

She kept her eyes on him as he told her about Sid and Earl and Tina gone. Couldn't phrase the words to say that his mother was gone too. She asked him, "And Darlene, where's she been all this time?" Her pale eyes were like moths. "Gone," he said.

Morning came when Timothy, Suzanne's dark-haired two-year-old, stumbled into the room with a thumb in his mouth and a wet diaper and legs that looked like they'd been shaped in a gale. His face full of red spots.

"What's that on his face?"

"Nerves," she said.

"A kid his age don't have nerves. . . ."

She kissed her son on the top of his head. He tried to remember last time someone kissed him like that. Closed his eyes as Suzanne went around the room changing and washing Timothy, and with a full bottle of apple juice they came back to bed and she read a story about three little wolves and a big bad pig. He wanted to tell her she had it all wrong, that everyone knew it was the other way around, bad wolves, good pigs, but he listened and fell asleep.

He woke and dressed and rushed out the door before anyone could stop him and ask where he was going. Walked along the waterfront, saw the pale blue mountains across the lake, and wondered if that was what the ridge looked like from a distance, soft and pretty. Seagulls perched on pilings and their wings turned silver in flight. He knew this lake was where his river ended up, where it lost its rage. Sound of the water lapping soothed him. Freezing cold water, if he should fall he wondered what he would feel. Stretched his arm out and cast his shadow over the water and spoke his brother's name. *Sid. Sid Summer*. The cold wind on his face reminded him of who he was—his father's son, his mother's son, his brother's keeper.

Suzanne's place was quiet and she had piles of clothes in her arms when he walked in. Ssshhh, she said. Nap time.

Butch picked up a little pair of pants with a dozen snap buttons down its legs. A little red shirt with a teddy bear pocket, and he folded it. "I'd like to stay," he said. He'd tell her other words later.

She didn't look up and for a moment he thought she was going to say no, that he had to go, then he saw she was crying. They clutched each other and said nothing for a long time. Then she pulled herself away from him and held her hands tight and looked straight at him. She was short, with long hair and a long neck and a painful look to her eyes. She wore silver earrings with tiny white feathers. "I can't promise anything," she said, "and you don't have to either. . . ."

"I can promise, I want to promise. I'm promising now."

She watched his expression and wondered if he'd make a good husband, a good father, if he had a good heart, if he meant well, and if the two of them meeting again was not some mere thing having to do with need. If she was a trickle of water that had escaped from the ridge, then he was the current to which she belonged. "Okay," she said.

He learned fast. Changed diapers, made funny faces, poured juice in a bottle, mashed bananas, kept an eye on the stove, on the windows, on the phone. He bought Suzanne a secondhand sewing machine but she had no patience for the threading so he mended everything. Made curtains, a tablecloth, bibs.

He fixed the vacuum, threw out old rugs, caulked bath tiles, bought new toothbrushes, a book on building boats, and got a nine-to-five job at the hardware store. Felt like a married man. Called Suzanne Mommy. Called Timothy baby. Making love with Suzanne one day, she said, "You be careful."

"Am I hurting you?"

"That's not what I mean."

"I'll pull out in time, don't worry."

"That's not what I mean, either, I mean be careful."

Love, of course. Be careful with love.

Thursday was visiting day with Sid, and Butch drove there, and after an hour he said he had to go. *Everyone says hello and for you to get well soon.* Then he drove down the interstate and into the small village and across the covered bridge. The closer he got to the house, the slower he drove. Looked to see if Earl's truck was there, whether anybody was looking out the windows, whether the dog was still barking out back, whether *she* was home. Didn't stop, didn't see the truck, didn't see a soul. Drove by the tepee and wanted to go in and tell the woman he was sorry. Wanted to tell her the story of his life and maybe in the telling he'd come up with the single fact, the truth to the whole thing. But he didn't go to her. Instead he drove back to the house and rushed straight up his room and grabbed as many clothes as he could and ran back to the car and drove fast, out of the ridge. It wasn't until he had reached Suzanne's house and climbed the twenty-three steps up that he thought of the boats. He'd forgotten to take his carved boats.

"So, did you find them?" Suzanne said as soon as he caught his breath.

"Who?"

"You know what I'm talking about, Butch. I know you go there, to the house. You don't just go to see Sid. I know."

There was a small rattle with a plastic head and two beady eyes on the table. He picked it up and shook it and watched the eyes roll around. Felt the same thing was happening to his head, nothing in place. He didn't say a thing for a long time.

"You think she'd of come home by now," Suzanne said.

"Who?"

"Your sister. Though I don't suppose she'd want to come back, with Darlene being gone and all. I know if I were her I wouldn't go back. I'd find a place to hole myself up for winter. Lots of places to hole up in out where you live."

"You make her sound like an animal. Animals hole themselves in. She doesn't know the slightest thing about being out there, that's what bothers me most," he said.

"Tell me one thing, Butch, in your mind, do you see her dead or alive?"

He lost his breath again and reached out to the wall and leaned hard against it. "Alive," he said. "Alive."

In his mind he'd seen his sister mauled by a bear, fallen into a trap, blown down a ravine, frozen right through. Those were fears, not the truth. "She can't be dead," he said.

"She might be. I can't imagine someone like her—"

He pushed himself away from the wall and grabbed Suzanne. "Shut up! Stop!" He felt crazy. Saw the table and wanted to hurl it, to do damage.

She took his hands off her and moved away from him and said, "You're not like them, Butch, you're not like Earl or Sid, and I'm sorry for the way things are, the way things turned out for all of you, but you've still got a chance. You found me. You found a way into my heart. That's something. So don't fight me, Butch. I'm done fighting. I won't let you."

She came to his arms and he stroked her hair away from her face and he felt the long scars on her forehead from all those accidents with her father. She'd told him, *My dad had an accident with my face.*

That night he found a blue pen and yellow paper and wrote a letter. *Dear Mom.* He told her about Sid and Tina. *Nobody's home*, he wrote. He told her the house didn't look real anymore and sometimes he wondered if it had all been real, the five of them there. He told her that as soon as she left there was no anchor, no nothing, and did she understand what he was saying. Told her the dog was gone. Told her about Suzanne and Timothy. Told her it hurt. Said he was sorry for all of it. Said he hoped she was all right.

Wrote a number she could call. He signed the letter, *With love, your son*. He folded it and put it in his pocket. It had no way of reaching her.

■   ■   ■

Earl was at the sink the day Butch came by. He was washing his hands and face with pink dish detergent, scrubbing grease off his knuckles, grit under the fingernails. He was thinking about all the things he'd done with his hands, and how his hands had the marks of everything he'd touched. Hands like an album. Dirt from years and years ago; gashes and burns and the white furled skin of the real deep cuts. Remembered everything he'd touched. Some of it shamed him, some would never wash away.

Filled a pot with water, set it on the woodstove to heat up. He'd wash later with his butt toward the stove's heat, he'd sponge himself and take his shivering body to the couch and sleep.

Couldn't go near the rooms upstairs. Their rooms scared him. His own room was unbearable. She was in there, in the photo. Couldn't take it down, couldn't look at it.

But he could look at the ridge and its configuration, watched it change from moment to moment. It was white capped and the sky was purple like a bruise and the river was like blackened silver. The river looked still but it was breaking underneath.

Heard the Lincoln stall on the bridge, the timing was all wrong, it stalled again in the drive. He heard his son's steps on the porch and then the door opened. The cold hit him around the legs. Butch held the door slightly open, and peered in, surprised to see him. For a moment Earl didn't know him. Something about the way he was framed in the light, way he hesitated by the door, plus his hair looked all wrong, cropped too tight to his head.

"Hey, son. Come in, close the door." No use being cantankerous or angry, he thought. He wiped his hands on his pants and tried to find a way to smile.

"Jesus, Dad, it stinks in here."

"Stinks? What stinks?" God almighty, he thought, boy is telling me the place smells, no, not smells, stinks. His mother would have said more: *Your armpit stinks, your socks, your breath, God, Earl, you stink something awful.*

"So it smells, okay, so let the door open, let the air in, don't come in, talk to me from out there." He made a show of it. "Hell, I don't care. Let the goddamn cold in." It was already bad, out of control.

"Dad."

"Yeah?" He felt as if he were hanging upside down, watching his son from the wrong perspective. He wanted to make peace, to let him know how wretched he felt; he'd offer him a job, pay him. He'd square his shoulders against those of his son and not make a big deal about him not being quite as tall as he imagined he'd be, not quite the man either. He'd let bygones be bygones, hell, he'd shake his hand. And if he wanted to talk about Darlene, he would. He'd take that bottle of whiskey and the two of them alone, sitting by the fire, they'd talk.

"Son, come in. Come in." He dropped his eyes to the dirty linoleum, picked up an empty wrapper. Held it up. "Beef jerky, son, sorry, it was the last one." Folded it in half and carefully put it on the counter. He wasn't funny, he shouldn't even try to be funny, he thought, not now, damn it, not now. He stood as he always did, as if something were between his legs.

Butch kept the door open with a foot and looked at the river and at his father, trying to see if that light in the river had a way of attaching itself to one's eyes. It wasn't in Earl's eyes. But he noticed the screen door was still on. That had been *her* job, to take it down for the winter, to put the storm windows in, put summer clothes away, bring out the boots, coats, hats, scarves. She wouldn't let the place stink.

"Well." Earl faced his son, gave him time to say something, but nothing came of that so he turned the water on in the sink and squirted a long stream of soap on the pots. He'd burned eggs that morning, boiled until the water evaporated. The pot was black inside and out. Last night he'd burned the fish, didn't put enough butter in the pan. He'd opened a tin of ham and the tin, rimmed in pinkish gelatinous layers, was in the sink filling up with water.

"Well, son?" He was offering conversation and still his son said nothing. "What do you want? What are you doing here? You standing there like a stranger. Come in or get out." He turned the water off, dried his hands on his shirt, and looked at Butch.

"I feel like a parrot here talking to myself. Cat got your tongue or what? Where you been hiding?"

"You really don't care, do you, Dad? About Sid or Mom or any of us. Tina's been gone for months now. Sid's dying. You haven't been to see him. I came to tell you that I can't do this anymore. . . ."

"*This?* What do you mean *this?*" He had to keep his voice low, he had to keep his eyes from burning into his son's. He studied his shirt, the stitching around the collar. He had to find a way to keep him there, near him, long enough to tell him a truth, any truth. "I'm listening."

"I mean I can't live here anymore, with you, like this. . . ." Chill in his eyes passed through him and locked into Earl's heart. Butch closed his eyes but Earl had seen the watery look in them. Goddamn, his son was about to cry. Hadn't seen him do that in years, years. Not since he impaled himself, left leg, on raw timber in the path by the shed. He'd run out with the prospect of doing something and Earl had called for him not to run, *Don't run, son,* then the thud, the impact of flesh on the jagged two-foot spike. When he reached him he knew the kind of pain he was in, could tell by the water in his eyes.

"You mean something else, son. You want out."

"Yes. Out."

"Then you're out. Don't stay. I ain't asking. You hear me asking?"

"Don't, Dad, don't."

"Don't what?"

Earl could see past his son to the ridge and it didn't look real, not the ridge, not the light, not the house, and not his son. None of it was real. His son's face was shaven, red as usual. And his hair was cut like an official, sideburns a quarter of an inch down the ears, a shine to his hair, a smell to him, so official, as if at any moment he would slap him with papers, a warrant, an arrest, and take him in. He felt envy. His son's pants were clean. His boots had new laces.

"You despise me, don't you?" Earl said.

"Don't know if I do."

"Someone taking care of you," Earl said. "Who is it? Nobody from around here, is it?"

Just then a sudden change of light happened, sunset light, liquid. Fairy light, Darlene called it. The dainty light mixed with the smell of the house and made everything more unreal than it had been.

"You ought to get your things out of here," Earl said. "And while you're at it take your brother's things too. Come spring I'll burn what ain't claimed."

"That's all you have to say?"

Earl lit a cigarette and squinted at his son and surveyed the kitchen. Saw his clothes piled by the couch, blanket and pillow, phone off the hook, curtains drawn. "Yeah, that's about it. What else is there?"

He was hungry. He'd have to fix his own dinner again. Wash his own pants. Make his own bed. Drink his own whiskey. No family stuff. Too late for that. It was clear. To hell with his son if he didn't think he loved him. To hell with Sid, too, if he wanted to die. To hell with his daughter, his wife too.

"To hell with it," he finally said. His son took on the dimensions of a stranger. Never liked strangers.

"Where's Missy?" Butch said.

"The dog? She comes and goes but you can take her, too, if

you want. What else do you want, let's see. . . ." And he made a show of looking around like he always did when he was offended. "Want the chairs, the table? Pots and pans?" He lifted a cast iron skillet out of the sink. He dropped it on a cup, heard it break. "Want something to remember me by? Take this." And he shoved his hands deep in the garbage and pulled out wads of wet towels, broken things, cigarette butts.

"You just don't get it, do you?"

"I get it. Here it is. See for yourself." He shoved his hand deeper into the trash to show him the burnt remains of his dinners.

Butch looked away and closed the door softly. It had been a mistake. He shouldn't have come. Good-bye, he said to the house, to the yellowed photograph, the mismatched furniture, the rows of canned soup, the four crystal goblets which his mom kept in the attic so no one could break them in a fit. Props, all of it. The only real thing was the light on the river, changed already. He turned to see his father on the porch, both shabby, brittle, old.

Earl held the door open and couldn't believe his son was going without a word, not even a curse, not even one. That bothered him more than anything.

And when night came the whiskey was gone but he didn't feel drunk, felt lucid, deprived and lucid, though his head felt heavier than a maul. He waited for the ugly black thoughts. Turned to the mirror. Watched them come.

You old fart.

Shot of hair over his forehead. Tried not to cry, said, What the hell, what the hell. He'd grown old and sad. No light in his eyes. He'd seen men like him before and hadn't understood how it was possible to have no light in the eyes. No smile. Didn't even try.

Can't smile, can you?

Old man's tears. Swollen ears, gummy eyes. Buried his head in his pillow and cried like a crow. *Caw-caw-caw.*

Moon died over the ridge.

"Darlene," he whispered to the pillow. *Darlene.* Occurred to him he was crazy. Pieces of conversations, snapshots of days. The two of them lying on a grassy knoll, head up to the sky. The two of them making love, then arguing. *You're such a disappointment, Earl! Nice, Darlene, you forgot how to be nice!* Then the note: *If I take you back shoot me.*

Thinking, sweating it out, alone. All of them gone. And then night came like it had to. Real and solid and cold. Pulled the smelly blankets over his head and dreamt he was a bloated bird struggling to get off the ground but he was wingless. The phone rang and he stared at it wishing it would stop.

"Hello?"

"Earl, is that you? I almost gave up, I was just about to hang up but I told myself someone had to be there. I've been calling for hours!"

"Mattie?"

"Earl? You don't sound like yourself. Where's Darlene? How come she hasn't called? Nobody's called me in ages."

"Mattie, Aunt Mattie?" He cleared his throat and closed his eyes. "I thought you knew. Everybody knows."

"Knows what? What are you talking about? Is something wrong? How's Darlene?"

"She's not here. She's been gone."

"Gone where? She's out or what?"

"She packed up and left. Months ago."

"Damn it, Earl, why didn't you call sooner to tell me? Why is it I have to call and find out the bad news? Why is it you don't stay in touch?"

"Sorry." She made him feel small, childish.

"What happened? You quarreled or what? Don't tell me if it's something I don't want to know, don't tell me."

"I don't know what to say. She's just gone. Things gone to hell since then. Tina's gone. Butch too. And Sid, well, Sid, he cracked up."

"Damn it."

"Tried to kill himself. He's in a hospital and all."

"Damn it. What happened to Tina?"

"Don't know."

"You're the father, what do you mean you don't know?"

"I don't know where she is."

"Damn it, Earl. Your uncle Tom passed away. That's why *I'm* calling, in case you're wondering. Just two days ago and, yes, I'm doing fine and all. But it seems to me we have to get some things clear before either one of us says another word."

Neither one spoke. It was that kind of silence. And if either one had spoken they would have said the wrong thing. Like I'm sorry.

"I'm sorry," Earl said.

"Don't be. Your uncle passed on, Earl, he was smiling when I found him, smiling like a goat on a sunny day."

"Aunt Mattie, you don't have to . . ."

"Have to what? Talk? Let me talk. I don't think you're in the position to tell me what I can and can't do. I'm not calling for condolence, I don't need pity. Earl, the man I loved is gone. That's all there is to that."

"Aunt Mattie, really, you don't have to—"

"Be quiet, Earl, this call is costing me money. I know what you want to say, and you want to say it because you think it's the right thing to say. Grief requires some talking, that's fine and dandy, but that's not what I want to hear from you. I'm up to my ears in words of condolence. I've had it with the preacher, the neighbors. You know how many casseroles have been left in my kitchen in the past day? The words get to me, Earl, that's maybe why I called you, although I thought I'd get Darlene, you know. She wouldn't give me nonsense about grief and all, she wouldn't call it a process. I hate that word. Process. Imagine that. Well, like I said, I was hoping Darlene was there and she'd come over and get me out of the house."

"I'll come over."

"I was hoping you'd say that." After a long silence she said, "Listen me out here for a minute and I won't have to tell you later."

She told him what Tom ate that morning. Two sausages, two eggs, toast burned on the edges, apricot jelly. Cup of coffee, no sugar. "Put on his coat, said I'm going out and I remember looking over my shoulder at him. Ten times a day, your uncle Tom said the same thing. Going out."

She told him she found him an hour later. "Hands folded, head up, no hat, snow on his head. And I thought, well, the old fool, catching a cold. That's exactly what I thought, damn fool. So I come up to him fixing to tell him to get up and I see. I knew."

Earl heard a deep drawing in of air, heard her blow her nose, clear her throat.

"Well, there I was, and there he was, and I'm thinking, Christ, this thing has finally happened between us. You know . . . death. You still there, Earl?"

"Yes, I'm here."

"Listen. Find yourself a good shirt and a clean pair of trousers and wash up and get in the car and come over."

"I can't do that."

"What do you mean you can't do that? I'm asking you to come to the funeral of your uncle, your father's brother. You're the only one he cared about. Your brother, you know, once he moved to Florida, it was like he died to him. Yes, he sent us oranges in a basket with a big red bow, arrived UPS every year. Tom never touched any of them. Year after year, every Christmas, all those oranges just sitting there in the back room till mold took over. Threw them out in the compost, watched the crows flying off with orange peels in their beaks. That's how much he cared for your brother."

"I never sent Uncle Tom a card, not for his birthday, or—"

"I know that. And it wasn't the sending of things that mattered to him. It was in the other things. Fixing his chain saw, plowing, saving his life. Don't tell me you forgot that. If you hadn't been there to pull him out of the wreck he'd have died. Two seconds after you pulled him out the whole thing exploded. You remember that? Those two seconds gave him ten years."

Earl remembered.

"Come down, Earl."

Light shone over his shoulder, spooked him to see his flesh lit up like that. "Okay, Mattie, I'll get ready."

"One more thing. When you leave, don't lock your doors."

"I don't think you understand, Mattie. Darlene's had it with me. . . ."

"I'm not talking about her. I'm talking about your children. Leave the doors open, Earl. Doors are like hearts, don't shut them."

It was his turn to cry, holding the phone in both hands, cupping it so she wouldn't hear.

"What I'm saying is what's lost is lost, but you never know what'll show up just when you think you got nothing left."

■ ■ ■

Fox couldn't see the serpentine row of stones because they were buried under snow. They surrounded the stone chamber in concentric circles, widening around and around for hundreds of miles. She was at the heart of a labyrinth made of stones and stones have spirits and she was in the spirit of the mountain completely.

She was hungry and thought of the hare and willed it to come and give itself to her. *Now.* The hare was waiting for her outside and when she saw it she followed. This was a game, the ritual before the feast. It hid behind trees. She hid behind trees. She fell, it waited. This went on all day. Her fingers were frozen around the rock she held. It was a flat broad rock the size of her palm and for a moment she thought it was part of her hand and was surprised to see the other hand so different. She walked until she fell and rose again, dragging her body. Her face was bleeding, blood was on the snow. She wanted the hare. She wanted to put her mouth inside its warm cavity. And then she saw them, the boulders of Mercy Road.

When she was a child she followed Earl into the woods and he told her there was no sense in her following him because he was only going up to the boulders. This is where the curse begins, he squinted at her in a way she knew was meant to scare her away.

What's ahead?

Nothing you need to know.

But she insisted and he told her. *I found a man hanging from a tree right up there. The man's wife drowned right around here, there, in the shallow. Then I heard the children, they were whiter than death itself. And they had no eyes.*

What else?

He told her. *Some nights you can hear the children singing. Spinning wheels turning. Goats bleating, wind sifting from the ground up, wind full of ghosts.*

Ghosts?

Ghosts.

She didn't believe a word.

That was the first time she heard of the curse.

The hare appeared between the boulders and she followed it to the house. The front door was an icy mesh of brambles. The windows were boarded up. A wooden wheel jutted out of the ground, splintered spokes with ice daggers.

A heavy tree had fallen on the roof but the roof was intact and the tree had gone on growing and its branches draped around the house like black icy fingers. The chimney was intact too. The ancient lilacs and hydrangeas were iced over and so were the beds of irises, which had spread for miles so that in summer, the wild purple color was all one could see.

Floods, blizzards and metal-bright starlight had touched the land and the house. The foundation, the stone cellar, the wide planks, the fieldstones laid out in the path, it had all been for nothing; a ruin of hope. Even in her stunned body Fox felt another kind of cold move in her.

What happened to the children? she'd asked Earl.

Gone. Funny what a life comes to, Earl had said.

Those were the strangest words she'd ever heard him say.

The hare leapt in and out of her vision, into deep holes, out again. And then she heard faint cries that changed to singing and then clear as anything she heard voices. *Over here!*

She followed the voices to the side door.

Here, here!

Around back, cellar door buried under snow, steep stone steps.

Here, here!

A window, no, not that one. The small door in the back. Leaned against it and it flew open.

Chairs, tables, a cupboard with plates. A loom threaded in wool: rotted warp, a shuttle laid down, brown wool the color of chestnuts left to dry in the sun, long-handled scissors, a cloth tape measure, a red pincushion, catalogs open to pages showing wheelbarrows, shovels; a man's boots by the door, the mirror streaked with age, a straw hat on the peg by the door, children's toys, a child's crocheted cap in blue and white, a fiddle in its case, a shortstemmed pipe still smelling of maple, a woman's comb, silver turned black. A pantry door with a bunch of dried grasses and dried roses, faint plaid ribbon. Carpets with the pattern of huge green leaves on vines. Water stains on ceiling, along walls. Smells of chipmunk, mice. Enchanted and spooked. A wide armchair by the fireplace, its cushions ripped open. Acorns. Husks of nuts. She turned the cushion over, equally ruined, and she sat, pulled her coat tight around her neck, and heard them again.

Find me, find me!
Grab a toad and find me!

A white skirt dashed behind the wall, a glimpse of a red bow, a slice of a little girl's pale face, hair like moonlight.

Find me, find me!
Foxes' tails can't hide me!

Spinning motion to the side; that was the boy, quick and small. Blue sleeve of his shirt, same pale white hair.

Find me, find me!
Lose your life and find me!

∎ ∎ ∎

MATTIE PLUCKED the flowers from the vase and spilled the water on the rocks. Kicked snow over the petals. Patted down the stems. Shoved the purple ribbons deep in the snow. Couldn't stand the smell of hothouse flowers. Stink of lifelessness in them. She emptied several foil-wrapped casseroles into the garbage but she bagged the sweet buns, caramel rolls, cinnamon bread, and apple tarts and stacked them in the freezer. Put aside the pots of raspberry jam. Grief offerings.

Washed her hands and made herself a cup of coffee and toast and he came back to her that way, Tom. He was in the breakfast smell of her kitchen, chasing the smell of his own death away.

"So, we're going to lay you down in a shiny brown coffin," she said to the air charged with Tom's presence. She'd cut down his pillow, small enough to fit the coffin.

"Goose feathers. You always liked a soft pillow, didn't you?"

She tucked in the cotton folds, stitched the hem. Small feathers scattered around the floor, in the air.

"Tom, you listening?"

I'm listening.

She knew he couldn't help but listen, even now.

"So, then, I guess that's all there is to it."

She wasn't quite sure what she meant by that. Smoothed her dress down. Opened her purse, took everything out. A hankie, a coin purse, a pink lipstick, a few dollar bills, coupons for birdseed, matches. Put everything back in. Set the purse by the door and thinking, or not thinking, said, "Tom, you think I need a hat?"

February, it's colder than a duck's ass.

"Ground's frozen, Tom."

Harder than a nail.

"You know we can't put you in the ground, Tom, you know that, don't you? We'll have to keep you like a turkey, frozen till springtime."

Never cared for turkeys like that.

"I know you didn't, Tom. I know that."

Opened the door, cold air whipped around her. Feathers took off in the wind.

"Tell you what, Tom."

In a few months there'd be signs of life everywhere. Lilies of the valley, green soaking wet grass. Life. But that was later. May, June.

"Oh, Lord. This won't do." She faced the dust motes in the light, said, "Tom, I got plans for you."

From the bread box she pulled out a loaf of rye and sliced two thin wedges, one for the bird and one for her. Heard the bird twittering in the cage. She whistled, bird whistled back. All her life she'd had parakeets, blue ones.

"Jericho, good morning, good morning." Finger in the cage, the bird quickly perched up on it and walked up her arm, made his way up her neck, under her thick wad of gray hair, pecked her ear, whistled, then flew to the window, where he cocked his head and watched a large bird swoop down out of the blue. Crow making a fuss.

It had snowed overnight, February snow, thick and wet. Walked to the garden, where nothing showed except a bale of hay left out since fall. Looked around for the prints and found them.

Tom's. Set her feet next to his. It would take a rain, more snow, and all trace of him would be erased from the land forever.

Followed his tracks to the wall of spruce planted when they married. *That'll keep the north winds out,* he'd said. They were a foot high then and she'd laughed to think those trees would offer them any sort of protection, but they had. His tracks led to the apple tree, and up to the woods, but he hadn't gone in there. Never did. Something in them, disorder, darkness. His parents were buried in there but goldenrod and thistle grew taller than the stones, and their names were gone, worn away.

Sat in the snow-dented spot where she'd found him and put hands out to the air where he'd been. She cupped the empty air and brought it to her heart.

In the house the bird pecked at the toast on the plate. The doorbell rang and the door opened. "Aunt Mattie? You in here?"

"Come in, I'm in here, Earl."

"It's dark in here. Where are you?" Bird took flight and found Earl. "Damn this bird, get him off me!"

"He's just greeting you."

"Get him off!"

"Come here, Jericho."

"It's dark in here."

"Plenty of light. I can see you and you look different."

He shifted his feet.

"Look at me, Earl."

He walked toward the small frame of his aunt. "It's too dark to see."

"Yes, something's different."

"I told you. She left me."

"No, something else left you."

Earl brushed the hair off his forehead and felt the sting of tears. Tried to act as if it had nothing to do with him, all those tears. Mouth forced open, gasping. It had never happened like that before. "I just don't know what to do."

"Oh, let it happen, Earl. It's just life. You just got this one life to cram everything in. That's the problem. It's not enough, one life."

She held his hands and looked at him. Everything about him was in need of repair. Buttons hung loose, hair part was not right, fingernails chewed to the bloody edge, rubbed the bone where a finger used to be. Burns, scars, cuts, and scratches.

"When's the service?" he said.

She let go of his hands. "I ain't burying him. I decided against it on account of the ground being frozen and all. And he wouldn't like being in an icebox all winter, so I decided. Cremation. I'm sprinkling his ashes in the river."

■ ■ ■

EARL SQUEEZED through the narrow passage up the stairs to the attic bedroom with its crooked door, low ceiling, stained wallpaper buckling where snowmelt had set in. Heat vents with rust spots. Dusty smell of heat. Sat on the featherbed, which folded around him like dough. Lay down, feet off the side, too tired to untie his boots. Closed his eyes and tears started. It was Aunt Mattie's fault, she'd made him feel like a child, made him eat more than he'd eaten in months, made him cry, and what was worse she'd made him talk about Darlene and say words he hadn't said in ages or ever. Like *love*, like *mine*. *She was mine and I loved her.* . . . Well, don't go off putting in the past what's still in the present, she'd said, rubbing his knuckles hard.

She'd made him drink a glass of warm milk with whiskey, saying, *That ought to do it*. And she'd pointed up the stairs, saying, *The little room on the right. Window on the front has a nice view of the moon when it's full. It ain't full tonight, is it?*

Thought of the moon brought back a jolting pain. Sleep came in the absolute quiet of a winter night and nothing moved. Love should be like this, he thought, just like this.

And he dreamt of his family coming at him like apparitions. Gray-clad creatures bristling with ice. Kind faces. Like deer. Was not ready when they all turned on him with gaping red mouths, catlike demons. Woke himself in a scream.

Mattie heard him fall into bed. Didn't want to tell him about Darlene's call. Weeks or months ago. Couldn't tell him, afraid he'd go. When she heard him scream, she knew the kind of dream he was having. A white scrap of light fell through the sky. Stars. "Let him find his way, Lord," she said, "burn a hole in the sky, make it big as you need to, just let him see the way."

She meant Tom, she meant Earl. "I mean all of us, Lord."

Face turned toward Tom's side of the bed. Imagined his naked arm out for her to put her head on. Caressed the pillow thinking of Tom's thick yellow-white hair, looked at a certain spot in the pillow where she knew his eyes would be. Closed her eyes eventually. *All right, I'll sleep now.*

* * *

WEATHER HAD changed overnight. He woke to the sound of hail and sleet pounding on the roof. Felt like a lonely turtle after the deluge.

"Let's take my car. It's got gas and it don't sound like the Fourth of July on wheels." Her car was a rusted Toyota, red plastic strip tied to the antenna, a wiper missing, seats covered in white fake fur.

Mattie slowed down, tires grated on snow. She pointed to a fancy house that looked like a museum, its path lined with wooden sculptures of bears. "Carla's place."

Carla was the first girl he'd ever seen naked. She'd shed all her clothes and flung herself into the air, forming a perfect human arc before she hit the icy waters of the quarry. He'd gone after her but she was fast and dove deep, surfaced on the other side, taunting him.

"She's a big-shot lawyer, made a lot of money from the cow case, man who was caught by a neighbor doing you-know-what to his cow. It was big news in the paper for weeks. Case got into court. Abuse and unlawful conduct with an animal. Carla got the man off easy. A slap on the hand and off the farm he went."

Earl could imagine Carla in court, saying, *Now, Your Honor* . . . pacing, looking around her, grabbing words out of the air.

The day he finally thought he had her, an August day, both naked on a huge boulder and nobody around, he watched drops of water trail down her breasts and was overcome. *Now, Earl, this is quite ridiculous, I mean here you are sucking on my mammalian glands* . . . and he'd let go of her fast and asked, *What are you talking about? What glands?* Pulled away from her fast and felt like a freak, tampering with glands. Still wondered what she meant. Why had she undressed if she didn't want him touching her?

Mattie pointed at new houses, old houses, mixed gossip and news. Talked about the blue heron on the pond. "Stood there all day long. Night came and it was still there, hadn't moved an inch. Pitch black but I could still make out its shape." Saw a man on the banks of the broken river, a speck of a man with a rod, preparing for the thaw and the run. "Fool," she said. "It ain't time."

Pointed at a growth of red-tipped sumacs. "Orioles nest there." When they reached Exit 10 she told Earl to stick his hand out. "I'm turning here. Signals don't work."

"You're supposed to signal on the driver's side."

"Can't drive and stick my hand out at the same time." She drove across the intersection without looking, didn't stop on the high incline where red lights flashed. The car didn't hold on a hill. She did not yield to traffic. "*Yield,* ain't that a funny word to find on the road?" Then she said, "There it is, ugliest thing you ever saw."

Central Hospital was a redbrick contraption with ten or more sooty chimneys. She parked by letting the car ram up against the concrete ramp. He rushed to keep up with her. She walked across the road without stopping to look both ways. He did the same. She clutched her purse like a bomb and she held the door open for him, said, "After you."

The heat of the building paralyzed them temporarily. Two nurses at the desk looked at them.

"Want me to stay here or what?" Earl said.

"Do what you want." And she marched to the reception area. "I'm here to see about my husband. His name's Tom. He's dead. I called about him. I'm here to pick up his ashes."

She let him drive this time. The box of ashes between them.

"Would you like some coffee, something to eat?" Earl said.

"Plenty of food at home."

Earl's stomach tightened, he felt dizzy. Drove with fear.

"Let me tell you something, Earl. About Tom. There was a woman. Name of Edna."

Earl looked out the window. Poplars branched out in untended fields like waves. Everything seemed familiar. Hemlock, beech, black cherry, basswood, butternut. Felt he had driven through here many times, seen the same sky, on a day just like that day. Even Mattie's words seemed familiar.

"Edna, well, it's been a long time since I said her name. She had the kind of looks a man, any man, could fall for. Too tall to go unnoticed, not easily overlooked, especially with the colors she put on. Bright reds. Coming down the road like a planet on fire."

Earl chewed on fingers.

"You wondering why I'm telling you this? What it has to do with you and me and Tom and your dad? I'll tell you but pull over here. I want to see the river."

A park with a sign and three wooden tables, a steep ravine with a manmade footwalk leading to the pebbled banks. Snow and ice over everything. Black icy pools where the river refused to freeze. Large boulders rose off the banks like stone beasts. Low clouds on the distant ridge. Mattie sighed and looked at Earl.

"This woman, Edna, came on a train all the way from California, but before that she was from Pennsylvania. She moved after her husband died. It was the war then, you know. Anyway, she came north, a widow in bright feathers. Flaunting her sorrow, if you ask me."

Earl tugged on his raw flesh. Paid little mind to what Mattie was saying, figured she was pouring her grief out. And this Edna stuff, that was a blanket over the grief, one she had to air out properly.

"What makes a man think he can take and take is the same thing that keeps a woman giving and giving. It's like taffy, stretching till it snaps."

Earl, head hurting, bladder full, stomach aching for cinnamon rolls, apple tarts. The only green for miles was up in the mountain, a stand of pure pine. There was life in there. Deer waiting out the long cold spell. Wondered what they knew about time.

The deer, the ice, the empty pain in him, reminded him of his daughter. He'd dreamt about her, first and only dream since she'd gone. Same night he dreamt of his father, Lucky, and thought it was some kind of sign. Imagined she'd hitched out, gone west, like Lucky.

"Well, to make a long story short, Edna died. In the bathtub, upstairs, in our house. She'd settled with us until she could find a place and of course, she never did. I found her floating, head down, in two feet of soapy water. Papers floating in the tub. I call out for Tom and what do you think he does? He grabs the ink-stained papers and reads them. Letter was addressed to your dad. His brother. Lucky."

The ridge growled, the sky arranged itself in layers. The river was a wild thing but not now, not in winter. They walked back to the car. His hunger, the way the trees bent toward the bottomlands instead of toward the rise, everything seemed out of sorts.

"Loved her like a dry-rock wall. That's what Tom said after Edna died. Said he loved her like a dry-rock wall." She lit a cigarette. "It's taken me all these years but I've taken her apart, rock by rock."

She reached into the car and got the box of ashes.

"This is a pretty place in spring," Mattie said. She held the box in one hand and turned back toward the river and let herself down. He followed.

She grabbed a heavy rock and dropped it on the ice until the water appeared and she grabbed more rocks and smashed the ice, making a flow that was deep enough, fast enough. And when she was sure the water would keep on moving, she let the ashes go. "Go on, Tom, go on out."

■   ■   ■

SID THE color of snow, skin like ice, eyes like cracks.

He'd been down. Gone. At the bottom of the lake. Taking in water. Hands out to the silt, the weeds. All night wondering how long he could hold it all in. Now he was awake, on the surface again, above water. Soon they'd be here again. They'd touch him, force his eyes open, take his hands. Turn him on the bed. They'd change his bandages. He'd feel their hot hands on his cool flesh, burning him. They'd talk as if he weren't there, but he was underneath it all. He wanted to tell them about the silt, the weeds, the dark bottom. He wanted to tell them where he lived.

"Well, there you are!" The nurse sucked in a mouthful of air and circled him. "Another day, another miracle." She always said that, she admired his wounds, said they were looking better now. "Lovely! Lovely! You're doing just fine!" She wrapped him up, blessed him.

"You have visitors today. Sid-ney?" She said his name in two distinct syllables. She forced her hand under his head. Then she moved him sideways as if he were made of nothing.

Inside, he was animated, alive.

"What do you think of miracles, Sidney? You ready for one yet?"

He rode a wave of pain that drove him out and back to the bottom again. He did not see her pull the silver cross from under her blouse, nor did he see her hold it in her hands, but he heard her pray. The words were generic. Water pushed him down. He was without pain. In the bottom there is no pain.

Part Five

SHE WAS no longer herself. The cold had taken her senses away. The wind had forced her to move like wind itself. She was a glowing piece of ice. She was lace and silver rain. She was no more than a thread and her eyes were done with seeing completely.

She thought she had to be close to death, or dead already. Why else could she see and hear the Mercie children? They were ghosts, and maybe she was one too. Their faces were like pinwheels, powder white, with their dark eyes whirling around her. They woke her, pulled her up, and forced her to make the fires.

She was nothing more than a tassel attached to their dream coats. Shivering, she followed those faces through the rooms, sour rooms smelling of pulp and boiling syrup. She was led to a room with a featherbed, feathers scattered, highboy with a tin box in which lay a rosary; she was made to hold the glass beads, and a brooch the color of a pickle, and lace, miraculously intact; all this the children put in her hands.

The children, flying knee-deep in old feathers, laughed. Their voices like percolated coffee, saying, *Now, now!*

Amber floors of wood, rooms dripping with childhood. Beds, so small, so perfect, and upon each a moth-eaten doll with a rotten stitch for a smile. Heavy muslin curtains, torn. Walnut smell to the rooms. Dressers with tiny jars full of buttons, stones. The hot pungent smell of time.

They were so impatient, the children, and they led her with

their sour sweet smell down the cellar where the wood was stacked. Brown rotten wood.

I can't. You don't understand. She pleaded.

They did not understand. They wanted a fire.

Like little goats they prodded her up and down and up again. She carried a log at a time. The queer little faces looked on. She was shoved toward the hearth. She made the fire. It was glorious. Fox clapped her hands and the children pebbled her with praise.

She kept the fire going and in the strength of heat she slept. Later she smelled the rich incense of berries steeping in a pot. She drank the juice, she slept. She woke to children's fingers on her body and on her hair and in her mouth. She was fed pulp, of what, she didn't know. Cucumber smell to the air. Stickiness to her. She slept and woke, stifling in the fanned heat and the smell of boiling sugar.

She was without voice but spoke with gestures to the wild-eyed children who flew in and out of her vision. This is all so odd, Fox wanted to say, and found the children listening, nodding their heads, looking out to the midmorning grizzle of light through the windows. They were such sad children, brooding, needy, absorbed in a dream-story and she was a mere word in it.

Roots, roasted like nuts. Wheat berries. Old jars of preserves which they opened by dropping and brought to her, scoops of fruit in their hands. Everything so sour. She slept, the children too. Sighs as long as the night.

The little freaks had what they wanted. Company and a warm house. The smell of food. They chased each other around the dusty rooms with arms out, never touching. They climbed the stairs and stopped at the door by the room with the damaged featherbed. There they wailed.

She comforted them, brought them down to her, and they sat in the big talon-legged chair through the night.

She boiled water and coaxed them to bathe. A cloth around

their faces and necks. Skin so glossy when wet, then quickly evaporating into dust.

Just when she was getting used to being inside, to seeing the snow and shadows out there and the fires inside, when her life had become the absorption of a dream not of her own making, when her thoughts were turning to need again, when the children's high laughter seemed endless—they would cackle like little hens for no reason at all—in the white light of another winter day they decided it was enough and put her out.

She had made a bed for herself near the fire, had enough wood, enough water. The children had looked at her feet and laid their hands so gently above them, not touching, never touching. Such sad faces. And just as she was thinking the cold had ended, it started again.

Light became dark. The children put out her fires. The little red fires. They did not want her anymore. She was not like them and they made her leave. They pulled her by the hair and pushed her out. They screamed. They spat at her. They took her food away. She'd had food, the berries, the wheat; she'd caught a squirrel with her bare hands, and hares, many of them. Their long ears hung by the mantel. They, the children, had led her to the river one day and showed her the beaver lodge and together, in single file, they crept on hands and knees over the rough wood. Nothing but darkness in there, and poplar bark and duckweed.

She said she'd take them there for more, she pointed out the window. She rushed out alone and brought them food, *See, look, look what I have,* but they turned their faces. They waited until she slept and then screamed, *Mommy! Mommy!* And she ran to them saying, *I'm here, here I am, what is it, what do you want?* and they threw their wild little bodies on her and dragged her out.

She didn't want to go. She whispered, *Oh please don't,* but the children held hands and turned their backs. They had their thick woven coats on, the blue and green with red chevrons, the long tassels on their hats. She was left with the sight of someone's meticulous handwork with wool and the children's nasty faces.

They were cunning. They would wait for another visitor to tease and chase into the house for a little bit of company, for a reasonable amount of time, for a hot soapy bath and some stewed rabbit. They would play games in the house. But now they were done playing and they were tired and they wanted nothing more than their old dead silence, the good rest of the long dead, and so they steadied themselves as they stepped up on the rotten porch, the girl holding the boy's hands, and they vanished, dissipated.

Inside, the grand house had already lost its warmth and the scent of good air. The mice quickly came back. The chipmunks and squirrels too; they burrowed in the neat wool and tore open the seams of cushions and made new nests. And the children settled in for a long sleep.

She felt the swell of her lids but wasn't sure if they had always been shut like that, or if her mouth was always so tight, hurting, and if her feet, too, had always hurt like this. The cold blue pain was back and she couldn't walk. Dragged herself over the land on her hands. When her hands couldn't move, she used her shoulders and her chin, digging into the snow to move up, forward. *Go on.*

. . .

JIGGER'S WEATHER station involved shadows, feathers, and sweetness. The shadows had to come on a slant and thin out by three o'clock. The feather was a turkey feather and was ten inches long and the tip had to point north when the wind was idle. The sweetness had to be in the air. All of that meant winter would be around another three months.

The cabin roof was weighed down with two feet of snow, he'd have to shovel it off. Watched Caroline through the steamy window chopping onions and crying. The house would smell of onions for days. Strapped on his snowshoes, and fell into the rhythm of snow travel over deep and solid drifts. Found a small bird frozen, tiny black feet up. Bitter, bitter, bitter. These were the dying days, the holding-on-to-nothing weeks of winter, the very heart of winter. Brutal. Thirty-two below. The Hopeless Ridge in all its glory.

Thought he saw a phoebe in flight but no, couldn't be. Too early. Come March they'd be back, and the warblers, vireos, and redstarts, but for now it was silent, snowbound.

Was thinking about the deer he'd seen in the fall, whitetails, grazing. And how he wished he could travel like them and grow thick then lean, scavenge, live. His greatest disappointment was knowing he'd always be just a man.

When he saw the dark shape against the tree he pulled out his knife, crouched, and fell sideways. Thought it was a bear and then he saw what it was. It was the girl, the girl in her fur.

"I won't hurt you, I promise. I mean no harm." Saw her frostbitten purple hole of a mouth, her sunken unfocused eyes.

She opened her mouth and made no sound and he knew she wasn't strong enough to knock him down and run. He put his arms around her and picked her up and heard her legs clanking together with solid ice.

The bird rises from its fern bed, shakes its wings, and flies over her, saying, Fly, fly, come on, come on. Twilight in the hills, pale blue then purple. The owls are awake. They fly across the open land like smoke.

Fox says no.

Owl says, Stay with me.

Crow wants to know if she is dead. Are you dead, dead, dead?

The ridge like a whale rising out of silt and granite and moss and lake weed and tree rot and bird plumage and ox and blood and song of love and time. The ridge like a wingbeat. The ridge hissing out with mist and wind and burning fires and smoldering ash and bark and barge and river creek. Mist singing wind.

The ridge with its captured souls released her.

You've passed on.
You're coming in.
You're going back.
You're going home.

■ ■ ■

JUST AS he thought, the house smelled of onion.

"Jigger! What is that?"

"It's the girl and she's near froze." He put her face under the light and they both saw.

"She's alive?"

"Yes, she's still alive."

"My God."

They laid her on the bed and wrapped her in quilts.

Jigger boiled water. Caroline opened the girl's coat and found a crust of ice, leaves, bark, matted wool. She smelled urine and blood, burnt skin, ice.

Kerosene lamps burned all night and they looked at the girl who was more like a horrible growth, like something sprouted out of rock and ice with a human face. She didn't look human at all. "I've never seen anything like this in all my years."

"She look like a Summer to you?"

"No."

"Yes, she does."

"No, she don't look like them at all."

They knew it, they both knew it. She was a Summer. But she was on their land now, theirs for now. They watched her lids tremble and her mouth open and shut and every now and then a huge tremor would fall on her and leave her in a deeper sleep.

They wrapped hot towels around her boots and peeled, then cut them off and with the sole of the boot came strips of flesh. The toes were hard and enlarged to twice their size and you could see the ice under the flesh. Caroline scraped the bark and cloth of one foot and then the other. She peeled and cut the clothes off. The zipper was frozen to her skin. The hair below was covered in blood. Caroline wiped the girl's body with a hot towel and rubbed the spots that were pure white, then waited to see if anything had changed. She rubbed the arms gently and smeared her chest with comfrey balm. Flesh came off in her hands.

Jigger kept the water boiling. He cut towels into strips. He made a sling for her legs from the ceiling to the bed. He moved the table close to the bed. "Her legs have to hang," Caroline said. "When her feet come off, her legs got to hang. There's going to be a lot of blood," she said.

Coydogs laughed in the hills. Owls hooted. Fox heard it all, laughing, thinking, *No, I'm not there, I'm in here. Here, come here, no not here, there.*

"She's convulsing. She's coming to. Put that chair on the door. She's going to bolt."

"She's not going anywhere."

The girl's movements consisted of swelling tremors that shook the whole bed and rattled the lamp on the table.

The kettle whistled. The wind howled. The girl lay on the table, eyes opened and closed again, crazy dry eyes.

Her color changed but not for the better. Around the scraped-off flesh on her feet the skin was gray and swollen. Her arms were still frost white and her chest and belly were swelling pink like cooked meat.

"Heavens." Caroline said the word over and over. The roof creaked, the storm mounted. Jigger sighed. The girl lay like a stone in her private depth.

On the stove potatoes boiled slowly. Somewhere she'd heard that potato water did good and Caroline put drops of it in the girl's mouth. They didn't sleep that night and whatever miracle they expected didn't happen. They kept the cabin searing hot. They kept her wrapped in blankets. The girl's feet turned blue, then, very quickly, right before their eyes, they turned black. The soles were spongy. Caroline poked what was left of her heels with the edge of the knife and it went right through.

Frostbite turned into gangrene. The cabin filled with the odor of putrefaction. In a cabin heated by wood, a hundred and twenty miles from the nearest hospital, without a phone, with a storm settling down on them again, they did what they thought best.

"I saw my ma do this once, took a man's leg off to save him. Tree fell on him and crushed both legs. Being the only woman around, they went and got Ma, thinking she'd know what to do. The man's legs were nothing but pulp and the man begging to die. She used a handsaw. Hot cured on a fire. I saw it."

Her mind worked independently now. The smell of rubbing alcohol stung her eyes. She rubbed the girl's legs one more time, hard, leaving dented finger marks on the white flesh, saying, *Come on, come on.* She was talking to the blood. She was thinking of the cut and how to save the ankle, a toe, the big one. Without the big toe she'd never walk again. But it was useless. "She'll have stumps. No feet."

Jigger held the butcher knife over the fire till it turned shiny blue. Did the same with the saw. Felt his stomach turning, his head was dizzy. Felt worse than the time the river swallowed him and he with his eyes open watched the roiling white water above him and the dark shapes of his log death approaching. Was a log that knocked him, a log that saved him, shoved him up from the bottom and heaved him up onto the bateau, where the men looked at him as if he were a dead one. They were ready to heave him out again when Jigger spit a mile of water and they knew he'd come back from the dead for good. Same water feeling in him now, something deep and pressing on him. He stood by her side in case she started to move. He'd have to hold her down and pray she wouldn't fight him.

Caroline scraped more dead flesh away like it was spun lard. The legs up to her knees were swollen like water-logged weasels. She made an S-shape over the bone above the ankles, left enough flesh to wrap around the stump. She'd laid plenty of rabbit on the block. Never liked the sound of bone cutting. Ate a pigeon once, teeth grating on the thin bones. Thought of that as she cut.

Jigger turned his back. Couldn't stand the sound of metal on bone. "Get the bucket ready. When it's full take it out," she said. A metal bucket, a large sponge.

The remains of the girl's boots were by the fireplace. Thin black boots. The label said Taiwan. Her coat hung on a peg by the door. It looked alive, ready to spring on him.

If she died they'd have to keep her out in the snow until spring. Then they'd bury her.

The wind howled.

The girl heard the wind and saw through the walls and into the night, where she burned with white light.

Caroline wrapped the tourniquet around the girl's legs and slipped them into the sling. "It's done, Jigger, it's done."

She wiped blood off her arms. "Take that out, Jigger." The bucket with the bloody feet, unrecognizable as such except for the shrunken dark toes. The flat nails looked foreign in there. Jigger bent to pick up the bucket and fell at Caroline's feet.

She stepped over him, grabbed the bucket, and put it outside. It was morning and the cackling crows screamed because they were alive or maybe because they smelled death. She closed the door and went to see about Jigger. She tossed another log in the fire. She had a whiskey.

• • •

*S*TONES, MARKED *by time, by sunset and sunrise, flushed out of sediment, carved in ice, wait to be held in the palm of a hand. What is there if not a world waiting to be held, a world of stones?*

Sid struggled in the green foam looking for a hand to pull him out. But Earl's face appeared. *Drown, boy, drown if you want.*

How long do you figure on being there? said Tina, flipping her hair side to side. *Huh, huh?*

Boy, look at that, Butch said, *just look at that one go.* He had no way of knowing it was Sid, not a fish, under the current-strewn wake, not a goddamn fish but Sid.

Sid, his mother said, *Sid, if you want to come up now, you can, you know, you can come up now, it's all right, nobody here except me, nobody's trying to keep you down, so come on up, Sid, you hear me? I know you hear me, come on up.*

"Sid? Can you hear me?" the nurse asked. The doctor next to her had Sid's file in his hands but he wasn't looking at it.

"When's the last time you had one of these?" the doctor said.

"Never."

"You get used to them. Coma. Never-never land."

"Sid." The nurse sat on the edge of his bed after the doctor left. "Sid, my name is right here on the tag, just open your eyes and read it. I know you can. I've been waiting for you to open your eyes and see me. I know your name. I want you to know mine. Come on, Sid."

Sid, wrapped in grass weeds, fish eyes staring at him. Sid, at the bottom of the lake, eellike. Placid. Cold.

"Come on, Sid."

Sid, letting the last of the air leave him, not needing it anymore. *So give up, you son of a bitch, go on, you've always been a quitter.*

Like I said, Sid, Tina said, *like I said, your time is up, you know what I mean, like I can't wait forever.*

Sid darling, Sid, what did we do, what in the world did we do? His mom, lying on the river bottom with him, fanning her tail, kicking up silt, muddy and black.

Sid, you remember that car you and I used to take out, that ugly green Lincoln Dad had? Remember that day with Suzanne? Well, let me tell you, let me tell you . . .

Sid could see Butch's hands in the water, above him, flat white hands, like angel wings. What was he trying to do?

"Sid, open your eyes," the nurse said.

Sid, deluded, rose from the bottom of the lake with great effort and opened his land-blind eyes to see the face of a woman who scared him. She seemed to want too much.

"Tippy, my name is Tippy, short for Temperance," the nurse said.

. . .

EARL IN the shower, plastic curtain, Mattie's pink shower cap hanging over the edge. Small window with a half shade. View of Mattie's garden, clumps of mulch snowed over. The stone wall was crumbling with age and he remembered how as a boy he and Tom had set the stones. Years and years ago. Thought maybe he'd ask Mattie if he could stay long enough to set the stones right. That would be spring. That would buy time and he needed time now.

Knew exactly how he wanted those stones to lie, from the drive to the house to the shed. He'd build her a new stone chimney, stone fireplace, more wall. There were enough stones to build a house and he thought he might just do that.

Remembered his mother with hoe in the yard digging around the asparagus, the rhubarb, cursing the stones in the garden. *You'd think rocks have a life, you'd think they climb down from the mountains and walk over here where the soil is good and rich and set themselves here just to aggravate me. Look at them all, propagating. Earl, you think rocks have a life?* He couldn't remember what he'd said to that. Couldn't remember his mother's face.

Naked and waiting for hot water to steam up the bathroom, to fog up the view. In the medicine cabinet, Tom's shaving brush dried and cakey, shaving soap, two-sided razors, toothbrush, bristles splayed to one side. Saw his own body in the long mirror. Hanging balls. A sad old man.

"I feel sick to my stomach," Aunt Mattie said, bird on her shoulder, dry toast on plate. "You feeling fine, Earl?"

"I guess. Clean, anyhow."

"You want to eat? Help yourself to everything in the fridge. There's plenty of cake. Heat up the casserole if you want. Take it with you."

"Take it with me? Where am I going?"

"Home. You got a home to go to." Mattie watched the little bird on the plate of crumbs. Little beak tapping the china. "You know, it gives me some comfort to know Tom's in the river. Might come back like a fish next time."

Earl imagined Tom as a fish. He'd never be a fingerling. He'd come back fully grown, a twenty-pounder. A fish who'd take to the dark waters and live there all his life, refusing the lures of men.

"I meant to tell you this, in a roundabout way, but it didn't come out the other day so here it is. Edna was your mother, though she didn't bring you up. She had you. Lila brought you up until she couldn't take Lucky anymore and she left. But Lila's the woman you should think of as your mother. I say that in case you're wondering. Only reason I told you about Edna was because of Tom. You take a man like him, a woman like me, then you take a woman like Edna . . ." She shrugged.

So, he wasn't who he thought he was. The image of his mother scrambled in his head like a pack of cards, all queens. Queens wearing flaming reds, widowed queens with thin black veils, lonely queens riding a train going west, drowned queens, queens holding a muddy hoe, cursing queens, pretty queens sitting in a tub of water. So, he was a bastard after all.

Mattie sat on the small rocker with a seat cushion the color of rotten mushrooms. Matched the floor, the couch, the chair, and the tables. Matched the color of her china and her eyes.

"Dreamt of her last night. Edna. Dreamt she'd traveled a great distance and was glad to be here. Ever had a dream like that?"

"No, I never dream," Earl said. "Sleep like a rock."

"Like a rock, huh? You think rocks have a life?"

When the phone rang Mattie said, "Get that, will you?"

Earl said hello and looked up in time to see the bird, Jericho, the little bulletlike shape of its body, as it hit the window and fell. Expected to see shattered glass and for Mattie to scream but the only sound was his son's voice at the other end saying, "This is Butch, I want to talk to Mattie."

Mattie was on the floor, on her knees. Blue bathrobe opened at the legs. Bird in her hands. Little moan escaped her lips.

"Mattie, it's Butch. He wants to talk to you." He twisted the cord around his hand, hoping to squeeze a sound out of it.

Mattie took the phone out of Earl's hands, said yes several times, said Christ once. She hung up. Looked from the bird to Earl, said, "I can't believe this. It's your son. Sid. He's dying."

There was a tiny smudge where the bird's beak hit the window. A dark bird circled above the old stone wall.

Earl went outside and smoked. It was so cold. His lungs ached. Thought of Sid was like the cold. Too cold to reckon with.

Never understood Sid. Never liked him. Thought he was an aberration. Something sent down to punish him. Told Darlene it was her fault. *You brought that child into the world but he didn't want to come.* Told her the way of nature was unkind but fair. Mother hens kill their weak chicks if they have to, he said, and for that he didn't get supper for weeks, and when Darlene saw him she'd leave the room like he was the plague itself until one day he'd had enough and cornered her and she'd struggled but he won, he always won. He told her he would have helped her do it, twist its little neck. *You've got no heart, Earl. No heart.* Maybe she was right. That was it. He'd plucked too many hearts out and in doing so he'd taken his own.

Clouds formed huge and horrendous shapes. *Son's dying*, he said to the big ugly sky. *Son's dying*. Fists in his pockets.

Head faced north, out there where the mountains bottomed out, where Canada began, where geese nested and mated for life, where mammals, thick with muscle, longed to escape. True north.

Mattie came out of the house with her coat on, and in her hand a scarf with the bird in there. When Earl asked her what happened to the bird, she said, "He's stunned, that's all. He'll come out of it." Then she got in the car, laid the bird on her lap, and told Earl to drive.

. . .

*M*OUNTAIN *CRANBERRY; alpine bilberry with its leathery and rubbery leaves to drink in the dew; sandwort in rock crevices; three-footed cinquefoil and fir-club moss in the path. Purple mountain, saxi-frage, carnivorous butterwort whose sticky leaves attract insects for food. Here, everything evolved out of stringent conditions.*

The girl was in the fever. Caroline sponged sweat off her forehead and the girl moaned. Every time she moved her hands down, the girl would move them back to her heart. Sat by her side and talked to her. Told her about her life in the ridge and the things she'd seen. Said she knew how it was, how people turned sharp corners in their lives and that one turn changed everything. *Just one turn, and it's all different from then on.*

Jigger left early to get groceries, petroleum jelly, menthol, sanitary napkins, and clothes from the Salvation Army. It was late when he walked in. He turned to the girl. "Any change?"

"No. Did you see anyone, talk to anyone?" she said.

"Saw Carm but didn't ask."

Caroline went through the clothes. They were all wrong. Too small or too big. She put the groceries away. Tinned milk, crackers, bag of apples, bag of oranges, chocolate bars.

"Did you drive by their house, the Summers'?" Caroline said.

"Nobody around. No car, no fires, nothing. Saw a dog, rabid, came at me like a drunken devil, then it hid under the house."

"Did you check their mailbox?"

"Why would I do a thing like that, peek into somebody's mailbox?"

"See if they're all gone or something. You go to the Pig's Eye?"

"Stopped in. One drink."

"Who was there?"

"Nobody but Carm and I told you, I didn't say a word."

"What are we going to do?"

"Do? About what?"

Caroline put her arms around herself. "We have to do something."

He didn't tell her he'd seen Butch by Porcupine Bog. "You looking for something in there?" he'd asked, and the boy looked around as if getting his bearings and after a long while he found his voice and said, "Yes." And the boy let it out. A maddened tale. "You know my sister? You seen her, any trace?" Beyond the boy was a shadow so long it looked like a tunnel. "No, I don't see anyone around here. Nobody comes up this way unless they're poaching or lost." His hands hung at his side and he moved to block the shadow from the boy's view, didn't want him seeing things. The boy stood and looked to the shadows.

"What makes you think she's around here?" Jigger asked. And the boy said she had to be.

"What if you find her, then what, what would you do with her then?"

"Nothing, I wouldn't do nothing. I wouldn't harm her."

"Well, I hope you find her or whatever it is you need to find."

／ ■ ■ ■

THE BUS stopped three times to let the passengers off and each time it did Darlene got out, walked to the restaurant, and sat at the counter. Ordered a bowl of hot soup. Smell of onion, celery, garlic. It smelled like her life, the salt and pepper of it. Looked like it too. A thick concoction of dissolution. Spoon in hand, didn't dare disturb any of it. Watched it congeal, the thin glaze of animal fat riding the surface.

Soup came with crackers in a pack. A glass of water with a thin sliver of ice.

The sign on the bus said NORTHERN TRAILS and she was being driven into the country like a flatlander. She recognized the signs: in the rock of the rising hills were shortcomings, dead ends; in the amorphous land, blurred by handling, scarred by construction, was the inane mingling with the barren. Through the greasy stained window everything seemed too distant to matter. Closed her eyes, weary, tired of seeing, then snapped them open, afraid she'd miss out on some slight revelation. In a clothesline, in a heap of junk cars, in a girl with a coat the color of cantaloupe, in the blur of whitened trees, in the look of the big brown dog by the side of the road, there was something she needed to know.

No river yet. The land south of the ridge was too shriveled to produce streams that mattered. Stiff necked, cranelike, she waited for light on the water, the snaking shape of its old trajectory.

What the hell you come back here for?

For the river's sake, I just came back for the river.

Shut her eyes for what seemed a short while and when she heard the name of the town, Smallford, she was startled. She'd been asleep for miles. "This is where I get off," she said, disoriented, and looked around, waiting to be reassured by the other passengers. Lady with knitting needles worked a furious stitch and glanced up briefly. Darlene grabbed her purse and made her way out.

Ridge air greeted her, cold and snapping. A patch of blue sky, a string of clouds. She dug her heels into the slush. She'd been let out at the same spot she'd left from. Something about that made her laugh, as if all she'd done was take a circuitous route around the ridge. She'd have to tell Earl there were places in the world where you could walk and not see the ridge. She'd have to tell him the ridge ended a hundred miles south. He wouldn't believe her.

In the parking lot were dozens of cars with kids strapped in the backseats, windows fogged over, howling babies. The mothers were in the store filling up carts with canned beans, canned corn, warehouse buys on potatoes and oranges, jumbo-sized bags of chips, sixty-four-pack diapers; mothers with coupons in their wallets, rusted cars, bruised, weather-beaten, breathless women smelling of coffee and Marlboros, and those howling babies waiting for them.

Rushed into the drugstore with head down. Felt like a movie character, an extra in a scene of no consequence waiting to be discovered. *Woman enters drugstore.* She'd been there a million times. Bought her dishtowels, tampons, nail clippers, lipsticks from the discount bin. Two for a dollar. Bought small presents. Stopped to see the glass case with silver chains and pendants of tiny angels. Nineteen dollars and ninety-nine cents. Wanted to get one for Tina but imagined her dangling the angel on a chain like a worm on a hook, saying, *What's this shit?* That's exactly what she'd say.

Turned to go when she heard her name called. Neal, of all
people.

"Hey," he said, "what's the good word?" He always said that.
Hands out in a high five. "You coming or going?"

"Both," she said.

Neal, an adolescent fifty-year-old with scaly skin and pimples.
A neighbor's son, working for the A&P, collecting carts off the
parking lot. Had no real sense of time but probably knew she'd been
gone because he'd heard someone say, *Earl's wife just up and left*.
And now here she was. He'd give the news over supper. *Guess
what?* and he'd make everyone guess. *Give up?* Then he'd tell them.
I saw Earl's wife getting off the bus. He wouldn't say Darlene, but
Earl's *wife*. And the word would be out by tomorrow that she was
back. There'd be talk at the gas station, at the feed lot, at the post
office, at the Pig's Eye, and Earl would not sleep, would load his
rifles, then hide them, and drink too much, and sit by the stove. It
would be stinking hot in there. It would smell of smoke and gas.
And there'd be no sound except the fridge going on and off. The
dog would bark at her as if she were a stranger. Her children would
be alarmed.

Walked down Main Street with her suitcase. Down Brook
Road, across Hoot Meadow Drive. A man on a porch lit a cigarette.
Large white thermometer behind him read twenty degrees. Across
the metal bridge, the river, finally, gray and white below her. Lifted
the suitcase and swung it over the metal guardrails and let it go.
Ran to the other side to see the black shape sink, then rise. The
metal clasps flashed. It swirled around an eddy and got stuck.

A red pickup slowed next to her, the driver's hand out the
window, beet-red face. "Wanna ride?"

"No, thank you."

"You look like you wanna get in."

"I said I don't." She didn't look at him.

"Suit yourself." The truck roared off and hit a frost heave. His
license plate read M-HORNY.

It could have been worse. He could have insisted and she would
have picked up a rock and struck him dead. Saw the rock she would
have used. It would have been a fatal blow.

The road that led out of the town thinned out, and she paused
to look at the houses with yellow light, and saw women cooking,
children by TVs, a man standing still as if waiting to be called. It
seemed calm, normal. Everything appeared just as it was supposed
to be. She pulled on her coat collar, found the bag of crackers, and
ate them. Ahead were the blue blinking lights of the Last Ditch Café
and six miles beyond was home.

The Last Ditch, she could have passed it by but didn't even try.
Pushed the heavy door open to the smoke and boozy air. Touched
the side of her sore face, wondered if anybody would notice. Sat on
a barstool and fished for change in her purse. Twelve ones and two
twenties.

"Bourbon," she said.

"That's on me," a man behind her said.

She turned around to see blue jeans, pressed and creased. All of
a sudden the thought of drinking didn't seem like such a good one
and she turned to go.

"Whoa, you're not leaving so soon, are you? What's the rush?"

Her eyes focused first on the man's belt buckle with a fist-sized
turquoise, then she smelled musk and baby powder, and then she
saw his pointy boots, too out-West, a driving cowboy. The first
notes of a Patsy Cline tune filled the place. The man said some
words and moved his hands around her but she was gone, out the
door, down the parking lot, away from the sounds of an ordinary
love song.

The road was dark but there was light above the tree line, gray
cardboard light, enough for her to see where she was going. Her
legs felt strong. She'd done enough walking in the city to make her
feel she could walk clear across the ridge and back again. She was
walking home.

．　．　．

THE RIDGE. At times it is purple and lavender, coated in evening mist. Other times it's brazen, orange. The whole face of the mountain is clay and sand, metamorphosed. Magma, erosion, intense pressure. It all adds up to change but what with the ice and the fog, it is hard to know time has passed.

Earl gripped the wheel. Car with New York plates splattered ice slush on the window. "Damn! I can't see a thing," Earl said. "You're out of wiper fluid." Wipers squeaked and smeared the windows.

Another car passed them. "I can't see a goddamn!"

"Then slow down. Don't rush."

"I ain't rushing."

He was doing fifty. A quick tap on the brakes, and they'd go flying. Laughed.

"What's so funny?" Mattie.

"Nothing, nothing at all." The car was too small for him, his head touched the ceiling, his thighs rubbed the wheel, and there was no place to put his arms. The sleet and snow, all that whiteness, tired him the most.

Wasn't ready for what Mattie said. Out of the blue she asked, "You ever kill a man, Earl?" Mattie turned abruptly in her seat to face him.

"What?"

"You heard me. You ever shot a man?"

No. He'd never shot a man but he meant to, came close to it one day, close enough to see the man's eyes through the barrel of his rifle, could still see him not as a whole man but as a pair of disembodied eyes at the bottom of the Fulfillment River.

The man's name was J.J., Jeffrey Johnson III, son of two generations of flatlanders. He'd been a hunting buddy for a season, but the man was the wrong kind of man to be out in the woods. He talked too much. Stopped to look at trees and said, Now, isn't that beautiful. Earl didn't call trees beautiful, the only thing beautiful in life was his wife, and he never called her that, knowing in his superstitious way that to call attention to beauty was to lose it.

Last time he saw J.J. they'd been together out by the river, tracking deer. They were drinking from the same Thermos full of strong coffee and whiskey, when a huge buck sprung from the banks and cleared the river, a twenty-foot leap clear across. Earl got to his feet and looked at the expanse of water the buck had crossed, he turned, picked up his rifle and aimed it at J.J. *You think you can do that? Jump clear across this river?* For once J.J. had nothing to say. Earl told him to try, told him to take his pants and boots off and jump the goddamn river. He wanted to humiliate the man, to make him fall into the icy water and drown. Didn't think of shooting him until the man flung his arms out and came close to him and said, *Earl, if this is about Darlene, I can explain.* That was it. That was exactly it. Earl had seen Darlene fluttering like a bluebird out to the birches by the shed, he'd seen the black-and-white shirt that belonged to J.J., he'd heard her laugh, seen them vanish out where the shadows turned into things he couldn't make out.

But it had been her laugh that rang in him over and over, a high, pretty laugh, one he hadn't heard come out of her in years. For weeks she had been wordless, dinner, bed, dinner and bed again, and not a word out of her. Then she was out there laughing. When she came home that night she laughed at the pile of dishes in the sink. For dinner she served radishes, a whole plate of scrubbed radishes, and laughed. He hated radishes.

All he had to do was shoot. Then the man would be gone. Nobody would wonder about him being gone. The town folk, when they found him floating down the river with his legs jutting out of a log jam, would say the man was in waters where he shouldn't have been, and that would be that.

But he didn't shoot him because he didn't want the man's blood and flesh in his river. He didn't want to step into that wild, wonderful river one summer day and find the likeness of the man's eyes down there, like living stones. Didn't want this kind of filth ruining his waters.

"Well?" Mattie said, shifting in her seat. "Did you or didn't you?"

"No, I never did."

"Reason I'm asking is this. When Darlene comes back, and she's bound to, she's got those children to look into, I don't want you laying a hand on her. Not a finger. Not ever. You got to promise me that."

"I don't promise things, Mattie."

"You're going to have to or I jump out of the car right now."

The thought of Mattie hurtling out the car and into the gray slush of ice was real to him. "You could kill yourself that way."

"I know it. And it would be another death on your mind."

"Another?"

They didn't say a word for a long time. Mattie lit a cigarette and opened the window a crack to let the smoke out. The road followed the river. The road, like a snapshot of the road, wet and dark.

Up ahead was the turnoff point for the village. After that there'd be no detours, no exits. One way in and one way out.

"You want to stop for coffee somewhere?" Aunt Mattie said.

"No. But I want to stop at the house. Got something I need to get."

"You ought to make it fast, then, I'll use the bathroom there. You have any coffee at the house?"

"I got plenty of coffee."

He turned off the main road and down the logging road, which was clear, plowed. It led to Brook Road, which was also plowed.

From there he hit the paved road, through Smallford. He didn't know why he was going back to the house but he had a strong feeling driving him there.

· · ·

"I NEVER liked this town. So dreary," Aunt Mattie said.

"It's not a town."

"Whatever it is. Don't like it. Don't know how anybody can live here."

The painted sign of the Last Ditch swung in the strong wind. Used to be the Howling Moon Café, before that it was the River Run Tavern, and before that it was a blacksmith shop. Soot of smoldering iron still hung in the cellar and in the rafters.

The constable was in the parking lot, making his rounds. "Sonofabitch," mumbled Earl, and ducked low, then remembered he was in Mattie's car. The constable hounded him all summer about the traps.

Earl, your neighbors down the road, they got a dog, a small spaniel, well, they say it's been missing and they sent me up here to see if you'd seen any such dog. You checked your traps lately?

There'd been several dogs, lots of cats, quite a few raccoons. Constable knocked on his door all summer long. By fall Earl pulled out the traps. Then it was the shooting.

Neighbors reporting lots of shooting in the woods here, you and the boys doing target practice?

That's right, Earl had said. Tires were stacked up in the yard, the plastic doe set up between bales of hay. Doe's body was pocked with shots. *Any law against target practice?*

No, Earl, there ain't a law against that yet.

Across the bridge, slowly, tires grating on the icy metal. Earl looked on his side down to the steep ravine where the river plunged twenty feet or so, mist and plumes of icy water. Mattie leaned over and caught sight of the black suitcase swinging back and forth in a shallows, but because her eyes were poor she thought it was a dog.

"That a dog going down?" Mattie said.

"What?" Earl looked over Mattie's head.

"Big black shape I just saw, down there. You see it?"

"Probably a rock," Earl said.

"No, it's floating."

"Yeah, well, maybe it's a dog. Think they can walk across it."

"Get off the bridge, Earl, before a car hits us from behind."

Earl turned. "Nobody's coming."

"Just the same. Get off the bridge." She stroked the little bird. Kept her head down. "I wish none of this had happened. I wish Tom wasn't dead. Just now, I wish he wasn't dead."

Hangdog Field, Porcupine Bog—not a real bog, just a vast wet patch of farmland—past the spot where he'd seen the large cat bound across the road. Catamount. He was sure of it. Long muscle in the air, it had crossed the road in seconds. Nothing else moved like a big cat. They weren't extinct, just hiding out in the big woods, protecting themselves.

Drove with brights on. Skunk crossed the road. Hated skunks. Ahead, like a dent in the darkness ahead, always ahead, not far, where stars fell and the moon hung and the sun never hit, the ridge.

"Wonder how Lucky's doing?" he said.

"Fine, I'm sure. What made you think of him just now?"

"Just thinking. I'm sure Tina's out there. Gone west."

She didn't say anything for a long time, then she said some words meant to stir him up. "Family tied together by strings. Nothing but strings. And strings break, you know, strings break."

Thought came to him clearly. There'd be no more Summers and no more Hanks in the ridge. No children would be born to his children in the ridge. No more stones to set.

"Your circumstances, Earl, they seem to have changed on you."

"My circumstances haven't changed, Mattie. Nothing has." He

was about to tell her he'd always seen himself alone in the ridge. "Nothing's changed."

If he had gone on with this thought he might have surprised himself, might have come to a conclusion of sorts, but what happened next veered him off that course. What he was seeing was the last thing he expected to find on the road. She looked small. She was walking home on the wrong side of the road. If a car had come swerving off the curve it wouldn't have seen her. He flashed his brights on and off and pounded on the horn.

"Jesus, holy Jesus, Earl, who is that, Darlene?" Mattie sat forward, opened the glove compartment, and put the little bird in there. "Slow down, Earl."

"What the hell is she doing out here?"

Darlene didn't stop, nor show signs that she'd heard the car. Mattie rolled her window down and hollered her name. Darlene didn't stop then either. When the car pulled up alongside of her she was looking at the ridge ahead, she was counting her steps.

"Darlene! for God's sake, what are you doing here?" Mattie.

He said nothing, afraid one word from him and she'd throw herself over the edge. Darlene finally stopped and walked to Mattie's side of the car. Hair around her face like a dark curtain.

Before Mattie had a chance to say anything, Earl blurted out, "Sid's dying."

One minute she was there looking at him, the next she was down, a heap on the ground.

"Jesus, Earl, you shouldn't have said that."

They lifted her and put her in the seat between them. "Don't say a word, Earl. Just drive. Keep your mouth shut and drive. Turn around right now and drive to the hospital. Now." Darlene came to and saw Earl on one side and Mattie on the other. Her head fell on Mattie's tiny shoulder. Earl fumbled with the heat vents. The cold coming off Darlene's body chilled him. Her coat was dripping wet, her hair smelled metallic, her hands were trembling. It was irrational, but he wanted to say he loved her.

■ ■ ■

A SUMMER, many years ago, they'd had a birthday party for the kids. One birthday party in the middle of summer for all of them. The boys got new bikes with wide speckled seats. Tina got a dollhouse with thimble-sized lamps, beds, teapots, chairs, and couches. She rearranged the furniture—the bed in the kitchen, couch on the porch. Got bored and went to the river carrying spoons and plastic containers. Balloons hung from strings tied to the rain gutter. Blue and pink balloons. A car drove up and down the road. "You invite any kids over?" Darlene asked Earl. "Nope, thought you would." The boys raced each other on the road. Sid pedaling furiously, stuck in a pothole, wheels spinning but going nowhere, and then Tina screamed.

She was sitting on the sand, knife in hand. She had a green dress, something Darlene had bought, not made. Green and white with a large bow at the back. Tina had sliced a frog in half with a kitchen knife, the serrated kind. "That's all right, honey," Darlene said, "that's all right, frogs got lots of hearts. You take this part, the legs, and this part, the head, and in no time at all you'll see, they'll grow the right parts again. It's okay." She took the two halves, legs still kicking, head attached to scarlet membrane, and she put both parts back in the river.

That night Earl asked Darlene why she lied. "Frogs don't have more than two hearts."

"You expect me to tell that to a child?" she said.

The dollhouse rusted in the shed. Over the years Earl came across a small table, a lamp, a slender, smooth-legged mother with molded hair, in the dusty floors of the shed, or in the grass outside. He found dice, bingo dots. Kept the tiny pieces in glass jars.

■ ■ ■

EARL MADE a wide sweeping turn into the other lane. Butter-yellow moon straight ahead. Sound of Darlene's breath, a whistling through half-open lips. "I'm starving," he said.

Mattie shushed him and told him it was no time to think of himself. Darlene, her legs twisted away from him, mumbled and cried and Mattie said, *It's all right,* and other words Earl couldn't make out. He was hungry, wanted to be led back to the house for supper, now that she was back.

Off the highway, down a town road, dark houses with plastic in their windows, snowmobiles and washtubs in the yard, witch-elder trees and valley marsh frozen over, the boarded-up sheds, ramshackle barns, winter-stained roads leading to the dead-ahead glow of city lights. The carcass of the night, like bones, pressing down. The smell of women and wool in the car.

Darlene was back. The stunned bird was dead. When Darlene stirred, Mattie stroked her hands. He was too much of a coward to touch her like that and clutched the skinny wheel, though he felt incapable of steering. The snow turned to sleet and the wipers were useless. And Mattie began to tell Darlene what she knew, said it was true that Sid was dying, told her how Butch had found him, told her all. And when Darlene gasped for air and clutched his arm, he said, *It's true, all of it's true.*

At the hospital, in the parking lot, Mattie put her hands out to Darlene but Earl told her to go on, to give them a minute alone. The lights of an ambulance fell on them, turned them blue, then ghostly white.

"This ain't the time to talk, Earl, so it's going to have to wait, whatever it is." She reached out for Darlene and pulled her on. The snow was ice and it bounced off their heads and they had to walk with their faces shielded. The two women rushed, Earl ran to catch up. Inside, they shook snow off their heads and stomped their boots as if to announce their arrival, and they all turned around to see where they'd come from. He saw her eyes then, cold, real cold.

A nurse led them past the swinging doors, down a muffled corridor, to the elevator. They felt themselves rise, and when the doors opened they rushed out fast as if the spot where they stood were mined.

Darlene waited till Mattie was ahead of her and she told him, "I didn't come back for you, Earl."

"I ain't asking nothing."

"And in case you're wondering where I was . . ."

"I ain't wondering. I don't care to know."

The nurse opened the door. Butch was leaning against the far wall. A young woman in jeans by his side. When Darlene walked in, Butch made a small move toward her but she put her hand out, meaning *later*. His girl pushed him back.

Darlene's thin legs muddied in the back. A blue thread hung down her leg. Stockings torn. Her shoes were ruined. The door swung shut on Earl's face. He didn't want to go in. Knew there'd be a doctor who'd see the likeness between father and son and talk to him as if he cared, as if he should know things, and he'd put out a hand and shake it as if a deal had been struck. Heard the elevator doors open. He could go now, he could leave.

"Earl, *Earl* . . ." Mattie pulled him in and the first thing he saw was Butch, like a dark dog in the corner. Couldn't look at him. Darlene slipped out of her shoes and sat on the side of the bed, eyes on Sid and on the thin green lines running off the screen. To her, Sid didn't look like himself. He didn't look like the boy she had nursed back to life. She'd do it again. Now that she was back. He'd get better. She'd done it before, she'd do it again.

"Is he all right?" Earl's voice lower than he intended, the voice of a grown man unaccustomed to whispering. He was suddenly tired and wanted to tell them all to go to hell. Felt useless and unloved and dirty and hungry and tired, more than anything he was tired. Tired of thinking, tired of knowing what he knew.

"So is he all right or what?" He said it loud this time, loud enough to startle everyone. Sid heard and his hands twittered, confirming the unasked: *Yes, I am alive.*

Sid's head was covered in bandages. Yellowish flesh. Eyes rimmed red. Mouth cracked, bloated. Thin plastic tubes in his nose. Wet sounds like something underwater.

"What the hell did he do this time?" Earl said.

"Your son is heavily sedated now," a nurse said. Nobody looked at her, not even Earl. Her voice irritated him. He knew he wouldn't like her face.

She spoke quickly, said they'd found him on the floor, that he'd pounded his head against the walls, cracked his skull.

"Jesus," Earl said.

Nobody was crying.

"This boy here, he's my son, I know this boy." Earl talked to the square room, to the monitor, to the empty chairs. "This boy here never wanted to live, so none of this comes as a surprise. None of it."

Darlene turned slowly and faced Earl and slapped him.

"You know better than me, better than all of us! If it hadn't been for you keeping him alive, forcing him to live like you did, he wouldn't be in this now. The poor bastard wanted to die all his life. Let him, for God's sake, let him die."

Darlene hit him again and again but she'd heard his words. The nurse grabbed Darlene by the shoulder and forced her away from Earl.

"Anybody know what's going on here? You have any clue?" He turned to Butch, but his girl held him back. He stepped toward Sid, but Mattie moved fast between them.

"Stop this, Earl. You're mad."

"That I am. Look at him, for Christsakes! What the fuck are we here for? To stand here and watch him die?"

Earl was wrong. They weren't there to watch Sid die of self-inflicted wounds, nor to think about how they, each in his own way, had contributed to Sid's pain. They were there because of their tragic assumption that by blood they were a family and therefore had to come together no matter what. But it was too late. They hadn't known how to love each other. They had known only their own wretched pain. It was all they had.

Mattie pulled herself away from the bed where she'd spread her arms over Sid. "Everybody come here, stand together, there's something to be done now. Let's pray."

Nobody came to her so she went to them and took their hands and forced them to hold on and she began her words.

"Lord, heal this child, let him know you are ever present, let him know you got powers that are greater than his, let him know of your will, Lord, hold him, hold him, Lord, don't let him fall, don't let him leave this world in a silent spell like this. Wake him, Lord, open his eyes so he can see us, his family, Lord, give him the power that is his, has always been his, let him speak to us, Lord, let thy will be done."

The doctor came in.

Earl broke out of the circle and touched his son's hands. "Let it go, Sid."

The doctor, a young man with small Chinese eyes and a thick black wristwatch, a gold wedding band, said, "Your son is in a very precarious state right now." He looked from Earl to Darlene.

"We know. We know that." Earl shivered. He'd seen his son as a child in teddy-bear pajamas, a toddler under the kitchen table, a boy in a dark room clutching an old bunny, a boy in summer dragging sticks on the road, a sunburnt boy in a boat, in a lake, flailing his arms like a drowning man, a boy who hated the hunt, the life, the blood of life, a boy who desperately wanted to be left alone. A dying boy, all his life.

Sid was in the bottom of the great silent waters. He looked

above and saw no shadows, heard no voices, felt nothing. He was not lonely. He muttered something but it had no sound. He was relieved. And when he turned slowly he saw a small light behind him. It did not seem possible but there it was. He had a tail, and a light on his tail. He was amused and turned around and around to see it. A tail. A light on his tail. It was nothing at all like he had expected. He was a creature of the depths with a light to guide him through the deep. Gradually the light moved up and took over his entire body. He was glowing.

The water was cool. And he watched the water become a beautiful blue, the blue of maps, the blue of the world seen from the moon. He saw the ridge and its rise and its rock and its icy cap, all blue. It was beautiful. And he was happy because he was exactly where he wanted to be. Saw the faces of his family, the emptiness, the great misery.

They were watching the sleet-shaved window when Sid opened his eyes. The nurse registered the move, she saw him scan the room quickly and close his eyes. She looked at the monitors and said, "Something's happened."

Earl and Darlene knew it before the doctor raised his head and said, "He's gone." They had been looking the other way when it happened.

At last, Earl thought, at last.

∎ ∎ ∎

MATTIE'S ARMS fell around her now. Butch stood by the foot of the bed. Earl waited for someone to hit him. Darlene lifted Sid and brought him to her and rocked him. Arms around him, she rocked him. Sid's arm slipped out of Darlene's hold and swung lifeless at her side. She stared at his arm as if she didn't understand.

Everyone saw it. Her eyes opened wide as she lifted the arm and put it over her shoulder again. *Not now,* she cried, *not now.*

She signed the papers because Earl refused to. She sat in the tiny office and looked around for familiar things. She looked at the nurse, who asked if she could please sign here. She tried to remember her name, her address, her relationship to Sid, who was now called the deceased. She sat there and listened to the words. *I am sorry for your loss.* She wondered what loss, then she remembered. The nurse said her name was Temperance. "I don't think he was ever aware of being here." And her eyes looked past Darlene, down the long corridor. "I think he was in a place of enormous peace and he didn't want to leave." Darlene nodded, yes, she wanted to know about this place.

Earl slumped against the wall while Mattie paced. "I know, Earl, I know how it is." She could see how he'd be later that night, and the next, and a month from now and a year from now. He'd stay in the ridge and harden like a lonely son of a bitch, wedded to the dark bag of weary seasons, a dull man, hurting, loving nothing, a lonely bastard. "I know, Earl, I know."

She saw through his greasy hair down to the pink scalp. She'd known him as a boy, *a problem* Lucky called him, and sent him to her and Tom in summer to mow, rake, set stones, burn brush, and help with pig butchering. He was always good with a knife. He wasn't eager or lazy, never asked for a penny. She liked him then. He was six feet tall by the time he was thirteen. Took a photograph of him sitting cross-legged in a field one year. Head down, hands twisting a stem, twirling a yellow flower. Same man, same boy. Still didn't know what to do with himself.

"Earl, listen to me. What's done is done. . . ." She couldn't. Didn't have it in her to offer a bit of hope.

"I'm tired, Earl, I think I'll get a cab and stay somewhere for the night. Too tired to drive. Take my car and drive Darlene to the house. She needs to be there. The two of you do." Her hand fell on his shoulder and she let it sit there for a while before she walked away.

Watched her go, but it was a long while before he stood and ran down the hall calling her name. Outside, the red taillights of a cab pulled into the cold night and the sleet still fell.

A couple embraced by an open car, a big man with his head on the shoulders of a small woman. It was always like that. Big things gave in, fell, broke down. Even the big ridge with its miles of rock and canyons flattened out. Its long trail ended in a small hole where a fox slept.

Butch's eyes were on the figure of his dad, who was outside lighting a cigarette like a man who's had a satisfying meal or some kind of deep pleasure. Looked hard and long, memorizing the moment. His father, out in the cold, alone.

Suzanne nudged him, said, "Your mom's there."

Darlene was in the darkest corner of the lobby with her legs crossed, head turned sideways.

Butch knelt in front of her and touched her cold hands. She tried to smile, said his name, but he knew she was seeing beyond him, and not seeing him at all.

"Mom, I'm sorry. . . ."

"Shh, don't, don't say it. It's all right. I'm back."

"I wrote to you. I wrote to tell you about all of this, but I didn't know how to find you. None of us knew where you were."

"I'm sorry, Butch, I'm so sorry. Someday I'll explain."

"You don't have to. I don't want to know. I'm just glad you're back."

It was remarkable. None of them wanted to know where she'd been, what she'd done. When she tried to tell Mattie she'd turned her face and said, *That's none of my business, that's yours, keep it to yourself.* Now her son was telling her the same. It was as if she'd been in a deep sleep and no one cared to intrude in her dream.

"I'll never leave again, Butch. Never. Not you, not the ridge. I'm home." A flow of words, promises, new ones. She hadn't known until then she could never leave again. The difficulty was knowing whether anyone cared.

He let his head fall on her lap and she rocked him as she had when there were babies in her arms.

"Mrs. Summer? I just want you to know that I'm real sorry about Sid and all." Suzanne had her hands on Butch's shoulders.

"Hello, Suzanne." Darlene took her hands and held them, resisting the urge to turn her palms up and read her love line—was it deep, long, was it there? The girl had soft hands and her eyes looked hurt but kind, and by the way she leaned over Butch, Darlene knew she cared for him.

"We're getting married," Butch said. "We're living out of the ridge, up north by the lake. You can stay with us tonight, stay as long as you want."

"Married?" she said. She wanted them to speak. Anything to keep her from her own thoughts.

"The old house is empty," Butch said.

"What old house? You mean our house?"

He nodded.

"What do you mean it's empty? What about all the things, your things, and Sid's?" It was unbearable.

"I got all I need from there." He didn't know how to tell her that it was empty in different ways now.

"You got everything? All your things?"

"Yes. Everything." He thought of his room, his childhood room: the dresser with sixteen coats of paint, the lamp with a headless eagle, the poster of a fish, clinically open, with arrows and names for its parts: gills, heart, stomach. The red chair, the brown heater, the speakers and the radio. The racks. Under the bed was the boxful of boat drawings. There had been a summer when all he wanted was a small boat. She'd told him they'd build it together. He was sorry they hadn't.

She, too, remembered his room. "I'm sorry, Butch. I'm so sorry." She remembered the promises.

"Is there really nothing left?"

How could he tell her there hadn't been much?

She smoothed her skirt over her knees.

"Mom?"

"Yes?"

"Tina's gone. . . ."

"I know, Mattie told me."

"She's gone, Mom. She's not coming back. I know."

"Since when did you become an expert on things like that? What makes you so sure?"

"She's not coming back."

"She has to."

"No, Mom, she doesn't have to."

It was horrible. What was he was saying? "I've come back, haven't I?"

"That's not the same."

"What do you mean? I've come back to you and—"

"She's not you. She won't be back."

"I'll stay until she comes back."

"Dad says she's out West, thinks she hitched a ride all the way to Montana, out West somewhere with Lucky."

"Out West?" She could not imagine her daughter beyond the ridge. "Do you believe that?"

"No, I think she's on the ridge somewhere."

"On the ridge?"

She shook her head and pulled on her hair as if to straighten out her thoughts. Something was wrong. She gave out a little laugh that sounded like a cry. "I can't picture her face, imagine that, my own daughter's face." And though she worked her mind like a scroll, a long thin white paper upon which were snapshots of the cabin, the house, Sid with his nose scrunched up next to the dog's snout, Butch swinging from a tree rope, Earl swinging the ax—the scroll came to an end with no picture of Tina. None.

"I'll never see her again." Darlene shook her head back and forth.

A mother can prophesy such events. Time would pass and she would wonder how it was, why she willed her daughter gone. Vanished from her heart.

"Mom, don't cry. . . ." He held her hand and was tempted to put his head on her lap and wanted nothing more than to be stroked. But the hand that fell on his shoulders was Suzanne's. "Butch, honey, please don't." So many tears, who ever thought one could hold so many tears? Darlene saw Earl outside. "Look at him, catching a cold."

Suzanne said, "Butch, honey, we have to get going."

"I wish you wouldn't go back there, Mom, you don't have to."

"I have to, Butch, you know that."

He kissed her cheek and hugged her and said they had to go, but they lingered, the two of them, afraid of another separation.

"Your father, you should say good-bye to your father, tell him you're leaving. The two of you. You should say something. It's not his fault, you know. None of it is."

Butch pulled back. He wanted to say, *I love you, Mom,* but didn't. Next time, he thought, I'll tell her next time. He took the letter he had written months ago and gave it to her. "Here's something I meant to tell you a long time ago." It was signed *With love, your son.*

Earl felt his son approach and looked at him but had to close his eyes. Like looking into the sun with naked eyes, it was bad for you.

"Son, please." Somebody had to speak.

The girl stood close to his boy and Earl could see she was

straining to keep him back. Women get killed for that, he thought, for stepping in, for being a shield. She said some words to Butch, and then she moved aside.

Butch stepped close to his father, inches away from his face. He saw his pores, the hairy nostrils black with snot and cold. His mind was raging with all the ugly words he'd been taught. He would never call him a bastard, he wouldn't call him anything at all. In his father's eyes he saw all he had been and would never be again. A coward, an ignorant man, innocent too. It was there, everything that mattered. He didn't need to know anything else. Didn't have to get closer. He'd been close enough, all his life, he'd been too close and it almost killed him. He stepped back, said nothing, and walked away. Suzanne's hands in his.

Earl watched them go. *Bye, son, bye.* He couldn't locate the source of his tears, couldn't stop saying, *Son, son . . .*

She never noticed how different they were until then. Though they were almost the same height, their heads at the same angle, their hands in the same position as if holding down something heavy, they were different. She watched Butch's lips and knew he hadn't said a word. Poor Earl, she thought.

She went to him then and he dropped his head to the side like she often did. A borrowed gesture. He searched for his cigarettes and quickly shook one out and lit it.

"How come there ain't no stars out tonight?" he was crying. "How come, Darlene? That's all I want to know. Where the fuck are the stars?"

"It's snowing, Earl. You know you can't see stars when it's snowing."

"Is this what it comes to, then? A sky with nothing in it?"

"There are things in the sky, Earl. We just can't see them."

He didn't want to hear explanations, nothing was simple as that, he wasn't after words. He tossed the cigarette out, far. "We made it all go bad, didn't we, it was us, we made them all go. Spoiled them, ruined them, looked at them the wrong way, said the wrong things, made them stay up when they should've been asleep, what else, what else did we do wrong?"

There was more to it, maybe they'd seen something he hadn't, something bigger than all of them put together. What had it been? And what about all those years hunting together, hadn't they learned? Hadn't they come along to watch life, to laugh at death? Hadn't they felt it, didn't they know? He raised his head to the snow. "Didn't I teach them to love this?"

"This?" she said. "This?" What was he talking about? The ice, the cold, the dark pain, the night. "What are you talking about?"

"Something happened to them out there."

He'd shown them, taken them out there and shown them how some animals, when wounded, lie down and wait to die, others thrash and resist it, knowing death is a terrible stillness. Death is what must be resisted. He'd *shown* them, he hadn't put it in words, but he'd shown them.

She reached out for his hand but he jolted away from her. She hadn't come for him, she'd said so. She wouldn't stay. She might as well go too.

"We'll have to bury him. Do it right and all," she said.

"That's up to you. Do what you want."

What she said next surprised him. "You mind holding me, Earl?"

She was thinking of Sid. She felt him around her, hovering, watching to see how it had all turned out. Thought he'd be pleased to see them in each other's arms, for once. She didn't want to disappoint him and closed her eyes and swayed in Earl's arms, rocking the three of them.

"We should just get going, this weather won't get better," Earl said pulling away from her. "All right." She followed him to Mattie's car.

"Here." He opened the door. *Here* is what he'd said the first time he took her hand and laid it on his heart. A long time ago there was a place called *here*.

He'd always thought the people of the ridge had a mark only other ridge dwellers could see, like a third eye, invisible, but clearly there, passed on like a kiss, or mother's milk, or a promise. It marked you for life. His children had it, he had it, but it wasn't in her anymore. Something about her. Wondered what she'd had to do to lose it, how did she let it go.

They drove in silence, each looking at the houses and thinking of their own. It would always be known as *the house* from now on and not home. It would stand with or without them in the worm-scented earth until it, too, gave in. They'd be dead by then, of course, all of them. They wouldn't live to see the house go down.

· · ·

JIGGER AND Caroline ate ham sandwiches on crusty bread and the girl watched from the bed and she remembered many things of a life she didn't think she had lived, couldn't have. It was in the smell of that food that she remembered her mother. A rich meaty smell. But she couldn't remember her mother's face and when she asked Jigger, he said, *She was a Hank before she was a Summer.* The words meant nothing. He told her about the others, two brothers, a father and leaning close to her, he told her, *You're safe here, nobody's going to harm you here.*

She heard their talk at night.

"Seems like she's not afraid of us."

"Seems like it."

But they were afraid of her. They took turns going to the outhouse twenty yards away and sat there with the door wide open. Caroline put away the stove poke, the gun, the rifle, the kitchen knives, the saw.

Fox knew by the smells of her body that she was not the same. Her feet were gone. The old woman told her they were gone. She said they were gone when they found her and there was no sense in keeping what was gone.

The old woman washed her flesh and combed her hair and helped her dress and Fox couldn't remember ever being touched or cared for like that. Was sure she'd been born alone, and the old man confirmed it when he told her, *You're a creature of the ridge, sprung out of the ridge, birthed by rock*. He seemed proud of her.

The old woman made her mittens of lamb's wool, coon hat, and a pouch with a strand of crow feathers. She made her a pair of long wool leggings.

At night their voices put her to sleep. The chink of their plates, the pouring of water in a glass, the opening of the woodstove, even the closing of the door, the laying down of their old bodies, made a nice soft sound. Nights when dreams came to her the old people were by her side telling her it was passing, it was gone now. The dream was always the same: A man came out of the bog and shot her.

The old man made crutches out of red maple, a fox head carved on each. The old people held her up and helped her walk around. They looked away long enough so she could look at them without being watched. Soon she was able to swing from bed to crutches alone. "You can go anytime you want," the old man said. "You can stay, you can go, it's up to you." And she looked at the old woman with her fine hands working a hooked rug and the woman nodded and said, "He's right. You're good as new."

Jigger watched the turkey feather swing in the wind. It never failed him. Any day now it would show signs of what was to come. The land was quiet as the night-passing deer searched for whatever had slipped between the seasons. One morning he made a circle on the snow with a stick and stepped out of it carefully. In its center he placed birch bark, three hollow reeds, dried singing grass, snow-shoes, bow and arrow. The girl watched.

She had on a green shirt of thick wool and a long brown skirt and a thick shawl. She had the coat on and she was leaning forward with the crutches.

The old man placed a pouch of juniper berries, a sumac cluster, dandelion roots, wild ginger, cattails, three pickled eggs. The girl watched. He tied the pouch with a strand of leather and gave it to her. He wasn't holding her to the place. *You're free, you know. Wild. You can come, you can go.*

That night he placed two round stones next to her bed. Holy things, he said. His eyes said so. She fell asleep and dreamt of the house that night, remembered it completely, every door and every window and every picture on the wall, remembered her room as it had been, white and empty with her in the center of it, remembered her fear of leaving the house, the fear of what held her in there. Now she was in another house and again she was being told to go.

Snow fell for days like a mantle of down, soft and light. The old man walked with her in the deep snow and instructed her, made her stop and listen to the short-winged bird as it settled on a nearby branch, a timber doodle. A male. He told her that soon it would start its peculiar mating habits, rising two hundred feet straight in the air then dropping straight down to the same spot and calling out the high buzzing notes, *Peeent, peeent,* that would make the female fluff her feathers and strut on a limb and wait for him to come and mate her.

He told her it was March. Said he never liked March. Too wet, too grizzly, too long, an old month which made him aware of his own old life.

They walked to the wolf tree, the council tree, the very old tree that had sheltered her, and he circled around the tree three times with a handful of coins, and made a wish and touched his heart. She touched hers.

"When I die you place my bones under this tree, you hear what I'm saying?" She nodded yes. "I want my bones here, right here," he said. "Yes," she said. They heard a rattling of leaves. "Promise me," he said. "I promise," she said.

"You being here is no accident. Don't know what it is, call it what you want, but whatever you're running from is still out there," he said. It was important she knew that. Day later he showed her the big white mare.

"She's yours," he said.

The mare looked at her and lowered its head and sniffed the ground she stood on. Jigger slacked the rope and hesitated. He twined the rope in one hand, then the other, and looked from girl to beast and back again. "She won't need much, but you'll have to care for her."

Again he looked at Fox, wondering if she knew he was entrusting her with more than a way to travel. It was a new way to live, one he now wished were his own. "If I were younger, I'd go off with the two of you."

Fox smiled, her first.

The mare backed away and waited with her nose in the air, and her beautiful head made motions of impatience or something else.

"I've never ridden a horse." She put her hand to the soft depression in the mare's forehead and the mare came forward to her touch.

"See that, she's already taken to you." He held the rope in his outstretched hands, and Fox took them.

They gathered kindling and dragged wood in a sled to the mound. Lambskins, furs for bedding. She stayed three nights and on the fourth she came to the cabin, knocked, and was let in. "I thought you'd be here by now," he said, and they served food and she ate. Jigger had a shot of whiskey. Caroline braided her hair, unbraided it, braided it again. Moon hung high in a twisted arc of light and Fox stepped out. Heard the owls. She heard a hare, its scream was terrifying only for a second, but the screech of the owl, the glory of its power, filled the woods for a long time. The mare came to her, nudging her.

She tested the depth of the snow with her crutches. *You were lost in all this whiteness*, the old people said but they were wrong. She'd never been lost.

She slept in the mound under the tree and dreamt she was a dressed-up doll in an open coffin and when no one was watching she shed her skin and slipped out.

She became adept at pulling hearts. With a deft hand under the rib cage where the small hearts thumped she pulled downward until the heartstrings snapped.

The rabbit trails were a maze of crossings through the willows and the birches, they were meant to confuse the common eye but she had learned to read animal sign. It was everywhere, in all things, the snow marks of foot and trail and wing. In some uncanny way she'd known this language all her life, as if born to it. She listened to the far high sound of the wind above the ridge. Mornings came with a glitter of frost and the light was diffused. She entered the time of the ridge, soft as a ghost. Every now and then came the vague menace of a big cat passing through, that or its shadow.

And every now and then she saw a young man in the snow, sitting still and waiting. The day gray-white, rain splattered. She leaned back on the big soft-throated mare and watched the rain making long holes in the snow.

■   ■   ■

THE RIDGE lay ahead in the whiteness, in fine mist and in sleet which pounded the car with the sound of a thousand hands clapping. The car's headlights split the night into distinct paths, top and bottom, what was and wasn't, and Earl could not tell what was solid in all that whiteness. He turned the wheel in a guessing way, not sure the road would be there under the tires. Earl looked at her and then at the road. He was not sure they were moving at all. It appeared that only the ridge was moving, pushing them on.

"Darlene, I was wondering . . ."

"I can tell you. If you want to know where I was, I can tell you."

"No. I don't want to know, that's the last thing I want to know about, and I don't want to apologize or have you apologize either. I never want to hear the word *sorry* as long as I live. What I'm trying to say is that things turned out just the way I was afraid they would. I'm not sorry, I'm real surprised is what it is.

"You remember what you wrote in that note, the one you left behind?" he said.

"I remember," she said.

"You don't know me, Darlene, you really don't if you think I would . . ."

"Shoot me?"

He slammed his fist on the wheel and he gripped it hard.

"I didn't intend on coming back, Earl. I didn't think I could."

"You were wanted here."

"I don't know if I ever loved you, Earl."

"That's something, isn't it, Darlene? That's something to say after all these years."

"I became your wife, Earl, I became a mother. That's what I did. I'm not sure love had anything to do with it."

It was unwinding—the ball of thoughts, the thread, the long skinny thread from the ragged quilt. The trail of the ridge.

The car went in and out of skids. Pure driving hell. As the road goes, so will life, so will the night. Three miles up the lower ridge and then a bottoming out, a steep drop, and then the winding road to the valley.

"There's just so much a man can take." He was crying.

"Yes, I know, Earl, I know," she said.

They were above the clouds and the storm was below.

They took the ridge road regardless of the signs warning them of snowslides, blizzards, the probability of death.

"Ten minutes," Earl said.

By tomorrow she figured the sad pastor and the well-intentioned parishioners would know about Sid and come knocking like pale messengers and offer pale hands, old words, sad ones. They'd connect the two events, Sid's death and her being back, and the stories would start. Someone would say they had a dream about it. Something about a hen laying black eggs. Or a storm that blew the tops of mountains off. Stories about the common made uncommon, and they'd shake their heads and darn socks late into the night and poke the fire and put off haying or butchering, depending on the season. *Them Hanks. Them Summers.*

She wouldn't let the pastor in. She'd give him Sid's Bible. Say, Here, take this.

"Here we are." He let the car idle in the drive, the lights on.

She climbed the steps after him. He held the door open for her. Something rushed in before them, something uninvited, unwanted.

"What's that smell?" she said. Gas. The house always smelled of gas or kerosene or diesel. It came with the men and settled in her cupboards.

"I don't smell a thing," he said.

The screen door slammed shut. "The screen door's still up." She looked around. Snow slid off the roof. "It's cold in here."

Earl saw her framed in the light of the kitchen. Coat wrapped around her. Arms clutching her sides. He could see the toaster beside her, the kettle, the coffee machine. Dishes in the drain. The square tins, small, medium, and large, sugar, tea, flour. He saw her and still he didn't know her.

"Do you love me?" she said.

"Jesus . . ."

"Say it."

He'd thought of it, thought he could say it, just this once, but he couldn't. "What's the use?" No, he shook his head. *No.*

It was a matter of sharp breaths going in and out of their respective bodies, then silence. A little wind moved across the dried silver leaves on the ash, on the snow, wind across the face of the sky.

He switched the hallway light on and the living room lamp but not the light by the bathroom. He grabbed a few logs stacked against the wall and opened the stove's side door and emptied the ashes into a metal bucket. He rolled a few paper logs, then put some twigs in, then he laid the logs in. He was glad to have it arranged right, the papers and the logs. Sometimes he spent a lot of time trying to shortcut the fire, to make it go, although he knew the paper wouldn't catch, or the kindling was wet. But this time he could see it was all right, it would catch.

The clock on the wall said eleven-thirty. She looked at the sink and at the stove for an indication of what to do next. She watched Earl rearrange a log in the stove. He moved fast, knowing exactly what he wanted. She wanted a fire. Was about to ask him something when she saw him reach for the matches. Thought she'd had a dream about this very same thing: he leaning over the open stove, the cold out, the dark in, the matches, then Earl rushing toward her making a loud *whoooosssh*. White light bursting behind him, pushing him forward, onto her, his hair on fire.

"Earl," she said, and he struck a match and it didn't catch. "Earl," she said again. He dropped the matches and looked at her. Normally he would have ignored her and gone on doing what he needed to do. Normally, he would have said, *What do you want?*

"I think the snow's stopped." She opened the door, felt the stinging cold, closed her eyes. He was at her side.

They walked to the maple, the branches touched Sid's window. From outside, the house didn't look so empty. They could see through the windows, the angles of the walls, the doorway in the big room looked like a child's secret entrance to a place of wonder.

The snow had stopped but the wind picked up.

They would go inside later and make a fire and stay up all night. So much had passed between them in a day.

The night had its risen ghost, they felt him, the son, rising fearlessly above them, locking himself in the substance of something other than rock, deeper than a chasm, and so unlike the ridge, made of nothing now, free of it all.

"I can't see the ridge," she said.

The terror in him was considerable.

"Earl? I was thinking of staying the night and then . . ."

"Heading out bright and early. You don't have to stay, not even for Sid's sake. He won't even know you're gone. I'll drive you out." He wanted to say, *Take me with you.*

"You're crying, Earl. I never seen you cry before."

"I don't know what to do, I haven't a clue. . . ."

"You'll figure it out."

They went inside and had coffee and every now and then Earl opened the door wide to let the cold air in. She said she'd see about getting a room at the Marshalls' place. "They always have a room or two to let." She'd get a job as a seamstress, do fine needlework, work her fingers and her eyes. Maybe she'd get a job at the store too.

Then in spring, they'd bury Sid. It would be green then. The river would flow wild and then calm down again. Sid's stone would have simple words: *His mercy endures forever.*

Earl would stay on in the house. He'd let everything go. What there was to the shed he'd set on fire and watch it burn while town folk stood around and mumbled. *There wasn't much in there, was there, Earl, nothing you wanted saved?*

· · ·

I т was the last storm of April and it happened like he knew it would. Heard the hooves first and then the animal was there at his side, the long white mare's legs, thick with good bone and the horse neighed and he smelled the horse's breath and when he looked, he saw her legs wrapped in lamb's wool jutting out by the mare's flanks and he saw the fox coat, heavy and rich and bigger than he remembered and there, above it all, above the mare and the coat, was her face, no longer childish, no longer fierce. *Tina,* he said and put his hand on the mare.

She looked at him for a long time. She had seen him climb the ridge. She had seen his tracks, watched him without being watched. She saw sadness in him and nothing else. When his face filled with tears she wondered what emotion had caused that. To anyone looking it would have appeared like a reunion cast out of visions.

"Sid's gone," he said, "he's dead." The memory of his brother was profound and he was sorry he had said his name and the word *dead* at the same time.

Her eyes fell low to the ground and the horse stomped its feet and Butch moved aside and she rode off.

He had no way of knowing she was of two minds now. One brimming, uneasy, and scrambled so she didn't know him anymore, and one that was clear and lucid and knew he was part of the ruined stronghold. To her, he seemed to be made of drifting snow, creeping and depthless.

■   ■   ■

*I*T *IS incidental, the idea of hope; a mere whim, hardly a need, forgivable.*

It is the accumulated grief over the years that gave the ridge its violent name, hopeless. One can imagine the stillness, the transparent winds, the icy dawns. One can project a human mind onto it and be lost, plagued by its unapproachability. Dark clouds, always. Huge and dark, always. It is easy to dream and be lost in the dream.

But who in a world that offers places of kindness, would want to spill seed in this soil, and why? Who is that innocent and in such violent need of defeat?

■ ■ ■

ON THE solstice, every year, she brings skinned hares for the old people. The hares come easy to her now. They fall in her hands. She mumbles words to let them know they have done the right thing, and their large dark eyes stare unblinking into hers as she severs their heartstrings.

A feast, Caroline says, always.

A feast, Jigger says.

They've seen the girl riding the big white mare. Her mane matches the girl's hair. White, silver, like a field of stars. Flying at times. Other times they saunter, girl and beast, they sink deep into the folds of snow, rising in waves of white to the crest, to the whitened rock where they ride. Saddlebags, snowshoes, bow and arrow strapped across her back. Raccoon mitts. Her great fox coat. Deerskin wrappings up to her knees.

Jigger's seen her wild hair and a hint of her wizened eyes. The light in them. He's heard the hooves, the thud and pound, the vibration in the land. He's felt how the hardened earth gives in to their weight. He's seen the owl and the crow alight in the path. Seen her out by the great tree; smoke in the chamber. She'll take his bones there soon.

■ ■ ■

SOME SAY they've seen a wild thing up there. They narrow their eyes. A huge hulking beast on horseback, they say, a thing covered with fur. But then nobody believes what they see up on the ridge is real. Things there, they know, are made out of quivering air.

And stories are told late at night when thunder rolls off the cliffs and blue rivers bulge with the strain of natural forces. The stories are hushed, embroidered, calamitous. The people speak of near death and frights that turned hairs on end. Things that, like a man said late one night in the Pig's Eye, *just send my innards aquivering, it just gives me the willies all over, makes my blood curl.* Makes some curse and shiver. Others rush home to find a woman to hold. *Quick, hold me,* they say.

Some nights, all over the valley, the whole of the land hums with secrets, lies, and legends, and in the telling of stories half true, half not quite true, all who listen and those who speak make themselves up like clouds, particle by particle. *It's being so alone,* some say. *It's being so cold, so goddamn cold,* others say.

And when strangers come around and ask about that road, they're never told much except it's known as Mercy Road.

© Adrienne Aurichio

DALIA PAGANI grew up in Alaska and Latin America. She is a recipient of a fellowship from the Vermont Council of the Arts, and her short fiction has been nominated for several awards, including the Pushcart Prize and the Iowa Short Fiction Award. Formerly a journalist, she now teaches fiction writing at a college in New Hampshire, where she lives with her husband and two children.